CAST A SHADOW OF DOUBT

D1082514

Cast a Shadow of Doubt
Christiane Knight

Published by:
Three Ravens Press
PO Box 502
White Marsh MD 21162
USA
Contact publisher for permission requests.

Front cover photo manipulation by Christiane Knight
Cover design and interior book design & formatting
by Leesa Ellis ⊷→ *www.3fernsbooks.com*

Library of Congress Control Number: 2021925327

ISBN (e-book): 978-1-7368503-2-9
ISBN (paperback): 978-1-7368503-3-6

CAST A SHADOW OF DOUBT

CHRISTIANE KNIGHT

three ravens
PRESS

TABLE OF CONTENTS

To all the dreamers, magic seekers,
and the ones keeping hope alive.

SPOTIFY PLAYLIST

https://spoti.fi/3F17mM8

MUSIC: STRANGE BOUTIQUE
The Kindest Worlds

The bolt of energy was a crackling beam of blue-tinged lightning, and it arced through the air as it caught Lucee off-guard and sent her flying backwards. She hit the ground with an audible "oof" followed by an exasperated groan. That groan didn't come from Lucee, though. It was an expression of long-suffering frustration from the one who had blasted her, and she knew she merited it.

She used to hate seeing the look of disappointment on her boyfriend Cullen's handsome face because she was afraid he'd realize that she was nothing like how he saw her. Now, she was just tired of being a failure, and even more exhausted by his efforts to teach her how to handle magic. She couldn't seem to get a grip on how it all worked and the longer it went on, the less she felt motivated to try. That lack of motivation was starting to show in their practice sessions, and Lucee felt like she was trapped in a loop of diminishing returns.

Cullen crossed the yard to her and offered a hand up. Lucee took it ruefully and pulled herself up off the ground. She sighed as she caught a flash of pink on the warm brown skin of her arm, and realized she'd scraped herself up nicely from her fall.

"You've got every right to be angry with me. I just can't seem to get this. I feel so stupid," she confessed.

"Lucee, you are not stupid! That is what is so frustrating. I know you can do this." Some of his blond hair had escaped the loose ponytail at the nape of his neck, and he moved it out of his eyes, tucking it behind one pointy ear. "It feels like you have not improved at all since we started these sessions. Tell me the truth—are you practicing?"

She sighed, a long exhale, hating every moment of this conversation. "Remember when we used to flirt, Cullen? That was fun. Even when things were the worst, you always believed in me."

Lucee turned away from Cullen and focused on the ground. She didn't want him to see her self-loathing, her disgust at her lack of ability to grasp what he was trying to teach her.

"Hey." He touched her shoulder tentatively, but she wouldn't meet his eyes. "Hey now, Lucee. I still believe in you. That is why I asked if you have been practicing, because I know you can do this. And I know you hate feeling inadequate, you will do anything to avoid that feeling."

"Ow, that was uncomfortably close to a direct hit. I know you didn't mean it that way. I know. But could you just—could you just not?" She tried to hold back tears, and mostly succeeded.

Cullen's shoulders sagged a little. "The last thing I want to do is hurt you. I wish I understood you better, so I could just tell you how to overcome this and be your hero when you did it perfectly. I do not know how to teach you, I'm afraid. I thought I could do it; I even risked angering The Ladies by insisting that I was up to the task. They will gloat when they hear me admit that I was wrong and they were right. That will perhaps make them more charitable with you, at least."

Lucee sighed and twirled one of her acid green and black braids of hair around her finger, tugging it lightly. It was a nervous tic, but one that never failed to make Cullen smile. She finally managed to meet his gaze and decided humor was the way to break the tension.

"I'm not looking forward to switching teachers, you know. The current one is much handsomer than the alternatives."

It worked; his smile widened and he pulled her into a hug. Lucee let it happen, grateful for a moment where she felt secure and confident. She took a deep breath and rested her head against his shoulder. He smelled of oakmoss and lavender, as always. It was a soothing scent that she knew she would smell on her own clothes later.

He kissed the top of her head, and she gave him a gentle squeeze. He was always doing his best to support her, she just wished that she could live up to that.

"I hate to break the mood," she sighed, "But a responsible version of me would be insisting that we go talk to The Ladies now, before she lost her nerve. And I guess that responsible version had better be in charge right now."

The first time that Lucee met The Ladies, she had been afraid of them.

Her best friend, Merrick, had tangled with The Ladies on the first day he met the Eleriannan, after crashing a Halloween party at their house. One of them had forced her way into his head and tried to push his boundaries so that he would submit. He told Lucee that it had felt like a fight for his life, and he had basically spent the entire time trying to hide his secret thoughts. After Merrick had shared this tale, Lucee had been understandably wary. The Ladies would have agreed with her fear, had she revealed it to them. They were small in stature, but quite intimidating.

At first glance, they appeared to be young women, about twelve years of age, dressed in clothes that were wholly inappropriate for their youth. They favored corsets, plunging necklines, and dresses that might be considered High Gothic in style. That was the first unsettling thing about them. But only when you got closer to them did things really start to get weird. For one, their skin was covered in hairline cracks. It reminded Lucee of old porcelain dolls, with the crazing that happened with age. Their eyes were also a bit creepy. Sometimes they were dark pools that felt like you could fall into them and never escape. Other times, they were as green as a slime-covered pond.

The Ladies were always found together. Lucee and Merrick had often wondered if they were actually one being split into three bodies, each with their own names. Most often Morgance was the leader with Morgandy and Ula following and adding commentary. Morgandy was least likely to speak, but she was uncommonly insightful when she did.

After some searching, Lucee and Cullen found The Ladies in the Tower room, sitting in three chairs of green velvet that were arranged to face another similar chair. It seemed to Lucee like they had been waiting there for a while, and they made it clear immediately that she was correct.

"It is about time you thought to come to us," Morgance said. "We knew it would have to be this way. This one," she gestured with a small hand in Cullen's direction, "is never going to be able to tutor you properly." Her expression held a whisper of contempt, as if she found it insulting that he'd even thought to try.

Lucee sighed, and glanced at Cullen. He was wisely keeping his expression neutral, but she knew how much he wanted to help her and how frustrating it was that she didn't seem to respond well to his lessons.

"It's not his fault. I seem to be a terrible student," Lucee admitted.

"Knowing one's weaknesses is an important part of being teachable," Morgance said. She addressed Cullen. "And as much as it pains us to admit it, you are wise to bring her to us for these sessions. You are too close to her to be an effective teacher. She needs someone who will push her in ways that you will not because of your feelings for her."

Cullen's handsome face stayed free of emotion, which impressed Lucee.

"As always, you are correct, Morgance. I did my best, but she needs someone more experienced than I, and less emotionally connected. And you have already stood with her to support her, so she knows you are on her side." He was referring to Lucee's initiation into the court of House Mirabilis, after their leader Fallon had chosen Lucee to be her heir.

The Ladies nodded in agreement, and Ula stood to speak.

"When we said that we would be by Lucee's side when we brought her into the Eleriannan, we meant in every way needed. That includes tutoring her in how to use magic and control her power, as well as protecting herself and others." She spoke directly to Lucee. "You observed how we instructed Merrick in how to use his powers, so you are familiar with the process. Sit you down now and we will decide how to proceed."

Lucee did as she was told, and asked nervously, "Will Cullen be able to stay, if he's quiet?"

Morgance considered this for a moment.

"I am unsure what he could bring to this task, other than distractions. Yes, you will say that he shall lend support, but was that not a failure when you worked together? No, he may support you from another room."

Lucee looked as if she wanted to argue, but Cullen ignored the small dig from Morgance and gave Lucee an encouraging smile.

"You may find me on the balcony porch when you are finished. I will try to gather up some snacks for you in the meantime. You will do much better with The Ladies, I know."

"Sit before us. We are going to assess you now. You will not enjoy it." A sly smile played across Morgance's lips.

Lucee was not excited at all by this idea, but did as she was told, trying to keep her face as expressionless as possible.

For a moment, it felt like nothing at all was going to happen. She sat there in front of the three tiny, witchy women while they stared at her, which was uncomfortable, but hardly a challenge. Her mind started to wander a bit, and she began thinking about what they might teach her. Could she be a shapeshifter, like Merrick or Cullen? Would she get a talent like Vali's graffiti—

WHAM!

She found herself on the floor, her head spinning and shrill laughter ringing in her ears.

"What—what happened?" She tried to sit up, and the room tilted, making her stomach flip-flop.

"You stopped paying attention, and we took advantage of that! Surely you know better than to daydream in front of your opponents," Ula scolded her.

"Do not let your guard down for a moment with us. Ever," Morgance added.

"Use this as your first lesson. When your enemies are distracted, it is a fine time to throw them off guard," Morgandy advised. Out of the three, she seemed the least terrifying, Lucee decided.

"Message received, Ladies. My apologies," Lucee said as she picked herself up off the floor, righted her chair, and sat back down. "Can I try again?"

Morgance grinned one of her alarmingly toothy grins. "You are at least as brave as you are foolish. Let us see how you handle yourself now that you have been shown the folly of your ways."

In what felt like a heartbeat, Morgance was across the space between them, and she grabbed Lucee's arm to pull her out of the chair and down to her knees. Her small hand fastened around Lucee's chin, forcing her to meet Morgance's gaze.

Then she was in Lucee's head.

Lucee was hiding in her room again, listening to Ma and Da arguing in their bedroom. Their words were muffled by the wall but still clear enough for her to know that they were talking about her. There were some shouts and thumps, and then her bedroom door opened with a slam, and Da stood there towering over her as she cowered on the floor.

"I know she bought it for you. Where is it? You both know that you can't keep wasting your time on this nonsense. You need to concentrate on your studies if you're ever going to get into college. Look at you, you're a mess, you look ridiculous! I'm embarrassed to even take you to university functions!"

He began to tear through her room, starting with the closet, throwing clothes everywhere as he searched for the one thing that mattered to Lucee—her guitar, the one Ma had secretly saved up to buy for her. It wasn't much of a guitar, but when she'd played it, she felt more whole than she ever had in her life. And now Da wanted to take that from her.

"You can't have it. It isn't yours." Her voice shook, but she stood her ground anyway.

He turned on a dime to face her, his entire body tense, his eyes reflecting disbelief that was turning to rage as she watched.

"What did you say? Every single thing in this house is mine, young lady, including you. You will give it to me, or I'll take everything in here until you do."

A feeling started in her center, expanding out and filling her with an energy and clarity that she'd never experienced before. This was the past! She was not this child anymore, forced to live in a room without a door, in a life where she wasn't allowed to make her own choices. She wasn't powerless at all.

She scrambled to the bed and pulled the guitar from under the covers where she'd hidden it. She held it in one hand, her arm outstretched before her, a gesture both defiant and challenging.

"You can't have it. You can't have me. But you are welcome to try and take us both."

The figure clothed in the likeness of Da lunged forward, and Lucee took the guitar by the headstock and swung it in an arc in front of her. There was an unearthly sound as the instrument smashed into the man, and everyone flew back—

She gasped as she fell backwards, away from Morgance's grip, and Morgance staggered back a bit. Lucee felt tears on her face and wiped them away with a trembling hand. For a moment, the room was unbearably quiet, and then all three of The Ladies started cackling and clapping their hands in appreciation.

"Well done, Lucee Fearney! I dare say that you did better at that than our Blackbird did when I challenged him. Quite impressive!" Morgance seemed as pleased as Lucee had ever seen her, and a feeling of relief washed over her.

"Does this mean that I could have magic abilities too?"

"Pssh, child. When Fallon gave you her essence, she imbued you with magic. You just need to learn how to trust yourself. Today's work should go far with that, yes?"

"I suppose?" Lucee blushed when The Ladies cackled at that. "How do you do that, though? How do you reach into my mind and pull out memories like that?"

Ula was thoughtful. "I believe you could learn this skill, you were so comfortable in it once you realized what was happening. Mind connecting is something all Fae have the ability to do, but not all are skilled at it. You have had several experiences with it now and seem to move naturally in that space."

"Feelings bring memories, and those memories are easy to enter for those who do not school their feelings carefully, or protect themselves well," Morgandy added, her eyes focused tightly on Lucee.

"I hear you, Morgandy. I need to work on protecting myself, as I am excessively full of feelings," Lucee agreed. Morgandy held her gaze for a moment more, then slowly nodded.

"Yet you must remember: your feelings are your greatest asset. Guard them well," Morgandy intoned, and the other two sisters turned to stare at her, surprised.

"You may be the first and only one to have such advice from one of us," Morgance said, sounding a little shook. "As always, Morgandy has the wisest words. Heed her well."

MUSIC: FLOWERS
Not My Kind

S ometimes, Cullen thought, *Food is the best comfort I can offer. Which is a sad state of affairs.*

If there was one thing that held true about working magic, it was that it generated a ravenous appetite. Cullen went to the kitchen in search of whatever might help Lucee recover once she was finished with her lesson.

The secretive Fae that managed the domestic details of House Mirabilis were quick to know what the residents needed at any given time. Cullen found a tray of little sandwiches made with soft cheese and vegetables waiting for him on the counter, along with pastries, and a pitcher of something purple that Cullen couldn't name. He trusted that it would be delicious, as was everything that came out of the kitchen.

"Hmm, three plates, that is odd," he said to himself, then he heard the loud voice of the unexpected third party.

"Helloooooooo, who's around?"

"In the kitchen! I expect you are hungry?" Cullen grinned as Sousa came into the kitchen. "I see you did not dress up for your visit," he joked.

Joseph Sousa, Souz to his friends, usually described himself as a dirty punk, and he was not wrong. He also happened to be Fae, and the owner—although he referred to himself as the caretaker—of the giant brick building known as The Maithe in downtown Baltimore City. For the longest time, it sat mostly unused, seemingly abandoned, and ignored by the Mortals who lived around it. It wasn't until recently that it came to light that Sousa had, in the late 1800s, built the building to protect a magical forest space that he referred to as the Heart of the City. The personification of that entity now used his girlfriend Vali as a conduit to speak to the Fae.

All of these things had done nothing to refine Sousa, who was unrepentant and comfortable in his guise as a dirty punk. He hadn't even wanted to become friendly with the more lordly Eleriannan of House Mirabilis until his mortal friend Merrick had forced his hand when he swore a seven year bond with them.

He'd eventually gotten over it. It didn't hurt that Lucee was now the leader of House Mirabilis, since she was also a close friend and bandmate in The Drawback, along with Merrick.

"What? I put my hair up, that's damn festive!" Sousa patted his rooster--comb hair, then glanced at the tray and frowned. "This looks great. Except where's the beer? Do you need help with this?"

"Grab beers for you, and the pitcher, and I will take the rest. I am meeting Lucee on the balcony after she finishes up with The Ladies."

Sousa cringed a little, then looked confused. "I don't envy her, but weren't you going to teach her?"

"Let us get this upstairs and I will tell you about that," Cullen sighed.

The balcony porch was atthe front of the house on the second floor and faced the road. The magic that surrounded House Mirabilis did a fine job of obscuring the intrusive traffic passing by, which made it a peaceful retreat. It was a beautiful space, exuding charm the entire Queen Anne-style house had, with gingerbread trim around the edge of the roof and a lovely hardwood floor. Cullen placed the tray on a café table and Sousa did the same with the pitcher and the beer he'd grabbed for himself. They settled down and Cullen leaned back in his chair before he told Sousa the whole story about his attempt to train Lucee.

"Oh damn." Sousa winced. "That definitely did not go well. At least she willingly switched to training with The Ladies. She's not giving up. Though our Lucee, she's not a quitter. She just needs to be challenged the right way."

Cullen tilted his head, considering, and then said, "I am not sure I know what you mean by the right way to challenge her."

"Look, man," Sousa said around a bite of sandwich. "It's like this. Lemme tell you a story."

Here's the thing you don't understand about Lucee: she needs nurturing.

She's the boldest, most authentic person I know. But, as you know, she sometimes suffers from a lack of self-confidence. And when she doesn't feel adequate, or she's faced with a situation that feels stacked against her, she's liable to act rashly. She's really good at recovering in a way that makes the end results pay off for her, but she does so much better when she's supported in a way that keeps her hand from being forced, y'know? If you give her a little room, you'll be amazed at how she blooms.

Let me tell you about how we met, and you'll see what I mean.

I had decided on a whim to check out guitars at Tom's Music. I can play passably, but usually on acoustics, and I wanted to try an electric out and see if one felt good to me. I don't know how familiar you are with places that sell instruments, but a lot of those shops are a testosterone-and-ego pageant. You walk in and there's a wall of glistening guitars, all ready for anyone to pick them up and try them out. But what I've experienced is that you get a bunch of guys who come to drool over axes they can't possibly afford, and show off how badass they are at playing. Basically to weep and wank, I like to say.

So here I am, eying all these guitars, and the guy working there is this third-rate musician who plays in a couple of bands I can't stand, and he's trying to sell me on the most expensive guitars there. He puts this gorgeous white hollow body with a vibrato tailpiece in my hands, and I'm thinking to myself, do you even see me, dude? What part of me looks like I can afford this beast? I mean, of course I could afford it, but he doesn't know that. I'm my usual dirty punk self, and in no way should I have this guitar in my hands.

It plays beautifully, but there's something not quite right with it for me, and I can't figure out what that is. Dude is pitching it to me like his life depended on it, and I guess it's all about his commission, which I get, but it leaves me feeling dirty. Especially since this guitar and I aren't talking to each other the way we should be if I'm going to drop that amount on it.

Guy turns away to talk to another potential sale, and I hear this small voice behind me.

"Try that one to your left, on the bottom. It's not a looker, but the tone is amazing."

I bend down and see a grey knockoff brand hollow body, not as fancy but with the same basic setup. No vibrato, though. It wasn't pretty, but the details were all there, and when I picked it up and strummed, the tone was fantastic.

"This is really nice!" And I mean it, it feels as high-end as the other guitar, and sounds better by far.

"Well, I'm not trying to make money on you. I come in here and play all the guitars, just to see what they're like. These guys quit trying to sell me anything a while back when they realized they couldn't dupe me into spending a fortune on a guitar that doesn't suit me."

I turn to see this young woman standing there, I guess she's maybe twenty-two, and nervous as all get out. Not only do I not usually see women at Tom's, I definitely do not see young Black women who obviously know their shit about guitars. Like I said, that place is a testosterone pit. And I could tell that she probably didn't talk much to those dudely dudes because they weren't going to be interested in what she had to say. Those types really only like hearing the sound of their own voices or the coos of women swooning over them. And I assess immediately that the woman next to me is not a swooning type.

I decide to address her nervousness by asking her more about guitars.

"So, which one do you play? I'd love to hear your style, if you've got the time." I make sure to give her an out, as she strikes me as the type who needs an escape plan if she feels trapped.

"Eh, mine's too cheap for Tom to carry it here." She shrugs, trying to hide her embarrassment with nonchalance. I'm not fooled.

"Okay, which one would you play if you could afford it? Like, if you had all the money in the world to spend on guitars, which one here would you pick for yourself? I really wanna hear what that one sounds like."

She bites her lip for a minute, and at first, I think she's considering which guitar to choose. But no, she's weighing how she feels about playing in front of a stranger because once she decides, she immediately stands up and reaches up for a guitar on the top row. It's a solid body, not flashy in the slightest at first glance, just a basic, warm maple wood with a matching neck and headstock. It's got two pickups and a pearly pickguard, and clear knobs with a slider underneath to switch between pickups. It wasn't until she sits with it that I notice that it has this sparkly clearcoat over the maple on the body and headstock that glints with purple and green. It's so subtle that I almost miss it.

And then she plugs into a nearby amp, and starts playing, and it's like the whole shop comes to a screeching halt.

I know you've seen us play with The Drawback, and you probably think you know what I'm talking about. But this was different. She starts off with this quiet fingerpicking, a version of a Nick Drake song without using the capo. The music begins to build speed and intensity, until she's riffing her own tune, changing keys. It finally ended in a wild solo that has everyone in the shop staring at her with their mouths open. She lets the last note fade out, then looks up at me and said, "You see why I like it, right?"

I manage to blurt out, "Are you in a band?"

She was not. I stand there and wait for the other clueless dudes in the room to speak up and try to impress her, to snatch her up for their projects, but mysteriously, as soon as I break the spell with my question, they all turn away and are deeply interested in anything but the female guitarist who obviously can musically kick their asses.

"You have a thing going already?" She looks dubious.

"I'm wanting to start something. I usually play drums. I need every-thing else. I'm starting from scratch, so if you know anyone good you like to play with, you can bring 'em along."

She raises an eyebrow at that. "Drums, huh. Any good?"

I have to laugh at her sudden shift in attitude. It was like I kick-started her confidence just by letting her jam for me and responding positively, which I guess I had. So, I sit down at one of the drum kits they have set up on the sales floor, go at it like the beast I am for a bit, and she jams with me after a while. We rip that place up, let me tell you. No, not literally, you Fae numpkin! "Ripped up" means that we were playing so well together that we left everyone impressed. We were completely in tune with each other. I've jammed with a lot of people in my time, but I hadn't felt that sort of energy in ages.

"At this point, she has the full attention of everyone in Tom's Music. I suspect that some of those doofs had never expected that they could be outplayed by someone like her, and they wandered over just to verify that she was the one making all that noise. Lucee, to her credit, doesn't shove it in their faces, doesn't gloat or showboat. She just grins at me and says, "I guess we're in a band now." I had to agree.

"I know a guy you need to meet," she tells me. That turned out to be Merrick, of course. As we exchange info, I tell her we should get together immediately because I don't want her to get all twisted up and talk herself out of it.

And I have her hand the guitar to me, telling her I'd hang it back up, that I want to check it out first.

I'm going to tell you something that no one else knows, and I'm trusting you to keep this a secret, Cullen. I bought both those guitars that day. I put the one she played in storage because I knew if I gave it to her then, I'd scare her off, or make her feel like I was trying to buy her. And I wouldn't have blamed her for feeling that way. But that guitar was hers from the moment she started playing it, and I didn't want anyone else to grab it, after she blazed on it like she had. I bought it, and I've been holding onto it all this time. I'm thinking that I'm going to have to give it to her soon because she needs something to remind her of how powerful she actually is.

So yeah. Nurturing. That's what I'm talking about. I gave her a little room to show what she could do, and she blew everyone away. And I invested in the long game of being able to remind her of that in the future. That, my friend, is how you handle Lucee Fearney. You believe in her, and you invest in that belief.

Cullen listened to his friend's story intently, but at Sousa's last words, he frowned and leaned forward, clearly agitated.

"I do believe in her! She is brilliant, in every way possible."

Sousa said nothing, choosing to simply raise an eyebrow before tilting his head back to take a long draw from his beer. Before Cullen could protest further, Lucee showed up, flashing a tired smile at both of them as she walked in.

"Hey Souz, what a surprise!" She turned to Cullen after glancing over the refreshments on the table. "Oh Foxy, these look so good. I'm starving and exhausted!"

She flopped down on the chair next to Cullen and he poured her some of the purple beverage. She seemed suitably impressed. "Whaaaat is that? It has to be so refreshing!"

"It seems to be lavender lemonade. It is quite a treat. The sandwiches are very good, we made sure not to eat them all," Cullen told her. She smiled at his affectionate tone and grabbed one of the sandwiches.

"So... don't suppose you're still up for band practice today, then?" Sousa asked her, once she'd inhaled some of the food before her. She screwed up her face and groaned in disappointment.

"Awwwwww, man. I definitely do want to practice, especially since we've got big gigs in our future. I'm just so tired! Can we raincheck until tomorrow? I won't push myself trying to do magic until after we've got a band practice done, I promise. I just need some rest."

"Hey, I don't mind just dropping by for some excellent food with my friends." Sousa grinned, then added, "And beer, of course. Tomorrow, though, I'm not driving. You're gonna have to walk yourself there."

"I need more practice with the gates, anyway," Lucee agreed. Each of the Fae houses had a unique portal that connected to each other as well as many other, unexplored places. They were highly efficient methods of travel, but they required one to learn the magical signature or vibration for the gate that corresponded with where they wanted to go. Lucee had only been led through them so far, so her experience was still at a beginner's level.

"I'm gonna see if Merrick wants to come to The Maithe and hang, I'll catch you tomorrow," Sousa said and left the balcony, making sure to grab the other beer before he did. Lucee shook her head at that, amused.

"It's a good thing he's got Fae-level tolerance, I swear," she said, then her face became serious. When she turned to Cullen, there was a haunted look in her eyes.

"Hey there, my beauty, is all well? You look like you have seen a ghost. Was it the training?" Cullen tried to keep his tone light, but his concern seeped through his words.

"Can we go lie down, and I'll tell you all about it? I just want to be close to you when I relive all of that." Her smile wavered, and Cullen, seeing that, immediately agreed.

"Nothing would be better. I want to hear everything you choose to share, always." He stood, and offered her a hand up, which she gratefully took.

"Friends," he addressed the air, knowing that those who were meant to hear his words would get the message. "The meal was perfect. I can return to clean up after I care for our Lady. Please forgive the mess."

"You are aware that they know you never actually come back to clean up, right?" Lucee chuckled.

"I always mean to, but circumstances often prevail. But I do my best to atone with gifts of fine chocolate whenever possible." He winked at her and continued as they walked to their room, "It never hurts to add an extra bar or two when I know I have been particularly negligent."

MUSIC: SEXTILE
Visions of You

The room that Cullen and Lucee shared was technically Cullen's. Lucee had her own room at The Maithe, which had been a point of contention for the Eleriannan of House Mirabilis. Their view was that as the leader of the House, she should be living there. While Lucee did find that reasonable, she also knew that it was still too early in her relationship with Cullen to share a room full time with him. Even having her own room at House Mirabilis felt like it would push those boundaries too much. She also thought it was good for her to have a place where she could retreat from everything and just think or have time to herself. Even Sousa would leave her alone at The Maithe if she told him to, and it was his house. Well, his and Vali's house.

Although Cullen generally dressed like a dandy, with richly colored fabrics and well-tailored fits, his room was a soothing wash of white, with voile sheer curtains and a crisp white comforter on the bed. It was sparsely furnished and open, and next to the balcony porch, it was Lucee's favorite place in the big house.

She sat on the bed and before she could start unlacing her boots, Cullen had already knelt to do it for her. He was so good at smoothing out the little details for her. She dug in the pockets of the cargo mini skirt she was wearing, pulled out the contents—her phone, a small bag with a couple of charms that various Eleriannan had given her, wax paper wrapped lemon drops from Tully—and dropped them into one boot. Cullen chuckled at that.

"You know I could have put that on the bedside table for you, right?" He waited for her to stretch out on top of the covers before he laid down next to her.

"Sure, but old habits die hard. I bet Vali does something similar," she agreed, snuggling into his arms. She took a deep, calming breath, then added, "Why do you always smell so good? Sorry that I'm sniffing you all the time, but I guess that's the price you have to pay."

Cullen grinned. "You must have had some success with The Ladies, considering the mood you are in. I would love to hear all about it."

"Can I ask you something?"

"I would be a terrible boyfriend if you could not. You know you can ask me anything, Lucee." He squeezed her lightly to reassure her.

"Would it hurt your feelings if I have more success working with someone else? I mean, it wasn't Merrick-levels of magic, but something happened and I don't think I could have done it with you." She hid her face against his chest, holding her breath as she anticipated his answer.

"First of all, I want you to succeed! Yes, it makes me a little sad that I cannot be the one to teach you, but that is neither your fault nor mine. I am just not the one for this task. The Ladies were correct when they said that I am too close to you. I cannot push you the way that is needed. This is a healthier arrangement for us, as well. I do not want to be in a position of authority over you."

Relieved, Lucee slid up enough to kiss his cheek. "I think I didn't like that, either. The Ladies scare me enough to make me pay attention without getting mad. When my concentration did drift, they called me out on it and I knew they were right without feeling like I needed to defend myself."

"Oho! You were daydreaming?"

"Nothing was happening, or so I thought. I was shown the error of my ways." She waited for Cullen to stop laughing at that. "Look, Morgance went into my mind and something happened. Can I just—can I just show you, rather than trying to explain it?"

He was quiet for a moment, long enough to make Lucee wonder if he was going to deny her.

"I have not been in your mind since the day we were attacked by the ArDonnath. And I only did that because we were scared that you were hurt worse than we had realized. Are you sure? This is a very... It is an intimate step."

He sounded nervous, and she didn't understand why. It wasn't like he hadn't already been in her mind twice in the time they'd known each other! She sat up, pulling herself gently out of his arms enough to meet his gaze and spoke forthrightly.

"You and I have got to stop this dance."

He started to speak, and she gently put a finger on his lips to silence him for the moment.

"Let me finish, okay? Cullen, we spend almost all our time together. I guess I don't tell you everything because you'd be bored out of your mind, but I would if you asked. I respect how you give me room to make my own decisions. Honestly, you've been the best boyfriend I've ever had, and the best addition to my inner circle. You support me even when I'm being difficult. And I don't want to have secrets from you or have you feel like you don't know me completely. I love you. I trust you with my life. I think you and I can move forward with confidence to whatever level of intimacy comes next."

Cullen sat there, wide-eyed, and Lucee's brow furrowed.

"Did I break you?"

"That is...You are...You always know what to say to me. And I realize now that sharing this way has always been a part of who we are, from the first day that we met." He leaned forward to kiss her, then pulled her back down into his arms. "And this is also a way for your skills to grow, one that The Ladies cannot fuss about us pursuing together."

"I think you should try to lead the connection this time," Cullen advised Lucee as he moved himself into a slightly more comfortable position on the bed.

"I think that, for once in my life since I've met the Fae, I can handle this sort of magic," she agreed. "But what do I do?"

His voice was soft and lulling, which helped her relax even further.

"There are a few things we use to build the connection between minds. We are already touching, so that is the first step. We ask permission, and I give that to you. And we find our own personal way to visualize how we enter the shared space between us - that is a thing you must decide for yourself. My personal visual key is imagining a shadowed space between two rooms. When I see myself crossing it and arriving into the next circle of light, I am there in the mind of the person I am connecting with."

She thought about it for a moment, then asked, "What about a door between rooms? I know Merrick saw doors in his mind when Morgance attacked him, and shut them against her."

"If that speaks strongly to you, then give it a try. You will know if you succeed." He squeezed her arm lightly in reassurance.

She closed her eyes and took a few deep, slow breaths. *I can do this,* she thought. *We have made this connection before.* She tried to imagine what a door that connected to him would look like, and found herself painting it in her mind.

The door was old wood, a light color like oak, with inset panels and an ornate doorknob made of brass. She realized there was a knocker on the door, with a brass plate. The knocker itself was made like a bouquet of flowers, and that made her smile. She decided to use it, because it seemed polite, and because it was too pretty not to use.

Instead of the loud rap she expected, it made a sound like a bell being struck, pure and clear. She gasped in delight, and when Cullen opened the door, he was laughing.

"What is this that you've dreamed up, my love?" He looked at the outside of the door and smiled at her, and it felt like she'd stepped into a sunbeam. "This is beautiful imagery, Lucee! I am so impressed."

She felt the elation rise in her. He had praised her, and she was managing something Fae. Finally! He was looking at her with such affection. Was that just how her mind painted him?

"You know that your thoughts and feelings are right on the surface here, yes? I don't mean to be intrusive, but this is the very definition of intruding, and I am not sure you meant to share these thoughts with me. And before we go any further with this, you need to know that I am always impressed with you. You leave me in awe, Lucee Fearney. I am sorry if I ever gave you the impression that I felt differently." His mind-avatar stretched out hands to her, and she took them and stepped closer to him.

"I've just felt like such a failure lately, until I worked with The Ladies today, and now here with you. It wasn't you; it's been me—I guess me fighting myself, making it harder than it needs to be. I'm not going to be like Merrick, or Vali, because they're different people. And you're so supportive, but you're never going to push me out of my comfort zone, and it was wrong for me to look for that from you." She leaned forward and kissed him, then pulled back with a grin.

"That is the kiss I tried to steal when first we met." Cullen laughed. "I might deserve it more now."

"That you do! Hey, so I connected with you, but what next? Do you, um, do you wanna come over?"

That made him laugh again. "You wanted to show me how your first day of— what did Merrick call it, when The Ladies taught him? Oh, magical bootcamp. How did that go?"

When Lucee had finished showing him the replay, he pulled out of the connection and pinched the bridge of his nose while making a pained noise.

"Your visuals are so vibrant that it actually hurt a bit when Morgance walloped you! You really are quite talented at this." He took a moment to massage his forehead. "Did you truly hit your father with the guitar? Or was that just how you broke through the illusion with Morgance?"

"I wouldn't have wasted a guitar on him if we were face to face. When it really happened, when I was a kid, he took it away from me. And he tore the door off my room, and confiscated all my clothes that weren't school uniforms. Ma took the guitar and all of my clothes back from him, and all of her things. And then she left him. She wanted to take me too, but he petitioned the court and said that I needed to stay in school since I was on the fast track for college, which was already paid for because I was destined to go to the university where he taught. Everything fell apart for me that day."

She stopped for a minute and wiped away some tears, then smiled when Cullen offered her a lace trimmed handkerchief, which he pulled from wherever he hid his perpetual supply of such things.

"If it hadn't been for Merrick, I don't know what I would have done," she continued, her voice unsteady. "I was super annoying and clingy, because at that point, he was the only stability I had left. He actually kept a closet of clothes for me to wear when we went out, and he ended up keeping my guitar eventually—all the stuff Ma rescued. He bought a bass because he knew we were 'destined to be in a kickass band' and I think also because his parents hated it. We're both huge disappointments to our families, ha."

"Little do they know how important and successful you both are now," Cullen told her. "You should be proud because you are actually doing work that makes a difference."

"Look, Da, I'm Queen of the Fae!" Lucee snorted. "Yes, but will it get you *tenure* and *awards*?" she added, taking on her father's Irish accent. Cullen wrinkled his nose and she snorted again, this time at his reaction.

"It's *allll* about the acclaim and peer respect for him. He doesn't even love education that much, except as a vehicle for success. But at least his insistence that I stay in private school kept me connected to Merrick, and gave me some space away from Da's control. But let me ask you something," she said, switching topics. "What did Morgandy mean about my feelings, do you think? It seemed to throw Morgance and Ula pretty hard, and I'm not sure if that was because they didn't catch whatever she did, or because it seemed weird, or what?"

Cullen thought about it for a moment, stroking her arm idly with two fingers, which made her sigh happily.

"I think that maybe—and this is me attempting to interpret The Ladies, so let us take that with a large grain of salt—maybe she meant that your passion is what gives you power, but it also can make you vulnerable if you are careless. You must admit, Lucee, you care about things wholeheartedly."

"Hmm. So, I should beware of letting my feelings spiral out of control or risk being exposed?"

"It is solid advice. You may find that when you do let loose your emotions, the power you can draw from them will be impressive. However, you will need to guard yourself well. That is a skill you can work on, and The Ladies will be fully on board for that sort of training, trust me."

Lucee chuckled. "Knowing them, they'll probably squeal with glee at the prospect of attacking me again. It definitely seems like their idea of a good time."

MUSIC: LINEA ASPERA
Eviction

It had been a long afternoon at The Maithe, and the light coming through the library windows had shifted from a rosy-purpled tone to a proper dusk when the doorbell rang. It startled Vali so hard that Sousa and Merrick had both laughed at her.

She'd been concentrating on drawing in her black book, the collection of sketches she made for her tags and bigger graffiti pieces. She was trying to work out the concept for a tag that would magically ward community gardens to keep them free from pests—both rodents and humans—and it was a frustrating process. Merrick and Sousa had been planning ideas for the stage setup for The Drawback's upcoming show, a local summer festival called ArtPark. It wasn't the biggest festival to happen in Baltimore, but it was one of the wilder ones, and they thought their band would be a good fit. The tagline for this year's fest was "Anything Can Happen!"

"It's almost like they wanted the Fae to show up," Sousa had quipped.

The doorbell rang again, and Vali muttered, "Sure, sure, I'll get that, don't everyone get up at once." She sighed dramatically as she stood up.

"You're the best!" Sousa yelled as she headed down the stairs to the first-floor entrance.

"Yeah, yeah," she grumbled, then came to a sudden stop, shocked at what she saw through the glass of the door.

"Hey Souuuuuz… you're gonna want to come down here."

Sousa and Merrick, prompted by the tone of her voice, ran down the stairs as fast as they could. They turned the corner just in time to see Vali open the door to a tall, handsome man. He was very pale with silver hair that gleamed like starlight.

Camlin of The Grimshaw, their sworn enemy, stood at their door with an unconscious mortal woman in his arms. This was the foe who had led an army against them, who had captured Vali and used her as leverage to try and gain The Maithe. Worse yet, he was the villain that had almost killed Merrick in that battle, and had slain their ally Genaine. And for some reason that Merrick and Sousa didn't understand, Vali was pulling them inside The Maithe.

"What the *hell,* Vali?!" Merrick yelled, and Sousa surged forward to push Camlin back out, but Vali got in his way.

"Can't you see that she needs help? He can't hurt us. He's weak as a kitten—look at him!" She ushered Camlin past the gawping pair and into the ballroom, directing him to put the unknown woman on the couch nearest the door. He nodded nervously and laid her down across the cushions as if she was the most precious cargo in the world. Merrick and Sousa stared from the entryway. It was obvious that they had no clue what was happening or how to handle it.

Camlin turned to them, desperation written all over his face, and tried to appeal to them.

"I did my best to heal her. I just don't have enough power left in me, not right now. And she can't wait."

Merrick looked perplexed. Sousa stood there with his hands clenched into fists.

"I came to offer myself in exchange for your help. I know you hate me; you should hate me," Camlin said, his voice trembling. Softer, he added, "I even hate me. But for some reason, she saw someone worth caring about. That's worth saving, someone who can manage to care about a lowlife like myself."

"Is that supposed to excuse your sudden appearance here?" Sousa barked, followed closely by Merrick exclaiming, "I thought you were dead! I killed you—when you were trying to kill me, I might add!"

"I should be. I wished myself that way more than once," Camlin admitted. "And healing myself used up power I could have used on Emmaline, if only I'd known her then. But I don't have time to explain all that now. Would you please just do something to help her?" He turned to Vali. "Surely you have the ability?"

Before she could answer, the woman on the couch—Emmaline—groaned and tried to sit up. Camlin wanted her to stay prone, but she waved off his concern.

"I'm not dead yet. I'll be fine for now, Camlin, let me sit up and speak to these kind people." Her voice was soft, but with the sort of steel that said she was much stronger than her appearance let on.

Vali was surprised to notice that the woman was older than she'd originally thought—closer to forty than thirty, though she wore her age well. Her hair was long and thick, a dark brown with red strands throughout, and she was the sort of pale that Vali associated with chronically ill folk. She was so sickly that she was practically translucent, with dark circles under her eyes. She wasn't thin, but she seemed brittle.

"I'm Emmaline—Camlin told me that giving you my name is important, even though I shouldn't do that to just anyone? It wasn't my idea to come here. I'm not even sure what you're expected to do. I'm dying and even the doctors can't fix that. And Camlin tried and couldn't, either."

"Camlin brought you here because though he wasn't able to heal you himself. He knows this house is full of powerful people. And the house itself is…well, it's a sort of power nexus. Do you understand that he came here to basically trade his life for yours?" Vali said the last part while watching Sousa glower, standing near the doorway with his arms crossed. Merrick seemed more sympathetic, despite his shock at seeing Camlin alive and in front of him.

Emmaline looked around the room, taking a second to meet the gaze of each person there, saving Sousa for last. When she spoke next, she kept her eyes on him.

"I would have said no, had he asked. I've become resigned to my fate, and I wouldn't have traded a chance to live on the risk of him being hurt, or worse—dying." She paused to catch her breath. "I can see that you find that hard to believe, as you know him in quite a different way than I do. Look, I don't want anything from you. Camlin acted before asking me what I wanted, which isn't like him, but he acted in fear and from kindness, and now he's being asked to pay a price for goods I never requested. Can I at least explain why you should give him some consideration of mercy? Let us tell you our story. If nothing else, indulge a seriously ill woman. Please?"

Sousa made a noise that sounded to Vali a lot like someone had punched him in the gut. She knew why. Even if Emmaline didn't know it, she'd hit some of the words that most triggered Sousa's sense of responsibility. Certain things mattered to Sousa, and justice and hospitality were at the top of that list. He was angry, and now he felt trapped. This didn't bode well, but Vali intended to hear this story, and she knew that Sousa was going to have to go along with it.

Emmaline sat back, looking tired to the bone. She managed to smile weakly at Camlin, who had been hovering protectively. He turned to Vali and spoke to her in a quiet but urgent tone.

"You owe me nothing, and I have no illusions of that, but can't you see that she's worn down? Can you convince her to rest and continue later?"

Emmaline held a hand up and spoke loudly enough that Camlin turned away from Vali to listen to her.

"Let me do this. They need to understand why I defend you, why you are defensible. I'll be all right."

She smiled at him, and Vali could see a depth of emotion on her face, tempered by exhaustion, but obviously that emotion was what powered her to keep going. Vali nodded in agreement.

"I trust her to know her limits," she said to Camlin. "I understand you're trying to protect her, though."

"Will you let me be by her side when we tell our tale?" His tone was stoic, but his eyes were pleading with her to grant his request. "Let me lend her some of my energy, as meager as it is now. I can help her. If you fear my interference, she can ask me if I am dabbling. I cannot lie to her."

He looked ill when he confessed this to Vali, and the thought occurred to her that he meant something much more concrete than a basic declaration of respect.

"You swore an oath."

He looked trapped, but he nodded in the affirmative.

"You gave her that much power over you."

He glanced over at Emmaline, then back to Vali. He straightened up a bit, and looked Vali in the eyes as he explained.

"She has never, not once, expected me to be anything more or less than what I've presented to her. She has never demanded anything of me other than to be myself and to be utterly and completely honest. This was the way I could assure her that I would deliver on that request. I wanted to level the field between us. I have so much power, and she had very little. At least this way, we could be equals."

Vali felt something loosen inside, a tension that had felt knotted up for a long time. This enemy was so tender with the woman he had brought here to the house of his foes, knowing that he would certainly be the price for any help she received. It was nearly impossible to reconcile. But here he was, showing them how he had willingly made himself vulnerable in order to care for Emmaline. He had already weakened himself deeply by trying to heal her when he had hardly any energy to spare. But he was ready to give her more, and Vali was finding that her sympathies were leaning toward helping her former adversary.

She wasn't sure she liked that feeling. But she saw shadowed pain change to relief and comfort as Camlin sat next to Emmaline and took her hand. She saw Merrick's face was reflecting the sort of emotional turmoil that Vali herself was feeling, and she was reassured that at least she wasn't the only one to have those same reactions.

And then she looked to Sousa, and when she saw the hard set of his jaw, her heart sank. He didn't get angry often, but when he did, it was an epic, slow burn, and talking sense to him was difficult at best. Her shoulders slumped at that a bit, even as she registered surprise that she was quietly rooting for Camlin and Emmaline's plight to succeed with the group.

"Merrick?" He snapped to attention, like he'd been lost in thought. "I think we need to bring some folks from the other houses to hear this story and weigh in on what to do. What do you think?"

"I—You're right, of course. I can round up Lucee, Cullen, and Aisling, and Daro and Karsten from Tiennan House should come, at least. Who else?" Merrick looked to Sousa, recognized his fuming state for the dangerous situation it was, and mumbled, "Never mind, I'll figure it out myself."

Sousa's jaw worked for a moment, his brows knitted together, then he finally spoke, in a much calmer tone than one might expect if they didn't know him well.

"Ask The Ladies if they will join us. *Explain* the situation to them, if you would."

After Merrick left the room—and he looked extremely grateful to get out of The Maithe for a while, all things considered—Sousa turned to Vali and summoned her in the most controlled, tight voice she'd ever heard come from him.

"Vali? A word?"

He strode off to the opposite side of the ballroom. She followed, a feeling of dismay settling into her guts. He'd never been angry with her before, and she didn't like being on the receiving end of it.

"What is it exactly that you're doing here?" His ire was barely contained.

"I'm waiting until I have all the information possible before I do anything, Sousa. That's how I always try to operate. You know that." She kept her voice even, trying to project calm.

Sousa clenched his fists, closed his eyes, and took a few deep breaths. Vali said nothing, letting him take that moment to try and rein in his anger. Finally, he opened his eyes and met her own with an intense gaze.

"I know you're a kind person, Vali. I mean, you took on all of this at the House, you nurture people and gardens and the neighborhoods that need it most. But why, of all people in the world, would you want to give the man who threatened to slit your throat if I did not do as he said the *benefit of the doubt?*" He hissed the last words, his voice betraying his confusion and frustration at her stance.

"Look, Souz. I *want* to hate him. I do. But have you watched him with that woman? He's ready to give up his life to save hers. He didn't even hesitate to offer it. He came here knowing that we could, and probably would, punish him and possibly kill him. But he felt that was a fair trade for saving Emmaline, who, I might point out, is a mortal."

Vali took a second to gauge his reaction. Sousa was still staring at her intently, and she couldn't read him.

"What I need to know is this, Sousa. Do we have room in ourselves to allow others to grow, to change, to become better people? Can we allow our enemies to repent and absolve themselves? And if not, can we live with ourselves?"

Her eyes were welling up, and she realized that she was shaking. Sousa blanched and looked as if she had punched him. He looked past her to the couple on the couch, watching as Camlin put an arm around Emmaline protectively and let her head rest on his chest.

"I need to think." He frowned, then, unsure of what to do. Vali reached over and touched him gently.

"Maybe take a walk to the gate and meet everyone when they get here? I can watch over these two until you return. And Souz?"

"Yeah."

"No matter what, we'll get through this. We always do."

Impulsively, she threw her arms around him and hugged him. He didn't hug her back, but she could feel the stiffness of his back and shoulders ease just a little. That was enough, she thought. He hadn't totally shut her out.

He strode off, leaving her to watch over their unexpected guests. Vali noticed that Emmaline was shivering and huddled up to Camlin, so she found a throw stashed away inside the storage area of one of the window benches and brought it to them.

"Here, this might help a little," she said to Camlin, who gave her a grateful look and carefully, if a bit awkwardly, draped it around Emmaline.

"She gets really cold when she's tired," he explained, and glanced down at her with such affection in his eyes that Vali had to comment.

"Is she asleep?"

He nodded in confirmation.

"She doesn't know, does she."

Camlin narrowed his eyes and cocked his head, confused.

"She doesn't know that you're in love with her."

Vali watched Camlin's emotions play out across his face—panic, anxiety, a touch of hopelessness. She didn't say anything, she just let him decide how he was going to answer.

"I can't—I shouldn't answer that. Just being near her puts her in danger."

"We wouldn't hurt her. But you don't necessarily mean us, do you?"

Camlin shook his head. It was obvious to Vali that he didn't want to use any names, just in case he somehow conjured up The Grimshaw.

"It didn't matter when I first met her, there was no reason to care about the consequences. And now it does."

Vali said nothing. What could she say? Camlin knew what his history was with all of them. When he'd held her captive, he had tried—unsuccessfully—to break into her mind and control her. He had used her as a bargaining chip to try and force Sousa into ceding The Maithe to him. She certainly wasn't going to gush over Camlin's seemingly newfound ability to love.

Yet... there was something inside her that urged her to weigh the possibility of change, just as she had asked Sousa to do. She had seen people grow and redeem themselves in her time on the street, even folks who she knew had done heinous things. And she certainly wasn't innocent. Living on the street and trying to survive opened one up to making choices that were often questionable at best.

But she'd never killed anyone. Camlin had killed. He had led an army against the Eleriannan and Gwyliannan factions. People had been hurt. Some had died.

Vali knew she needed to reconcile all of this soon because when the Fae showed up, things were bound to get heated fast.

As she had predicted, no one was happy when they walked into the ballroom of The Maithe.

Sousa had wisely waited until the folks from both Tiennan House and House Mirabilis arrived before he returned inside. Vali could hear arguing voices that announced them before they even entered. She rose from her chair near the couch but didn't move to greet them; she wanted to give them the impression that she was carefully guarding Camlin and Emmaline. A bit of security theater for their comfort, to be sure.

"Why is this villain not in chains? What is the meaning of this?" It was Daro, one of the Gwyliannan leaders, and Vali had expected that reaction from him. Tiennan House had suffered many losses from their interactions with The Grimshaw. It was going to be difficult to get him to listen objectively.

Karsten, who was next to him, was harder to read. They looked alarmed, but Vali couldn't tell if it was because Camlin was there, or because Daro was angry. Usually, Karsten was a gentle soul from whom Vali would expect compassion, but there was no telling what might happen today.

But when Lucee, Cullen, Aisling, and Merrick entered the room, Vali held her breath. Cullen's hands were balled into fists, and he tensed up when he saw Camlin. Aisling wrung her hands nervously. Surprisingly, Lucee showed no reaction at all. Vali couldn't decide if this was a good thing, or a bad one.

The Ladies were the last to enter, their childlike stature at odds with the power and wits they wielded. Upon seeing Camlin, Morgance made a face that could have either been a grin or a grimace, but was certainly filled with pointy teeth.

"Well, what have we here," Morgance hissed. It wasn't a question; it was an accusation. One of her sisters—Ula, Vali thought—sniffed, then made a disappointed face.

"He is laid low. He is no threat to any at this moment. A shame." She looked as if she'd been denied a favorite meal. Vali shivered, glad they were on the same side.

Merrick chimed in. "He wants something from us."

"And desperate he must be to come to those with whom he made war!" Morgance turned to Merrick. "He holds the reason in his arms. See there, his weakness revealed."

Emmaline did her best to sit up when Morgance referenced her. She looked at the newest arrivals with naked awe on her face. Of course, Vali thought, because until now the only Fae she'd met all looked like unreasonably attractive mortals.

The Ladies were completely different. Despite their small size, they were dressed in sweeping, Gothic dresses of black and green. They had wild black hair that was long and tousled, and of course those jagged teeth.

Daro and Karsten also were the sort of eye-catching that was beyond just being beautiful. Daro's dark skin was covered in golden swirls that traveled up his bare arms, and his almond-shaped eyes were a beautiful matching amber shade. And of course, he had those elegant horns that curved upwards from his forehead over his spiky, golden-tipped, black hair and his pointed ears.

Karsten was both muscular and androgynous, with strong features that somehow worked perfectly with their beautiful eyes and full lips. Karsten's hair always confused Vali. It was short on the sides, but the middle was a thick crest that spilled down their back in long tendrils that moved independently, much like snakes. Merrick had once confessed to Vali that he was afraid to ask if they actually were snakes. As kind as Karsten usually was, Vali wouldn't have been comfortable asking either.

"She sees through our glamour, I take it." Daro's deep voice echoed in the ballroom. "What else is there to know about this mortal?" His eyes narrowed as he looked Camlin and Emmaline up and down. "I thought you despised mortals, Grimshaw. What could she offer you that would change such a hatred to a warm embrace?"

Camlin swallowed visibly, and Vali could see him trembling nervously. His voice was subdued and humble. "She gave me the chance to be better, at least to one person, without asking me to justify that chance. She saw me and who I might be, given time."

He swallowed again, and Vali thought that he might be pushing back tears. Camlin, crying! What on earth?

"I owe her everything. And so, when she needed the help I cannot give, I brought her here to those I knew had the only chance to save her. Even if it costs me everything."

Morgance spoke up then, stepping forward to stare at him in her most challenging manner.

"So, you came here, to your enemies, to ask for succor for a mortal none here know? And you give yourself as forfeit for this aid?" She looked terrifying in that moment, like she could jump forward and eat him in one bite if he answered in a way she disliked. Camlin, however, seemed to accept this possibility and maybe even welcomed it.

"I did."

He paused, letting that answer sink in before he continued.

"Do with me what you will. But I am begging you, save Emmaline. She has the sort of inner light that you lot talk about wanting to attract and support. But she is dying, and I cannot help her more than I have."

A quiet fell over the room, as those assembled contemplated what Camlin had said.

Morgandy, the third Sister, who had been quiet until that point, spoke up. "You, mortal. Did you ask for this aid? Was this your idea?"

Emmaline gulped at being addressed by that small, fierce being, but she answered in a clear and strong voice. "I did not ask. I must have passed out, and Camlin couldn't wake me because when I did wake, I was here. This was the first I knew of his plan. I would have refused if I had known because I could never trade his life for my own."

"What has he offered you, then?" Morgandy's green eyes glittered as she challenged the woman.

"He—he offered me nothing? He gave freely to me." Emmaline looked confused.

"And what did he give freely to you?"

The whole room seemed to lean in to hear her answer.

"Friendship. Care. And most importantly, honesty. The thing I needed most."

Morgandy took a step closer, her teeth slightly bared. One would be foolish to lie or annoy her, Vali thought. Emmaline should have been terrified, but she held steady.

"And how could you know that he was honest with you?"

"He swore a vow to me. Before you ask, unprompted."

Morgandy turned to Morgance and nodded. Morgance spoke up then.

"We wish to hear this story." She pointed at Camlin, then addressed him in a steely voice. "And you shall answer questions. She will ask them for us, and we will know you speak true."

Camlin inclined his head and murmured, "Yes, of course. Whatever you desire."

"Oh, you shall do it whether you will or not," Morgance cackled.

MUSIC: HANTE.
I Don't Need A Hero

Camlin stood, taking only a moment to ensure that Emmaline was supported and comfortable before he rose to speak to the assembled Fae. He squared his shoulders, and his voice became haughty, disdainful—the first time that he had used that tone since his arrival at The Maithe.

"I know what I am. I'm the one who brought destruction to your peaceful, special little lives. I'm the villain who led my faction through the powers of my mind and will. I'm the one who strove to divide you from your precious Maithe House and your charge to protect the Lady of the City. I captured Vali and tried to force her mind to fall under my control, and I used Genaine in that very same way. And then I killed Genaine.

"I know that is all you see when you see me. I am dangerous, untrustworthy, evil."

Camlin paused, then licked his lips. His hands were clenching and unclenching at his sides as he spoke. Vali glanced over the room, noting the reactions of the Fae gathered there as Camlin spoke. Sousa was still seething under the surface. Merrick leaned forward, as if getting closer would help everything make more sense. Aisling clutched his arm as though she wanted to hold him back. Lucee was still unreadable, her face blank, but her eyes wide. And the rest of the Fae in the room were either angry or appalled, from what Vali could see. She wasn't sure what she felt yet. Her intuition was telling her to reserve judgment until the whole story was told, so she was doing her best.

"There is so much you don't know about me, and about what has truly happened," Camlin spoke quietly in the silence. "The Grimshaw are not what you think they are."

"What are you trying to sell us, enemy? We are not so simply swayed that you can convince us that evil is actually good," Daro spit out at Camlin. "Why are we even listening to you?"

"Because you need to, in order to understand what you are truly up against, Gwyliannan. You have allied with the Eleriannan and beat back The Grimshaw for now, but they are much more than you suspect. You know that much of the ranks of Grimshaw come from your own people. And you have wondered, I am sure, how I managed to control so many—how I pressed them into my service, how I knew how to capitalize on their hatreds and fears."

He stopped, and looked around the room, meeting the eyes of as many as would match his gaze, before he went on.

"I, too, was controlled."

The room broke out into chaos, with yells and gasps from those assembled.

"What do you mean 'controlled?' And who could do such a thing?" Merrick asked, his voice cutting through the din. At his question, a nervous silence fell over the group.

"As surely as I held the minds of those who were under my command, I too was captive. The Grimshaw is more than the people who gather together under that banner. There is a force of deep malice, of cunning and rot and entropy at the center of The Grimshaw, one that eats at the heart of everything it occupies. Its power flowed through me, and I am ashamed to admit that I welcomed it for far longer than I should have."

"So, you claim that you weren't responsible, that this evil force is to blame?" Sousa broke in, contempt in his voice. Camlin acknowledged his question by raising a hand, signaling for Sousa to stop and listen.

"I was a willing partner when all this started. I was angry and damaged, filled with hate for mortals who had rejected and feared me throughout my life, and who were responsible for the death of my mother. I despised the Gentry for abandoning me and then shunning me when I finally discovered who I was. I was a perfect vehicle for the seductive song that was spun for me. I offered myself gladly to the force that whispered secrets and ideas to me, that agreed with all I felt, and offered more examples of how terrible those I despised were." Camlin paused for a moment, then added, "Its control was so deep in me that even after I failed, and it rejected me as a proper vessel to carry it, I still...I still followed that path. It corrupts all that it touches, and that corruption runs deep."

Morgance walked right up to Camlin and inspected him for a moment, seemingly to seek out any sign of lies or subterfuge.

"Although this one reeks of past lies, he speaks the truth." She backed up and looked to Morgandy, who was in agreement with her sister. She looked thoughtful.

"Long ago, there was known to be a creeping malady, an infection that would slip into the minds of those ripest for the taking, usually those of us who were untrained, unaware, agitated, and alone. Like you, I wager," Morgandy directed to Camlin.

He nodded, his eyes downcast in shame.

She continued, "We called this the Mealladhan, they who beguile and deceive, for that was their true path. It has been an age and then more since any I knew saw activity from them."

"The eldest of us worked to root the Mealladhan from this world, and those who left to the Misty Lands did so believing that their task was complete," Ula added. Out of the three of the Sisters, she looked the most concerned. Morgandy wore a thoughtful gaze, and Morgance seemed prepared to poke Camlin to see if she could rouse whatever evil might be inside him.

"They are unbodied spirits, nigh impossible to detect. They seep into the minds and thoughts of those of us who are the depths of the most negative emotions or circumstances. They cause chaos and destruction when this happens, but usually not in such an organized manner. Their primary targets are those who are young and untrained because they do not have the discernment to sense what is happening. They feed on the energy of their host and will often compel the host to act irrationally, so that they might get access to that energy even more easily." Ula paused for a moment, then added, "Something has changed. Your interactions with the Mealladhan are different than any known to us."

Merrick frowned at this. "What does that mean, Ula? Something has changed?"

"It means," Camlin answered with a thoughtful tone, "she believes that something about me caused the Mealladhan to operate differently. It used me to gain control of others, ones it normally would not have been able to reach. Is this correct, Ladies?"

Morgance grimaced, as if she disliked greatly having to agree with Camlin.

"It is correct. Through you, it spread like a virus, setting each one controlled like a puppet dancing at the end of a string. Or rather, you set them to dancing, and it pulled your strings." She paced back and forth while she spoke, her small steps echoing in the ballroom. Vali realized that she had never seen The Ladies this agitated before, not even when they prepared to go to war with The Grimshaw.

"How do we fight something like this, then?" Merrick asked, his voice low, unsure.

"I do not know," Camlin admitted. "It released me, not the other way. When you defeated me, it was not just in body, but in spirit as well. I was broken, dying, and ready for that fate. I did not expect to be dragged away by The Grimshaw. I was certain they would leave me there to die in the street, as befitted a failure of their leader.

"Yet they did take me. I awoke on the dirty floor of a collapsing warehouse, my wounds bound and a jug of water by my side. Nothing more; I was alone and left to heal or die. I suppose some of the Gwyliannan felt the pang of guilt at the idea of leaving me without the barest of tending. But the most disconcerting thing to me was this."

Camlin paused, gathering the attention to focus on his next words.

"My head was finally clear. I was truly alone, for not even the whispers that had controlled me lingered. Hurt as I was, I was of no use to The Grimshaw."

"And they threw you to the wayside as easily as you had tossed Genaine at Sousa and The Blackbird when you were finished using her, then?" Daro's accusation rang out across the room, and energy crackled around him in his anger. Camlin acknowledged it with the bow of his head.

"I was under their control, but yes." He hesitated, then added, "It knew how I felt about Genaine, and it used my feelings to bend my actions in ways that sicken me now. I understand that you may never be able to see the difference, and I accept that and whatever punishment you hand me. I cannot undo what was done, I can only pay the price now."

Vali was tired of all this talk about things that, in her mind, could be solved later. She spoke into the silence that followed Camlin's last words, chiding them all.

"This is all well and good, and certainly needs to be discussed at length. Later. Because right now? There's a woman who needs our help. I see no evidence that she is part of some plot against us. She is an innocent bystander who actually deserves some saving. And we're supposed to be saving things and making things better, right? Isn't this our calling?"

"Hmmph."

Sousa stood there, arms crossed on his chest, and Vali's heart sunk a little when she looked at his stance. He was such a great guy, but when he made up his mind about something, he could be incredibly stubborn.

She looked at him and raised an eyebrow. "You have thoughts?"

"What I want to know is this: why her? That one has hated mortals with more vitriol than any of us I've known, so what could be so special about her that he would change his mind? A spark? We see mortals with that spark all the time. It hasn't tempted any of us to switch sides." His words dripped with distrust and contempt. "And how did he get close enough in the first place to know anything about her? He hasn't said a fuckin' word about any of that. You'd think he would have led with it, y'know?"

Sousa glared at the woman on the couch, leaning into the armrest in a way that looked precarious at best, thanks to her illness.

"I wanted to use her. That's what you want to hear, isn't it? It is the truth, and yet only the surface of the truth. But perhaps that is all you need to know," Camlin sighed. He looked incredibly tired, like he just wanted it all to be over.

Sousa gestured for him to go on, the look on his face impenetrable to Vali. She glanced around the room, trying to gauge how everyone else felt. Daro's handsome face reflected disdain, which Vali expected. After all, Camlin had killed one of his court, and he had been the one to influence her to betray them before that. Genaine's death obviously weighed heavily over all of them.

Karsten, standing tall next to Daro, seemed to Vali to be a bit more interested in hearing the rest of the tale, or they at least held less contempt for Camlin than Daro did. The Ladies seemed distracted, and Vali guessed that they might be contemplating what Camlin had told them of the Mealladhan. Merrick looked nervous and edgy, like he didn't know what to do with himself. And Lucee and Cullen? They both looked sick. Lucee was biting her lower lip, something Vali had learned over time meant that she wasn't sure of what she should do. Cullen was staring at Emmaline with a haunted look on his face, and Vali had no idea at all what that meant.

She turned her attention back to Camlin, who was explaining how he came to meet Emmaline.

"When I saw her the first few times at the café, I saw her shine from across the room. I wasn't looking for anyone like her, I was trying to avoid being seen. I was still weak from healing myself, practically useless. My only trick left to me, really, was basic glamour like avoiding being noticed.

"I first thought about how I could use her energy to my benefit, as I am sure you expected. The Mealladhan had taught me well. I would go to the café to steal food right from under their noses, and I would contemplate how I would introduce myself to her. But she beat me to it, because somehow she saw me, even though I had cast my glamour to avoid being seen. And that threw me off my game so much that when she spied me, I went to her with no plan, and I just—I talked to her."

Emmaline broke in then, her voice soft but clear.

"He reached behind the glass and took a cinnamon roll, put it on a plate, and walked away with it. Not a soul there even batted an eye, everyone just treated it as if it was normal behavior. They *saw* it, but they just accepted it. At that point, I couldn't help it, I started laughing and he must have heard me because he turned on a dime to stare in my direction, a look of total disbelief on his face. And that made me laugh even harder, and I waved him over to my table in the corner while I tried to get myself together.

"I have no idea why I beckoned him my way. Maybe it was because in that moment, I felt a weird kinship with him? Two people in this crowded coffee shop, and no one really paid attention to either of us. And in the back of my mind, I knew it was foolhardy of me, but you see, these days I really don't worry about things like that much, not anymore.

"He came over and the first thing he did was pull out a chair and sit down, all princely, like he owned everything in that café. I raised an eyebrow at that, because really? I mean, for all I knew, he did own the place, and that's why no one said a thing, but somehow I doubted that."

Morgance snorted at that. "This story is quite believable so far!"

Emmaline turned to look at Morgance directly, which Vali thought was impressively brave. She addressed Morgance in a firm tone, sitting up as straight as she seemed able to manage. "Honesty is the thing I value more than anything. You will see."

"Continue on, mortal, I wish to hear the rest of your tale," Morgandy encouraged her.

"I just ask that everyone let me tell it without interruption, and then we can answer questions." Emmaline looked around the room for agreement, ending with Camlin, who sighed and nodded.

"Please don't wear yourself out, Emmaline."

"I'll do what needs to be done, especially as you've left me no choice."

He clenched his jaw at that and looked away. Vali thought to herself, *This should be interesting to hear.* She decided to bring some chairs over for everyone to sit in a loose semi-circle around the unwelcome couple, and then Emmaline began to tell the rest of her story.

As I said, he came over and the first thing he did was pull out a chair and sit down. And he seemed confused by me, which didn't make sense until he started to talk.

"How in the world did you see me? That's not a thing mortals are usually able to do when I want to be unnoticed!"

It almost slipped by me that he said "mortals" and I decided to call him on it and see what happened. Maybe he was delusional; I'd talked with enough folks who had mental illnesses during all my trips to run-down free clinics to know how to roll with that.

"Mortals, you say. As if you aren't one? Interesting." I tried to strike a tone that passed it off as no big deal. "My question was more wondering why no one else paid attention to you. But if you are the only non-mortal here, then I suppose that's my answer?"

I guess I'd thrown him off his game.

"I—" He paused for a second, I assume to get himself together. "That is, I asked first."

I said nothing, just waited.

"How much did you see?"

"I was watching you from about the moment you walked in."

His face registered his surprise at that, the reaction of someone who isn't used to people who don't perform as expected. Not the first time I've seen that reaction in regards to me, let me tell you.

"So why take things? Are you broke, or do you do it because you can get away with it?"

"I'm supposed to be asking you the questions." He sighed. "But it's a little of both. I do admit the idea of moving unnoticed amongst these slow and unobservant people is a thrill. And I am hungry."

"Please don't stand on ceremony on my account, go ahead and dig in! But surely that's not enough to fill you up."

He looked relieved and tore into the cinnamon roll in a way that made me realize that he must have been starving, but was polite enough to not eat in front of me uninvited. Which was another piece in this very odd puzzle because most street people I've encountered wouldn't care enough to worry about being rude when it came time to eat. Anyway, he didn't look like that type of person, he was much too refined.

I drank the rest of my tea while he finished the roll, then drank a bottle of expensive juice and started on some water. I played it cool, but I could tell that he was looking me over, assessing me. I was curious what he was thinking, but I learned long ago that if you're patient, most people will tell you what you want to know, so I waited in silence. Finally, he leaned forward and squinted at me a little, then nodded as though he'd solved a mystery.

"You're sick, right? That's why you're used to people watching. You sit back here and observe people because it's the level of socialization you can handle. You have a frailness about you, and a way of moving languidly, conserving energy. And you've got dark circles. They do play up the green in your eyes, though." He looked pleased with himself.

"Not the most tactful way to bring it up, but yes. I am chronically ill, and it's a chore to even walk around some days, much less interact with people. But I still get lonely, so I drag myself down the street from my apartment to this café, and I sit here and people-watch. And usually, people notice me about as much as they did you, today."

"I hope I did not offend—"

"Ha! I bet that's not a phrase that comes out of your mouth often, is it?" I laughed again when he nodded, looking a bit abashed. I figured that he didn't get that look frequently. "It's fine, I find your straightforwardness refreshing. You say what you mean, and so many just don't. Or they don't know how to act around me. Another reason to sit here and watch them, rather than try to interact. I would guess that you know exactly how that feels."

I sipped my tea, gazing at him over the rim of my cup. It was obvious that he wasn't used to being examined so closely, and he ran a hand through that spiky silvery-white hair of his.

"I make you nervous. Why is that? Surely if you are more than mortal, you have no reason to fear me?"

It was a genuine question, though I did take a lightly teasing tone when I asked it.

"I don't open up to mortals. I don't open up to anyone, actually. Despite how little I have shared, I have told you more today than I have any anyone at all in quite some time. I'm confused by it, but I suppose I find your straightforwardness refreshing."

He did look confused. I also got a hint that, just possibly, he was as entertained talking to me as I was with him.

"That's rare enough to impress me. Most people say they want frankness and honesty, until they get it and realize that they prefer the beautiful lie. Not me, give me the ugly truth. Even if I hate it, it's real, not some bullshit to make me feel better or be more compliant."

I guess I let some of my emotions show on my face because his demeanor shifted just a touch. Maybe I'd triggered some empathy in him.

"I respect that." He finished off the water in one gulp, then added, "Until recently, I had a lot of people surrounding me who liked to tell me what they thought I wanted to hear. Or what would keep me happy, even if it wasn't the truth. I fostered that environment, to be fair. But it ended up being a cage because I was lulled into a false sense of security." He shrugged and smiled ruefully. "I paid for that dearly, and now I'm on my own."

I don't know how he did it, but that admission just broke through any reservations I'd had about him. It was ludicrous, really - this handsome man that no one seemed to take note of, talking to this broken, ill-looking Gothy woman in the corner like she was the most interesting person in the place. He's got that charm, as you know. But he wasn't using it on me; he was actually talking to me like he was the one who couldn't resist my charms. And normally that wouldn't get to me, so maybe I was vulnerable, or maybe he worked some of his—as he called it—glamour on me. I extended my hand, and after looking at it for a moment like he wasn't sure what to do, he took it.

"I'm Emmaline. And *that* is the first time I've told anyone who isn't a doctor my name in ages."

"Giving names to others is something my people do with great caution, but as you offered yours first, I shall do the same. I am Camlin."

He looked like it pained him to say it out loud. I didn't understand that look until later, of course, when I learned about The Grimshaw and what had happened. He let go of my hand, a slow withdrawal that under other circumstances would have creeped me out, but I found that I hadn't wanted to let go either.

"Why do I get the impression that I'm an entire package of 'things you don't do or don't often do?' And despite that, you're kind of enjoying it, aren't you?"

"You are not wrong," he admitted.

"So tell me, why don't your people like giving names? Is it a power thing?"

I thought at first that I'd caught him off guard with my question, but it turns out that it was because I had guessed correctly.

"Exactly right. Names hold power. Knowing the proper name for something, or someone, can confer great control over them. Offering one's name to another is a gift of trust. And when a name is given generously, without thought to power plays, it is generally considered good manners to respond in like. Manners also matter to my people." He made a face, then, and added, "Not that I really can call them my people these days."

"Why aren't they your people anymore? Or is that too forward to ask at this point in our conversation?"

"I have managed to alienate myself from all of them, even those who were supposedly on my side. But that is a tale I'm not ready to tell yet. Perhaps in the future."

"I get that. I don't have people anymore, either." I paused for a second, then added, "I mean, this should go without saying, but because life is what it is, I'm going to say it anyway. If there's anything you don't want to tell me, don't. I won't push you, ever. You give what you feel like giving, and it'll be a gift."

He considered that a moment, and I let him, while I finished my tea.

"That is more than I expect or receive from the rest of the world, a generous offer that I will uphold with you in return. And because you have been so straightforward in your desire for honesty, I offer that as well. The truth may be ugly, but I won't lie to you."

"In my experience, it is the liar who insists on being believed." I said it flippantly, but something about it must have struck a nerve with him. He sat up stiffly in his chair and slapped his open palms down on the table with a smack. He had my full attention.

"I know you're teasing me, but it's important to me that you understand that I am telling the truth. I am saying this once, and only once. I promise that I will only speak the truth to you."

As soon as he spoke the words, there was a ripple of energy that radiated out from him, in blues and golds, rustling papers and blowing the napkins off the table.

I couldn't help it, I blurted out, "What the hell!" and moved back suddenly.

"That's the sort of half-witted decision that one of my kind makes when they have been deprived of good company for too long, I fear." He had the nerve to look amused at my reaction, and in that moment, I admit that I was reconsidering my rash decision to talk to this man.

"You—you did some—Something weird happened." I sat there and thought about it a moment, my head spinning. "You made some sort of... of...a magical vow?"

Wow, did that sound ridiculous.

"Let me reassure you, that is exactly what my foolish words did. Well, I suppose that time will tell if I am the fool. My instincts pushed me to trust you, so here I am, trusting you by offering you a bit of power over me. Please do not abuse it." He actually looked uncomfortable, it was obvious that whatever had happened, it left him feeling off-kilter, and that was another feeling he was not accustomed to having.

I sat there in silence for a few moments. I'm sure it was killing him to have that tension hanging over us while I took in what had happened.

"Would it be ungrateful of me to use that as little as possible? I would rather you offer up what you choose to share than to ask you a ton of probing questions. But thank you for the consideration you're obviously giving to my needs."

"Don't use those words. Don't thank me. It is not a welcome exchange to my kind, though I appreciate your impulse. Be grateful, be pleased, be honored. Don't say thank you." He paused to make sure I nodded in agreement before he went on. "Power is best saved for the most important moments to be used. Though any question you ask is fine; if I don't wish to answer, I won't. That is my counter to your power, you see." He smiled at me, then, and it was like the sun shining on an icy road - blinding in its beauty, possibly hiding hazards behind the dazzle.

"So—why me? Why decide that I'm the one to trust?" I had to know, because seriously, who makes a vow like that with someone they've known for less than an hour? He took a moment and considered the answer, his brow furrowed a bit. He even frowned handsomely, of course.

"I expect you to scoff at this, but there's something compelling about interacting with you. You've taken everything I've said to you in stride, which is a rarity. You have asked me reasonable questions and accepted every answer. And you offered me respect without any strings attached. I think I'd be a fool to ignore these things, so I am choosing to trust you." He paused, then added, "To be honest, I need to have someone I can trust in my life. It's been such a long time."

His eyes immediately widened, and it was obvious he'd had no intention of saying that last part out loud. If it had been anyone else, I would have laughed at that reaction. Instead, I looked him straight in the eyes, and reassured him.

"I'll do my best to deserve that trust. And I understand. I've been alone for a long time too. The longer you're alone, the harder it gets to be around people."

I was surprised at how sad he looked at that.

"You previously said you are alone, and that perplexes me. You're a perfectly pleasant companion, why are you without friends or family? Or a lover, for that matter?"

It was my turn to look uncomfortable. I didn't much like talking about how being sick changed my life.

"People started treating me differently when I got ill. Some wanted to fix me, and no matter what I did, it was never enough. Others started out supportive, but after a while, they got tired of my complaining, my attitude, the fact that most of my life revolves around being ill. I wasn't as much fun; I couldn't do all the things I used to do with them. And being sick makes you poor, too, so that changed me. Eventually people drifted away, and I let them. And I don't really have family. They're all terrible and I'm estranged from them. Soooo… yeah."

As I talked, I watched his face change emotions from sad, to a flash of anger. Then his jaw set and his eyes narrowed a little, and I wondered what he was thinking.

"Are you here daily?"

"Most days. Unless I'm too sick. This is my big outing, such as it is. I can watch people, and write." I indicated my laptop, which had sat closed the entire time.

He nodded, and then stood up abruptly.

"I will see you here tomorrow. Until then."

And he was gone, like he'd never been there.

The next few weeks, he came every day, without fail. He learned what I liked to eat and how I took my tea, and suddenly he was there before I arrived, everything waiting for me. When I protested, he got mad at me and told me that if I didn't accept his gifts, he would be highly insulted, and no mortal wanted to insult his people.

I laughed at that and he wouldn't talk to me for the rest of the day. He didn't leave, he just sat there, sullen, until the usual time that we parted ways. He then bowed to me! Bowed and left! The next day, he acted like it had never happened, and I drank the tea and ate the food without protest.

Over time, we began to ask each other questions ruthlessly. Who we were, what we did outside of our meetings was considered less important than what we liked and disliked, what we observed around us, what mattered to us. He would read my writing and laugh or look thoughtful at my observations of the people that passed all around us. He told me that he understood why I did well in my job as a writer.

I eventually figured out what to call his kind—your kind—accidentally, during a conversation where we were teasing each other.

"If you don't finish your food, you will disappoint me. You don't want to do that."

"Oh sure, my Lord of Faerie, I'll do exactly as you bid!"

He sat back suddenly, like I'd slapped him. I felt myself flush, realizing

I'd said something bad and I was in danger of him storming off or worse.

"I'm sorry! Did I insult you? I didn't know, I'm so sorry!"

His face softened at my emotional apology.

"Of course, you couldn't know, could you. The Gentry—actual Fae lords—are everything I hate, and calling me one of them insults me deeply. I am no lord, and they despise me as much as I do them."

I sat there, digesting what he'd just told me. He actually looked like he regretted his reaction, which was a surprise to me. For someone who hated lords, he sure could act the part sometimes.

"You don't believe me? They are so full of themselves, you see. They hold so much power, and yet choose to sit back and hoard it, only getting involved in the world outside when it comes to their doorstep and drags them into it."

"I believe you." I bit my lip, unsure if I should go on. "I just—I didn't know that you actually are...Fae?" I stumbled over the word as it just seemed weird coming out of my mouth. "I mean, I knew you were something different than me, I guess you'd say. Help me here, I'm stumbling around, trying to figure out how to word this and not inadvertently insult you further."

That got an honest-to-god laugh out of him. I guess I'd managed to break the tension with my incompetent attempt at honesty.

"I'm not insulted, not anymore. I see that you were just teasing, and how could you know you would get that reaction from me? I've never told you a thing of my background, and to your credit, you've never pried or pushed me. It's one of the reasons I enjoy your company, Emmaline."

He became serious then and leaned forward towards me, as if he was sharing a deep, dark secret. I did the same, and we must have looked like two gossips sharing an exceptionally juicy bit of news.

"I'll tell you all about me if you want to hear my tale. But I won't do that here, where those I seek to avoid might overhear and make my life... complicated. But if I share this with you, then I ask a return of equal value."

He couldn't just say that he wanted to know more about me. Not this guy, not ever. It had to be couched in some sort of tit-for-tat game, like he couldn't just be interested because he liked me and wanted to know me better. Walls behind walls, that's how Camlin is. Sorry, Camlin, you know that I'm right.

So that's how he ended up walking me home—to my tiny, sad little one room apartment—and how I learned about who he is and was. And yes, he told me everything about The Grimshaw, and how he was in opposition to all of you. And the battle, and what came after, at least for him.

We sat there for hours on my sofa-bed while he explained the intricacies of his world. He only left when it became obvious that I was exhausted and was trying to hide it so that he would keep telling me more about his mysterious life.

The next day, I was sick. So sick that I couldn't make it to our usual meeting, which had never happened before. I was distraught, because not only did I hate missing our date, but getting ill in that way was a bad sign. I've been living with this disease for a while because I'm poor and uninsured, and I've learned to pay attention when my body tells me things. In this case, the message was that I wasn't going anywhere. And I had no way to get in touch with Camlin to tell him, which made me feel worse, like I was letting him down.

When he showed up at my door, I honestly didn't expect it. I was barely able to get up and answer it, and as soon as he saw me, he just... well, he swept in and started taking care of me. Not in some knight-in-shining-armor sort of move, either. He was so careful to ask me what I really needed, how he could be helpful.

He said, "I won't do anything without getting your direct consent unless you are unconscious, then all bets are off." And I agreed, with the caveat that he was under no circumstances to take me to a hospital or doctor, because I couldn't afford it. He didn't like that, but he reluctantly agreed.

He got me into my sofa-bed, and then he left, promising to be right back. When he returned, he had a huge bag of food from my favorite restaurant, the Lucky Duck.

"I saw the menu on the counter, so I went there and asked what you usually ordered. Then I got some other things too. You should have some food for the next few days, easy to reheat whenever you need it."

"I thought you were broke? I guess I should be grateful, huh. I'm sorry, I'm so crabby when I feel like this." I was embarrassed, he was being kind to me and here I was, questioning him.

"When I said I was broke, it wasn't untrue, exactly..." He trailed off for a moment, then added, "I don't have much money, so I save it for situations where I don't want to use glamour to get what I want. The people at the place where I got this food were nice, and they seemed to care when I said you didn't feel well, so I wanted to make sure they got paid fairly." His face colored a little bit, and I couldn't decide if he was embarrassed about ripping people off, or admitting that he cared enough about my friends at the restaurant to not cheat them. Maybe it was both. I would bet that he didn't usually feel bad about ripping off mortals, though. It felt like this was a new consideration.

I got sicker. I was pretty scared and tried not to let on to Camlin, but I've been hospitalized once, and I was afraid it was coming again. There was no way I could afford a hospital visit. It terrified me that I might actually die this time—a pretty terrible death at that—but what was I going to do?

He didn't want to leave me alone. I fell asleep with him stretched out there next to me, chattering away on some topic on another. When I woke back up, I saw that he'd fallen asleep too, slumped over with his head resting on the arm of the sofa-bed. And from that point on, he just started staying over every night. We would talk until I passed out. Or I would type up my column and send it in to the online publication that published me and paid me a modest salary, and he would sit and read one of the many paperbacks off my shelves, or take a shower, or wash clothes. This immortal, stunningly handsome being, someone out of a fantasy tale, and there he was, doing our laundry. It was too ridiculous to be true, but there we were, being domestic and hermit-like roommates together.

I could tell he was worried about me, about my deteriorating health. It's my immune system, it attacks me from the inside out, and the meds I could afford hadn't helped. He told me that because I was around him all the time, I benefited from his presence. At first, I laughed because it sounded like a humblebrag or something, but he explained that actually being near him conveyed some strength and health benefits. Just—it wasn't enough to heal me, because he had used so much of his energy on healing himself. It was only enough to keep me going, but even that was becoming more difficult.

"Your health is getting worse by the day," he told me, and his voice was so full of concern that it made me sad, because I'd hoped he hadn't noticed. I mean, of course he did, he's magical and all that, right? But I hated how worried he looked. I know, I see the skepticism on your faces, but this was two days ago, and here I am now. I didn't expect that he was going to bring me here to you. He didn't even tell me that he was thinking about this before he did it, or even that he thought there was a possible option. He just brought me here when I collapsed.

When I came to and realized where I was, I knew that he had just bargained his life for mine. How on Earth could I ever rate that? I'm as mystified as you seem to be.

MUSIC: THE BRAVERY
Believe

As Emmaline told her story, her face first reflected her sense of humor and awe at getting to know Camlin. Vali had to admit that she'd been captivated by the tale, as Emmaline was a good storyteller. It was obvious why she was employed to share her tales. Everyone in the room, even Sousa, had seemed to get sucked into listening. But at the end, as Emmaline described becoming more ill, her face changed—the humor trickled away and left a haunted, tense expression.

Emmaline turned to Camlin and spoke in a soft voice, one that Vali had to strain to hear.

"When did you get this idea, make this plan?"

"Should I answer the unasked question as well as the one you're voicing?" Camlin's voice cracked a little, and Emmaline waved her hand to indicate that he should go on, her eyes downcast.

"When I first saw you, I saw the sort of hidden spark that often goes unnoticed, which makes it even more precious. And yes, I wanted that for my own. I was consumed with the idea that a mortal could be the answer to my downfall. I studied you from a distance for many days before you actually noticed me. And then when you revealed that you saw me, I enacted my plan to charm you, to get close to you for your energy."

There were noises of outrage, contempt from the assembled Fae, and Camlin let their reactions roll over him before he continued.

"Yes, I deserve that, and more. I was still Grimshaw, despite my freedom from the grip of the Mealladhan. But... I actually liked Emmaline. And the longer I spent time around her, the more I hated the part of me that ever saw her and wanted to use her for my own gain. For one, she accepted me immediately, and even when I told her about the things I did, who I was—I know that you would say who I am, still—she accepted me."

Merrick broke in, then, his voice incredulous, and he directed his question to Emmaline. "How could you accept one who admitted to hating mortals like us? Or, even worse, who killed people?"

She turned to him, her gaze intense, accusing.

"And you? Did you not also kill? Was it not a war?" She cast that same look around the room. "You all fought. Wars have sides, winners and losers, and each side believes their cause to be the right one. It doesn't mean that I agree with Camlin's choices, but I understand to some degree how he arrived there. And are any of you guiltless of hating or mistrusting another group without a real reason? Don't tell me you are, because Camlin explained to me how he used the hatred between the Eleriannan and Gwyliannan against you both."

"Biases are easy to exploit, and we were all used," Lucee's voice cut in, quiet but powerful. Emmaline looked to her and raised her hand in agreement.

"This is the moral of the whole story, right? This thing—the Mealladhan? It has used everyone. It taught Camlin how to use others and it spread its poison that way."

"It used me to infect the Gwyliannan and Eleriannan, to rip apart Houses and deepen the already existing mistrust for its own benefit," Camlin added. "It wasn't until you were able to unite and defeat me that it let me go, and even then, the poison took a long time to leave me, as you see. I suppose I am always going to be fighting it in some way for as long as I live. But now, at least, I know what it is. Understanding that it is there helps me to resist the call."

Vali thought that he looked embarrassed, and she realized that when he said he hated himself, he might not be just saying it for effect.

"We did not heal the rift between the Houses until our mortals joined us and pointed out the follies of our ways," Morgance said in a thoughtful tone. "It was The Blackbird who bade us go directly to Tiennan House and address our issues with each other."

"No, that was Sousa," Merrick corrected, and Sousa made a dismissive sound.

"I would never have thought to go there and ask them if you hadn't admonished us all the night before. And you agreed to go right away. Then, when we met with them, you cut right to the heart of the matter between us and helped us start to build an alliance. None of that would have happened if you had not fallen in with the Eleriannan. Everything changed when they took you in."

The room echoed with the sounds of agreement from the rest of the Fae there. It was then that Vali noticed Emmaline's expression—her face was tight, the rigid mask of someone who was in pain and trying to hide it. Her skin had grown even paler, and she was shaking, despite her best attempts to conceal that.

"Camlin, is Emmaline okay? She looks terrible!" Vali watched in horror as the frail woman turned away from them, a small gasp escaping her before she managed to bend over and became sick on the floor in front of the couch. Camlin reached out to give her some support, then looked up and met Vali's eyes, silently pleading with her. The message was clear: do something.

"Are we going to help her, or sit here arguing over all of this until she wastes away right in front of us?" Vali snapped, and she felt the mood of the room shift as she scolded them.

Karsten stood up and looked around the room, then turned to Vali.

"We have no healer. But I would make an elixir for her, if some of the others here would contribute to it." They spoke to Camlin then. "This is the outcome you wished for, correct? To give her some of our essence? You know that she will be bound to us, not to you. You cannot even contribute; you are too weak."

"This is one of the scenarios I hoped might play out, yes. And if she is bound to you, that is an extra layer of protection for her," he agreed, the relief obvious on his face. Vali considered that a moment, then filed it away to ask him about later.

"We will help her. If she was able to see one such as Camlin when he did not want to be seen, having her bound to our side is a wise decision," Morgance declared. There were some assorted murmurs across the room at that, then Cullen spoke up.

"I trust The Ladies in their assessment. I will assist," he volunteered. Beside him, Lucee nodded.

"This isn't a thing that I can help with, is it? Because I'm not Fae born?" She leaned forward, eager to be included if possible.

"You may stand with us as we prepare the elixir, but your essence needs to stay with you. Having you by our side will ensure that you are included in the connection," Morgance reassured her. Lucee looked thrilled to be able to help in any way she could.

"Fine, I'm in. We need to make this happen quickly. She is fading fast!" Sousa broke in, surprising everyone with his apparent change of heart. That was how Sousa was, though, Vali recognized. He could get angry and stubborn when things called for it, but in an emergency, he could be counted on. And he was secretly much softer-hearted than a lot of people suspected.

"I'll stay here with Camlin, or are you going to use the ballroom?" she asked, and Sousa shook his head.

"We need privacy. We can take her to a room upstairs."

Camlin started to move to scoop up Emmaline, but Sousa stepped forward and gestured for him to move back. "We need you to stay here. I can handle this," Sousa said, then bent down next to Emmaline and asked in a gentle voice, "Is it okay with you that I carry you upstairs? We all want to help you; I just need your permission."

Until Sousa spoke to her, she had been cradling her head in her hands, leaning over with her elbows propped on her knees. She lifted her head just enough to stutter out an agreement, then dropped her head back into her hands. She looked miserable and deathly white.

"Here, I'm going to pick you up now," Sousa warned her before carefully gathering Emmaline up in his arms and heading towards the stairs. Camlin and Vali stood there, surrounded by empty chairs, as they watched the group file out on their way to try and save the sick mortal.

"I know she is hating every moment of this," Camlin muttered. "She's told me that she despises how weak her body has become, and she always complains that I've been doing too much to take care of her."

He made a gesture of powerlessness, his hands in the air, and sighed. "She will be furious with me when she feels better, and she should be, I suppose. But I'd do it again if I had to. She's worth it."

Vali said nothing and just nodded absently. She felt at a loss, left here alone with this seemingly very different version of the adversary she knew. She didn't feel any more in control of her feelings when he casually asked her where things to clean up the mess on the floor could be found. She walked him to a closet that was filled with cleaning supplies and gestured widely at the array of things to choose from.

"Things I didn't expect to be doing today include instructing Camlin of The Grimshaw about where to find rags to clean up after his sick mortal girlfriend," she grumbled, then sighed and added, "Sorry. At least you offered to clean it. And I guess it says something that you decided to come to us for help. Though the less charitable parts of my brain are waiting for the other shoe to drop."

Camlin grabbed an armful of rags and set to cleaning up the mess. He looked up at Vali from where he was down on his knees scrubbing, and addressed her last comment while he worked.

"I would think you a fool to trust me, to be sure. If our positions were reversed, I would certainly suspect a trick to come." He paused for a moment, looking over the floor to make sure that it was clean, then looked back at her. "And I find myself in a similar position—waiting for the other shoe. Because one doesn't walk into the house of one's enemy and offer their life in trade without understanding that this offer can be redeemed at any time."

He scooped up the rags and took them back to the closet, where he dumped them in a bin for such things. Vali heard him wash his hands, then he came out and started pacing back and forth in front of the windows. She watched him for a moment, studying his face and the way he carried his lean form as he walked and worried. Finally, she flopped down into one of the chairs with a sigh, and pulled over another so she could prop her combat-booted feet on it.

"You might as well sit, before you wear a groove in The Maithe's gorgeous ballroom floor, and then Souz will really have something to be mad about." She pointed at the couch and raised her eyebrow for emphasis. Camlin's shoulders slumped as he obeyed by flopping down on the couch.

"I know. The waiting is the worst."

Vali didn't know why she was offering comforting words. Really, she knew she should be angrier, or cautious, or something other than this calm, accepting version of herself. There was just something different about him, something unsteady and unsure, that made her feel sincerity in his words and actions. That, and she privately agreed with Emmaline—none of them were perfect, and Vali had a policy of believing that even the worst people had good in them. No one was irredeemable, not in her mind.

She realized that Camlin was staring at her intently, and she cringed a little inside, hoping she hadn't been making stupid faces while she'd been thinking or anything like that.

"What? Do I have something on my face? Did I finally grow those cool pointy ears that everyone else has?" He snorted at that.

"So cool that we have to hide them from every mortal so we aren't killed for being monsters. Besides, I saw what you can do. It is pretty spectacular, even without the ears."

It was Vali's turn to snort, and she made a dismissive wave of her hand.

"Here we are, making jokes about how I crushed your troops after my friend stabbed you with an expanding thorn. We truly must be on the road to friendship now," she quipped.

In the back of her mind, she knew that her joke could be walking on the razor's edge, but if he reacted poorly, it would tell her something about how volatile he truly was. In the battle between The Grimshaw and the Fae that Merrick had led, Vali had broken free and called upon the power of the Lady of the City in a wild rage after Merrick had managed to stab Camlin. She had brought down buildings on The Grimshaw without a second thought, sealing their victory as their adversaries fled for their lives. If anything was going to make Camlin touchy, it would be that subject.

To her surprise—and his credit—he took the comment in stride.

"If I can't be friends with those who thoroughly defeated me, who can I truly befriend?" He didn't look exactly comfortable making the joke in return, but Vali suspected it was more from being out of practice with the art of self-deprecating jokes, rather than the subject matter itself. She decided to distract him with that line of thought, which might get them more information as a tasty extra as well.

"I guess you don't have a lot of people lining up for that job, anyway. Not these days, at least."

"Right to the bone, you cut me. But yes, I'm not—I have never been—good at making friends. Or allies. Or connections at all, until I fell in with The Grimshaw." He shrugged, playing at being careless, but Vali could tell that under that cool facade, it bothered him. She decided to pull at that thread.

"You've been an outcast. The Grimshaw were the first to make you feel like you belonged," she guessed.

"Shrewd observation, Priestess of the City. You're quite observant and thoughtful," he said, looking uncomfortable. "Did you know that in Middle English, the word 'shrewd' used to refer to a villain? Not a comment on our situation, merely my mind finding random connections to distract itself."

"You like to play with words. You must have been quite a bookworm growing up. Of course, loners often are."

"And you must have dreamt of being a therapist as a child."

"I have a lot of time invested in understanding people. It helps me be able to navigate the world a bit easier, and sometimes I can aid them too. Trying to give back for all the times other people helped me, you know." She leaned forward a little, knowing it was probably a bit reckless, but she needed him to feel that sense of closeness for what she was going to say next.

"People who had shitty, abusive childhoods recognize each other."

She watched him drop a mask over his face like a brick wall, his expression blanking out to something cold and haughty. *There it is,* she thought. *That's where it started for him.* She decided to turn the lights on herself for a moment, let him regroup and think about what she was saying.

"You know, when I met Sousa, I was living on the streets. I slept on the regular in some big cement pipes over by the Jones Falls, in an abandoned construction site. I've been squatting since I was fifteen, and before that, I was tossed around between relatives and foster families. Somewhere in there, one of my parents—I guess—must have been Fae, but there's no way to know who. So that was a surprise when I found out, you know?"

She took a pause, and realized he was listening to her intently, so she decided to keep going.

"Some foster families are great, but some are godawful, and the last one I had before I got out of there...Well, they were monsters. They used the foster kids as cheap labor. They didn't feed us well. We slept on the floor. They locked us in the closet as a punishment, which was all the time, because we could never do anything right in their eyes. And then the husband came and got me out of the closet one night and just—he just beat me for no reason, until I could hardly stand. And that was the last straw, I knew I had to get out of there.

"I don't know what happened to the others after I left. That haunts me to this day."

The room was unbearably silent for a few moments, then Camlin's voice, soft and full of emotion, broke that silence.

"No one can fault you for running from the monsters. You were a child."

"I tell myself that all the time. One of these days, I might believe it."

"You're shaking."

She was, and she felt vulnerable being called out on it, but she just nodded. She wasn't going to let him think her vulnerability was a weak point, even if she wasn't always sure that was the case.

"They killed my mother because they feared me and my magic." His voice was so soft, she almost missed this confession.

"...Oh. Holy shit."

"My mother was mortal, and had no way to defend herself. She tried so much to find ways to support us after my impossibly handsome, ice-cold father left, I suppose to rejoin the other Gentry of the Fae. I didn't know at first what he was. I had no idea. It wasn't until much later, when she explained where my powers came from. That was why I had no one to teach me how to control them or use them properly. I ruined so many opportunities for us because I would make some mistake, let my magic be seen, and we would be chased out of town. We often would only escape with our lives and the barest amount of our belongings.

"She met a man. He was cruel, and he despised me. I had stopped going to school. It was torture for me. I was bullied constantly and it was almost impossible to control my magic when they were trying to hurt me. And one day, I awoke from a deep sleep and he was beating my mother black and blue, and she was crying and screaming, and people were pounding on our door—and something snapped in me.

"I attacked him with a blast as the door flew open. And they saw the attack. In that moment, I was suddenly the villain, and my mother must be just like me. Why else would he have been attacking her? And they went after us, and I escaped.

"And she did not."

He looked up and locked eyes with Vali, his icy blue gaze penetrating and intense.

"If I had been there when your foster father had been beating you, I would've killed him too. As much a monster I may be, even I have lines that must never be crossed."

"Do you still see yourself as a monster?" she asked breathlessly. Her heart was pounding in her chest so loud he surely could hear it.

He sat there, motionless, still holding her gaze, then finally broke it and looked away. He wrapped his arms around himself, his hands moving nervously, pale against his black T-shirt.

"I would kill all the monsters if I could. Even the one inside me, and me with it, if I cannot purge it."

Vali felt a wave of profound sadness and empathy wash over her.

"You don't think you can purge it."

Silence.

"You don't have to do it alone. Not everyone here would help, but I would. You might be surprised who will step up to your aid."

He turned his gaze back to her, his face once again masked.

"In my experience, people don't offer to help unless there's something in it for them," he said in a flat tone.

"The world's a transactional place, but that doesn't mean that we all want you to pay an unbearable price. What I want is the chance to reduce pain and improve life for those who need it. That's what gives me joy."

She jumped up then, a sudden movement that made Camlin blink and pull back quickly.

"I'm sorry, I didn't mean to startle you, I just had an idea. Hold on a sec, let me grab my bag and I'll show you." She retrieved her backpack and pulled a black hardback artist's notebook out of it.

"This is my black book, where I make the magic happen. Literally."

She grinned and flipped it open, and he gasped as he realized exactly what she meant. Each page was covered with graffiti in small-scale mockups for future tags, to recreate in large scale on walls. Each tag shimmered with stored energy and purpose.

"These are incredible!" Camlin exclaimed as he examined them carefully. "You've charged them for different purposes?"

"We use them for many things, including warding doors. That's how we kept you out of The Maithe until Genaine brought you in. I probably shouldn't be telling you that, but it's long done by now." She laughed. "Souz is going to kill me, but it's my magic to show off, I guess. And I want to make something for you, which he's also going to hate, I'm sure."

"I don't think that's ever going to change. I threatened everything he holds dear. I would despise me too, were I in his shoes. Or boots, I suppose."

Vali had taken out a plastic bag filled with all sorts of pens, markers, and paint pens in the meantime, and she squinted at the blank paper for a moment before starting to work. First, sweeping lines that seemed to undulate together, into letters that were almost readable, and then back to other twisted creations. She swept her pens across the paper in rhythmic motions, and although Camlin watched intently, he couldn't seem to get the grasp of what she was creating. Colors built and overlapped, a deep blue and lavender and a mossy green that changed textures depending on which way Camlin looked at it. Then Vali had a marker with a chartreuse yellow-green and she was layering the tiniest dots here and there in the design.

And then she was finished and when Camlin looked at the drawing, it seemed to hover over the page, and glow with an inner light that he had a difficult time looking away from.

"What—what *is* it?" he breathed, entranced.

Vali grinned and looked pleased with herself.

"It's belief."

MUSIC: DEPECHE MODE
Wrong

What do you mean by 'belief?' I don't understand." Camlin frowned at the little piece of magic, then reached out a finger to touch it gingerly. Vali grinned even wider at that. He was like a little boy with his curiosity.

He gasped a little when his fingers seemed to pass right through the drawing as it hovered over the page, and he closed his eyes for a moment to steady himself.

"That is the oddest feeling—it seemed to want to attach to me! What does this mean, Vali?" Camlin was starting to look spooked, so Vali took pity on him and explained what it was meant to do.

"If there's one thing I have in surplus, it's a positive outlook. So, I took some of that energy and wrapped it up in this tag. I guess you could say I imbued it with belief in goodness—in something better, you know?" She leaned forward in a gentle, encouraging movement. "I think you might need some of that. Maybe that's insulting, but I hope not. Sometimes we all need some help, when things get dark and difficult."

Camlin considered that a moment, then picked up the notebook and looked at the tag a little more closely, bending his head close to the paper. Vali wondered if he was hiding a reaction from her.

"So how does it work?" he asked, his voice a bit deeper and softer, which seemed to confirm Vali's suspicion that he was feeling emotional.

"You can just carry it like a talisman if you want, but I do have something I've been practicing, if you wanted to have it on you at all times." She gestured for him to set the notebook down, and he did so. The tag still hovered over the open page, and she leaned over, biting her lip a little in concentration as she moved her hand next to the tag, and scooped it into her cupped palm.

Camlin sputtered a bit in surprise, and she shot him a look of pride.

"Wasn't sure if it would work in front of others, but here we go! Now here's the cool thing. I can place this anywhere I like, and it will meld seamlessly with it. And once I do that, no one will know that it is made of magic except those who are attuned to it. So, it could effectively work as a tattoo, for example, and none would be wiser."

"Do you think...Would you...Ah, could I do that?" He looked embarrassed to be asking it of her, and Vali thought on that for a moment before she answered.

"I can, but you'll have to let me touch you for that. Which might be weird for us both, but I'm game. And you need to tell me why asking for that bothers you."

He shifted in his seat nervously, then sighed and looked up to meet her gaze.

"It seems intimate, and I don't think I rate that from you. I feel like seeing it every day would be an excellent reminder of what it is for, but again, your friends may find it objectionable. And they will surely think I am attempting to manipulate you, and I would not blame them for that."

"Anyone who knows me will tell you that the opinions of others have been less than successful in keeping me from doing what I want to do. And what I want to do is help you find some joy in life, so you can feel some hope. People without hope do stupid things, like let evil fungus in their minds to control them."

The smallest smile pulled at the corners of her mouth. Camlin closed his eyes and shook his head at that.

"You are a force of nature, I have to admit. No wonder the City chose you."

"It couldn't have been anyone else, it's true. Now, where do you want this?"

Camlin thought about it, then stuck out his left arm, presenting his forearm to her. She looked at his pale skin and nodded, then stopped.

"You know this is going to be very visible, right? On your complexion, it'll look amazing but everyone is going to see it immediately. I think I can move it after I place it, but I've never done this on skin, so..."

"I'll see it too. And I don't want to hide it. It'll remind me that things can be better. That I can be better. Let the symbolism shine forth." His voice was resolute, and she smiled at his determined tone.

She moved forward with the tag hovering over her palm, gently sparkling as she carefully positioned it. A voice in the back of her mind reminded her that this was the closest to him that she'd been since he'd captured her, and she quietly told it to shut up. She refocused at the task at hand, and with a flick of her wrist, the image jumped over to his arm.

He breathed in sharply, and she asked, "Did that hurt?" He shook his head, and she reached out gingerly, touched the tag, and was able to slide it around to the perfect position on his forearm. She tapped it twice and felt the smallest wave of vertigo—which by his reaction, he seemed to share—and then she stepped back and the tag was emblazoned on his arm. It glowed against his skin and it looked like something only the most talented tattoo artist could have applied.

"Um, what the hell is that?"

Vali turned to face Sousa and Lucee, standing at the threshold of the ballroom. Lucee looked confused, though Vali could tell that she was intrigued by the art that was now on Camlin's arm. Sousa, predictably, looked angry, with more than a touch of concern. Vali sighed internally, careful to keep her frustration off her face. She knew that Sousa was generally more suspicious and cautious than Vali tended to be, but she chafed a little at the idea that she couldn't handle herself.

"Guess you're finished with Emmaline? We kept ourselves busy down here," she said in an upbeat tone, flashing Sousa a brilliant smile. Behind him, Lucee shot her a look that obviously was meant to ask if she was okay, but Vali didn't know how to convey "My enemy and I had a fine time alone, but my boyfriend is angry" with facial expressions.

"What is it, Vali? It's beautiful," Lucee said. The unasked "Why?" hovered between everyone in the room.

"I had an idea. Camlin was game to play along with it. I made a piece of magic specifically for him, to assist him in his work of changing himself, and in seeing the good parts of the world. It's like a talisman of how I move through life. It is a small magic I've been working on, and it felt like he needed it," she explained. She was gratified to see Lucee's face soften and relax at that. Sousa didn't seem as ready to accept that, but he didn't push it right then and there.

"You'll have to explain that one to me in more detail later," he said to her with a penetrating look. "Emmaline is going to be out of it for a while, and she was pretty upset that he"— he indicated Camlin with a roll of his eyes— "couldn't be a part of bringing her into our ranks." He turned to Camlin then and addressed him directly.

"I know you understand that I don't like you, and that has small chance of ever changing. I don't take well to people who threaten those I love and protect. And that one upstairs? She's under my protection now. For some reason, she sees more in you than I'm able to understand. Me, though? I'm still suspicious. That hasn't changed. I'll be watching you." He narrowed his eyes, staring at Camlin intently.

"That's nothing less than what I would expect," Camlin answered in a subdued voice. "And you'll discount it, but I want you to keep that suspicion about me. Watch me like a hawk; it'll make both of us feel better. As for Emmaline? She's the last person on Earth I would want to hurt. I'm sure you can see that she is precious to me." He turned away from Sousa then, as if he had said too much.

Sousa sniffed and looked up to the ceiling for a moment like he was exasperated, but Vali knew that reaction. He was conflicted about his feelings, and he didn't know what to do next. *Me too, Souz, me too,* she thought.

Lucee broke the tension with a deep sigh.

"I don't know how all of you aren't ravenous. I didn't even do magic and I'm ready for a plate stacked with food! Surely there's something to eat around this magnificent pile o' bricks you call home, Souz?" She gave him her saddest puppy-dog eyes.

"I don't know what I did to deserve this," he said in long-suffering tone. "There'll be food up in the library when you go up. Take Camlin too. Vali?" She turned, having already started to head towards the stairs. "A moment, if you don't mind?"

She made a face that clearly demonstrated just how fun she expected the next few moments were going to be, but she came back to Sousa, flopping down on the couch where Camlin had sat earlier. She decided to let Sousa say whatever he was going to tell her first before she opened her mouth. Maybe it wouldn't be that bad.

He did wait until Lucee and Camlin were out of earshot before he let loose at least.

"Vali, what the hell are you up to with this? You're playing with fucking fire!"

Okay, maybe it would be that bad.

"Before I say anything, what do you want from me? Do you just want to yell, or do you actually want to hear my thoughts? Because I need to know how to react to you right now." She kept her face and voice calm, and her tone reasonable, but she could feel her considerable patience starting to run out.

"What? When have I ever wanted to yell at you?" Sousa looked shocked, then his whole demeanor changed as he realized how he'd been acting. "Oh wow, I'm an ass. I'm sorry, Vali."

"You're scared. I get it. But you do realize that, despite my propensity to see the good in everything, I actually have pretty good survival skills. And also, let's not forget that I have the powers of the Lady of the City in my back pocket."

He had the sense to look embarrassed at that. "You're right."

"And I appreciate you worrying about me. I do. But I have things that I need to do, and one of them is to keep pulling Camlin towards our side of the field. Because that guy? He's got a lost, scared, hurting kid inside him under a mantle of a lot of power. It's no wonder that whatever it is that's powering The Grimshaw snatched him up when it found him."

Vali patted the sofa next to her and looked up at Sousa with a questioning gaze. He still had that embarrassed look about him, but he sank down on the cushion next to her, and she turned and hugged him. A tiny noise escaped from him, almost like a gasp or a sob, then he wrapped his arms around her and pulled her close.

"I really am sorry. That guy, he just pings me on every level, you know? But you didn't deserve that," he mumbled into her hair after a few moments. She made a shushing noise and tilted her head to kiss him, and she felt the tension leave him.

"It's natural that we're going to be feeling like this," she said after they pulled back a little, and she leaned into his embrace, her head against his shoulder. "He was our enemy, and he brought so much destruction. But he says that he was used, and he wants to do better, and I want to give him that chance. And we have Emmaline with us now, so that's going to affect how we move forward as well. I want us to be smart, and also kind. That's the brand we strive for, right?" She smiled at him, then reached up to trace the edge of one of his pointy ears affectionately.

"If you're trying to distract me by doing that, I'm not going to stop you," he said, laughing. "I don't trust him. But he said all the right things. But I still don't trust him. I'll stop being a raging asshole though. It's tiring anyway." That made Vali snort in response.

"I want to stay here cuddled up with you, but I'm awfully hungry too. Guess that's my fault for giving away tag tattoos," she lamented jokingly. "Mr. Joseph Sousa, will you take me to dinner?"

"I hear that the library is serving currently. What exactly it is serving is, of course, beyond my pay grade. I'm definitely not the one in charge here."

Lucee had discovered something about Camlin that wasn't obvious—not until they went to the library and found a bounteous spread of all kinds of finger foods waiting for them. Camlin had gaped at the selection, picking up an hors d'oeuvre-sized quiche of egg and spinach and studying it curiously.

"This is...well, unexpected. Excessive!" He popped the quiche in his mouth, and his eyes grew wide. "And delicious," he added after he got the quiche down. "Is there a reason for this? Or is this normal?"

"Oh, this isn't even as fancy as it gets around here," Lucee said, filling a plate with tiny cheese-filled croissants. "I have never eaten better than I do now that I'm with the Fae. But surely this is something you've experienced? I feel like all I do these days is eat, and every meal is better than the next."

Camlin had been studying each platter of food carefully while she talked, as if he was trying to decide which things were best to concentrate on. Lucee shook her head at this.

"You can take as much as you want, Camlin. There'll be plenty for everyone, and our friends who make the food will feel quite complimented that you wanted to try it all. No one goes hungry here at The Maithe."

He stopped to regard her for a moment, and she thought he looked a little shocked. His jaw worked for a second before he answered her, and it was obvious that he was fighting some strong emotions.

"I've never been extended such hospitality before today. And to think that it's in the house of my once-enemy." He paused, then looked away. "The welcome you have given me is kinder than I deserve and I am both grateful and ashamed."

Lucee didn't know what to say to that, so she decided to shift the focus of their conversation.

"Surely you've had tables piled with food like this before? I mean, you're Fae, it's something I've associated with any gathering of Fae around me, at least."

She pointed at two of the comfortable velvet armchairs that were nearby, indicating that they should sit. Camlin pulled the small side table that was between their chairs forward a bit, so that they could rest their plates on it while they ate. He sat back in the chair and considered what she'd asked for a moment before answering.

"It might surprise you to learn that I didn't grow up around other Fae, and I hadn't even crossed the path of another of my kind until about forty years ago. My mother had given me a fanciful explanation of what I was when I was young, but after my father disappeared, I saw not one other face like mine until much later. All that time in between, I was on my own, growing sadder, then angrier. I never had the opportunity to experience the magics of a proper Fae House."

He paused for a moment as Sousa and Vali entered, then shrugged in a way that seemed almost flippant to Lucee, and continued.

"When I learned about the Eleriannan, at first I longed to meet them, to join them. But they were unapproachable, locked away in their great Houses, impossible to gain audience with unless you already knew another Eleriannan. The first Fae I truly met were a troop of Gwyliannan, who harbored a dislike for the Eleriannan, because they treated the Gwyliannan as lesser. We bonded over those shared dislikes, and they took me in. They were eventually to become The Grimshaw, as dislike turned to enmity, fostered by myself, directed by the influence of the Mealladhan."

"You were alone for all that time? Wait, I thought you were Highborn. Oh wow, so many things suddenly make sense," Lucee said, a sad look on her face. "You were ripe for the picking for that M-Mealladhan," she stumbled over the last word, still unfamiliar to her tongue.

"Half Highborn. Half mortal. The product of two worlds, belonging to neither," Sousa muttered. Vali turned and glanced at him, and his expression changed enough to tell her that he was affected by Camlin's story, but he didn't want anyone to know that. At least not yet.

"I suppose I was," Camlin replied to Lucee. "Almost everything I had seen of the world at that point was ugly, harsh, cruel. I hadn't wanted to be the same as what I saw around me, but slowly that changed; I changed. I won't place the blame on the Mealladhan—that would be too simple and unfair. It obviously saw a rich medium in me where it could grow and spread." His voice took on the bitter tone of self-hatred, and for a moment his jaw tightened. Then he gathered himself together and turned to take a bite from one of the things on his plate, trying to turn the attention away from himself and his emotions.

The room fell silent for a few moments, and everyone followed his lead and ate some of the food placed before them. The silence was broken by the entrance of the rest of the group that had been with Emmaline, except for Karsten.

The Ladies went straight for a bottle of dark liqueur that Lucee could have sworn was not there earlier. Three small goblets were poured and gulped down before any of them even looked at another person in the room. Lucee exchanged a wide-eyed impressed look with Vali at that.

"I don't think I've been this tired in ages," Merrick said and sank down on one of the couches with a small grunt. Aisling flopped down next to him and leaned her head on his shoulder wearily. "I had no idea it was just as intense to be on the giving side as it was the receiving when it comes to the elixir," he confessed.

"It is easier with a larger group, especially one that is more used to working together like this than we are," Cullen said as he slid to the floor next to Lucee's chair and leaned back against her. She leaned forward to touch his shoulder, and he reached up to cover her hand with his. As they basked in each other's presence, Vali happened to glance toward Camlin, and she caught his wistful expression.

She leaned close to Sousa and whispered to him, "Do you think we can let Camlin see Emmaline? He's being incredibly reserved about it, but I can tell he's worried." Sousa's brow furrowed, then he squeezed her hand before he walked over to The Ladies and spoke quietly to them.

There was a bit of back and forth before Morgance strode over to where Camlin was sitting and spoke to him in a voice that was much less bell-like than usual. She sounded tired and suspicious.

"Tell me then, our enemy who sits comfortably in our midst, was it your idea?" She glared at him, fierce despite her small stature.

"I can't answer until I know of what idea you speak?" Camlin, genuinely confused, scrambled for a response.

"To go to see the one you brought to us, lying there helpless as she re-covers, of course," Morgance snapped. Her eyes were hard as she looked him up and down, looking for any sign of bad intent. Finally, she made a dismissive noise and said, "No, I see you are clueless and without motive. Fine, go see her, though she will surely sleep all night. There is much to repair, but she is strong-willed and given time, she will recover."

Camlin's eyes darted around as he looked at every person in the room until he came to Vali. When their eyes met, his shoulders relaxed a little, and he nodded with the recognition that she was the one who had set this up.

"Would you be kind enough to escort me? I don't know where she was taken, and it might ease the minds of those here if I was accompanied," he asked, his demeanor humble.

Vali agreed and led him down the hall to the room with the open door.

She could see warm light from the sconces in the hallway spilling into the darker room. The windows along the wall that faced outside were dark, which meant that hours had passed since Camlin and Emmaline had arrived. Vali had barely noticed; everything had been so tense.

They found Karsten dozing in an armchair that had been pushed against the wall just inside the doorway. Vali coughed lightly, trying to let Karsten know that she was there without startling them, and Karsten's eyes flickered open.

"Ah, I should have known you would want to check on her," they said in their soft voice, then covered a yawn. "Apologies, this was unexpected work and we had little time to prepare. But the woman did well, and we believe that she will recover fully." They stretched gracefully and pushed back their rippling hair, then addressed Camlin. "She will be glad to see you once she wakes."

They paused for a moment to level a stern gaze at Camlin before continuing.

"Take care that you do not use her as the balm for your own damage. She is strong but fragile, despite how she hides that. You did the right thing to bring her to this house."

"My goal is to spare her from any pain caused by me or any others," Camlin answered in a subdued tone. "You were kind to help her, despite my involvement."

"Hmm." Karsten tilted their head, studying Camlin's face before they responded. "I have been thinking on all you said. I do not think you were blameless, and all you have said tells me that you agree. That gives me hope for you. Let that hope not be misplaced, Camlin-who-was-Grimshaw."

Camlin nodded, solemn and thoughtful. "I will hold that hope as my balm, then."

MUSIC: SISTERS OF MERCY
Some Kind of Stranger

The room was dark, and every part of her ached.

Emmaline couldn't figure out why she hurt so much or—after a moment of lying there as she tried to get her bearings—where she was. She decided that maybe she should sit up, but her body shut that idea down, and she thudded back to the mattress with an "oof!"

"You're awake! How are you feeling?" Camlin's voice was a comforting sound in the darkness. She heard some rustling, then he asked in a gentle voice, "Should I turn on a lamp, or is darkness preferred right now? Here, squeeze my hand if you want some light."

She felt his hand, cool and reassuring, take hers. She squeezed it weakly, and he withdrew it. A moment later, soft light illuminated the far corner of the room, and she was glad that he had been thoughtful enough to not blind her with a closer source.

"Um… Hi. I'm not sure how I feel, actually." Her voice was rough, raspy.

"I suppose that makes sense, given that you just awoke," he said reassuringly as he crossed the room and sat in a chair next to the bed.

She decided to attempt turning onto her side so that she could face him, and after struggling with that task for a moment, she managed it. She was grateful that he didn't try to help her, because she already felt awkward enough with the situation they were in. Then she looked at his face and inhaled sharply.

"You told me that I saw you properly before. But you look…You are…" She trailed off, embarrassed at her lack of eloquence. She knew she was staring, but she couldn't seem to help herself.

He'd been handsome before she'd drank the elixir, but now it was almost unbearable. His skin practically glowed. His eyes were an even icier blue and his hair more silvery-white. Everything she had found attractive about him before was even more pronounced. Even his pointed ears, which he often took pains to hide, were on full display and only added to his striking looks.

"I see." He cleared his throat nervously. "I truly thought you saw entirely through the glamour and treated me as you have, despite what you saw."

She realized he was blushing, which seemed utterly ridiculous to her. Surely, he was aware of his looks!

"Evidently, I did not. But you mean that you thought I treated you like a normal person, rather than some hottie, right?" He made a sputtering sound at that which might have been laughter or indignation; she really couldn't tell.

"Well, you must be feeling better then," he managed to get out, and she decided he must be laughing. He finally got himself together and added, "To answer your question, yes. I am loath to admit it to you, but the fact is that I've been quite talented at using my looks to inspire trust and convince others to follow me. Because evil never comes in beautiful packages, of course."

She started to answer that, but he didn't give her a chance to address it.

"But please tell me, truly, how you are feeling? I've been so worried." His voice trembled a little at the end, and she frowned at that.

"Would you sit with me? I'm a wobbly mess, but I miss being close to you. Maybe I shouldn't be that straightforward, but I almost died. That gives me the leeway to say whatever I'm feeling, if you ask me." She patted the space on the bed next to her and carefully moved away from him to make more room.

"Are you sure? I don't want to hurt you..."

She looked at him beseechingly, and she was rewarded with the faintest whisper of a smile before he gently eased onto the bed.

"I really want to hug you," she blurted out, feeling herself blush. That won her a genuine smile from Camlin.

"Come here then, because that is something I would very much like."

She slid into his arms, laid her head on his shoulder, and wrapped her arms around him, sighing deeply. They stayed like that for a few minutes, saying nothing, the two of them just basking in each other's presence. Finally, she said in a quiet voice, "I've been better. But I have been much worse. Right now, I'm grateful for this moment with you. I'm afraid about the possibility that there won't be many more of them, and that isn't making me feel very hopeful."

"I don't think you have to worry about them hurting me, at least. Not after the speech you made."

"Camlin"—she sighed, pulling back so that she could look at him—"there are so many ways to hurt someone that aren't physical, and you know that. What if they decided that your punishment was to separate us?"

He was silent for a moment, and when he finally answered her, his voice was mild. "Perhaps that is what I deserve. Perhaps that would be better for you as well."

"...Oh."

"I hope you understand that I don't want to be parted from you. I'll accept whatever atonement is demanded of me, but that would be a bitter price to pay."

"I don't want to lose you." Her voice was firm, and she clung to him in a way she had never felt comfortable with before. Funny how almost dying seemed to make that seem irrelevant now. She decided to put everything she'd been thinking since they came to The Maithe out into the open, because what did she have to lose? "The others, those who gave me the elixir, told me that the bond with them is unbreakable now. How is it that I don't know any of them at all, and I have that sort of connection, but I don't with you? Or is that too much to ask? Do I want too much?"

She realized his eyes were glistening with tears. Camlin, crying? That seemed wrong to her.

"I have had bonds with so many of my kind, with The Grimshaw. I ruled their minds and wished in my heart that it was something more real, a true connection and not the controlling grip that the Mealladhan encouraged in me. I have never had the pure sort of partnership that you are suggesting, not once in all my days." He took a deep, staggered breath, his face paler than she'd ever seen.

"I need to explain something to you, and I'm not proud of it, but you need to know it to understand what sort of man I was— and am, I suppose, as that man is still part of me.

"You understand that the Gwyliannan hate me because I'm responsible for the death of Genaine, who was one of their own? I used her to get information about The Maithe, and to help The Grimshaw capture Vali and hold her hostage. I forced her to let me inside The Maithe so that I could demand that Sousa step aside and let The Grimshaw take the Heart of the City. Yes, I know that you don't know what that means, but trust me, The Grimshaw have no business with their hands on that.

"Most importantly, though, I betrayed Genaine, and the reason that I hated her was that the Mealladhan told me that I should, because she made me weaker. What was the weakness she exposed in me? I was vulnerable because I cared about her."

He paused, letting that sink in, and Emmaline took that moment to ask the obvious question.

"Did you love her? Was that what made you vulnerable?"

"I wouldn't say that I loved her. I don't think I was actually capable of an emotion that deep that wasn't focused on me and the goals that the Mealladhan had convinced me were important. But somewhere inside me, I wanted to, and I think that alarmed the Mealladhan, because that threatened its grip on me.

"It started twisting my thoughts, eroding my self-confidence. It whispered doubts in my mind, poisoning my feelings about her, and of course it worked. I began to grow paranoid about how much access she had to me, how much she knew about me and The Grimshaw. And eventually I used her to destroy another house of Fae—Tiennan House, which lies to the west of here. Her House, her friends. They hadn't known that she had taken up with The Grimshaw, and she didn't know that we had planned to take down the House. I betrayed her, and left her there to die when she tried to stop me."

Emmaline felt like she had been slapped. It was a sickening feeling.

"How did she finally die? Did you—was it you?" She didn't want to know. But she needed to hear it all, every sickening detail.

"We were at war, in the street outside. The Blackbird—Merrick—was my target, and we had given each other a terrible fight. I had him at my mercy, my arm around his throat, choking the life out of him. And at that moment, Genaine struck me with a blast of energy, distracting me.

"And then she cursed me. 'You shall have no rest, no growth, no success, no home.' When I retaliated with a powerful blast, I dropped Merrick. I hit Genaine full on, and she did not survive. And The Blackbird stabbed me with a thorn that grew into a branch inside me, and I almost died."

Emmaline realized that she had been holding her breath throughout the last bit of his story, and she let it out with a gasp. Camlin looked tired, beaten, and when he continued, his voice shook.

"As you see, I told you the tale, but not all of it. You compelled me to tell the truth, but even that compulsion couldn't force me to give you every detail. I didn't withhold it to hurt you, but because of my deep shame at who I was. Who I am, even though I wish with every fiber of my being that

I wasn't still the monster that I had been. And now you understand why Tiennan House will never forgive me, nor should they."

"Camlin. Stop. You have said yourself that the Mealladhan has broken the bond with you, that it rejected you when you lost. Isn't it possible that you were cast aside because it knew you would never be suitable to serve it again? It had already sensed what it would consider weaknesses in you, that you could care for another."

"And it took that weakness and made me hurt the one I cared for anyway. I hurt her deeply and repeatedly. And she cursed me for it, Emmaline. Do you understand what that means, what happens when a Fae casts their energies in that way? You saw the effects when I took a vow, and that was made in the spur of the moment, not in the heat of battle before striking what might be a death blow." He paused, and Emmaline could feel that he was shaking. "Everything I touch has always been corrupted. I have no hope that things might improve now."

Emmaline reached out and placed her hand on his chest, over his heart. "You saved me. I'm not corrupted. Thanks to you, I've been connected with the most powerful, positive people you know, and you did it full well knowing what it might cost you. I think that is the opposite of corruption. That is heroism."

He looked skeptical, and she could feel a sense of urgency rising in her, a need to convince him that she was right.

"Look. Everything you have told me is disturbing, yes. But it also goes along with what you have already shared with me. You did bad things, and you feel appropriately responsible, even though you were under the control of something that used you for its own goals. I can appreciate that. You are flawed, as are we all. But you are willing to make amends! You're doing the work."

She paused, studying his face to see if anything she was saying was taking hold in him.

"I'm listening," he said, and he moved his hand slowly to cover hers, which were still on his chest. "I'll confess this to you. I am afraid to believe what you're telling me. I am afraid that if I relax, for even a minute, and believe that I have become someone good, I will fail. I am afraid that the Mealladhan will find a way back in, and infect you, even though I have no proof that is possible, as you are mortal born. And I am desperately afraid that it is somehow still deep inside me, just waiting for a way to loose itself into the Eleriannan and Gwyliannan.

"That's why I am so hard on myself, and why I still hold parts of me at arm's length from you. I am afraid that it is the only way to protect you—to protect you all."

He turned his head to face the door during his last few words, and Emmaline followed his gaze to find Sousa and Vali standing in the doorway. Vali looked sad, and Sousa was obviously disturbed.

"Y'know, I didn't want to believe that you'd changed. Maybe you're full of shit, and I'm getting soft, but I don't think so. Fuck, I hate that you're making me not hate you." Sousa kicked the door frame with a booted foot, hard enough to express the frustration he was feeling and punctuate his last words.

"I'm sorry if we intruded," Vali, the gracious host as always, said to the couple. "We had come to see if Emmaline was awake yet and, well - I guess she is." She looked uncomfortable and glanced over to Sousa with a raised eyebrow. "Help me here."

Sousa frowned, then raised his eyebrows in a way that conveyed that he'd come up with an idea. "You should know that this is your room for as long as you want and need it. And Camlin can stay here, or in a different room, whatever you both want. We're not going to keep you apart, all right? That's not how we work here."

He was rewarded with a grateful look on Emmaline's face, and astonishment on Camlin's.

"That is more than I deserve—" Camlin began to answer, but Sousa broke in before he could say more.

"Maybe so, although I'm beginning to disagree with you. Either way, Emmaline doesn't deserve to be punished for what you did in the past." The look on Sousa's face said plainly that Camlin should stop arguing with him and just accept what was happening.

"You're probably starving, so we can send up some food," Vali added. "And we can get some or all of your things for you and bring them here. I don't think you'll be able to go back to your apartment for a while, but we can take care of all the details for you."

"I think—That is really kind of you." Emmaline stumbled over her words, trying not to thank Vali and Sousa for their efforts. "I think I need to rest. But food would be really welcome, I'm definitely starting to feel hungry." She turned to Camlin. "Will you stay here with me?"

"There is no place I would rather be."

After Sousa and Vali left, Emmaline sank back against the pillows with a deep sigh.

"My life is completely changed, and I should be happy about that. I'm alive, because of you. You're here next to me, and you want to be here. That should be enough."

She could feel his gaze on her as he contemplated what she'd just said. She stared at a shadow on the ceiling, waiting for him to say something, anything. Finally, she felt him slide down on the mattress as he laid back, settling down next to her.

"You deserve things that I cannot give you, at least not now."

She felt his hand searching until it found hers, and he entwined his fingers with hers. A flush overtook her with that contact from him. They had been close, and he had even helped her change clothes and bathe when she needed it, but he had never held her hand. It was such a simple, yet intimate gesture.

"I don't know about that." Her voice trembled. "Who am I to expect anything more than what I've already been given?"

"Someone who has always seen through my facade to the truth of who I am."

"That doesn't mean I deserve—"

"Love?"

Time seemed to slow down to Emmaline. She was acutely aware in that moment of Camlin's voice, the feel of their entwined fingers, the pounding of her heart, that felt so strong that it could shake the bed.

"You deserve love, Emmaline. More than anyone I know."

She sat in silence for a beat before responding.

"So do you, Camlin. Even though you don't believe it."

"Emmaline." A deep breath, an exhale. "You know how I feel."

"About many things, I do." She swallowed hard, pushing down the things she really wanted to say. "Some things need to be said plainly, though. Not left open to interpretation."

The doubt that she'd said too much, pushed too hard, made a sick feeling flood through her. She felt Camlin let her hand go, and in that moment, she knew everything was ruined.

She closed her eyes, willing herself not to cry. When she opened them, Camlin was there at her side, propped up on an elbow so that he could look her in the face.

"Everything I have done has been to protect you, Emmaline." His voice was soft but full of emotion. "I have tried to demonstrate how I feel about you, in every way I know because using words to declare those feelings could put you in even more danger. I know that it isn't fair to you. None of this is."

He reached out to trace her cheek gently with the back of his hand. "Please know that all the words you want to hear from me are yours, even if I cannot yet speak them."

"It makes no sense, Camlin. Surely there aren't creatures listening, waiting around for you to say something they can use against you. What a terrible job that would be."

He chuckled softly at her halfhearted attempt at humor. "Incredibly boring. But no, they aren't hovering nearby, waiting for a chance word. The reality is much more straightforward. Words have power. Emotional declarations resonate deeply. They send reverberations across energy fields. Anyone who has stayed attuned to my whereabouts would be able to detect such disturbances."

She turned to face Camlin, ready to question him further. The movement caused her to slide toward him, and he reached forward to brace her. Instead of holding her back, however, he pulled Emmaline into his embrace and took her by surprise as he kissed her tenderly.

"Is this another demonstration?" Emmaline murmured as he held her close.

"Sometimes words are not needed," he replied before kissing her again.

MUSIC: HOLYGRAM
A Faction

The next morning, Sousa and Vali were finishing up a leisurely breakfast in the library when Camlin walked in. Sousa motioned him over to their table, indicating that he should help himself to the food and drink laid out for them.

Camlin nodded and poured a cup of coffee, then sat across from the couple. He looked uncharacteristically nervous, and Vali was curious to know what was going on in his mind.

"We need to get things for Emmaline. And I'd like to go. Vali, as well, if you would indulge me."

"Sure, besides, I can't count on two dudes to know what she'll need," she said in a teasing tone. Sousa didn't look pleased, but he didn't disagree.

"I'm not thrilled with taking you outside The Maithe yet. If The Grimshaw are looking for you, surely they'd spot you at Emmaline's?"

Sousa isn't wrong, Vali thought.

"That's actually part of what I want to talk to you about," Camlin said, looking like someone would overhear. He gulped down the rest of the coffee. "Let us continue this on the way?"

Sousa sighed and gestured for him to follow, and Vali took up the rear. She had no idea what Camlin had in mind, but at least she could keep an eye out for any surprises.

Once they were in the van and Camlin had given Sousa the address of Emmaline's apartment, he began to explain.

"I have an idea. I'll say up front, neither of you will probably like it, but hear me out." He paused.

"Go on, I'm listening," Sousa said.

"I've been thinking on what we can do about the Mealladhan. Left unchecked, we'll have to face it sooner or later. I don't know how it restructured The Grimshaw since it rejected me, but the longer we wait, the stronger and bolder it will get. That puts everyone in danger, not just the Fae." He sighed. "I'm aware that you know that. I just want you to be sure that I understand it and that it matters to me. I don't want to bring harm to mortals anymore, or drive them from the city. I was consumed by my hate, and I'll regret that for the rest of my days."

"We know, Camlin. You don't have to convince us anymore. What is your plan?" Vali asked, encouraging him to continue.

"It involves subterfuge, and your magic, if you'll agree. None will be at risk but myself, if it goes the way I envision."

"Wait, what?" Sousa barked. Vali, who was in the passenger seat of the van, turned to face him when he referenced her magic, an eager look on her face.

"Souz, look, here's a parking spot, right in front of her place. We can sit here while he explains," Vali said in a calming voice. "Go on, Camlin, I'm interested."

Camlin's plan was fairly simple. If Vali would create a magical tag tattoo designed to help him take down the Mealladhan, Camlin could act as a Trojan horse and once he was in place, activate it. It would require a few things for the plan to work, though, including as few people as possible knowing about it.

"Everyone must believe that my re-insertion into The Grimshaw is a surprise to all, or this will never work. If they suspect me, I won't be able to get into place close enough to accomplish this task. Of course, this is all assuming that Vali can create something that will achieve what I am wanting, and that she's willing to use her magic in this way."

Sousa sat there and listened to Camlin with a surprised look on his face, and when he realized it, he exhaled loudly.

"Well, damn. I don't know what to say. Vali, do you think this is possible?"

"I think I see a few ways I could take this. Some I feel more comfortable with than others. I don't want to use my tags to bring destruction, but I could make a trap? I would need some time to really work out the details." She ran a hand through her purple hair, agitated. "What about you, Camlin? I don't think I can protect you with that tag, not without drawing attention to what the tag is for. That might jeopardize the whole attempt."

"I'll figure it out. That's not a worry right now. First things first: are you on board for this? Because what we do next is a setup for the future, if so."

"What do you mean?" Vali tilted her head, confused.

"I get it," Sousa answered. "We're going to use getting Emmaline's things as an act to show that we don't trust Camlin, and that he's our captive. Assuming that The Grimshaw have eyes on this place."

"I have been operating with the assumption that they have spies watching me," Camlin agreed. "Even though they released me, they know I am not harmless, and I have a reputation for ruthlessness, so..." He trailed off ruefully. Vali noticed that he was fidgeting, running the fingers of his right hand back and forth over the tattoo she'd given him.

"So let us march you to the door, so we can get this done and get to work," Sousa said, breaking the tension. "Stay there. Let me, um, *help* you out of the van."

Sousa did exactly that. He put on a scowl and marched around to Camlin's door and jerked it open as if he was angry. He then grabbed Camlin's arm and yanked him out of his seat.

"Open the door!" he barked, pushing Camlin towards Emmaline's apartment.

Vali thought that he might be enjoying this scene a bit too much. She scrambled to follow them, looking around the street as though she was watching for enemies to pop out of the shadows. "I guess I am," she said to herself as she hustled to get into the building and off the street.

"Well, that was fun!" Sousa laughed, then stopped when he realized that he was standing in the middle of a huge mess. "Did the place look like this when you left?"

"It did not. Emmaline is quite neat, and so am I," Camlin said in an affronted tone. "Someone has ransacked the place. Be careful."

Vali could tell that Camlin was seething at the destruction, but he kept it in check and busied himself by finding a couple of travel bags and gathering some of Emmaline's clothes. Vali helped him by looking for the essentials, neatly tucking them into the bags.

"I appreciate the help," Camlin said in a low tone meant only for her ears. She nodded absently and muttered, "You think they're listening?"

He shrugged, nonchalantly, but his face said otherwise. She nodded again and said, in a louder voice, "This place gives me the creeps, and so do you. Hurry up so we can get out of here."

Sousa's eyes widened and she could tell he was trying not to laugh. But what almost broke her was seeing Camlin's shoulders shake in barely contained laughter. She huffed and grumbled, "What I have to put up with, I swear," to distract anyone who might be spying.

They finally made it back to the van, Camlin playing up stumbling a bit as Sousa gave him the lightest shove towards the door to the vehicle. Sousa managed to keep himself in character until they made it down the street, and then he busted out laughing.

"Holy shit, Vali, I almost died trying to hold it in when you called Camlin a creep!"

"I did not call him a creep, I said he *gives me the creeps*. If you're going to quote me, get it right," she laughed. "Sorry, Camlin," she added.

"Despite the fact that I was unprepared for that, it was brilliant," he chuckled. "You sold your distaste well."

"I hate to bring this heartwarming moment to an end, but before we get back to The Maithe, we need to decide a few things," Sousa said. "First, how are we going to work on this while keeping it secret? And second, who gets to know about the plan?"

"The less people, the better," Camlin asserted, and Vali nodded in agreement. He added, "My guts say that it should be as need-to-know as can be."

"What about Emmaline?" Vali's voice was quiet, but cut through the road noise like an arrow to the heart of the matter.

"She cannot know. I would rather her be angry with me than worry. And I want her as protected as can be," Camlin said in a firm tone. Vali turned in her seat to look at him, and he shook his head. "I don't want her to know," he said again, his voice trembling as he looked away from Vali.

"All right," she answered, in that same quiet voice.

As soon as they had returned, Vali started thinking about how she would create the magical graffiti tattoo that Camlin would bear to help defeat the Mealladhan. She knew it was going to take some careful planning and visualizing in order to make things work correctly.

The intent had to be hidden inside the art, making it look and feel as innocuous as possible. Hiding the intent was the easier of the two tasks. She had thrown many tags that were obviously magical, but didn't give away what their purpose was. But even the pieces that she'd thrown before she had learned to infuse her art with magical skill had stood out and had drawn attention. Now she needed to be subtle, and she hoped her talent was up to the challenge.

Once Camlin was finished with delivering all of Emmaline's things from the apartment to her, Vali invited him to sit down while she worked at one of the big wooden tables in the library. He took a seat opposite her and watched as she drew great sweeping, unconnected lines across a sketchbook.

"That's not the black sketchbook, I see. Does that make a difference?"

She grinned for a moment, then picked up a thicker marker and drew a few more bold sweeps of ink. "The black book is for more finished concepts. This sketchbook is about working out the basic ideas. Or as is the case now, doodling until inspiration strikes."

Sousa walked in a moment later, carrying a large, covered tray. "Just your friendly punk server with refreshments, no tipping please," he grinned, then sat the tray at the end of the big table and uncovered it.

"So thoughtful," Vali said, and grabbed a sandwich from the tray. "You know how hungry this work makes me."

"You and everyone else," Sousa agreed, taking a beer from the middle of the tray. He indicated to Camlin that he should help himself, and Camlin walked over to look over the offerings.

"The food here is delicious." He sighed after taking a bite of a croissant that was stuffed with ham and melted cheese.

Sousa raised his beer in agreement. "I count myself lucky to be taken care of so well. The house never seems to be thrown by whatever random guests that show up, either. Speaking of, you know we should talk Emmaline into moving into The Maithe, right?"

Camlin blinked a few times, obviously surprised by that thought. "Well, I hadn't thought of that at all, but you are right. It would be smart for her to live here, well protected amongst her new family. It would certainly take a weight off of my mind."

"Camlin, is she up for joining us, do you think? We could broach the subject now, while we're thinking about it. Anyway, it'll take me a while to make anything happen with what I'm working on currently. Might as well give her some company if she is ready for that," Vali suggested, still hard at work on her dark sweeping lines, which were now covering most of the page.

"That's a wonderful idea," Camlin agreed, wiping the crumbs from his hands as he stood up. Vali watched as he left the room, then she leaned towards Sousa, who had taken the seat at the head of the table.

"What are you thinking, Souz?'

"Hmm. Mostly about what we discussed in the van, and how to pull it off. And who to tell."

"Lucee. Merrick. Someone from Tiennan, and by someone, I mean probably Karsten, as they are the most even-tempered person we know in that House."

He snorted and leaned back a little. "I see you haven't been thinking about this at all. I don't even know why I ask you anything." She stuck her tongue out at him. He laughed, then said, "Of course you had answers right away. But do you think this will work?"

"I think it's a brave plan. Maybe too brave, and I'm still not sure we'll be able to make it work, but when has that stopped us?" She looked up from her sketch and caught his expression. "What is it?"

"Just thinking that at least we had a few months where nothing happened, so we got to enjoy just being together. Kick me the next time I say that things are getting boring."

"I don't think I recall you ever saying that, you goofball."

They were laughing when Camlin walked in with an unsteady but upbeat Emmaline. Vali cheered when she came in, and Emmaline grinned and held up a fist in victory.

"I don't know what that is on that tray, but I want five of them," she said, agog at all the choices of sandwiches available.

"The croissant ones are particularly good," Camlin suggested.

Sousa added, "There's also water, tea, or coffee on the table over there. I'll bring one of the cozier armchairs over here in the meantime."

When she was settled, she looked around the room and said, "Camlin says that I can't thank you. But you need to know how grateful I am for all your help."

"We know, no worries," Vali told her, smiling.

"You're part of our people now, Emmaline," Sousa reassured her. "And speaking of that, there's something important we need to talk about. Did Camlin tell you what we found when we went to your apartment?"

"He didn't. But to be fair, I was a bit excited about having some of my stuff in my hands."

"I didn't want to upset you," Camlin explained. "Your home was ransacked. We're sure it was The Grimshaw. They made a big mess, but it's mostly salvageable. We don't know what they were looking for, but it's obvious that they had been watching."

Emmaline gasped and started crying, and Camlin looked like someone had punched him.

"I'm so sorry. This is my fault," he muttered.

"Nonsense," she answered. She wiped tears from her face with the back of her hand and straightened up in her chair. "I apologize for crying like that. I'm just...It caught me off guard. It's all just stuff, no one is hurt. That's the most important thing."

"You've been through a lot. Crying is normal, you know," Vali told her in a soothing voice.

"My reason for bringing this up is that I think it would be a good idea if you permanently moved into The Maithe." Sousa got to the point. "There's so much room here you could avoid us all if you wanted, and we can take care of the moving part, so you don't have to do anything. And you'll be safer here than anywhere else I know."

"Oh. Wow, I didn't expect that," Emmaline breathed, and her whole demeanor seemed to relax. She looked to Camlin, who nodded encouragingly. "I can do that. If Camlin is welcome too."

"He was a part of the discussion, so yes," Sousa agreed. He scowled at Camlin, and Vali had to look away so she wouldn't grin at that little detail Souz had thought to add for authenticity. "I can keep an eye on everyone this way."

"Trust me, I expect I will be well-monitored as long as I live here," Camlin said in a resigned voice.

"What about my work? I don't want to give that up if possible. It was the one part of my life I could hold onto and mostly maintain once I got sick. Losing it now would really hurt." Emmaline looked to Vali, then to Sousa. "I don't even know if you have an Internet connection here. It seems like something stupid to expect in a house full of...of magical people."

"Fae. You can call us Fae," Sousa explained, and then snorted. "Lucee would insist on that, actually. There's a lot of debate about who wants to be addressed as what amongst our alliance, but you can't go wrong with Fae. And yes, we're connected to the Internet here, and it's fast, because I don't mess around. Also, because I'm really the only one who uses it much."

"You and the Fae-adjacent, and even them not so much," Vali interjected, then added to Emmaline, "Fae-adjacent refers to once-mortals, Fae bound, like you and Merrick and Lucee. You're not really mortal anymore, but you're not born Fae either. And there's half-bloods, like me. Just to keep it spicy, you know." She spread her hands in front of her and wiggled her fingers, and Emmaline laughed at that.

"Sure, spicy is certainly a word. But let me get this right. There are three...*factions*? Is that the right term?" Vali nodded in agreement with Emmaline's word choice. "Okay, so I know one is The Grimshaw, the faction that Camlin led when you warred with them. And two different ones helped me, that was made *abundantly* clear to me as the elixir was being prepared."

"You certainly got that right!" Sousa guffawed. "Actually, you got contributions from the Eleriannan, Gwyliannan, and me. I'm my own sort of weirdness that doesn't fit into either faction comfortably. And that's how I like it."

Camlin leaned forward, interested. "I always assumed you were Eleriannan. You're so tightly associated with them through Lucee and The Blackbird."

"You know that you can call him Merrick, right?" Sousa rolled his eyes. "I once would have called myself Eleriannan, before I grew tired of their ways. And yet their beliefs had steeped into me enough that when I met the Gwyliannan, I carried all the prejudices against them that the Eleriannan did and was shocked to find that I—that all of us were wrong. And I align much more with them in many ways than I do the Eleriannan.

"But no, I keep The Maithe neutral, and I try to move between the various Houses as a friend to all. That also leaves me free to call them on their bullshit, which comes in handy."

"I expect when some of the folk from both houses hear that Camlin will be living here, they'll be ready to call us on our perceived bullshit as well," Vali noted, one eyebrow raised. "Which is fine. It won't be the first time we've been controversial."

MUSIC: EMPATHY TEST
Monsters

Slowly, the plan began to build.

Vali worked on the art for what she privately referred to as the spell, bringing her concepts for the art together with the intentions she wanted to set into motion. She had several concepts that needed to be contained in her work, and bringing them all into a cohesive whole was proving to be challenging, but not daunting, because she was so exhilarated when something she did worked.

The first concern was aesthetics. She needed the tag to hold all the elements of her goal in a way that was beautifully hidden within the work. It shouldn't give away what it was designed to do in any way, whether seen or touched. But touching was how she planned to have it activated, and for that, she needed Camlin's approval.

"Look, to deliver its magic, it will either need to be touched or applied to one of the people who carries the taint of Mealladhan within. That means that you'll either need to be able to remove it and apply it to another, or you will have to be comfortable with being touched to have it activated on yourself. That's an ethical line that I need your permission to bake into this. Do you agree?"

Camlin's eyebrows shot up, and he sat back a little from her and the table where they were sitting as she worked.

"I'll do whatever's necessary, of course. But your kindness in asking is unexpected." His voice shook, and he spoke quietly so that it wouldn't carry to Emmaline, who was in the middle of a deep conversation with Karsten.

"We believe deeply in consent in this house. No one should be forced to take actions that go against their will unless there is no other way. Too many of us know how it feels to have our choices removed," Vali explained in a reassuring tone. "I'll do my best to give you as many options as possible as far as our collaboration in this scheme goes."

"That's appreciated, especially as I have no idea what path will open for me as far as deploying this. I have a few ideas, but nothing— Emmaline! Look at these stunning works that Vali has been doing!" He went from an intense mood to smiling in an instant as Emmaline sat in the chair next to him. She looked at Vali's art with interest. Karsten joined them as well and leaned over the table to study Vali's efforts.

"I almost see... something. I am not sure," Karsten said in their soft voice. "Something compelling lurks under the surface of this one, Vali." They looked up to meet Vali's gaze and held it for a moment, then nodded once, their expression changing to a lighter one. "I will learn how to understand these someday, but this is not that day!"

Emmaline smiled at that and asked, "So does no one actually understand your magic besides you, Vali? I find it fascinating to look at, so many colors and so much movement, and sometimes I almost feel like I could read it or understand what it means. Then a moment later, it feels like it twists away and becomes something else!"

"I get that a lot, actually. Karsten's come the closest to seeing what I'm about with my tags, everyone else just *oohs* and *aahs* and happily accepts the magic that they serve up. I'm kinda unique, at least so far!"

"You know, I think your uniqueness is due in part to your youth and growing up outside of the control of the Gentry, or the Fae in general. You didn't know what to expect, so you developed without influences telling you what is supposed to happen, or what is the right way to channel your magic. You didn't even know you were working them!" Sousa interjected from across the room, where he was working on connecting Emmaline's laptop to The Maithe's wifi. He scowled at the computer and added, "The House doesn't like your laptop. Would you object to getting a new one? It can be really picky sometimes, especially when it thinks something doesn't live up to its standards."

"The house? The *house* has opinions?" Emmaline looked around the room suspiciously, her eyes wide. "I don't really have money for a new laptop..."

"No, no, no, that's not an issue. You're one of us, we'll take care of that. But yes. The Maithe is...well, I hesitate to call it 'alive' in the sense that most people would mean, but it, or something I might call the spirit that inhabits it, has very specific preferences, opinions, agendas, and allegiances." Sousa turned to Camlin and addressed him. "And that is just a part of why when you demanded that I give up The Maithe, I was so angry. I am no more the owner of it than it is of me. I am a protector, a caretaker, and a partner. And of course, Vali now has a deeper connection to everything The Maithe is and holds than even I do."

"I learned that the hard way. I was a fool to underestimate you, and I see now that even had The Grimshaw won, this house would have done everything to reject us, and surely would have succeeded." Camlin rested his chin on his fist, thoughtfully. "It makes being welcomed in when I arrived with Emmaline even more surprising. I'll keep that kindness in mind."

Vali smiled to herself at that, and Sousa mock-grumbled, "Trust me, the House certainly will."

"Hellooooooo! Where is everyone?" Lucee's voice echoed from downstairs, and Sousa grimaced.

"Damn, time just flew by. They're here for band practice. Feel free to come down and listen if you like."

He hustled out of the library and thundered down the stairs, his boots clomping on each wooden tread. Vali shook her head at that.

"As much as he moons over that woodwork, and then he tromps over everything in those damn boots. I keep telling him that we should set a no shoes policy, at least upstairs, but he just laughs at me." She grinned at Camlin and Emmaline. "You haven't experienced the magic—and loudness—that is The Drawback. You should totally go watch them practice. I mean, if that's your thing? This house is all about music, I should warn you now."

Seeing Emmaline's eyes light up, Camlin answered affirmatively, "Of course, we must go downstairs!" Privately, Vali wondered how excited he actually was by that prospect. She guessed that with their future plans hanging over his head, he was going to agree to anything Emmaline wanted them to do.

"You go ahead, I'll be with you in just a minute, I need to clean up my mess," she said, but stopped Karsten before they followed the couple downstairs.

"Did Sousa speak to you about our plan?" Vali asked as soon as they were alone.

"He did. It is a bold idea, one that depends much on Camlin. Do you truly think him capable of success?" Karsten's snakelike hair curled around their neck in copper-toned coils, and they idly pushed it back. "I understood your sketch as a building block for your part in this plan, although I do not grasp the mechanism you are trying to create. So you must be confident, as it seems that you are moving forward with this idea."

"I would worry at this puzzle until I solved it, no matter what, to be honest. It is a fascinating challenge." Vali closed her black book and scooped all her markers into a pen bag, then put all of that into her backpack. "I don't know if he can pull this off, no. But he wants to try, and I don't have any other ideas about how we can weaken the Mealladhan. This is what we've got."

Karsten touched Vali's arm, gently. "He will sacrifice himself to assuage his guilt. I do not believe that to be in alignment with our values. I see his worth in our alliance, even if others do not. What can be done to help him succeed without losing his life, or his way?"

"I don't know, my friend. But I'll do my best to build protections for him into my tag. And we will need to keep our plans as secret as possible so that he isn't accidentally revealed to our enemies. All must believe that he has abandoned us to return to The Grimshaw, even Emmaline, or this won't work."

They descended the stairs, came around the corner into the ballroom, and saw Camlin making a face at the noise that Sousa's drums were making as he tuned the heads. Emmaline was laughing at him. They both looked carefree in that moment.

Karsten turned to Vali and said in an undertone, "Someone will need to be there for Emmaline when this plan is enacted. He is her anchor."

Lucee felt uncomfortable at first when Camlin had walked into their practice. It was already an adjustment to see him as anything other than the enemy. And practices were a place where things could be extremely powerful, but also deeply vulnerable. Trying out new songs sometimes left the band feeling raw and exposed, because a million mistakes could happen until the song gelled for them. Merrick shot her a look that she knew all too well—it was the "whatever you decide, I've got your back" look. That was enough to shake her out of her discomfort. She grinned back at Merrick and gave him a thumbs up.

"Hey, I've been practicing something. Wanna see?" she asked her friend.

Merrick ran a hand through his black, spiky 'do before answering. "Of course!"

Normally he does that when he's nervous, Lucee thought. *Maybe he's uncomfortable with Camlin here too. Well, maybe this will distract him.*

She held her hands in front of her, concentrating on the space above them. She imagined a sphere floating above them and filled it with starlight in her mind. She could feel the light, like tiny fireflies flocking to her imaginary sphere, swirling in to join all the other light she was collecting. Her face and hands lit up as the sphere began to glow in earnest.

"Lucee! That's amazing!" Merrick cheered.

Off to her side, she heard Cullen ask, "When did you learn to do that?"

"I remembered something Fallon did, and I wanted to try it! So, every time I had a moment alone, I worked on how to make it happen." She didn't look at him as she spoke, She kept her focus on the ball of light.

"Can you hand it to me? Have you tried that?" Cullen came up to her, and she glanced up and saw his encouraging smile. Just that bit of belief bolstered her, and she decided to try it.

She slowly stretched her hands before her, cupping the ball of light, and he brought his hands under hers, lightly touching.

"Try dropping it to me?" he suggested, his voice soft and supportive.

She took a few slow, deep breaths, then parted her hands, hoping for the best. The ball of light seemed to hover there for a moment before falling gently into Cullen's palms.

As soon as it touched his hands, the glow grew so bright she had to look away, and everyone watching gasped. As quickly as it had lit up, it seemed to melt across Cullen's palms, starlight trailing out and away in little curlicues as it dissipated.

Lucee let out a disappointed sigh, but Cullen grinned in delight.

"Well done! Most of us could not have managed to let go of it at all on the first try, Lucee. I think you tried so hard to give it to me that you actually overpowered it. I am so impressed!" He hugged her, and she giggled with relief.

"I didn't mess it up?" she asked as he released her from his embrace.

"Not a bit! And you even made it look pretty as it melted away, so you get extra points for style. Next time you try, you will remember how it felt when you gave it to me, and remember not to strain so much. I am so proud of you!" He was rewarded with Lucee's huge smile.

She turned to Merrick and said, "I guess that would be a walk in the park for you though, right? You lucky duck." She grinned at him, making sure he knew she wasn't resentful—though secretly, there was a tiny part of her that was envious at Merrick's ease with magic. As far as she knew, he'd never struggled at anything he'd tried to do with his powers, which was so typical with everything in his life.

"I dunno, I have always needed to have someone show me the

possibilities before I could create them. You figured that out on your own! That's an enviable gift," Merrick said, a wistful look on his face, which Lucee found utterly ridiculous to contemplate.

"I'll trade you for some shape-shifting ability," she joked, to cover her feelings and turned to pick up her guitar before he could answer.

She mentally kicked herself as she tuned up. What was wrong with her today? She usually didn't get bothered by things like how much harder than Merrick she had to work in order to succeed, at least not anymore. It wasn't really fair of her, she knew, because Merrick's journey as The Blackbird had been filled with plenty of challenges. And he'd almost died in their battle with The Grimshaw.

Although she'd almost died too, when they'd been attacked by the ArDonnath at House Mirabilis. That was one of the events that precipitated her becoming the leader of the Eleriannan, and it was the point when she realized how dangerous The Grimshaw were.

She stole a look at Camlin and Emmaline, who were on a couch with their heads together, laughing. She still didn't know how to feel about his presence in The Maithe, walking around freely. She liked Emmaline, who reminded her a bit of Vali, with her kind heart and positive attitude. Lucee wanted to believe that her influence could truly help to turn around a former villain like Camlin, but she couldn't help but doubt.

Sousa knocked her off her train of thought with a loud drum roll that ended with a cymbal crash. "Let's get down to it!" he yelled into his mic, and Merrick whooped in response.

They began with a couple of covers of Joy Division and Delphine Coma tracks, then segued into an original song that they had been working on. Merrick and Sousa started it off with a soft rat-a-tat of snare that Merrick's bass droned over with deep, throbbing notes. Lucee's guitar swirled over top of that backbone, a shimmer of feedback pulling it all together.

Merrick sang the lyrics in a direct, plaintive style, with a slight echo on his vocals.

Lying back in piles of Autumn leaves
Under the ancient oaks
You and I could spend September days
Curled together, whispering thoughts

Lucee began to build the guitar with a shoegaze buzz, and they burst into the chorus like the sun coming out on a cloudy day.

Let's run through the trees
Let's dance in the meadow
Let's sing to the open skies

The stars get all our secrets
The moon gets all our lies

Lucee and Merrick sang the last lines together, twining harmonies in a way that made the listeners want to sing along.

And when we fall back down
When we tumble to the earth
You and I will be one, my love
You and I will be one

The song ended almost as it started, with Sousa's snare and Merrick's bass drone, and Lucee took her last fuzzed out notes and held them until they faded out alone.

The first person to speak was Emmaline, who broke the silence with a hushed, "Oh wow."

"Does that mean that you liked it?" Lucee asked, elated at this response.

"I do not think you can call yourself a 'crappy garage band' anymore," Cullen said, a look of awe on his face. "When did you manage to write this, that I have not heard it until now? That was astonishingly good."

"We've been working on it right in front of you, Foxy! It just suddenly came together for us."

"It means a lot that you think it's good," Merrick added. "I know that our music doesn't always connect with you."

"I have to admit, it has grown on me," Cullen admitted, sheepishly. "I know I have complained in the past that it was loud and...well...odd to my ears. But either I have changed, or you have improved, and I have it under good authority that you have always been quite talented at what you do." His smile was lighthearted, but she could sense his sincerity underneath his words. Two wins in a day! She felt like she could float across the room.

They ran through the rest of their set, which was becoming more originals than covers these days—something that excited Lucee to no end. Watching the growth of the band in such a small stretch of time was satisfying in a way that only learning magic had been able to match.

"You do realize that our first show was only in November, right?" She spoke into the mic because she wanted to be heard over Merrick's bass noodling. "At the tiniest club we know, even. And here we are, scheduled for stage time at one of the biggest summer festivals in Baltimore!"

Merrick stopped playing and looked up, his face a mixture of pride and nervousness.

Appropriate reaction, Lucee thought.

"We're going to kick all the asses at ArtPark this year!" Sousa crowed and thumped on his bass drum, followed by a rimshot. Everyone in the room laughed at that, which of course was what Sousa had intended.

"What's ArtPark?" Camlin asked once the laughter had died down.

"Every year, Baltimore hosts a bunch of summer festivals with live bands and performances, art, vendors, and sometimes games. ArtPark happens on the first weekend in August, so it's always incredibly hot, but somehow that never stops everyone in the city from attending," Vali explained. "The best part is that although they shut down a bunch of streets for the festival, the bands all play on a stage in a park, so there are trees everywhere. And they set up all these big art constructs, hence 'ArtPark.' It has a magical feel. People put down blankets and picnic all day. It's a really great event."

"Those fools put us on the main stage on Sunday," Sousa added, a mischievous twinkle in his eye. "It's not the busiest day but it's a damn good gig for a band of our size and experience. We're going to make the most of it!"

After practice, Sousa pulled Emmaline aside and informed her that when she wanted to get some work done, she would find everything she needed in her room, ready to go.

"You got my laptop to finally connect?" she asked in a confused tone. "When did you find time to make that happen?"

"I didn't, but you'll see that the solution is even better, or at least I hope you'll agree that it is." Sousa looked pleased with himself. She obviously didn't know what to think of that, so she turned to Camlin and made an 'I have no idea' face.

"Do you mind if I go and check on my email, and catch up on some work? I need to put in some updates on my current assignments. I'm sure they're wondering what's going on with me."

"I can certainly entertain myself," Camlin agreed and smiled encouragingly at her. "And you need to re-establish some routine, so take all the time you need."

Once she had gone upstairs, Sousa spoke up to the rest of the folk in the ballroom. "We need to discuss some things, and I really need a beer.

We've got refreshments and a nice space over there." He gestured toward the other end of the ballroom, where a table had mysteriously appeared, laden with food and beverages. There was a nook set up with some of the ubiquitous velvet couches and armchairs that were favored seating at The Maithe, a cozy space well away from the front entrance and main staircase.

Sousa had planned well. There was no way Emmaline would easily overhear their discussion, and no one was going to be able to come into the ballroom without one of them seeing that person first. Merrick and Lucee only saw the beers and food, though, and made their way to the table to gather platefuls before everyone settled down together.

After they had managed to get some food down and most of the post-practice joking and chatter out of the way, Sousa addressed the group.

"So, there's something important we need to talk about—" he started.

"I have some ideas about the show, should we write this stuff down?" Merrick interrupted, obviously excited by the upcoming gig.

"Dude. That is *so* not what this is about. I need you all to pay attention for a couple of minutes, okay? I know we're all amped up after that excellent practice, but we've been sitting on some news of a totally different nature, and this is the first chance we've had to talk to you about it." He looked around at everyone, making sure they were paying attention. Merrick and Lucee both looked confused, but Cullen's face gave away that he might have an inkling of what kind of subject they were going to address.

"We've been working on a plan to take down the Mealladhan."

"What?" Both Merrick and Lucee said at once. Cullen said nothing, but turned to look at Camlin, concern on his face. Camlin met his gaze and nodded once, and Cullen's expression deepened to distress.

"Camlin and I have been working on some ideas," Vali added, her voice confident but her face not as much. "He came to me with the germ of a plot and we filled it out together. We told Sousa, to see what he thought, and he told Karsten. They have been the only ones who know what we have been plotting, until now. And we want to keep this between us only, because the less people who know, the safer Camlin will be."

"Wait," Merrick's voice cracked a little as he spoke. "I think we need to hear this entire plan before you go any further."

Vali and Camlin laid out the proposal. They kept their voices calm and measured, both trying to instill the idea that they knew what they were doing as if they'd agreed to that method before they'd broached the subject. Surprisingly, the others managed to keep quiet the entire time, though they had plenty of questions after.

"You have tested this tattoo idea?" Cullen asked.

"I have no way to test the actions beforehand," Vali explained, her brow furrowed in frustration. "But I trust my magic. And the mechanics are sound, I have already made movable tags that look like tattoos."

She gestured to Camlin, and he pulled up his shirtsleeve to show Cullen the tag that Vali had given him on his first day there, and Cullen's mouth fell open.

"That—that moves? It looks like it was done directly on his skin!"

Vali showed Cullen how she could pick it up. "This one is made so only I can move it around. But I know how to fix it so that Camlin could move the one I'm designing to trap the Mealladhan, if needed. The trick is that he needs to be close enough to his target to affix it, and it must be to skin." She made a face. "I know that's a lot of specifics."

"But I'm willing to take the risk to do this. I think if I act as if I've escaped from here, they will grab me up. They would rather hold onto me than willingly allow their enemy to keep me, even as broken as they think I am." He paused. "I think I can convince them that I'm no longer broken if I play it right. That could get me closer to my goal to get close enough to the one the Mealladhan has chosen to take my old place. I believe that I'll need to get to the root of the infestation."

"They'll have to believe that you are angry," Lucee said, her voice soft and thoughtful. "You're not the wrathful man that you used to be." She gasped as it hit her what he meant to do. "You aren't telling Emmaline. That's going to be your fuel, isn't it?"

The room fell silent and they all looked to Camlin, his jaw clenched and his eyes reflecting the pain he felt at this prospect. He drew in a great stuttering breath and then exhaled hard.

"This is the most difficult part of the plan. I'm willing to sacrifice myself for this. But knowing how much I'll hurt her is tearing me apart." His normally pale face flushed, color spreading across his cheeks and nose. In that moment, he was unrecognizable as the haughty man that had strode into the ballroom last year and threatened and insulted them all.

Lucee had the sudden urge to hug him, as improbable as that would have seemed just a few minutes before.

"I understand," she said instead, and he answered with a grateful look. "You need her to react naturally because The Grimshaw will certainly be spying on us. We must keep this a secret, both for this to work, and to keep you safe."

Merrick looked ill. "I don't like this at all. No matter how much I've disliked you, I wouldn't willingly send you into danger. Surely there's got to be a better way."

"I'm not sure there is," Sousa answered, shaking his head sadly. "I've been thinking about it, and we don't even know where The Grimshaw are hiding these days, just that they're around, and they're getting more active. They ripped apart Emmaline's apartment, did you know that?"

Merrick looked aghast.

"Vali and I made a big scene with Camlin like he was a prisoner when we went there. This was after he told us his idea. And it was a good thing we did, because they're definitely paying attention. It makes the setup for this feel like it could work, at least." Sousa took a long swig of his beer, which fooled no one. He wasn't thrilled with this plan either, it was obvious. But it was also plain to see that he didn't think there was any other way to fight the Mealladhan.

Karsten held up a hand for attention, worry plain to see on their face.

"They are growing bolder and stronger. We have been hearing stories of terrors in the night on the city streets, and it has emboldened the ones who run the gangs and sell the drugs. They claim the monsters are on their side, or that they are the monsters themselves. And those who want to just live in peace are quaking in fear." Karsten's usually gentle voice crackled with anger. "They are striving to undo all the progress our neighborhood, and the city, has made. And the unrest is spreading - violence in areas that are usually less prone to it, crime and chaos."

There was a murmur of dismay and concern from all gathered around, and Camlin's voice cut through them like a knife.

"This is why I need to try something, anything." The room grew silent, and Camlin continued, "I must try to make amends for my part in this. I was a fool, and I was wrong. And now innocent people are paying the price for that."

"When will you enact this plan?" Lucee found that, no matter how she felt about Camlin, having him go back to The Grimshaw was too much to ask. Even if it was his idea, it was too high a price to pay.

"Soon. When Vali and I know that her part of this will work, and when I am mentally prepared for the role I will need to play." Camlin's face was resigned, but his shoulders slumped. He no longer looked like an overly proud princeling, but more like a dog that had been kicked.

"What can we do to help?" Merrick, always the one to volunteer, asked. "And can I bring Aisling into this circle? I don't like keeping secrets from her, and she might have some ideas about how Camlin can hide his true intentions from others."

"I would appreciate The Dreamling's input," Camlin agreed.

"We keep this circle to us, and her, and that's it," Sousa confirmed. "It's not that I don't trust anyone else, but if too many people know, a secret is bound to reach the wrong ears."

MUSIC: DRAB MAJESTY
Kissing The Ground

They wrapped up the discussion with the agreement that Vali and Sousa would keep the others up to date on their progress, and that they would meet for another band practice in a few days. Merrick, Lucee, and Cullen headed to The Maithe's portal gate for their trip back to House Mirabilis.

While Merrick seemed deep in thought, Lucee was too nervous to keep quiet and chattered to Cullen while they walked down the stairs to the inner courtyard.

"This place never ceases to give me shivers when we enter, it's so majestic," Lucee remarked, her head swiveling from side to side in a vain attempt to take in the expanse of forest that stretched improbably before them.

The Maithe had been built by Sousa long ago in an attempt to preserve the last bit of primeval wilderness that was left inside the heart of Baltimore City. Other tiny stretches of green space in the city contained the same sort of vibe and connection, but the forest inside the inner walls of The Maithe was the most powerful, at least in the city center.

Sousa had placed a glamour over the space that blocked anyone who he didn't want to see the treasures hidden in that space. Instead of an endless expanse of trees, they saw a courtyard with benches and tables and a few, more reasonable trees. When Vali first came to the house, she managed to break through that glamour. She then connected with the being that lived there, unperceived by Sousa—The Lady of the City, a spirit of place. Sousa then decided that the time had come to allow anyone in their cohort to access the space. When the Gwyliannan started to explore the secret forest, they discovered a gate—a portal that would allow the Fae to travel to other portals through a liminal space—hidden along one of the walls.

The trio headed for that gate, and as always, Lucee was awestruck at the idea that they had this ability to travel from one place to another with such ease. She reached for Cullen's hand, and he took it and squeezed it as they walked.

"If it helps you, keep talking," he told her. He knew her well, and she took a second to relish that fact before she answered.

"I know that once we get to the House, we won't be able to discuss this much, so I'm just amped up. I hate secrets. I know you guys know that. I'm sorry."

"I'd be worried about you if you weren't babbling, honestly," Merrick broke out of his thoughts to tell her. "I think I can confidently say that neither of us are put off by that, Lucee." He gave her a reassuring, if distracted, smile.

As they approached the gate, Lucee stopped them.

"Look, I need to know. What did you guys think? I mean... do you believe Camlin? And do you think this is wise?"

"I guess I do? I trust Souz, and if he's going along with this, then that means he believes that Camlin is trustworthy. Or I guess he could be happy to get rid of him, but I don't think so. That guy's too powerful to risk turning back over to The Grimshaw without a good reason and a plan that has a chance of working." Merrick ran his hand through his hair, then straightened up and nodded, as if he was agreeing with himself. "Yeah. I trust Souz and Vali to have really thought this through."

Lucee turned to Cullen, who was pensive for a moment before he spoke and sounded a little unsure.

"I do not like it, but I agree with Merrick that Sousa would not have gone along with this if he did not believe it stood a chance of success. I dislike immensely that we are keeping Emmaline in the dark about this. I know how I would feel, were I in her shoes."

"Yeah. I hate that." Lucee, in frustration, kicked at a clump of grass growing at the base of the stone gate. "I think it's really eating at Camlin too. I couldn't do what he's volunteering to do."

Cullen and Merrick murmured agreement. No one felt very happy about the plan, but at least everyone seemed to agree that it wasn't because the plan was bad, but just that it was destined to hurt more than their foes.

"Do you still hate him?" Lucee asked Merrick. He raised an eyebrow in surprise at her question, and she added, "I don't know what compelled me to ask you that, sorry. I just...It seems like you've gotten past the battle, and that is huge. I don't know if I could have if it was me."

"It's a fair question, and you've got every right to ask me. You almost got killed by The Grimshaw under his lead too. Even if that wasn't the case, you know I expect you to ask me the tough questions." He grinned at her for a second, then his face became serious again. "I think I've mostly—*mostly*—forgiven him, which I know must sound like madness. But I get it. We've seen it before—people getting radicalized by having their hates and fears supported by powerful outside forces telling them what they want to hear. We've seen that get twisted into awful behavior from people who the world would never expect to act that way.

"Even the smartest guy in the room can get his head warped by forces like that. Sometimes *because* they're the smartest or most powerful guy in the room! And he seems to have developed some self-awareness now, maybe thanks to Emmaline, I dunno. But yeah. I can't hate him. Honestly, I sort of pity him now. He's going to have to carry what he's done with him for the rest of his life."

"That is what worries me, though," Cullen said in a somber tone. "Carrying a weight like that can cause one to take unnecessary risks. I hope he is not planning anything stupid."

Their trip through the gate took them to the misty woods, a liminal space that led to another gate where they exited. They found themselves in the fields behind House Mirabilis, and the walk home was a quiet and subdued one. At one point Cullen muttered his usual complaint about the gate being too far from the actual house, but his companions ignored it. The gate had been shaped from a living tree, bent into a gentle arc to the ground, making a loop high enough for all to walk through. They had no intention of moving it, but Cullen found it absurd that it was located at the far end of the property.

Upon entering the House, they were greeted warmly by Aisling, who had been waiting for Merrick patiently, and loudly by Sheridan, who—as usual—was drunk.

"You've been gone forever!" Aisling said and ran up to Merrick to kiss him. She pulled back a bit after embracing him and said quietly, so only he could hear, "Something happened, didn't it?"

He whispered in her ear, his face buried in her voluminous hair. "Don't worry, but I can't tell you until later." She squeezed him gently, acknowledging his plan.

"I was all set t'drink with you, and here y'are, late!" Sheridan boomed. The wild-looking man pounded a tankard on the kitchen counter, punctuating his last few words.

"Pretty sure that's never stopped you before, or even tonight." Merrick laughed. "Give me a few minutes to clean up and catch up with Aisling, and I'll drink a few with you."

"Y'look clean enough fer me, boy!" Sheridan hooted, waving him on. Cullen went to walk past him, but Sheridan caught his sleeve with a surprisingly quick hand.

"You come back too, eh? I've got some things w'need to talk on with you and th'lovely Lady there," and he bowed—deeply, if a little sloppily—to Lucee. She covered her mouth with a hand, trying to cover her giggles.

"I could use a beer, sure. I don't have anywhere to go, let's sit at the big table and wait for Merrick and Aisling." She laughed as she pulled Cullen through the doorway.

It took a bit longer than just a few minutes for Merrick to share what had happened with Aisling, who reacted much the same as he had to the ideas that had been laid forth.

"Vali can do this?" she had asked, keeping her voice soft so no one could overhear, despite them being behind the closed doors of their room.

"She believes that she can, and so do the others. I don't know how this will go, but they'll keep us updated. And they know I've told you everything; no one else at all is to know. This is going to be hard for us but even harder on Camlin."

"There's no plan to get him out if things go poorly?" Aisling was aghast. "We need a backup plan!"

"I wish I could tell you that we had one, or that we knew as of yet how that would work. There are so many unknowns. But I don't think we could stop him if we wanted to, Aisling. He's determined." Merrick gestured helplessly. "I didn't think he had it in him, honestly. There's still a part of me that doubts him, and I guess always will. I don't want to shove him out the door and back to our enemies, though. Especially not without backup."

"There has to be something we can do to help, Merrick. Let's keep thinking." She leaned against him with a sigh, and he put his arms around her and held her close as they grounded themselves in each other.

When they came back downstairs, they found a few more folks had joined the table, and Cullen was hyping the upcoming ArtPark show to the group.

"I am told that there will be music *all day* and massive artistic constructions everywhere! Merrick says that we will blend perfectly with the crowds. We could let our glamour down a little and truly draw admirers to inspire!" He sounded like a sideshow barker, but the folks at the table were eating it up.

"Merrick, is this true?" He grinned at the speaker, a lovely blonde Fae woman who radiated her sunny nature both in attitude and her mostly yellow clothing.

"Tully, you'll love ArtPark," he confirmed. "It's a weekend of merriment, but Sunday will be our day to truly shine. The band is playing that afternoon, and I'm hoping that many of us will want to be there. It's a perfect place for the Fae to bring their powers of inspiration, and soak up that energy from the crowd."

One of the first things that Merrick and Lucee had learned about the Fae was that they needed the creative energy of mortals around them to keep them from fading away. And in return, they inspired creativity and growth, but the Fae required mortal energy in order to thrive. The mortals could get along fine without an exchange with the Fae.

The Eleriannan had drifted from this sort of sharing before Merrick had stumbled into the group, and according to them, were on the brink of fading away. The addition of his energy, then Lucee's, had revitalized the group and given them new purpose. Now they were striving to find new ways to reconnect to the modern world and the mortals around them. Lucee and Merrick had both agreed that bringing the House to their show at the ArtPark would be an amazing way to do that.

Sheridan banged his tankard on the table, commanding the room's attention. "As much as I love a party, we need to talk about t'Grimshaw!"

The chatter from those at the table stopped abruptly.

"What's on your mind, Sheridan?" Merrick asked warily. There was no way he could know about Camlin's plans, but why was he bringing up their enemies now?

"We know they're planning somethin' and what better time to cause a mess than at this art-thing?" Sheridan swigged some beer, the added, "We'd best be prepared, is all I'm saying, if y'know what I mean."

"We've been thinking about that too," Lucee reassured the wild man, who looked both surprised and pleased to hear that. "I was going to call a house meeting to see what everyone else thought, but we can start talking about this now. I'm glad you brought it up."

Sheridan looked pleased at that. "Glad t'see that *some* people around here think I'm good for more than just drinking beer," he muttered.

Merrick grinned and thumped him on the back. "You're one of the people who believed in me first! Anyone who underestimates you is sorely mistaken," Merrick told him.

"I hate to say it, but if we are going to have this talk, we should have everyone here. And not everyone has your stamina, Sheridan," Cullen advised.

"Lightweights, the lot of ye," Sheridan declared.

"House meeting tomorrow afternoon, then," Lucee decided, thunking down her tankard in an imitation of Sheridan that set the whole table laughing.

The next morning was spent having a leisurely and delicious breakfast, as was usual around House Mirabilis. Lucee had told everyone the night before to get word around to the Eleriannan about the house meeting, but for now, she needed to have a magical bootcamp session with The Ladies.

"You have learned something without us," Morgandy said immediately upon Lucee's entrance into the tower room.

"How did you know that?" Lucee asked.

"We know many things, girl," Morgance answered, a sly and toothy smile on her face. "We keep our watchful eyes on all that concern us."

"You would be best to learn that and use it to your advantage," Ula added, and Lucee gave her a measuring look.

"You can spy for me, you're saying."

"We spy for ourselves, and we can be enticed to share," Morgance's smile widened and somehow grew even more toothful.

"Well... all right then," Lucee said, a tad awkwardly. "I'll keep that in mind."

"No plan stays hidden from us for long," Morgandy added. Lucee felt like she was staring a hole through her. What on earth?

"I'll remember that as well," Lucee managed to get out, then fumbled to change the subject. "Did you want to see what I learned?"

Her misdirection seemed to work. The tiny Ladies gathered around her and she brought up her sphere of light, cupped in her hands.

"You saw this done previously and recreated it from memory," Morgance said. It wasn't a question.

"Yes, when Fallon brought one forth to light our way to the gate. I remembered how it looked and felt, and I tried to tap into that memory. I'm having trouble giving it to anyone else, though."

Ula snorted and reached out a claw-like hand, plucking the globe from Lucee's outstretched palms easily. The light didn't even flicker.

"You overthink. The magic is well done, you just doubt yourself." Ula tossed it in an easy motion to Morgance, who caught it with her left hand.

"It is well made and well done," Morgance observed. Morgandy reached over and took it from her sister in a quick swiping motion, and Morgance's face twisted in annoyance.

"You are advancing well," Morgandy said. "But you will need more than this for the days to come." She tossed the globe into the air, where it disappeared in a glittering swirl of stars.

"Of course, you're right," Lucee said. She wondered what exactly Morgandy knew but wasn't saying. "What do you think I should learn next?"

Morgandy's hand suddenly shot out and she grabbed Lucee by the arm, pulling her close.

"How to protect yourself from those who want to get *in*," she whispered, her face too near for Lucee's comfort. "You fared well last time, but now you go against me."

There was a sickening, wrenching feeling, and Lucee felt the room tilt around her.

A clock was chiming, a grandfather clock like the one in Da's office at the university. Lucee opened her eyes to find herself there, in a room with dark paneling and too many books—they spilled off the shelves and were stacked in piles around the room. The large desk was covered with papers, books, research, and a typewriter, because Da hated writing on a computer. Sitting in the comfortable chair behind the desk was Morgandy, dwarfed by the huge upholstered back of the chair.

"This place brings strange emotions for you, Lucee Fearney. Tell me about this."

Lucee paused for a moment, trying to figure out what the play was here, what Morgandy's goal was. Then she answered honestly because she knew Morgandy would know if she didn't.

"The last time I spoke to Da was here. He was angry with me because I didn't plan to be an academic. I was leaving college after I got my B.A. He told me that he was disappointed in me, that he thought I'd never amount to anything. I was so angry! He never wanted to see me for who I was. I was always some failed extension of himself. I had a 4.0 grade average, but I didn't want to follow in his footsteps. I looked like a hoodlum in his words, and I spent too much time on frivolous things like music.

"I got angry, and I told him that when he was ready to see me as a real person with my own hopes and dreams, he would know where to find me, but until then, he should leave me alone, I'll figure it out on my own. And I guess that's what I've done since then."

Morgandy leaned forward across the desk towards Lucee.

"And he has never come to find you."

"He has not. Even Ma doesn't bother to check in anymore. It's been me and Merrick ever since. Both of us are disappointments to our parents, I guess." Lucee shrugged, then added, "But we always have each other's backs."

"*Even when it comes to keeping secrets.*"

Lucee blinked, confused.

"*Why don't you ask me what you want to know?*" *A realization dawned on her, and she asked pointedly,* "*Do your sisters even understand what you're doing right now?*"

Morgandy bared her teeth at the question and snapped, "*They do not, because they do not suspect the plots that are happening beneath their noses! I am always alert, even when they are not. I watch, and listen, and wait for what will happen. But you and The Blackbird have been plotting things without The Ladies, and I wish to know why!*" *In that moment, she looked even more terrifying than usual.*

Lucee gulped, and backed up a few steps involuntarily.

"*I-I'm not at liberty to say.*" *She scrunched her face up, waiting for the angry explosion from Morgandy. When it didn't come, she opened her eyes warily. She saw the Sister staring at her thoughtfully, her chin resting in one small, clawed hand.*

"*Is that so? You know I could come pluck the information from you as easily as one picks an apple from the tree.*" *She waited for Lucee's reaction and grinned approvingly when Lucee straightened up and confronted her.*

"*You could try. But neither of us would enjoy that,*" *Lucee hissed, full of bravado.*

"*Ah, girl! You are a spitfire, even when you are scared. This is why my sisters and I are drawn to support you. But we cannot if we are uninformed of the plans that are happening around us.*" *She paused, then her voice took on a conspiratorial tone.* "*I am aware of some of the facts, at any rate.*"

Seeing Lucee's disbelieving reaction, she continued, "*I know that your plans revolve around this event that is to come, and that Grimshaw hiding at Maithe House. Shall I go on?*" *Lucee just stared at her, so Morgandy added,* "*My guess is that you will allow him to rejoin the enemy, in hopes of destroying them somehow from the inside. And that is why you keep the secret close, so that none may give away his intentions.*"

Lucee felt like Morgandy was gazing deep into her soul, and it made her itch all over. She made a distressed sound and groaned, "*I don't know where you're getting all this from.*"

"*I am no fool. They will pull us apart in a moment so let me set this at your feet: you must be careful. Your foe sees deeper than I, and your Trojan Horse will be more exposed than you were to my eyes. We can help.*"

Lucee found herself sitting on the floor, her legs stretched in front of her. Morgance and Ula had pulled Morgandy back and were berating her in shrill voices, their sister standing defiantly between them.

Lucee took that opportunity to scramble to her feet and flee the room before the Ladies could turn on her and ask her anything at all.

MUSIC: HALLOWS
Her Thirst

Lucee rushed downstairs after the creepy interrogation from Morgandy and found that folks were already starting to assemble for the house meeting.

"I am so not ready for this," she groaned to herself and glanced around the room until she found Cullen. He waved her over with a smile that fell a little when he saw her face.

"Is everything all right?" he asked as she flung her arms around him and buried her face in his shoulder.

"No," she mumbled into his silken shirt, "It most certainly is not." She rose up a little to whisper in his ear. "We have a problem and I need to talk to you and Merrick and I won't be able to before the meeting."

He kept his voice low and his face expressionless. "Can you drop me a hint, at least?"

"Morgandy knows. At least some of what we're planning, anyway."

She felt his hands tighten on her reflexively and he inhaled sharply. "What did she say? And she alone? Not her sisters?"

"Just her, though I'm not sure that'll last after the stunt she pulled to tell me what she knows." Lucee shrugged when Cullen raised an eyebrow at that. "I'll tell you more later. Watch for reactions during this meeting, would you?"

"Well, this should be interesting." Cullen kissed her lightly, then turned to wave Merrick and Aisling over. "I would love to take a walk after this! Would you care to join us?" He widened his eyes and stressed the last words.

"Um, of course, that sounds like a great idea," Merrick said, a confused look on his face. Aisling cocked her head as if to ask "Is everything okay here?" Lucee smiled wanly.

"Cool, cool, I have to tell you about the *weird dream* I had," she said with the lightest stress on the words weird and dream. "But I guess now we need to have this meeting."

She gestured at the room, which had filled up with the residents of House Mirabilis. Lucee never tired of seeing the wild variety of Fae beings that made up their house of Eleriannan. Looking around the large room, she saw the ones that Camlin would call "Gentry." They were beautiful, intimidating beings, with regal stature and uncannily symmetric features—the ones that inspired ballads and legendary tales.

Cullen was one of them. In Lucee's eyes, he was far too handsome for her. This was a man who had confessed to her that his kind of Fae were known for taking mortals to bed, then abandoning them—leaving them lovelorn and wandering hopelessly in search of their Fae lovers until they died. She had sat there with her mouth open when he told her that bit of history. Cullen had been quick to reassure her that he had only ever left broken hearts, not dead lovers, and that was in the past for him. He was a changed man now.

Cullen shared another attribute with some of the other Eleriannan—he was a shapeshifter who could change into a fox. Lucee only knew a few others who she had seen change shapes. Merrick was called The Blackbird because he could take on the form of a raven. He knew at least one other shape, a bobcat. Camlin, too, could take multiple shapes and seemed quite talented at it.

Her next favorite shape-changer was Quillan, a young boy who had served as the page for Fallon and now Lucee since she had become leader of House Mirabilis. He was small and quiet with dark blue feathers for hair. He could change at will into a single bird or a flock of small birds when frightened or in danger. He was a calm presence at her or Merrick's side whenever they needed help, and she was glad to see him in the crowd. He smiled shyly at her when he saw her gaze sweep the room and land on him.

She caught sight of The Ladies near the fireplace and felt her heart start to pound. They seemed to be busy discussing something among themselves—probably Morgandy's stunt. Tully and a group of her friends stood nearby, all Gentry. And spread throughout the room were some of the more unusual, fantastical looking members of House Mirabilis. There were small, gnarled, gnomelike beings who all wore brown caps with feathers, and the beautifully graceful Ffyn, who looked like trees that swayed and waved their branches in the wind as they moved. Gathered toward the back of the room were a few small, round, spiky creatures that Merrick and Lucee agreed reminded them of hedgehogs. They never spoke to her, but they seemed to approve of everything that had happened in the House since Merrick arrived, at least as far as Lucee could tell.

Cullen stepped into the open space in the middle of the room and addressed the crowd. "Are we ready to begin?" After the noise died down, he said, "We wanted to talk to everyone about our upcoming plans and what they mean to House Mirabilis. Some of you are aware that Merrick and Lucee will take their band to perform at the mortal event called ArtPark. If we choose to accompany them, we have an opportunity to walk amongst the mortals and their energy in a scenario where we can let our glamour rest."

"The event is filled with music and performances and large art installations, and it is the perfect place for all of you to amble about and interact with the mortals who attend," Merrick said. "And yes, there will be beer and food, though of course nothing as delicious as what we have here." Sheridan hooted at that and lifted a tankard. Merrick laughed and saluted his friend.

"Here's something that Sheridan brought to the table, and we agree with him. Although this event will be a wonderful opportunity for us, there's also danger. We fear that The Grimshaw—who are quietly regrouping—will attempt to strike us on that day." Merrick paused to look around the room, seeing dismay and outrage on the faces of the Eleriannan.

"We hope for the best, but we must prepare for the worst," Lucee said. "I know none of us like this possibility, but it needs to be addressed. And as much as I'd want as many of you there as wish to attend, I want you all to understand the risks before making any decision." She frowned and said in a softer voice, "I hope that some of you will want to come. Merrick and Sousa and Vali are all pretty strong, but I don't think we can fight off The Grimshaw. And this is an opportunity for you to re-enter the mortal world for a bit, to spread wonder and spark imagination in ways that I know many of you crave more than ever."

"Our friends died trying to stop The Grimshaw from turning the city to the wrong path," Tully spoke up, her voice quivering a little. "We said we wanted to touch the lives of mortals again, to make a difference. This seems like the perfect time to do that, and to make sure that The Grimshaw do not re-emerge and regain strength. I am no fighter, but I stand ready to take this risk."

The Eleriannan seemed divided. Then, to the surprise of everyone, the group of Ffyn moved forward. They did not have the ability to speak aloud, but a feeling of approval, of alliance, and excitement washed over the room. Lucee stepped forward, and one of the Ffyn gently touched her with its branchlike appendage. She let the images it sent her wash over her, momentarily immersed in the peacefulness that came when she communicated with one of the creatures.

"The Ffyn want us to go to ArtPark. They are ready to feel the joy of being in the midst of mortals in that environment and," she paused a second, for effect, "will tear apart any Grimshaw that tries to ruin the day." She raised an eyebrow at that, and Sheridan hooted and clapped his hands.

"If th' gentlest beings here be that fierce, can the rest of us give any less?" he challenged the room.

The hedgehog people cheered and stepped forward, hands aloft in solidarity. That seemed to push everyone else over the cliff, and soon the entire room was loud with clapping and stomping. Lucee held her hands over her head and shouted for order.

"Quiet, my friends!" Once the noise died down, she continued, "Then we have a decision. I'll be glad to know my family and friends will be with us on this day!" That elicited more cheers.

Cullen spoke up. "We must plan now for any contingency so we may be prepared. We will scout the area well before the day, learn the lay of the land and places where we may retreat or take stands as needed. Merrick has the map of the event, and we will study that as well."

"We need you to think of how you will protect yourselves and the mortals around you if it comes to that," Merrick told the crowd. "And also, you must decide how you'd like to appear on that day! The festival is known for wild costumed and masked performers as well as the kinetic sculptures and installations. No one there will suspect anything beyond artistry, so you should find it easy to be yourselves. I expect many people to be inspired after this event!"

The room exploded into excited conversation and Merrick turned to Lucee and Cullen with a grin.

"I think this house is going to be busy for a while! We can let the event coordinators know that there'll be performers who support us in the audience so they'll have even less scrutiny."

They watched Tully round up the gnome people and hedgehoggy beings and usher them to her chambers, which Lucee knew were filled to bursting with outfits of all types and styles. Lucee pointed it out to Merrick, Cullen, and Aisling, and said with a laugh, "Guess Tully's going to make costumes for them all now."

"Oh, that is Tully's dream come true!" Aisling giggled. "She would dress us all if we allowed it. But she'll certainly have wonderful suggestions for those she is dragging away." That made Cullen look away, his face strained from trying to stifle laughter.

"Do you think they'll notice if we slip away for that walk now?" Lucee saw The Ladies and thought that they were attempting to approach her, but they were hindered by the crowd of Fae in the room. She really didn't want to be cornered by them before she could tell her friends what had happened.

"Yo, Sheridan," Merrick waved over the wild man. "We need to get out of here for a bit, can you hold down this horde while they talk things to death?"

Sheridan looked back and forth between the four of them and ended at Lucee. In that moment, she knew in the depths of her soul that he played up his drunken character a lot more than anyone suspected, and he knew more than he ever let on. He tilted his head and nodded sagely.

"Y'go on, now. I'll distract these fools, while you take care of th' details they'll never see. You can count on me." He reached over and awkwardly patted Lucee's arm, then turned away and walked into the middle of the crowd, yelling, "Beer is what we need for this! Let's get a keg open, friends!"

They managed to escape out the back door and away from the house, laughing at how Sheridan's plan for everything was beer-based. Once Merrick judged that they were far enough away, and Lucee had decided that they weren't being followed by The Ladies, he asked her, "So what's on your mind?"

She took a deep breath and told them everything that had happened with The Ladies. When she got to the point where she'd stood up to Morgandy, Aisling reacted with a gasp.

"That was quite bold, Lucee! Of all the Ladies, Morgandy is the one I fear the most."

"Well, I was pretty mad. And freaked out. That's usually when I'm the bravest. And the stupidest." She got laughs for that, but she brought the group back to the subject at hand. Once she was finished, they all walked in silence for a moment, contemplating what this all meant.

"She told you things that she has not shared with her sisters. I do not think I remember the like happening before now," Cullen said in a subdued tone. "She chose to anger her sisters in order to speak to you privately. She made sure that your secrets stayed your own until you choose to reveal them."

"They're angry with her," Lucee said. "They pulled us apart. Of all the places in the world I could be, standing between The Ladies is currently my least favorite." She plucked a soft blue chicory flower from its stem as they passed by and twiddled it between her fingers as she frowned at it.

"How can she know what we're planning? This is, you said that she spies on us?" Merrick's face was tight with concern.

"They said that they spy, and that they could do it for me. But only Morgandy knows—or has all too accurately guessed—what we're planning. She even referred to Camlin as a Trojan Horse." She said the last part in a whisper, afraid that, somehow, someone could hear her.

"She wants to help him hide his intentions," Aisling breathed. "Oh, she's right. We were foolish not to let The Ladies in. It is right in their wheelhouse to do something like this."

"Like what, exactly?" Merrick was plainly confused, and Cullen was as well.

"Merrick, think on it. Who but The Ladies are the ones that most understand the locked doors and secret spaces of the mind? If they hid away parts of Camlin's memories or feelings, none would find them until they unlocked the way."

Merrick's eyes widened as he realized what Aisling was saying.

"He would lose parts of himself until they allowed a reversal," Cullen said in a sick-sounding voice. He was pale and distressed, and Lucee dropped her flower to take his hand, worried. "I am sorry. That just sounds like one of my worst nightmares," he continued. "I do not think I could do it. Even if it could be reversed, my experiences and feelings are precious."

"I think he will, though," Merrick said, stopping in his tracks to look up at the sky. "I think he's ready to risk everything."

He sighed and leveled his gaze to look around at his friends.

"He makes it really difficult for me to hate him."

They walked on for a bit, and once Lucee realized where they were, she stumbled over her feet a little bit. Cullen steadied her, and she held onto him for a moment.

"The irony of this discussion just hit me. Look, we are where we first fought The Grimshaw! The day that changed everything."

She didn't need to say it aloud because they were all thinking the same thing—the day Lucee had almost died.

"This is just one of the things he's trying to atone for," she added. "And I don't hate him, either, Merrick. Maybe that's stupid. Maybe I should expect him to betray us—especially if we let The Ladies hide the motivations that I figure are what's driving him to be a better person. I have no idea. All I know is that he wants to do this, and if The Ladies can give him a better chance of success, I shouldn't stand in their way. If he agrees to their plan, of course."

She sat down abruptly, closing her eyes and putting her hands down on the ground as if she was trying to communicate with the Earth. She felt someone's movement as they sat next to her, then drew her in for a gentle hug. She hadn't expected it to be Aisling.

"You've been through so much," she murmured close to Lucee's ear, her voice kind and reassuring. "You are doing a great job at this, Lucee Fearney. I know it's such a heavy load for you to carry, but that is why we're here. Let us carry it with you. You may be in charge, but you are not alone."

Lucee started to object, but what came out was a great, stuttering sob. She found herself sitting on the ground, crying, while Aisling hugged her close. Merrick and Cullen were there as well, encircling her with their arms.

"No matter what you do, Lucee, I am at your side," Cullen reassured her.

"We are all in this together," Merrick agreed.

"I just...It's so...I don't want to be responsible for deaths! I don't want to make the mistake that gets people killed, even the guy who was our worst enemy. Maybe especially not then!" Lucee sobbed.

"Lucee, you always give them choices. I listen to what you say whenever we face a crisis, and you are consistently clear. Everyone chooses their path, and you honor that decision no matter what it is," Aisling told her distraught friend. "None in our house would call you less than fair and respectful as a leader and a friend."

After a moment more of tears, Lucee seemed to be gathering herself together, so they moved back and gave her room. She sniffed a few times and started to wipe her face with the back of her hand, only to be offered a handkerchief from Cullen's seemingly endless stash of them.

"I swear you must have hundreds of these in a pocket somewhere," she sniffled as she gratefully took it from him. "I'm sorry for dumping on everyone. It's just—it's a lot. I've never been responsible for so much before."

"Lucee, you know that Aisling's right. You need to lean on us more, you dingdong," Merrick said gently. "None of us can do this alone. Together, we're unbeatable. And you need to stop claiming responsibility for the paths that other people take. Anything that any of us undertake is a decision made ultimately by us alone, and that includes Camlin and the path before him. Okay?"

Lucee looked distraught, but sighed, "Okay." She then looked around at her friends and snorted, gesturing at all of them. "Here we are, sitting on the ground in a field while your illustrious leader cries her eyes out. What heroes we are! The legends that will be told about us!"

"Better than some of the other councils I've been to, honestly." Merrick laughed. "At least I like everyone here!"

"I really cannot imagine you not liking anyone," Cullen said. "You are even friendly enough with our enemy-turned-resident. That would be a stretch for most folks, to be cordial with the man who tried to kill you." He stood up and offered a hand to Lucee while Merrick did the same for Aisling.

"I'm glad you can't tell who I like or dislike. That means they probably don't know, either. I'll be honest. If circumstances were different and I'd met Camlin now, I would want to be his friend. Now? It's still going to take some time to forget his hands around my throat."

"He still has nightmares," Aisling added. "Though I should probably not tell you that. But he won't." She shot an accusing look at Merrick, and he held his hands up like he was surrendering.

"I do. You're right. I have nightmares about the whole battle, more often now that I see his face regularly. It's not like I can go to a therapist about it." Merrick shrugged. "But bringing this back to the original subject—are we going to include The Ladies? I think we should."

"Aye, you are right, Merrick. We were foolish to not include them in the first place. They are not known for giving secrets away." Cullen said.

"If any can navigate this without endangering themselves, it would be The Ladies. If, of course, Camlin says yes to this," Aisling agreed.

"This conversation will be fun." Lucee rolled her eyes. "At least I won't be having it alone."

MUSIC: THE MISSION
Drown In Blue

There was no outside evidence that The Ladies had been arguing among themselves. But when Lucee came to them to explain the secret plan, the conversation felt tense and weird, and she was glad when it was over.

The four friends asked The Ladies to meet them in the tower room to discuss something of importance. Morgandy looked pleased with the invitation.

Merrick held up a hand, then pulled out a clear glass bead on a string that hung around his neck.

"We need more privacy than this room offers. Let me take care of that," he said and held the bead in his hand, concentrating on it. The bead seemed to grow bigger, the edges of it glowing gently. It stopped growing once it reached the walls, encircling them in a globe of shimmering light.

"That should do," Morgance said curtly and turned to Lucee. "You have something you have held back from us. Tell us."

"Only a few know this plan. We wanted to make sure that it would stay a deep secret while it played out, and we need reactions to be… *appropriate*." Lucee frowned then added, "We were wrong to not include you. We were just acting out of an abundance of caution. And to be honest, this sort of secret keeping isn't really natural to me. Or Merrick, I think."

Morgandy made a rude noise, and her sisters swiveled to look at her.

"I like not this change in you of late, sister," Ula said reprovingly.

"Do tell us what you are thinking now that you have our attention," Morgance said in a sharp tone.

"What I am thinking is that my sisters have become soft!" Morgandy spit out. "How do you not see what has happened under your very watch when it is so obvious to me? The Grimshaw looks to return to those who cast him out, to play the prodigal with a hidden purpose! Am I wrong, Lucee Fearney?"

"You are not, Morgandy. There's a bit more than that, but that's the gist of it."

She explained the plan as best as she understood it and when she was finished, Morgance asked, "And we are expected to go into that one's mind and hide his secrets? Even though he fears spreading the contagion of the Mealladhan?"

"I am volunteering. None expect it of me. I have already pledged to help," Morgandy declared.

Morgance and Ula were incensed at this and both shouted at the same time.

"You cannot risk yourself!"

"You would put us in jeopardy!"

Lucee held up her hand and stepped into the middle of the circle, serving to create some space between Morgandy and her angry sisters.

"If it causes a rift between the three of you, it isn't worth it. We can find another way. You're too important to all of us to risk."

This caused Morgance to sputter indignantly, and Ula to clench her small clawed fists.

"*We* will be the ones to judge the risk and our importance! None shall keep us from this task if it is truly what is needed," Morgance snapped. She turned to Morgandy and asked, "If you say this is the way, we all work together, as it should be."

"We cannot risk all three of us becoming ensnared. If I go into his mind, I will need my sisters to ensure that I will leave again unscathed. You know that I am right. Think on it," Morgandy said, in a voice that made Lucee think of stagnant ponds—calm but with the potential for horrors to lurk under the surface. She wouldn't have wanted that tone directed at her. She glanced at Cullen. He looked like he was trying his best to hide his discomfort.

"None of this will matter if Camlin doesn't agree, let me remind you," Lucee said, trying to regain some control over the discussion. "I think it would be wise, but it's his plan, and more importantly, his mind."

Morgance made a dismissive noise. "He will agree if he wants this to work. Otherwise, he is walking into a death trap. Though perhaps that is his wish?"

"I sincerely hope not," Merrick said. "He's a lot of things, but he's never struck me as a fool."

"So... that was weird, right?" Lucee asked Cullen a bit later as they curled up on their bed together. They had decided that a nap seemed like a good idea, but once they crawled into bed, neither one could stop thinking about what had happened with The Ladies.

"Thoroughly strange, and I do not use those words lightly when it comes to anything pertaining to The Ladies," Cullen agreed. "I cannot remember them ever arguing with each other. I have to say that I mislike it greatly."

Lucee sighed and stretched out, lying on her stomach next to Cullen. He reached out to massage her back with one hand, and she sighed appreciatively.

"This is the best thing that has happened today. Keep that up and I'll make you king."

He snorted and leaned over to kiss her shoulder. "I know you better than that, you would not do that to someone you loved. Anyway, I am probably at my best as a consort and sounding board. And provider of handkerchiefs, of course."

"Where do they go, anyway? You always have a clean one, and I never find any of the ones I've soiled. I even tried to hide one once and it disappeared..."

"You did not!" He laughed as she nodded guiltily. "Let it be known that, despite as close as we are, I still need a secret or two. I am Fae, remember."

"What happens if I discover all your secrets? No, don't answer that. I suspect the answer to that is one of them. Keep a mystery or two, it's sexy." She giggled when that made him pink up a bit. "You're remarkably easy to make blush for someone who was such a playboy in the past!"

"I assure you, it is a power only you seem to wield over me." He covered his embarrassment by leaning in and rubbing her back a little harder. Lucee closed her eyes and enjoyed it for a moment.

"So, not to break this delicious mood we've got going here, but do you think they'll be okay?" Lucee kept her eyes closed, but she could feel Cullen's hands ease up a bit as he mulled over the question.

"I think... it seems as if they are in the throes of a power shift. Morgance has been the de facto leader for a very long time, and I am unsure if she came by that position through strength, cunning, or consensus. For as long as I have known them, she has been a small terror. When our Blackbird won her challenge, I suspect that started the changes in the dynamic of The Ladies."

"I got the impression from Morgandy that she found that her sisters are becoming soft. Which—well, if that's soft I don't want to see hard."

Cullen snickered at that. "It is certainly better that they are on our side!"

"So, I guess we'll be bringing them to The Maithe so we can watch Souz get mad that he wasn't consulted. Maybe I'll talk Sheridan into giving me some beer to bring. Or maybe we should all just get drunk and kick Camlin out at the end of the night." At that, Cullen fell over and buried his face in his pillow to keep from laughing too loudly.

"So much for a nap!" he wheezed. "That mental image of you and Sousa drunkenly booting a confused Camlin out the door of Maithe House was too much!"

"Wouldn't solve all our problems, but it would fix 'em for that night, at least," she said in an upbeat voice.

"And the next morning, you would be busy dealing with a hangover," he said.

"You know, it's funny. I haven't had a hangover since I met all of you. Maybe it's just Sheridan's superior brews?"

"Hello, silly girl. If I have said it once, I have said it a million times..."

"Fae!" They both said together, grinning.

No one at The Maithe was excited to see The Ladies.

Emmaline was obviously afraid of them, even though they'd contributed to the elixir that had brought her into the fold and was working to restore her health. When the strange little women walked into the ballroom, trailed by a contrite Merrick, Aisling, Lucee, and Cullen, Emmaline struggled to hide her reaction.

Camlin, next to her, visibly flinched. Vali, sitting in a chair facing the couch, didn't see at first what had caused the couple to behave like that. She whipped around, expecting something truly horrific, and sighed when she saw The Ladies standing there, imperious and glaring at everyone.

Vali turned back to Emmaline and her voice was as quiet as she could manage. "I think if you wanted to slip out of here for a while, none would fault you."

"Our reason for being here does not involve her," Morgance's voice rang out. "We have need to speak to that one." She pointed one clawed finger at Camlin.

Before anyone else could react, Lucee stepped forward and said, "I sure could use some coffee. Hey Emmaline, could you join me? I hate to drink alone." She made a face that plainly said, "Let's get out of here, quick."

Emmaline glanced over to Camlin, looking for guidance. He nodded briefly, and murmured, "Go on, I'll be fine. And everyone else will be here, nothing bad will happen."

She looked guilty, but relieved to get out of the room. Lucee smiled at her reassuringly and led her out of the ballroom and upstairs to the library.

"Lucee, what's going on? Do you know?" she asked once they were up the stairs. Lucee made a beeline for the side table where an urn of coffee was always available and fixed herself a mug. She gestured for Emmaline to join her and chose one of the velvety overstuffed armchairs to sit in.

"Might as well get comfy, I have no clue how long this will take," Lucee told her. "The Ladies want to talk to Camlin about Grimshaw stuff. Don't worry, they're not angry with him—well, not any angrier than they usually are."

"They frighten me, Lucee. I guess if I understood them better, I might be less scared of them."

Lucee chuckled at that. "Understanding The Ladies? Good luck. They're an enigma, wrapped in a riddle, shrouded in the kind of horror tales that made you afraid to sleep when you were a kid. Yet they've done much to train Merrick, and now me, in how to use our powers and be stronger. I guess braver too. No matter what, I know that they are one hundred percent on our side, and I would much rather that than the alternative, you know?"

"They *train* you?" Emmaline shivered at that. "How does that go?"

"It goes very fucking terribly sometimes, to be honest." Lucee took a swig of her coffee, then went on with a self-deprecating tone to her voice. "They're excellent, if harsh teachers. It's the student who tends to suck."

"I'm sure you're being hard on yourself. You're the leader. They're probably extra tough on you," Emmaline said in a soothing tone.

"I'm pretty sure they were harder on Merrick. But you know, he's a natural at all of this, so it came easy to him. Me, I have to work really hard for every success I get." She shrugged, then added, "I did figure out something on my own recently, and The Ladies seemed pleased. I know a lot of my problem is that I don't think I'm good at this. Mental blocks, impostor syndrome. Blah blah."

Lucee finished off the coffee and got up to refill her mug while thinking of a way to change the subject. She was so tired of that line of thought. Emmaline, though, wasn't ready to let her drop it.

"Lucee, you're so tough on yourself! I know I haven't known you long, but all I've done since I got here is sit around and watch everyone interact. And you handle all of this weirdness so well! Not to insult anyone," she added quickly, looking around the room worriedly. "Poor choice of words! But it is a beautifully strange world for mortals to navigate, and any of us might feel inadequate. Yet here you are, leading these amazing folks by being yourself. You're open and vulnerable, and you aren't afraid to say 'I don't know' or admit that you can't do something. That's a rare quality."

Lucee could feel her face getting hot, a feeling she would get right before she started to cry. She took her mug and quietly walked back to her chair, then sat in silence for a few moments before she responded.

"I-I appreciate your words." She gripped her cup tightly and stared into her drink while she collected her thoughts. "I feel like I don't know how to measure myself for successes or failures. The person I inherited this position from wasn't around me for very long, so I didn't have much chance to learn the craft of leadership from her. Especially not the delicate nature of being mortal born and guiding the Fae, which I don't even know if she could've taught me anyway. I'm constantly second-guessing myself, even with the excellent counsel that I get from my friends. It's a weird place to be, you know?"

"Well, feel free to ignore anything that I'm about to say, but what if you're looking at it the wrong way? I find it hard to believe that you weren't chosen specifically because of the differences you bring to the table. So, if I'm right, why are you trying to operate as anything other than your authentic self?" Emmaline shrugged, then looked over at the coffee stand. "I don't remember those cookies being there before. They look delicious!" She got up to grab a plateful. Lucee watched her, shaking her head.

"Fae tricks. They're always surprising you." She paused, then corrected herself. "*We're* always surprising you. Holy crap. I think it actually, finally just hit me. I really am one of them. Us."

"It's not a fluke, Lucee. I don't even know how you came to belong to this group, but I can see that you're one of the most important parts of it. It's obvious." Emmaline wiped cookie crumbs off of her chin, then smiled at Lucee. "You know, I'd really like to hear that story, whenever you feel like telling it."

"It's all Merrick's fault. I've never been more grateful for his impulsiveness in my life."

"Okay, now you *have* to tell me."

Downstairs, things were less pleasant.

"You left us out of your plans," Morgance seethed. "Foolish and short-sighted! Lucky for us all that our sister saw clearly what you strove to conceal."

Vali noted to herself that Morgance's expression as she glared at Morgandy appeared more accusatory than proud or pleased. She began to answer, but Sousa beat her to it.

"It wasn't a planned slight, Ladies. We wanted to keep our circle small to begin with, as rumors spread easily and reactions to our plot need to be genuine. And all of this has happened rather quickly, to be honest." He was trying to cover his exasperation at their ire by being as conciliatory as he could manage, but Vali knew that would wear off soon.

"Rather than arguing about what we should have done, perhaps you could share with us what you would like to do?" she said, smoothly interjecting herself between the angry sisters and Sousa. "I, for one, would welcome your suggestions." She held back the urge to smile, knowing that it would be wasted on The Ladies—especially right now.

Morgandy took a step back. "You are correct, Child of the City. We waste time with bruised egos and pointless arguing." She glared in Morgance's direction for a second, then pointed at Camlin, and addressed him. "You are planning to put yourself in peril. We can provide you with a way to help keep your secrets safe."

Camlin seemed surprised by the entire outburst happening in front of him and swallowed hard when Morgandy extended her offer.

"Forgive my shock, Ladies. You have caught me off guard. How much do you know? And what will you do to assist?"

"I traced the whispers of hopes and fears, boy, and they tell me all I need to know about what you wish to do," Morgandy hissed through her teeth. "Those with mortal blood all leak your emotions freely, leaving them available to all who care to see."

"Yes, yes, my mother was mortal," Camlin said in a curt, dismissive tone. "I leak emotions? What is this ridiculousness?"

Vali thought for sure that Morgandy would get angry at that, but instead she burst into shrill laughter.

"Your emotions are quite readable to those with the skill and desire to view them. And what I see is subterfuge, fear, and sadness. You cannot lie to a power that controls your will, and you are walking into a lion's den without that weapon at your command. If the enemy chooses to peer deeply into your mind, you will be lost, and so will the hopes of the Eleriannan to destroy that which threatens us."

Camlin's face blanched.

"I thought I could hide my intentions from them. If you could spot them from where you are, and even without a connection to me, then I'm lost."

"You are not lost," Morgance sighed impatiently. "You are not listening. We have the ability to lock these thoughts away safely where they will never see them. When you are triumphant, we will unlock them again, and all will be as it was."

"But what if the Mealladhan has left my mind full of traps? I don't want to spread the infection to anyone else."

"You let me worry about that, once-enemy. This is my realm, and the Mealladhan should be afraid of me." Morgandy cackled, her pointed teeth gleaming.

"You need to understand one thing, Camlin, before you agree to this. Your memories, anything that might give away your motives? You may not be able to access them, either. Not until The Ladies let them back out. You will have gaps in your memory until they do," Cullen broke in, his voice filled with concern.

Morgandy made a face. "And if you do not hide those all-important memories away, you will betray yourself and all who count on you. It is certainly your choice, of course."

Camlin's face reflected the tension he was feeling, and he paced back and forth for a moment. All eyes in the room were on him as he considered. Finally, he went down to one knee in front of Morgandy and addressed her in a soft, humble voice.

"You're correct, of course. But I want to hold onto myself until it's time to disappear. May I have a few more days before that happens?"

Morgandy sniffed, her face softer than it had been just a moment previously.

"Come this way, let us discuss our options." She turned away and gestured for him to follow, walking toward the far exit of the ballroom. Her sisters looked at each other, incredulous, then followed in Morgandy's wake.

Once they had left the room, Vali glanced over at Sousa and muttered, "That was weird, even for them, right? Not just me getting that?"

"Nope, not just you. I don't know what to make of any of that. But I'll tell you one thing." He addressed the last part to all those gathered around. "I expect our guest will be leaving us sooner than we thought. Things aren't going to get any less weird, that's for sure."

MUSIC: ALL ABOUT EVE
In The Clouds

The rest of that night was subdued. After The Ladies left without speaking to anyone, Camlin walked through the ballroom, looking like he'd lost everything he'd ever owned. He excused himself, saying that he would send Lucee down and that he wanted to spend some time with Emmaline. When he walked out, the room felt heavy and everyone was quiet, contemplating what the future might hold.

They had scheduled a band practice, but none of The Drawback felt particularly into it, and both Sousa and Merrick were drinking more beer than they probably should have been. Lucee spent most of the time noodling on her guitar and playing with effects pedals. Merrick messed up his lyrics five times in a row, the last time improvising with an imaginative string of curses that left Sousa sitting behind his drum kit with his mouth open.

"I didn't know you had it in you, my man," he quipped, then hit a cymbal for emphasis.

Merrick winced. "Sorry, sorry. I'm a dumbass tonight, sorry."

"We need to cover something ridiculous, that'll get us out of our misery," Lucee said. "I have no idea what, but there's gotta be something."

Merrick ran his fingers down the frets of his bass, then plucked out a sonorous note, followed by two more. Sousa instantly recognized the tune as "Bela Lugosi's Dead" and started the choppy drum hits that opened the tune. Lucee picked up on it and stomped on a couple of pedals before dropping into her best approximation of Daniel Ash's swirling, echoing guitar tone. Sousa yelled "NICE!" and they just let the tune build for a while before Merrick dropped in with the vocals, pitching his voice extra deep at the beginning.

The original version was already a good nine-and-a-half minutes of 'spooky goodness,' as Lucee put it. They managed to drag it out for almost fifteen, just by Lucee devolving her playing into the most godawful screeches and whines she could coax out of her guitar while Merrick and Sousa roared with laughter.

"Theydies and Gentlebeings, we are The Drawback! No refunds!" she yelled into the mic and dropped her guitar on the ground, causing one last terrible squeal.

Merrick looked over at the couch, where a horrified Cullen and Aisling sat next to a totally blasé Vali, who looked like she'd heard worse.

"Believe it or not, that's not the shittiest we've ever sounded," Merrick said and laughed at Aisling's wide eyes.

"I choose not to believe that," she answered and blew him a kiss.

"No comments, Cullen?" Lucee grinned at her scandalized boyfriend.

"I—um...no. Maybe not best to premiere that during the ArtPark show?" Cullen looked like he was doing his best to be diplomatic, and he relaxed visibly when she laughed at his comment.

"But do you feel better?" Vali asked, and Sousa raised two thumbs up over his cymbals, then went back to tightening something on his kit. She looked over at her friends on the couch and echoed his thumbs up at them.

"Who's ready to hear me say that I'm starving? Because it's true," Lucee announced, jumping off the small stage and running up to Cullen. She put her hands out and pulled him up. He wrapped her up in a quick hug, a pleased look on his face.

"I am actually hungry as well. Sousa, do you think the House will oblige feeding your wandering minstrels and entourage?" Cullen asked.

"I have it on good authority that the House would like nothing more," Sousa said and pointed upstairs. "Someone's going to have to fetch our lovebirds down, and if the rest of you can move some furniture around, I'll go grab the food. Lucee, wanna help me?"

He didn't wait for her answer. He just turned and headed out the far exit of the ballroom. She hustled to catch up and bounded up to him in the hallway.

"Where are we going? I never go past the door to the Forest!" She looked around with interest.

"There's actually a kitchen down here off of the dining room we never use! But we're just retrieving food. We have a big spread of everyone's favorite takeout waiting." He glanced at her while they walked. "I wanted to check in with you and make sure you're okay. Lots of weirdness going on for you lately, especially with The Ladies. You look together from my vantage point, but I don't wanna assume anything."

They entered a long kitchen space, all smooth marble counters and steel appliances. Everything in the room looked impeccably clean, relatively new, and professional quality. Lucee let out a long, appreciative whistle.

"This is one swank kitchen, Souz! If I could cook for anything, I'd want to have this space." She stepped over to where he was loading up trays with takeout boxes, plates, and silverware. "And I'm doing all right, I guess. The past couple of days have been an emotional rollercoaster, so I feel like I've been through the wringer. But I guess I'm starting to get used to that feeling." She laughed nervously.

"You need a break." Sousa gave her a meaningful look, then picked up the heaviest tray. "You can't keep that kind of stress level up, even with Fae backup. You should get that man of yours and go out on the town for a night or two. Something away from all of this mess."

"This must be two tons of food, dude!" Lucee huffed behind him with the other tray. "It's not a terrible idea—I mean, it's not like Cullen and I have ever had an actual date."

"Ha! That's not a big priority around here, is it!" Sousa banged his tray down, and Lucee followed suit. "Soup's on!" he shouted, grinning when everyone got excited about all the choices they faced.

There were cartons of Thai, Chinese, Mexican, and Indian cuisine—and randomly, one huge pizza. Sousa pulled a slice out of the box, threw it on a plate, and dumped some spicy broccoli from one of the boxes on top of the pizza.

"I'm not sure if that's gross or genius," Merrick commented, loading up his plate with a sampler from each country's offerings in a much more orderly manner.

"Half the fun is mixing things up!" Sousa retorted, adding a samosa to his pile. Aisling looked at Lucee and they both made a face that said exactly what they thought about that.

After everyone had gathered up a plateful, they found places to sit. Vali had grabbed a spot on the floor next to the armchair that Sousa claimed for himself. She put her plate on the floor and leaned over it as she ate.

"Camlin and Emmaline said they were tired and they'd eat something later," she said between bites. "I told 'em that we'd leave something for them. Don't make a liar out of me!"

That got her laughter from everyone in the room, who were all busy stuffing their faces.

"I think band practice makes me almost as hungry as doing magic," Merrick said. "And this day has felt endless, like a marathon." Lucee had to agree with that. She leaned close to Cullen, who was sitting next to her on one of the couches.

"Hey, want to just sleep here tonight? I am wiped out."

Merrick overheard her and said, "I know you're not talking to me, but that's a really good idea. I think I'd prefer to just crash and go back to House Mirabilis in the morning."

"That sounds like a splendid idea then," Cullen agreed. "No reason to drag ourselves down to the portal and back again."

Lucee poked Cullen gently. "Hey Foxy, Sousa said something tonight that made a lot of sense. He thinks I need a break, that I'm stressed out. And I'll be honest, that sounds pretty great, the idea of taking a break, that is. He said you should take me on a date." She paused, and gave him her most appealing look. "And we've never actually been on a date..."

"Oh. That is true." He looked aghast at that revelation. "I should remedy that immediately. Or immediately tomorrow, perhaps?"

"Not tonight, that's for sure!" She laughed at that thought. "But we could talk about it before we fall asleep. Or in the morning. I really don't need much, just getting to go someplace different with you would be a treat."

The room that Lucee had chosen as her own at The Maithe was just as beautiful as every other room there. But despite being hers, it showed almost no sign of her personality or even objects that belonged to her. She had a closet with extra clothes, including all her stage outfits, and she had placed a few photos along the mantle of the fireplace. Other than that, it didn't look like a room that Lucee lived in.

That's because I don't really live here, Lucee thought as she noted how little of herself was present in her space. She vastly preferred sleeping next to Cullen, who until recently hadn't wanted to spend the night at The Maithe. Lucee suspected that it was his way of feeling secure in the relationship, as his feelings had been hurt when she chose to take a room at Sousa's rather than one at House Mirabilis. Secretly, she feared being away from him too long, as though he would suddenly disappear or decide that he'd made a horrible mistake in choosing her.

The folks at House Mirabilis preferred that she stayed there as well, and she understood that desire since she was their leader. So, her room remained unoccupied and felt empty.

She went to the French doors leading to the balcony and pulled them open. The smells of the forest that hid inside the inner walls of The Maithe wafted into the room on a gentle breeze. Lucee took a deep breath happily, and behind her, she heard Cullen do the same.

"This is my favorite part of staying here," she said, letting the calming air flow over her.

"Watching you react to that the same way every time is my favorite part," Cullen said as he came up behind her and put his arms around her.

"Mmm, Foxy, you could hug me like that all the time." She sighed happily. "We could also snuggle in the bed, though I guarantee I won't be awake for long."

"Poor tired beauty. Let us remedy that now, and tomorrow we can think about what we would like to do for a date." He leaned over to kiss the top of her head, and she sighed again. She was grateful that he always seemed to go out of his way to make her feel loved.

After they woke up the next morning, they decided that a leisurely day of wandering around parts of the city and just letting things happen might be fun.

"I truly have no idea what the city holds these days," Cullen said. "I am familiar with some of the areas around The Maithe, but not nearly enough. And I would like to see the places you love with you to guide me. That seems like a perfect day to me."

Lucee smiled brilliantly at that. "What a wonderful plan! I think I know some places that'll tickle your fancy, or at least perplex you in the best way. Which seems like the quintessential Baltimore date, in my opinion."

She decided to dress up a little; of course, Cullen always was dressed impeccably, so she was going to have to up the ante a little bit to compete with that. When she checked in the closet, she found some clothes that she wasn't familiar with. They were obviously meant for her. They reflected her style perfectly.

"I wonder if Tully left these for me," she mused as she laid out several outfits. She picked up a dress and held it up against her body. Cullen made an approving noise so she went to the mirror next to the closet to check it out.

It was made in layers. The inner layer started from thin shoulder straps and a loose-fitting bodice that flowed into a lace-edged skirt, all in burgundy with green trims. The over-layers were gauze cotton and lace in a variety of green and burgundy shades made to flow around Lucee as she moved. It was a perfect dress for a summer day, as it would keep her cool but still look beautiful.

She slipped out of the tee she'd worn to bed, and into the dress in one fluid motion. Of course, it fit perfectly, and when she spun around, she could see how good it looked on her. She glanced over at Cullen to see his appreciative smile.

"You look stunning as always," he said, and she blew him a kiss.

"I think I'm ready for this day now. And maybe I'll be a proper match for you, my foxy fashion plate." She popped out to brush her teeth and finish her morning duties. When she came back, she found Cullen carefully rolling up the sleeves of a black, buffed silk button-down shirt that he had paired with baggy black linen pants, which were tucked into black boots. He had somehow found a narrow tie that matched the green of her dress, and he had tied it loosely, matching his not quite buttoned-up neckline.

"You really shouldn't look better than your date, you know," Lucee joked and kissed him. "Oh, that shirt is so soft! Maybe you should wear it more often?"

'Whatever my lady wants, of course," Cullen replied, "especially if it means she cannot keep her hands off of me!" He expertly dodged the smack to his rear she tried to give him. "Now, now, be kind to the man who plans to follow you all over town today!"

Before they left The Maithe, they ran into Sousa, who was drinking coffee and tinkering with their practice setup on the small stage in the ballroom.

"If you get tired of walking around, call Merrick and we'll come pick you up," Sousa advised. "I don't know what you have planned, but we'll be here all day, and I'm sure we'll be happy to get out of here by the time you're finished."

"You're the best, Souz," Lucee said and pulled Cullen by the hand out the door.

"I take it you are excited," Cullen said, laughing at her impulsiveness.

"I am! And I want to show you so much!" Lucee bounced up and down as they walked, as exuberant as he'd ever seen her. He entwined his fingers with hers, and they walked down Park Street with their hands swinging.

She took him to some vintage shops first since they were in the same neighborhood as The Maithe, just a few blocks over on Charles Street. They *oob*ed and *aab*ed over a perfectly tailored wool morning jacket, and Lucee almost bought another vintage prom gown. She ended up talking herself out of it when she decided that the aged tulle wouldn't hold up through her on-stage antics.

The couple walked up Charles Street, passed by the slightly shabby Beaux-Arts style train station, and over the bridge that spanned the Jones

Falls Expressway. They made sure to stop and watch the trainyard for a few moments and they talked about places that would be fun to visit together. They crossed the street near Club Marcada, where The Drawback had played their first gig—and where Lucee and Cullen had first kissed. He took that moment to kiss her again, and she decided that she'd never been happier.

When a guy rode by on a bike and cheered them on, they broke apart, laughing. Lucee steered Cullen around the corner and asked, "Up for a little more walking? I think you'll appreciate the path I'd like to take."

They crossed over Maryland Ave and went down a hill. Suddenly, everything felt different. Until then, the scenery had been typical of the city, with storefronts and restaurants and old apartment buildings with big stairs in the front. But the hilly street ended in a T, and they were facing the trainyard now. They turned to the right, and there was a train bridge that traveled over the long, curvy, two-lane road that looked completely out of place.

"The Jones Falls is running along the left side. The right is where the commercial trains go. And over on the other side of the Jones Falls is the light rail, but you can't get there from here. In front of us is the streetcar museum, then everything is industrial for a bit until we get to the condos that they built in old warehouses. I'm curious what you see and feel when we walk through here, because this bit of Falls Road has always left me with conflicted feelings." Lucee pointed to their left, where the water of the Jones Falls swirled by. A bunch of graffiti tags stretched across the retaining wall above the flow of the stream. "I wonder if Vali's ever tagged down here?"

As they walked, Cullen said he could feel the scattered pull of energies that Lucee had mentioned. "I think that Vali would have a lot to say about this place. It feels like nature is trying hard to reclaim what mortals attempted to tame and harness for their own gain."

He pointed to where a blue heron stood on a drainage pipe that spewed water into the stream. "That water is obviously tainted, but the animals still persevere." His voice sounded profoundly sad. "There are pieces of abandoned machinery, but they are swallowed up by the grasses and vines. Nature will win this battle."

"I want to show you something, Cullen. I feel like this space totally sums up my take on all of this." She led him to a path that diverged from the road into the trees. There were a couple of sets of stairs, steep and slowly eroding from exposure. As they carefully climbed down them, Lucee soundlessly pointed to a small clump of red-and-yellow columbine flowers growing in the shade.

Lucee balanced precariously on one half-step, hanging onto an overhead branch. They heard a small whuffing sound. They both stopped in their tracks and looked up to find a young doe standing on the hill, watching them curiously. Cullen made the smallest sound of surprise, and the doe swiveled her ears back and forth nervously, deciding if they were a threat to her.

They stood stock still as she moved forward uncertainly until she was right next to them. She whuffed again, then stretched her neck out to gently nuzzle Cullen's chest with her nose. Lucee watched with wide eyes as the doe came up to her and did the same.

Seemingly satisfied that these beings were of no harm, the deer calmly stepped away and continued on. Cullen and Lucee looked at each other in awe, and Cullen muttered softly, "That beats any magic I can do."

They continued down to the bottom of the hill, revealing their goal: a dilapidated deck, covered in graffiti, that overlooked the man-made semi-circular falls set into the stream. The noise from the waterfall drowned out the sounds of traffic passing above on the bridges that crossed the Jones Falls at that point. It was like they were in a little pocket of time outside of the regular world.

"This is delightful and uncomfortable all at once," Cullen said. "It is the most unsettling connection between humans and nature I think I have ever experienced."

Lucee nodded, pointing upward to the trees. "That's how I feel about it too. But look up there and tell me what you see."

Cullen peered into the trees for a moment, and eventually understood what she wanted him to notice. "Those are...heron nests?"

"There's at least ten nests up there. Look at them! They come here every year and raise their families in this strange, secluded place. I'd call it an oasis, but the water is so...not worthy of that."

They looked down over the rails where the brownish water swirled around, agitated by the waterfall. Lucee pointed again. "At least there's some fish? And it's cleaner-looking than the last time I was here. This is something I'd love to be able to help clean up. I just don't know how. Maybe Vali has ideas, I dunno. I have no idea where to start, but once we finish up with everything that's been happening, I think I'd like to learn more about what I can do to conserve this area at least. It feels like a place that the Fae could reclaim, you know?"

"I do. I feel that power underlying everything here, where nature has worked hard to stake her claim in the midst of the city. And this waterfall—made by mortals—it sits here abandoned by all but the creatures who live here. They are trying to keep what is theirs." He swept his gaze around the grotto, his face thoughtful. "I would like to help you, when the time comes. This place has stirred some deep feelings in me. And now that you have shared it with me, I feel protective of it." He turned, smiled at her, and took her hand.

"I know, this is the weirdest date ever, but something told me that it was important to show you this. You've wondered before about my love for the city, and this really encompasses some of the energy I've found here. I know lots of humans are responsible for the pollution that we see here, but there are many humans who want to fix it, and who care about preserving this thread of nature that runs through the heart of the city. It's not just what Sousa protects inside the walls of The Maithe. There's so much more."

They stood there for a while longer, listening to the rush of water over the falls and the wind in the trees. At one point, a heron took off from its nest, its huge wings unfurling as it swooped down and soared over the water. Cullen squeezed Lucee's hand, and she made a little sound of joy.

The rest of their walk was mostly silent—in part because they were thinking deeply about what they had seen, and in part because they had to walk up a steep hill. By the time they made it to 36th Street, a vibrant and quirky neighborhood of shops and restaurants, they were both huffing.

"Don't care how in shape you are, that hill's a killer!" Lucee joked as she tried to slow her breath. Cullen, his cheeks pink from exertion, just nodded.

They wandered through gift and antique shops, bookstores and boutiques, and grabbed iced coffee from a local roaster. To Lucee's surprise, Cullen confessed that he'd never tried iced coffee before. She laughed when he sucked it all down in record time, then expressed regret that there was no more coffee to be had.

"It's called pacing yourself, you know...Oh my. Oh wow." Lucee came to a full, abrupt stop on the sidewalk in front of a shop window. Cullen, absorbed in trying to get a few more drops of coffee out of his cup, almost ran into her.

"Whoa! What is it?"

"Look at *ALL! THOSE! RECORDS!*" Lucee exclaimed, bouncing up and down. "I have some vinyl, but I haven't bought anything in so long. Stores like this are dangerous for me."

"Well, that sounds like a place where we certainly should explore. Danger from music will be a pleasant change, if you ask me," Cullen said and pulled her into the shop with a look of glee.

"I don't have record money, Cullen," she objected, and Cullen made a *pfft* sound.

"It is a date, remember? Let your boyfriend treat you to something that will bring you joy."

They ended up spending an hour just shopping and standing at the listening booth while Lucee explained to Cullen why she liked or disliked what they were checking out. He listened attentively to everything she said, and by the end, he was starting to offer his own opinions.

"I think this is the first time I've heard you actually get excited about music," Lucee told Cullen after they'd checked out the big pile of vinyl she'd chosen.

"I have learned a lot about how to hear music, courtesy of you and your band. Before now, it was pleasant enough to have in the background, but I had not thought much about what it adds to my life. I never connected with music the way I do now, until you came into my life."

They stepped out onto the sidewalk, and crossed over the street to cut across the parking lot of a convenience store. They were in the middle of the lot, passing a couple of guys going the other direction, when the bigger of the two stepped over and crashed his shoulder into Cullen, pushing him back into Lucee.

"Hey!" Lucee yelled, trying to steady herself while wrangling her bag of records. Cullen took a moment to sweep her behind him protectively and turned to face the hulking man who stood there with a big, ugly grin on his face.

"What'cha gonna do about it... *Eleriannan?*" The man spat at Cullen, and Lucee gasped as the man slowly turned into something troll-like and terrifying before their eyes. His grin became wider and toothier as they stared, aghast.

"*Arswyd,*" Cullen hissed. Lucee could feel the anger and fear coming off of Cullen as she stood behind him. "Bold of you to show up in daylight hours, here in the midst of the mortal world."

"I don' fear the likes of you or that pretty morsel behind you neither." The brute laughed. The smaller one beside it morphed enough to show a sallow, greenish complexion and tiny, hard-looking eyes.

"Me too, nope," it agreed with a voice like metal scraping against metal.

"We come to tell you that if you don't give us back The Camlin, a world of hurt is comin' your way. Grimshaw ain't playing. You got what's ours and we want it back." The larger one leered at Lucee and added, "Couldn't hurt t'send this one too. Make up for the insult given. We won't hurt her, not too much. Not at first. Unless she like that, right?"

Cullen's hands balled into fists and Lucee knew that if he tried to swing at the creatures, they would be in a world of trouble. She was scared and furious, but she knew she had to keep her cool so that Cullen wouldn't lose his.

She decided to treat them like cat-callers in the street: with a hefty dose of disdain.

"Ew. Also, gross." She was answered by raucous laughter from the two terrors in front of her. "You won't touch us here. Not in front of the mortals. Don't even try to jerk our chains like that. As for the rest, you threw him away. What makes him worth wanting back now?" She was grateful that her voice didn't shake as she tried to radiate a nonchalance she certainly didn't feel.

"Even our trash is too good to be in yer hands," it said in a contemptuous tone. "Give it back."

Lucee made a show of nudging Cullen. "Get this, he's talking like we're walking around with a guy in our pocket, and we can just pull him out and hand him over. Or like we would. You know what they say about one man's trash."

Cullen snorted. "Actually, they probably do not."

Bless him for playing along, Lucee thought. "It's another Fae's treasure," she said in the sort of tone one would use to explain things to a toddler. The bigger one started to frown as he realized she was mocking him so she quickly added, "But we can't do anything about your—ahem—request right now. How about you beat it before I call those cops over here, and we'll consider what you said."

As if they were one person, the pair swiveled their heads towards the cops.

"A nice, polite fellow like my companion here versus two brutes who look like they're trying to make trouble? I wouldn't risk it, not out in daytime hours. But it's up to you. You delivered your message; you probably should leave."

She glared at both of the creatures, then made a big show out of stepping around to Cullen's left and taking his arm. She tugged on him gently, just enough so that he'd follow her lead without their opponents seeing her directions, and they walked away from the confused Grimshaw.

"Well, I think that's the end of our date, Foxy," she muttered as they walked away. Once they reached a busy restaurant on the corner, Lucee steered them onto the patio, where there were many customers seated at tables.

"Let's sit here, and I'll call Merrick to send Souz to pick us up. I don't want to risk walking back home, and Souz is going to want to hear all of this."

Cullen managed to order them beers while she called and navigated getting Sousa to come soon without telling him what happened. She knew if she let on that they'd had an encounter with The Grimshaw, he would lose it. She had no desire to ride in the van with Angry Sousa driving.

They had plenty of time to finish their beers before Sousa pulled up and honked. Cullen held Lucee's bag of records in the back and she climbed up front, trying to play it cool. They pulled away and Sousa started back toward The Maithe. Lucee turned to look at Cullen, unsure when she should bring up what happened.

"Okay, you two. Something's weird here. Did you have a bad time? I expected you to be out much later than this," Sousa asked in a worried tone.

"Oh Souz, you won't even believe it. Maybe you should pull over."

MUSIC: THE WOLFGANG PRESS
Cut The Tree

Sousa was furious.

"On the *street*? In broad *daylight*?" he yelled, and Lucee winced.

"This is why I had you pull over. I knew you were gonna blow your top, but ow, my ears," she complained, putting her hands up in protest.

Sousa gripped the steering wheel and fumed for a moment, working to get himself back under control. "I'm sorry for yelling. But this is some crazy shit, Lucee! That they were that bold...lucky for you both that you kept your cool. Arswyd are dangerous!"

"I remember that there were a few of them on the battlefield at The Maithe, but I do not recall ever seeing one amongst mortals like that. They must truly want Camlin back to risk that. They were so bold until Lucee threatened to draw attention to them," Cullen mused. "I assume that means that their glamour will not hold under close scrutiny from mortals, though I fully admit that to be an assumption."

Lucee glanced back to him and saw the fear in his eyes. She reached back to touch his shoulder, a quiet reassurance.

"We were both pretty clever and resourceful, but I don't want to have to do that again," she said, frowning. "And I guess this answers the questions we had about Camlin being able to get back in with The Grimshaw, though they acted more like he was a possession than a valued member of their scary little enclave."

"This sucks. Every single thing about this sucks," Sousa said, smacking the steering wheel. "And I'd better finish driving us back to The Maithe before I hurt my poor ol' van in a fit of rage."

They were silent for the rest of the short ride, each in their own bubble of worry. Lucee stared out the window, wondering if every person they passed was secretly one of The Grimshaw and how many creatures like the Arswyd she had seen every day and had never suspected to be anything other than mortals.

When they walked into The Maithe, they rounded up Merrick, Aisling, and Vali so they could explain what had happened.

"What about Camlin?" Lucee asked Sousa in a whisper. "Should we tell him about this now?"

Sousa subtly shook his head. "Let's tell our crew first. Then we'll worry about that."

Everyone was justifiably horrified by what had happened and after Lucee and Cullen finished their tale, they had questions.

"What's an Arswyd?" Vali asked first. "I know it's the thing you described, but tell me more about it?"

"Arswyd basically translates to 'terror' and that is what they are best at. You would definitely place them in the house of Unseelie Fae if you want to use that terminology. They are large, brutish, unpredictable fiends who enjoy nothing more than intimidating those they think are weaker than them. Which is why it started off with us like it did, to put us off guard and make us afraid," Cullen explained.

"You forgot smelly; those guys stunk!" Lucee added. "I think when we didn't cower like they expected—because I'm too stubborn to let them push me around, ha—It really threw them off."

"You implied that they were stupid right to their faces, which was not so off the mark. Took them a moment to catch on," Cullen laughed, but Lucee could still hear his fear underpinning the attempt at levity.

"Lucky for us that they weren't too bright, or I might've just managed to wind them up," she confessed. "I just knew we needed to not let on that they scared us. Like you do with bullies. You can't let them see the fear in your eyes."

"Question is, what do we do now? I'm not sure that them wanting Camlin back speaks well for his safety," Merrick said. "But at the same time, it does mean that he's on the right track with thinking that if he left, they'd pick him up."

"I don't like it," Aisling said, her face reflecting worry. "I know that this plan was never a safe path for him. But I wish we had more than an inkling of why they want him back so much that they would risk going out to confront you two during daylight hours."

"Souz, what do you think?" Merrick turned to his friend, hoping that his experience would give them the guidance they needed.

"I hate this. That's what I think." Sousa sighed deeply and thumped the table with his fist. "I've gone from despising Camlin to almost kinda liking him, at least a little. Even if I hated him, I guess I wouldn't feel good about this, if I'm being honest. I get mad and say things, but I don't want to be that vindictive guy, even if this is a problem that he brought on himself by his own choices."

Vali made a noise that sounded suspiciously like a raspberry, and Sousa looked embarrassed.

"Yeah, yeah, I get it. He made bad choices because his life was shitty. I'm trying to get over how I feel, because it's obvious that none of this is great. He is voluntarily going into danger to try and fix his mistakes. That's what matters. We need to tell him what happened."

"He was right when he said they have been watching him all along. I have no doubt that he knew that they would start petitioning for his return directly," Cullen said. "I wonder if he thought it would happen like it did today?"

"I wonder if their actions were because they were feeling bold, or feeling desperate," Vali said in a thoughtful tone. "We're locked up tightly here. The only reason Camlin has ever been able to set foot inside this place is because someone let him in."

"Ohhhhh," Lucee breathed. "Shit. Cullen and I were on full peacock display today around town. If they've been spying on the house, they would've had plenty of time to arrange that attempt to scare us into submission."

"We are lucky it didn't go worse than it did." Cullen's voice trembled a little as he thought about having to fight the Arswyd on the busiest street corner in Hampden.

They decided that Sousa and Vali would pull Camlin aside to update him on what had happened. The less people involved in that discussion, the less likely it would make Emmaline suspicious. The couple went off in search of Camlin after Sousa made sure to grab a beer because he thought he was going to need one to get through it.

After some debate about what the plan should be for everyone else, they decided to stick around and work on things like the stage layout and setlist for the upcoming ArtPark show. When Emmaline walked into the room, Lucee and Merrick were having a spirited discussion about what covers would be just the right ones for a blazingly hot summer festival. Cullen was looking through one of Vali's sketchbooks. Aisling was sitting in one of the sumptuous armchairs with a mug of coffee and a look on her face like she was trying hard not to be annoyed at the setlist argument.

She spotted Emmaline and waved her over enthusiastically. "Pull up a chair. Come save me from all of this," she said with a friendly smile. "The coffee is fresh and the scones are strawberry and delicious."

"Than—um, okay!" Emmaline slapped her hand over her mouth before the "thanks" could come out, and Aisling giggled.

"No worries, I know how difficult that restriction can be to mortals who were raised to be polite by your own standards. I'll tell you the truth"—she leaned in closer, as if revealing a secret—"I only find it offensive when used aggressively by mortals who know that it is distasteful to us and choose that wording anyway. But bear in mind, that's just me." She winked, and Emmaline looked at her with wide eyes.

"I'm so afraid of doing or saying the wrong thing! I don't want to insult any of you. Everyone's been so kind to me," Emmaline confessed. "You could've just as easily turned us away, or used me as leverage against Camlin. I am—is it okay to say that I'm grateful?"

Aisling winced. "It's edging along the sort of thing that makes us uncomfortable, but I understand what you're saying. We can be very intimidating. Intent means a lot—to our group, anyway, although that isn't always a reliable touchstone for dealing with other Fae. But politeness and honesty will take you far with my kind. Our kind, now. You are coming to realize that, yes? You are now more Fae than mortal. You're one of us."

Emmaline's pretty face revealed her wide array of emotions about that idea. She pushed back some of the thick, dark hair that had fallen into her face before she answered.

"I honestly don't feel it. I feel healthier, which is a miracle and should really drive home that things have changed. But I don't—I don't feel magical at all. I don't feel like I can do the things that you all do. And I thought I'd feel closer to all of you... and to Camlin." She paused for a moment. "And I don't. I don't feel it."

Aisling sighed, feeling a rush of empathy for this woman who had been through so much. It was obvious that Camlin was trying to spare her by holding her away from a deeper connection with him, and Emmaline knew that she was missing out.

"I know that he's afraid to connect with anyone in a meaningful way because he fears accidentally spreading the contagion of the Mealladhan. I would say that despite that, he's closer to you than to anyone else he's ever known. I'm sure that doesn't make you feel any better about it, though."

Aisling paused for a moment. "What if I showed you some other ways to find a connection with us? You should get training, and you can learn how to do mind work and protective exercises from me at least."

"Oh! Would that be allowed?" Emmaline was flabbergasted. "I could do actual magic? Fae magic?"

"Of course! Look, you're as much one of us as Merrick or Lucee. And they do magic! Oak and ash, Merrick can even change shapes. You certainly will have some amazing talents." At Emmaline's expression of surprise, Aisling added, "Do you want me to ask him to show you?"

Emmaline nodded wordlessly. Aisling grinned and raised her voice. "Blackbird, someone would like to see your namesake appear!"

Merrick, who had been in the middle of a rambling defense on why they should add their "Bela Lugosi's Dead" cover to the setlist, broke off and grinned at her. "That would be a nice reason to take a break!" He walked to the middle of the room, making sure there was enough space around him before he began, and said to Emmaline, "Do you want me to explain it as I go? So you can see how I think in order to make it happen?"

She nodded and he smiled reassuringly.

"I know, this probably seems like madness. Just wait, it gets weirder."

He closed his eyes for a moment and took a deep breath before he opened them again and began to talk her through the process.

"First, I need to see in my mind what I want to look like—in this case, a big raven. I hold that image in my mind, and I start to call up the things that make me think of birds. How they fly, their light bodies and hollow bones. The idea of flying, almost weightless, in the sky, light glinting off my feathers. Their voices, a strident caw..." He drifted off, and started to blur, like an unfocused lens.

Emmaline blinked, trying to bring him back into focus, and suddenly it wasn't Merrick standing there at all. It was a large black raven, flapping to keep aloft in the space where he had been standing in human form just a moment before.

Aisling stretched out her arm, and Merrick, in bird form, came to gingerly land on her forearm. She laughed and stroked his head gently.

"He doesn't want to scratch up my arm with his claws, which I appreciate. It took me a while to convince him that this was an okay move for us to do!"

"I'm having a difficult time believing that—that this is Merrick," Emmaline breathed, awed. "He's a beautiful raven!"

Merrick-the-bird made a soft clicking noise and flourished his wings a bit.

"Show off," Cullen said from his armchair.

"He's just mad that he's so much older than Merrick, but he only has one shape. Merrick can do others too." Aisling winked at Emmaline, who looked even more impressed.

"More shapes?" She turned to Cullen. "What shape do you take? Would you show me?" She looked confused when the whole room burst into laughter and Cullen turned pink.

"He's blushing because although he's got quite the handsome fox guise, he cannot shape it without taking off his clothes." Aisling giggled.

"Hey! I can indeed change guises while clothed, but... I will be a tangled mess when I do. It is practicality, not necessity," Cullen protested. "And changing back does not guarantee that the clothes will end up in the proper places. So it is best to start from a blank slate, as it were."

Merrick-the-raven cawed and took off from Aisling's arm then, distracting them all from Cullen's attempts to explain himself. As they watched, he morphed in the air and landed on the library floor in the shape of a sleek, black house cat. He immediately sat down and stared up at Emmaline and Aisling, the tip of his tail twitching. Then he was human Merrick again, sitting on the floor with a big grin on his face.

"That was fun. It's been a while! And that's the first time I tried the black cat. Did I look okay?"

"Didn't you do a bobcat the last time you were feline?" Lucee asked. "I think I like the black cat better. It suits you."

"I did, you're right. I was scrambling for an animal that I thought would give me an advantage against Camlin, and a house cat seemed too small to take on a falcon..."

"Excuse me, what?" Emmaline said, shocked.

"Oh shit. You didn't know that part of the story." Merrick looked like he wanted to sink into the floor. Emmaline nodded and gestured for him to tell it.

"In the battle, I turned into a raven so that I could get away, get some space. And he turned into a falcon and chased me all over the place. It was intense! I couldn't outrun him forever—he was faster than me in that shape—so I tried taking on a bobcat shape. And that worked. I was...You know what, let's just say I was successful." Merrick stopped abruptly and bit his lip nervously.

"I sometimes forget how hard you both tried to kill each other," Emmaline said, her voice so quiet that Merrick had to strain to hear it. "This is a reminder that you all really didn't have to be as kind as you have been. As uncomfortable as I think it's been for Camlin, it's been worse for all of you."

"I'll admit, we've been challenged. And if he had shown up here by himself, I can pretty safely speak for everyone when I say he wouldn't have had the reception the two of you have had," Merrick told her. "But Emmaline, we're all learning more about ourselves and how to be better people every day, and Camlin being here has certainly pushed us to work even harder, even if he didn't mean for that to happen."

Emmaline cast her eyes downward and nodded solemnly. "I guess so. He's changed a lot too, and I'm glad for that." She then looked up, and with a tentative smile, asked Merrick, "So what magic do you think I could learn?"

Sousa and Vali had found Camlin in the room he was sharing with Emmaline, stretched out on their bed while reading something on Emmaline's laptop. He startled a bit when they walked in but seemed to recover quickly.

"I wasn't expecting you to be coming through that door, sorry! I was reading some of Emmaline's articles—she writes for a magazine called *Whispers and Screams*. She's quite the writer, though I shouldn't be surprised. Articles, short stories, reviews..." He trailed off, seeing the look on their faces. "Something's happened."

"I don't think I want to tell you about this here. Why don't we choose some place less likely that Emmaline might walk into," Sousa said and gestured for Camlin to follow.

They walked silently through the hall, then up the stairs to the next floor, which looked much the same as the floor below. Sousa led them toward a space that corresponded with the library downstairs, except instead of bookshelves there was art on the walls. There were also more couches and armchairs than the library had, and Sousa led them to a circle of armchairs farthest away from the entry near the staircase.

"This should do," Sousa said as he sat, then he leaned forward and said to Camlin, "Arswyd."

Camlin looked puzzled at first, then his expression slowly changed to alarm as he started to understand. "Someone was attacked? Did anyone get hurt?"

"I hate to say this, but if you'd reacted in any other way, I would've been ready to punch you." Camlin nodded at Sousa's statement and waved him to go on. "I'm glad you get that. Everyone is fine, but two of the Arswyd confronted Lucee and Cullen on a busy street corner in Hampden today. In broad daylight, I should add."

He waited for Camlin's reaction, which was one of shock and confusion.

"They demanded your return."

"I... for them specifically, or for The Grimshaw?" Camlin sounded like he wasn't sure which answer he would prefer.

"The Grimshaw. Seems that, as they put it, even their trash is too good for us." Sousa paused a beat to let that sink in. "Lucee handled them with her usual skill and left them thinking that she was actually considering that we might return you. I don't know what that means in regards to our plans, but it seems that you were right to think that they would want you back."

"My guess is that they decided that if I am strong enough to recover on my own, then I am still valuable. And that you having that thing of value is intolerable. But to come out in public so boldly and threaten the leader of the Eleriannan...Unbelievable. I would never have allowed that when I was leading them. For one, Arswyd are too unpredictable and not clever enough for an assignment like that." Camlin scrunched his handsome face up, frowning as he weighed the possibilities.

"I think this pushes up our timetable," Vali said, and Camlin snapped to attention at those words.

"You're right. I need to fall into their hands soon, both for believability and to head off escalating things. If they are acting this recklessly, it bodes well for my attempt to wrestle back control."

For just a moment, Vali felt a chill of doubt go through her. What if he fell under the control of the Mealladhan again and became an even bigger threat to them? She shook off the thought, knowing that this was the only plan they had with any hope of success.

"We'll need to coordinate. I am almost ready with the drawing. Once I give you that, you will need to meet with The Ladies—"

Camlin cut her off by holding up a hand. "The Ladies and I have an arrangement already in place. They will take care of things once the tattoo is set and I leave. I'll place it in their hands to explain all to you once I enact the plan." He looked pained, and Vali wondered if that came from the knowledge that precious memories would be locked away soon.

"I'll work on finishing up in the next day, then," she said, feeling a pang of sadness. "I hate that this is the way."

"Me too," Camlin said, his voice subdued. "But I'll be glad to be past this painful waiting."

When they came down to the library and joined their friends, they found Merrick and Emmaline standing in the middle of the room, laughing hysterically. Lucee and Cullen were both crouched on the floor, trying to evade something flying around the room. Aisling was off to the side, sunk down in an armchair, one hand over her mouth as she laughed.

"What on earth is going on here?" Sousa boomed and then ducked as a book went sailing over his head, made a sharp turn, then made a nose dive and crashed directly into the floor in front of an embarrassed Emmaline.

"Oh no! I hope I didn't hurt it!" she exclaimed and bent down to pick it up. Vali noted that it was a huge leather-bound volume entitled *Great Men and Famous Women Vol V.* Emmaline turned it over to Sousa, who looked at the cover and laughed.

"Guess that'll show whoever decided that women couldn't be great, only famous," he joked and set the book on the table with a thud. "So, I see we missed some excitement, or maybe got here just in time for it?"

"I can't believe I did that! Merrick showed me how to do a magic, um, thing—but I'm not very good at controlling it yet," Emmaline confessed with a rueful look that made Sousa laugh again.

"It takes time and practice! You have nothing to be embarrassed about," he reassured her, with a big grin. "Wanna hear a confession?" She nodded. Sousa leaned in and whispered, "I can't even do what you just did."

"What?" Emmaline's exclamation was echoed by Vali and Merrick.

"It's true! I mean, I guess I *could* do it, but I really haven't tried doing much magic like that. I tend to stick to practical stuff. Think about it—what magic have you ever seen me do?" Sousa shrugged and plopped down on a couch with a contented sigh. "I'm the guy who uses his talents for useful things like keeping keys from jingling and building giant buildings that contain the heart of the city, no big deal."

As Vali sat down next to Souz, she happened to catch the look on Camlin's face when Sousa mentioned the heart of the city—awe, longing, and maybe a little confusion. It tugged at her and she lost track of what her friends were saying as she followed the thread of her thoughts.

She knew that Camlin understood that she was the connection to the Lady of the City—the living personification of the heart of the city. He had witnessed her channel that primordial power when she escaped the Grimshaw who had held her, and when she pulled buildings down all around her in her anger. The rubble from those buildings was still piled up across the street from The Maithe. But it occurred to her that he had never asked about the forest inside the inner walls of the building, and now Vali was curious - what if he didn't even know it was there? The first day she had come to The Maithe, she forced her way through a glamoured door and into the forest beyond it. Sousa told her that she wasn't supposed to be able to see any of it. She made a note to ask Sousa later if he'd blocked that aspect of The Maithe from Camlin.

The conversation was still focused on Sousa and his lack of magic-using.

"But you've been around for a long time! You never tried doing anything like the skills that Lucee and I are learning?" Merrick asked, incredulous.

"Like I said, practical stuff." Sousa shrugged. "I can make a light like Lucee can, but I'd rather flip a switch or even light a torch over that. I can throw energy like you or Camlin, but I'd rather swing my trusty bat. I dunno, I've just always been like this. I like engaging with the world in a way that doesn't make me feel like I'm set apart from the mortals around me. Does that make sense?"

"Sure, it does," Lucee said after she got up from the floor and found an armchair to sit in now that the air was free of flying books. "But now the mortals around you do magical things too, so maybe it's time to adopt a hybrid plan?" She grinned at him, but it was obvious that she was serious. He tilted his head and considered what she'd said.

"You want *me* to join the magical bootcamp? Because I can hear The Ladies cackling their little heads off from here at that thought." This made Cullen, who had joined Lucee and sat on the arm of her chair, start laughing so hard that he almost fell off his perch. Merrick barely managed to cover his amusement at this mental image.

"Why not? In fact, why aren't we sharing our skills with each other and training together? I don't even know what all the Eleriannan can do, and I suspect that I'm not the only one! We could have skillshare days where anyone who wants to can share something magical that they can do, and days where we all work on a skill together and help each other improve. Or does that seem too modern of an idea for you?" She looked comically fierce as she challenged him.

Aisling sat up straight in her chair, excited. "This is a brilliant idea! I would be pleased to teach any of you how to navigate the dreamlands, or even just how to contact each other in dreams. There are many useful things one can do with those skills."

"I would love to see if anyone else can learn how to work with charging art with intentions, as I do with my tags," Vali volunteered. "I'm not sure if I can teach it, but I'm willing to try."

Sousa looked back and forth between the two women, a look of amazement on his face. Finally, he let out a long breath and said, "Every time I think you can't possibly surprise me with your insight and clever ideas, here you come again to prove me wrong. I'll tell you what." He crossed his arms across his chest. "If anyone at House Mirabilis dares to object to this, I'll start holding sessions here at The Maithe."

Lucee grinned at that, and Merrick cheered.

"Actually, would you want to have them happen here? It's not like we don't have all the room in the world," Sousa added, gesturing widely to indicate the expanse of The Maithe.

"Not a bad idea, if you ask me," Cullen said, nodding. "It is neutral, there are spaces that are appropriate for all sorts of disciplines, and if folks need rest after there is a room for anyone who would want one."

"And that might encourage both houses to participate. I've been trying to prod the Tiennan House folks into coming here more to hang out, so they feel more welcome. That bond is going to take some time to build, so anything that helps the task sounds great to me," Sousa said.

"I'd like to be one of the first students," Emmaline said, excitement coloring her voice. "But for now, what else can I try?"

Lucee held out her hands, and a sphere of light formed in her cupped palms. "Wanna try making one of these?"

MUSIC: UNDERTHESKIN
Burn

Emmaline managed to create a tiny ball of light. Lucee cheered, then collapsed dramatically, and declared, "I'm pooped! I need to eat, and then maybe nap. I dunno. It's been a day!"

Everyone agreed that, indeed, it had been a day. Sousa disappeared and then returned with a large platter of fruit, cheese, meats, and all kinds of breads, piled high.

"There's your workout for the day," Merrick joked. He snagged a stack of plates from the side table and handed them out to everyone. A pleasant murmur of low conversation and folks eating and drinking fell over the room.

Camlin and Emmaline were at one of the long tables near the food. He smiled to himself, watching her eat heartily, remembering how difficult it had been for her to eat once her illness had spiraled out of control.

"It's all quite delicious, isn't it?"

She nodded vigorously, her eyes wide and her mouth full.

"I'm so glad I brought you here," he said. The tone was a happy one, but his face said otherwise.

Emmaline frowned and hurried to swallow her bite of food.

"If it wasn't for the fact that I know that you can't lie to me, I'd be accusing you of that," she said in a mildly reproving tone. "What's going on, Camlin?"

He pressed his lips together for a moment, then leaned in so that she could hear his whisper-soft words.

"I would very much like to have some time alone with you this evening.

Would that be acceptable? Please don't say no." He delivered the last few words with an edge of desperation.

"When have I ever not wanted time with you?" She pulled back a little, her face reflecting her surprise at his request. "Seriously, what's bothering you? I'm right here, I'm not going anywhere."

"I know." She watched him school his face to a more neutral expression. "I'm sorry. I'm feeling the preciousness of everything. Especially my connection with you." His gaze was direct, and she met it for a moment, staring into those icy blue eyes as she tried to gauge what he was feeling.

"I get that. You know I very much understand that feeling."

"I do. That's why I didn't want to burden you with my emotions. You've carried enough burdens of your own." He took her hand and raised it to his lips to kiss it. She felt a blush spread across her face.

"I-I think we should go have that time now, maybe?" she asked, her voice cracking a little.

They rose and walked out, hand in hand. Vali, noticing them leaving, poked Sousa surreptitiously. He was deeply engrossed in his thoughts and jerked his head up, startled. Vali nodded her head to indicate the couple leaving the library.

"I don't envy him," Sousa said. Vali raised an eyebrow at that. "He knows he's leaving very soon. He's got to get all the time he can with her while keeping his intentions to himself. I couldn't do it." He looked meaningfully at Vali.

"What was that look about?"

"Huh? I was thinking that I couldn't just disappear on you like that, you goof." He laughed a little self-deprecatingly. "Especially not after you worked so hard to get me to let you in."

"I'm glad you finally did. And I'd be less patient with you if you disappeared now than I was while you were figuring out what you wanted. Just so you know." She winked at him and grinned when he looked embarrassed.

"Well, I was being stupid. I think I'm mostly over that now. I mean, I'll always be a dumbass, but I'm your dumbass now." He gently kicked her booted foot with his own, affectionately, and she laughed.

Eventually, everyone else went to bed except Vali and Sousa, who were used to late-night hours.

"It's finished."

Vali sat back and inspected the drawing. Despite the feeling of accomplishment she always had when she created one of her magical tags, she had a sinking feeling in her guts. It took away any satisfaction she had for completing such a challenging task. All she could think about was what would happen next.

Sousa looked up from the couch where he was stretched out with a beat-up acoustic guitar, playing what he called "old home" music—ballads and drinking songs that he occasionally sang along with in his pleasant voice.

He stopped strumming when Vali spoke and asked, "How do you know?"

"Well, I can't exactly test it, but it *feels* right, if that counts for anything. It is easily the most complex thing I've ever attempted to create, so there are definitely things I'll worry about. But I can't do any more than what I've managed here. It's up to Camlin now."

Sousa went to set aside the guitar, but Vali shook her head.

"Can you play something happy? Or upbeat, or something where people don't all die at the end, at least," she requested, putting on her best begging face.

"Have you heard my repertoire?" he said with a big grin that dimmed when he saw that although she was trying to sound lighthearted, it was all a ruse. "Okay, lemme see what I've got. Why don't you tell me what you're thinking about while I'm playing. No pressure or anything."

She recognized a New Model Army song, "Queen of My Heart," and made a face. "That's pretty, but if this is your idea of happy, wow." He shrugged and kept strumming as softly as he could. After a pause, she started talking without looking at him, like she was speaking to herself.

"I feel guilty about all of this—my part in it, that I didn't do more to find a better solution, that we're keeping things from someone and that she'll be hurt more deeply than any of us because of that. And I'm worried, because despite how I've been around him, there's still a part of me that doesn't trust Camlin. I hope against the proof that the past has given us, and I put on a brave face for others to follow because I couldn't live with myself if I didn't give him the benefit of the doubt."

She stopped to wipe her eyes with the back of her hand, only realizing that she was crying when she couldn't see. When she started to speak again, her voice was shaking.

"Here I am, sending a man potentially to his death, or maybe worse, with an untested trick that may or may not work—and what happens when he locks down the Mealladhan, anyway? None of us have really discussed it further, leaving it all to Camlin. What happens if everything goes as planned? What happens if it doesn't?" She broke off with a sob, and Sousa laid down the guitar to put a comforting arm around her.

"Look, Vali, you can't take all this on yourself. He asked you to help, and you did, to the very best of your ability. He's his own man and he understands the risks. Do you want me to break the possibilities down as I see them? I mean, I agreed to this idea too, and believe me when I tell you that it wasn't an easy decision."

She nodded with her head in her hands.

"You know I didn't fully trust him. At first, it was because of what he did and who he was when he was with The Grimshaw. I'll never forget the way he threatened us. How he threatened you. But I do believe that he wasn't wholly his own man during that time, after talking to him and observing him recently. If he's still a horrible person, he's playing quite the long con, and that would make him a better actor than anyone I know.

"Here's the possibilities I see. They're going to grab him up, and if he's able to convince them that he escaped, he'll give them info about us, which is fine. I've kept him in the dark about the most important parts of The Maithe, and everything else he's learned while he's here is hardly a secret."

Vali lifted her head and said, "You did keep him from seeing the Forest."

"Of course I did, my girl. As far as he knows, the Heart of the City is this building and—well, you. He can't tell The Grimshaw what he doesn't know, even if they try to force information out of him." He gently squeezed her. "The other reason I did that is because I believe that he thinks that it's inevitable that he'll be a needed sacrifice in order for his plan to work."

"I know." A tear rolled down her cheek, and she angrily rubbed it away. "I know, and I helped him anyway."

"What else were you going to do? At least this way, you've given him things that he would've lacked otherwise. You offer him the possibility of destroying it, and you've given him something that only one other person has ever offered him, as far as I can see."

"Belief," she whispered.

"Even if you don't fully buy into believing him, you gave him possibilities. I can't see how you think that's not helping him in the best of ways. You can't stop him from doing this. And if, somehow, he *is* lying to us, you've done no harm—in fact, you gave him something better to strive for, which damn well is doing a good act." He furrowed his brow and made a face to drive his point home.

"I guess. All I know is that I'm not going to feel any better about this when he leaves and Emmaline is standing there, heartbroken."

"We'll deal with that when it happens," Sousa said with a sigh. "And we'll do our best to help her when we do."

The next morning, sunlight streaming through a window woke Vali up. She realized that she had fallen asleep on the couch, and Sousa wasn't there. *This is weird*, she thought. They had hardly slept a night apart since her first night at The Maithe, last year.

She heard a clinking sound behind her, on the other side of the couch where she couldn't see. After a second, her ears told her it was a spoon in a coffee cup.

"Good morning?" she called out, wondering who it could possibly be. A moment later, Camlin came around to her side of the couch, holding two mugs. He offered her one soundlessly. She struggled for a moment to sit up and then took the full mug of coffee gratefully. He sat in an armchair across from her and stretched his long legs out.

"Ugh, yes, I need this," she muttered and drank half of it right away. Camlin watched her, one raised eyebrow visible over the rim of his coffee cup.

"Sorry, I had a long night," she explained, gulping down the rest of the brew.

"That was freshly brewed and rather hot. I'm not sure if I am impressed, scared, or both."

"Drinking beverages the temperature of hot lava is my superpower." She got up, walked over to refill her mug, then sat back down with an "oof."

"So... I finished it. Last night." She took a gulp of coffee.

His other eyebrow raised, and she could see him tense up.

"May I see it? Once you're properly caffeinated, of course."

She gestured towards the table. He got up and retrieved the book, then sat down with it in his hands, looking at the black, textured cover with trepidation. She indicated that he should go ahead and open the book, and when he continued to hesitate, she sighed.

"I wish you just would, okay? I've been sick to death all night, thinking about what we are doing and the ramifications."

"Ramifications?"

"To you. To her."

"...Oh."

He looked like she'd kicked him, and if she was being honest with herself, she probably had. He was quiet for a bit, thinking. He still hadn't opened the book.

"Please don't beat yourself up over this. You have done more for me than almost anyone in my life has. Helping me was a kindness, and I hope you'll come to see it that way," he said in a soothing voice.

"Funny, that's basically what Souz said to me about it too."

"Despite all my flaws, he sees me clearly." Camlin's laugh had a bitter edge to it. "Perhaps one day I'll feel like I've earned the grace you've all given me."

Vali could tell that he wanted to open the book with an aggressive motion, but something about her black book caused people to handle it reverently, and he wasn't immune to that. He carefully flipped to the last page she'd worked on, and when it fell open to the tag she'd designed, he gasped.

"This is shockingly beautiful," he breathed out in a hushed tone.

The art was different from anything she'd ever done before. At first glance, it looked like a Celtic knotwork design or something inspired by Arabic calligraphy, except every twist and turn of the design hid any possible identification of letters or words. It was shaped like an anatomical heart, colored in shades of blue and black, with a glow behind it that made it seem like it was hovering over the paper. When he held his hand over it, he could see it pulse slightly.

"What—why does it do that?" he asked. As he moved his hand closer, the pulsing increased. He jerked his hand back as if he'd been burned.

"It wants to connect with you. It's waiting to be united with you, that's how it's charged to work." She watched him react with both fascination and some fear. "Once I place it, it won't be as obvious until you activate it and put it to work."

"Can we do it now? Before I change my mind."

"Not here. Not where anyone could see what we do."

He knew that she meant Emmaline. Though honestly, she didn't want anyone at The Maithe to see where she placed it or what it looked like—even though it was the finest work she'd ever done. The less who knew any of the details, the better.

In the end, they went upstairs to one of the unused rooms, and she closed the door and locked it.

"I've never locked a door inside The Maithe before," she muttered, and he looked surprised.

"Never? Even with your enemy inside these walls? Truly a feat," he said with only the faintest trace of sarcasm. She sniffed and rolled her eyes, but privately she was glad for the attempt to lighten the mood at least a little.

"I'll need to put this on your chest. I decided that it was the place that made the most sense and designed it with that in mind. You can reach it easily to activate it or move it to another person, and you can hide it under a shirt."

"Yes, that seems sensible and well thought out," he agreed, as he took off the loose, unbuttoned black shirt he was wearing over a plain charcoal-colored T-shirt.

As he pulled the tee over his head, Vali gasped involuntarily and one hand flew up over her mouth.

"Oh yes, I'm sorry. I didn't think to warn you," he said, an unreadable expression on his face.

He was a rather tall, thin man, though decently muscled. His skin was a perfectly even, pale ivory tone, the kind of pallor that a Goth might dream of having. But that skin was marred by a scattering of dark scars that started with a large one, low on his left side. They sprayed across his torso until they stopped at his right side. Vali realized that they told the story of how he had almost died at Merrick's hand, when a thorn, thrust as a weapon, expanded into a flowering branch inside and through Camlin.

"That must be very painful," she said, her voice quiet and her eyes wide.

"It was. Now, they twinge and remind me that I am lucky to be alive."

Vali had expected that he might react with embarrassment or shame—even anger—but his accepting nonchalance really threw her. She didn't know how to respond, so she decided that no reaction at all would be best.

Vali took her black book and laid it on a table, open to the page where she had drawn the heart-shaped tag. She gestured Camlin over and took a moment to center herself before she proceeded, closing her eyes and breathing deeply. When she felt herself slip into the right frame of mind, she stretched out her right hand and deftly plucked the design from the page. It hovered above her palm, glowing gently with an azure tone.

She waited, watching as Camlin steadied himself, preparing for what they were about to do.

"Will it—will I feel it?"

"It won't hurt. You won't feel it much after I place it unless it's activated. Once it's activated, only I can remove it. But before that, you can transfer it by picking it up just like you saw me do just a moment ago." She looked at him with sympathy in her eyes. "Did you have any other questions?"

"I don't believe so." He lifted his chin, steeling himself. "It all becomes real now, doesn't it?"

"That it does." She stepped forward, and with a flick, the image jumped from her palm to his chest.

He swallowed visibly, then nodded, a solemn look on his face. "I want to be a better man. I want to be the person Emmaline believes me to be," he added so softly that she had to strain to hear. "I'm afraid that I'll fail. But still, I am going to try."

As he put his shirt back on, he said to Vali, "I don't know how long this may take me to accomplish, if indeed I manage it at all. Will you do something for me?"

"How about you ask, then I'll let you know if it's possible. I've learned not to agree to conditions before they're told to me. Not my first time down this road, you know." She kept her tone light because she wasn't sure how many more heavy topics she could take.

"Just—I can't expect Emmaline to stay hidden away in Maithe House forever. But if you would try to keep her with you, it would ease my mind. For all that Merrick was the one to bring me down, I believe you to be the strongest one here. I won't be able to control what The Grimshaw do, and if they set their sights on coming after her, I want to know that the one person I believe could hold off their forces is by her side." He looked at her with a pleading look, his hands clenched together nervously in front of him.

She considered his request carefully before she answered.

"No, you're right." She ran a hand through her short purple hair and sighed. "I'm painfully aware of how powerful I can be, especially in clutch situations. And you're also right that Emmaline can't stay locked up in here. Even with as awesome as this place is, that's no way to live. So… I'll say that I'll do my best. Is that good enough? Will that ease your mind?"

"It will." The unspoken "thank you," hung between them.

She had him go downstairs using the other staircase, and she barreled down the front stairs to the first floor and ran to the kitchen, where she found a corked bottle of ale she knew was from Sheridan. She pulled the stopper and took a deep swig directly from the bottle while she stood there with the refrigerator door open, and she tried not to cry.

"I hate this so much," she said out loud, and her words echoed off the walls and rattled around in her brain until she wanted to scream. "I'm supposed to be a helper. I don't want to help like this!"

Sometimes, to help the most, you must allow harm to a few.

The voice was the sound of wisdom and age, from someone who had seen ages pass and had suffered disappointment and defeat and yet managed to keep faith. Vali felt it move through her with the whisper of a stream, but the unstoppable strength of a landslide.

The Lady of the City.

"Grandmother, did I do it right? Am I making a mistake?"

No way to know what mistakes are being made. You must choose with the information you have available. But child, you know that something needs to be done. You took action with good intention.

"I don't know if that's enough. I am afraid that I am sending a man on a suicide mission."

YOU did not choose the mission. You only gave them one of the weapons needed.

"One? Are there others needed?" Vali felt her heart beat faster. What else could she give?

Not from you. You will see what your next role will be soon enough.

Well, that's not comforting at all, Vali thought. Out loud, she said, "So what do I do now? I'm feeling so sad, Grandmother, so powerless. What can I do to change that?"

Child, you feel powerless but nothing is farther from the truth. Do what you do best: help people. Tend to my lands. Keep shining your light. That will drive your sadness away.

Vali felt a comforting energy move through her, and she closed her eyes and let herself feel that rooted connection to the land below her feet, and the entity that personified it. She smelled brackish water, concrete, and ozone for a moment.

When it is done, bring the new one to me.

Vali felt the disconnect with a jolt and stood there for a moment, in the middle of the kitchen while her chest heaved and her heart pounded.

"Well, that was unexpected," she murmured.

MUSIC: REM
Leave

Vali had decided that the best thing she could do right now was to throw herself into her work like the Lady of the City had advised her to do. She parked herself at a table in the library and started working on some new sketches.

She planned to try an experiment over at the big community garden near Greenmount Avenue. After working with Camlin, she needed to clear her head so she wandered over to check out the public plots. She lucked into meeting the folks who managed the project, and they were thrilled to talk about the garden and their successes and failures. They were also quick to point out some of the challenges, like keeping out rats and scaring off the people who wanted to tear down the garden.

Vali wasn't really shocked that some people would want to destroy a useful community project, but it still got to her. As the head gardener had pointed out, the whole reason for starting the plots had been to offset the lack of availability of fresh fruit and vegetables in the neighborhood.

"Anyone can come here and plant, or even take food from the free plots. It's just pure spite to ruin that and take food from the mouths of hungry folk," Shanice, the head gardener, had said as she pushed aside her locs so that she could wipe sweat from her forehead. "We had to fight with the city to get them to board up abandoned buildings"—she gestured toward dilapidated rowhouses across the street from the garden—"but now they wanna come rip up the garden because we didn't get permission? They won't even answer our emails or calls! And this was a shitty abandoned lot, all overgrown and full of trash. We took the time to clean it up, fix up the soil. Now they want to take it away."

It had inspired Vali to try something she'd been contemplating for a while. She pitched the plan as "adding art as enhancement" to the garden managers, suggesting that it might add to the community feel of the space and that she needed some big legal-ish walls to work on, with a wink. The gardeners had eagerly agreed, and Vali had made plans to throw up a colorful mural-style tag on the brick wall at the back of the garden. It wouldn't only declare the space "Official Community Garden," but she planned to work in some warding to keep the city government—and rats—away from the space. Of course, Vali didn't mention that part of the plan.

Shanice was excited to work with her and had many suggestions and ideas. She made sure to take Vali around the neighborhood so that they would know to expect her there when she came back to set up her mural. Everyone was so nice and happy to have her contribute art to the area! Vali had left with a bag of cherry tomatoes, the best she'd ever tasted. She finished eating them before she even made it back to The Maithe.

"Have you seen Camlin?"

When Emmaline's voice echoed up the stairwell, Vali's head snapped up from her work, her concentration broken. She felt a chill run through her. Surely, he hadn't left yet?

She heard Lucee answer in an upbeat tone. "I saw him with Souz earlier! Hey, can you help me for a sec?"

Vali couldn't tell if Lucee was stalling or if she was telling the truth. She also wasn't sure she wanted to know for sure yet. Vali had no wish to trip that whole cascade of events, she just wasn't mentally ready for it. She heard her name and turned to see Camlin in the doorway, a finger to his lips.

"I need your help again," he whispered. "One more favor for me, and I'll ask for no more. Please?"

"Ugh! Fine," she whispered back. "I hate this. I hate it."

He made a face that clearly conveyed how much he hated it too.

"Change the image you put on the front door to ensure that I'm not allowed back in, once I'm gone," he said, still whispering. "I want to leave nothing to chance." He looked ill as he said it. Vali didn't feel good about it either, but she nodded, understanding his motivation. Best not to tempt fate or the ability of The Grimshaw to take advantage of the possibility of getting inside The Maithe.

Camlin looked relieved when she agreed, then turned and headed *up* the stairs. "He's clever to hide away up there," she muttered. She wondered to herself when he was going to slip out and what would happen after that.

Judging by the paltry amount of light coming through the windows, it would be dark soon, and he would make his move after that.

"I think I'm starting to understand why Souz drinks so much beer," Vali said to herself. "Too bad there isn't any up here. Maybe we need a mini-fridge."

As she turned back to her sketch of the proposed garden mural, Emmaline burst into the library with an apologetic-looking Lucee in tow. "I can*not* catch a break," she muttered with an internal groan.

"I can't find Camlin anywhere," Emmaline said, sounding like someone who was trying to come off as unconcerned but clearly failing. The undertone of panic in her voice made Vali cringe.

"I'm guessing he's busy somewhere," Vali said, positive she sounded as unconvincing as possible. Lucee, behind Emmaline, made a face that Vali couldn't decipher.

"That's what Lucee said, but he never disappears like this." Emmaline looked like she was going to burst into tears, but she managed to school her face into a reasonable imitation of a stoic expression. She wasn't fooling either of the other women in the room. They exchanged glances of worry as Emmaline went to the closest couch and sat down, perched in a way that conveyed all the nervous energy and worry she was carrying.

"Look, I'm not stupid," she said in a flat voice. "Just tell me. Did he go? He would never tell me. He wouldn't want to make me worry, but I know he's been planning something. Like I said, I'm no fool."

"Fuck," Lucee said and sat down in one of the chairs at the table, hard.

"I *really* need a beer." Vali sighed.

"You know his plan," Emmaline stated. "I'm not even asking. I can tell by your reactions that you do." She collapsed back into the corner of the sofa. Vali was reminded of Emmaline's first day at The Maithe—she looked, in this moment, just as fragile and vulnerable. Vali opened her mouth in an attempt to explain, but Emmaline held up her hand.

"Don't tell it to me. There's a reason he didn't want me to know beyond not wanting to hurt me or argue with me about this, isn't there?"

Vali nodded mutely.

"He's afraid I'll somehow let details slip to the wrong person."

"Not just you, very few people knew of his plan. And also, he wanted to make sure everyone reacted appropriately; our foes are spying on us," Lucee said, her voice flat and subdued. "We've been his enemy. It's easier for us to channel the reactions that The Grimshaw would expect."

"I see." Emmaline turned away, leaning over the arm of the sofa while she contemplated what Lucee had said. Finally, she turned back to the other women and said, "I want to help."

"I don't think—" Vali started to say, but Emmaline cut her off.

"I can't help him other than to heed his wishes and not ask for details. But I can help around here! I am tired of recovering, of feeling helpless and useless, when I am definitely neither! Let me help, please?" She gestured emphatically as she spoke, then her hand fell to her side, and she seemed to deflate. "I just want to start living. I thought I would be doing that with Camlin. But he would want me to move forward, and... I'm going to need something to do." She sounded so sad, so defeated.

"It's time we did something about that," Lucee said in that brisk tone that she always got when she saw something she thought needed fixing. "You're part of this house and one of us. We'll help you make your place here." She got up and sat next to Emmaline and reached over to pat her arm awkwardly. "I don't know you very well yet, but I'm gonna make sure that changes."

"What she said," Vali added. "I'd love to show you some of what I do, and I can always use help. Lucee, you're welcome to come along if you want."

"I do! But I also think that... Ugh, I hate to say it. We should find everyone else and let them know what's changed."

"I can do that. I'll bring everyone. Just wait here." Vali paused, then asked Lucee, "Wait, do you have any idea where they are?"

"I think they were in the, um, courtyard? But they've got to be back in by now, it's dark out there!"

Vali took her time going down the spiral staircase because this was not a conversation she was looking forward to continuing. She was already exhausted by all of the emotions tied up with Camlin's plan. Although she had to admit she was grateful that Emmaline had figured things out, at least to some degree.

She paused when she reached the main floor and decided that she had better take care of the last task that Camlin had charged her to accomplish. She walked to the front door and crouched down to touch the wooden panel under the glass portion of the door.

After the great battle with The Grimshaw a few months ago, she had made some changes to her warding device that she'd created with a graffiti tag. Originally, she had made it so that it would repel anyone who was not physically introduced by someone already inside the protective shield it created. After they'd defeated The Grimshaw, she had gone back and made her tags more complex, so that she, or anyone she gave ownership of the tag to, could rescind permission to enter. It had ended up being a simple tweak once she understood how to do it.

Now she laid her hand over the tag she had carefully painted on the door—it seemed like ages ago that she'd put it there—and she whispered, "Camlin Grimshaw may not enter." She made sure to hold his image in her mind as she reset the permissions for him. She felt sadness wash over her yet again as she sensed the tag change slightly in response to her command. *This is a tragedy that just keeps going*, she thought, then steeled herself to find the guys and tell them what had happened.

It turned out that they were in the ballroom, which was starting to feel like Grand Central to Vali, what with all the traffic it was getting these days. The guys were sweaty, filthy, and covered in—dirt? Sawdust? Maybe both. It was hard for Vali to tell.

"What have you doofs been up to? You're a mess. I mean, I expect that from Souz, but not from our resident fashion plates," Vali teased, trying to lighten the mood before she broke her news.

"Can't tell you yet, it's a surprise," Sousa said with a self-satisfied smirk. "And I'd say that I resent that remark, but to be fair, you're not wrong."

"I mean, you're the one who calls yourself a 'dirty punk' all the time." Merrick laughed. "I'm just trying it on for size today."

Cullen shrugged and added, "I thought for once I would attempt an honest day's work. It turns out that I am best skilled at holding things." It was obvious that he was a little embarrassed about his lack of skills, but he had decided to use some gently self-deprecating humor to deflect that. He pushed back some loose strands of golden hair, which made Vali smile.

"You know, after all these years, you'd think you would have come up with a fix for that hair of yours always escaping your ponytail," she joked.

"Ah, but I have been told that it is endearing, and I certainly would not risk being less so. Especially not when I have been told by others that I am vexing," he answered with a wink.

Vali grinned at that, but then she remembered why she'd come looking for them and her smile faded. Sousa, who had been—of course—grabbing a beer, turned in time to see that change in her expression.

"Okay, so something's happened. Let me get you one of these too." He turned back, but she stopped him.

"I'm good for now. I really wanted one earlier, but right now I want to be clear-minded." She sat in one of the banquet chairs scattered around in front of the stage area and beckoned the others to come close.

"Two things. Either Camlin has left or is hiding somewhere with the intention to leave sometime tonight." She paused, watching their reactions of sadness and resolve, then she added, "And Emmaline knows that he's got a plan."

"What? How?" That was Sousa, incredulous.

"Were we not careful enough?" Merrick asked.

"She knows because she loves him, that is how," Cullen said. The other two men swiveled around to stare at him.

"Bingo," Vali agreed. "She figured it out because, in her words, she's not stupid. She knows the guy; they're in love—although I don't think either have admitted it to each other—and she wants to believe in him. However"—she held up a finger, cautioning them—"she doesn't want to know about any of the details of the plan. And I think that's both brave and clever of her. She understood immediately why Camlin wanted her shut out of our plans."

"Wow." Merrick looked stunned. "I don't think I could manage to do that."

Vali nodded. Sousa obviously was impressed, but Cullen just looked ill.

"This would be a nightmare for me, were I in her shoes," he murmured.

"I get that. I think she's going to need that sort of compassion in the upcoming days," Vali said. "And I was supposed to be gathering you all up so that we could talk about this as a group, but I guess I wanted to prepare you first."

"Here's what I think," Sousa said. "Let us go take showers because we're a mess. That'll also give us time to think about what to do next. And we can reconvene down here and have a discussion over dinner. What do you say?"

They all agreed. "I think I speak for everyone in the house that we would appreciate that!" Vali added. She ran back up to the library to let Lucee and Emmaline know what was happening and found the two of them tossing a globe of light back and forth across the couch to each other. Lucee's face was a study in concentration, her brow creased and her eyes squinted. Emmaline looked more relaxed, almost like she was meditating or daydreaming.

When Vali softly cleared her throat, Lucee dropped the light-ball, then exhaled explosively.

"Oh *damn*. I feel like I was almost connecting with it that time too!" Lucee gestured at Emmaline, who looked a little guilty for smiling when Lucee dropped the sphere. "She makes it look so easy, and I'm the one who showed her how to do this!"

"I don't try," Emmaline explained. "I think that might be the reason it seems easy—I'm not concerned about the outcome. It's fascinating to me that I'm able to make it happen at all. I think you put too much pressure on yourself, Lucee."

Vali started laughing. Lucee whirled to glare at her, then sighed and put her hands up, surrendering.

"Well, you've got me pegged for sure," she admitted.

"Seriously," Vali agreed. "You need to get out of your own head, my friend. Which is ironic because I'm sure that's why you two were playing around with light spheres, right?"

Lucee nodded, a sheepish look on her face. "Yes, yes, you're both right. I guess I need to listen to you and chill the hell out."

"Speaking of chilling out, I gave the guys the very basic rundown, and sent them to take showers before we discuss things. You'll be glad that I did that, trust me. We're going to meet up in the ballroom and have something to eat while we talk."

"Take a shower? What on earth were they doing?" Lucee asked, perplexed.

"Souz said that it's a surprise, which makes me both intrigued and a little afraid." Vali grinned. "He even roped Cullen into helping." That got a raised eyebrow from Lucee.

They trooped downstairs, and when they came around the corner from the staircase and into the ballroom, they gasped in tandem.

"I really don't know how they manage it," Vali said in amazement as she took in the table laid out in front of them.

In the time that she had gone upstairs and talked to Lucee and Emmaline, a round table had been moved into the middle of the floor, under one of the grand chandeliers, which was now lit. All the other tables, chairs, and couches that had been scattered around the room were now in small clusters along the walls.

The table was laid out with place settings for eleven and the center of the table held a bunch of platters with a variety of foods to choose from, as well as wine, beer, water in a crystal pitcher, and a strange corked bottle that could have been liquor.

"But there are too many places set..." Emmaline trailed off as the doorbell rang.

Vali had a moment of panic—the last time the bell rang, it was Camlin with Emmaline in his arms. She shook it off. "Well, this is weird." Before she could get there to answer it, she heard Sousa's voice.

"What a surprise! We were just gathering; your timing is impeccable."

He walked into the ballroom followed by Karsten and The Ladies.

Karsten looked pleased to be there and grinned when they saw the table in the middle of the room and the people next to it.

The Ladies, however, looked exhausted and even grimmer than usual. They trailed behind Sousa, their small heads down, their veils pulled over their faces. Vali heard Lucee's small intake of breath when they pulled their veils back, and as the tiny Fae turned to her, she saw what had caused that reaction.

Sunken eyes looked back at her. Wizened features betrayed the actual age of the trio of women who usually looked so childlike. Vali tried to control her reaction, but she was sure her shock was all over her face. Emmaline looked around the room and seemed unsure of what to think.

Of course, Vali thought, *she has no real baseline of what to expect. She just sees our reactions.* "L-Ladies," Vali stammered, "what can I get for you?" She gestured to the table, unsure of what else she could do. As Sousa had told her a while back, when in doubt, good manners were a smart default when dealing with the Fae.

One of the sisters pointed with a hand much more bare of flesh than normal, towards the strange corked bottle on the table. Lucee uncorked it and poured some into three small goblets. She offered them to The Ladies, who turned away from the women and towards Sousa and Karsten when they drank it. Vali caught Sousa's expression when he caught sight of them without their veils; he looked appalled.

They turned back, and finally Vali could tell the three apart again. They weren't fully restored to their usual witchy forms, but they didn't look like walking cadavers anymore, thankfully.

"A few more of those and we might begin to feel ourselves again," Morgance croaked, setting her glass on the table.

"Where is the Blackbird? We wish all to be gathered before we tell what we have done," Morgandy declared in a loud voice, and Morgance glared at her. Ula said nothing, instead upending her glass over her toothy mouth in order to catch the last drops of her drink.

"We're here, Ladies," Merrick called out as he, Aisling, and Cullen hurriedly entered the room. "We wouldn't have dawdled if we knew to expect you. My apologies."

The Ladies seemed appeased by that, and gestured for the tardy group to join them. Morgandy looked at Emmaline, then, and cackled.

"I told my sisters that you would see through his plans, yes I did." She seemed quite pleased with herself.

Morgance spat out, "Yes, yes. You have seen it all. So, I will leave it to you to tell them what you have done."

"I don't want to know," Emmaline said, voicing her protest in a mild voice. The Ladies all turned to her, and Morgance made a terrifying-looking grimace.

"What you want is hardly our concern. We are focused on what is needed, you silly child."

"What we have done will affect us all," Ula added.

"What *she* did!" Morgance hissed and pointed at Morgandy, who looked for a moment as though she was considering eating her sister.

"Ladies, please. Will you kindly tell us what happened? We can't afford to be fighting right now," Merrick said in a soothing, reasonable voice as he gestured for them to sit down. The Ladies made some angry noises but seemed to settle down as they took seats at the table.

"Emmaline doesn't want to know details because that was something that both she and Camlin understood—" Vali started, but Morgandy cut her off.

"We are aware of the reasoning. Nothing we tell you will change her reactions or endanger our little mole. In fact, you may find that our news will give you some relief."

Morgance looked skeptical but said nothing. Ula nodded, seemingly in agreement with her sister. Emmaline looked back and forth between the three of them, then indicated that Morgandy should go on. Her face was drawn and pale.

"Sit you down at the table, all of you, and we will tell you what we know," Morgance said.

MUSIC: ALL YOUR SISTERS
Come Feel

H e cannot betray himself now," Morgandy told the room. "His memories have been carefully edited, powerfully so. Locked away, so none can force the truth from him."

"What?" Emmaline's hands covered her mouth in shock and horror.

"How will he know what he meant to do?" Lucee asked, her eyes wide.

"Ah, *dear sister* Morgandy feels that she has this under control," Morgance spat, her eyes gleaming a deep, noxious green.

"This is where we see our once-enemy's true nature," Morgandy hissed, clearly becoming agitated by Morgance's opposition. "He still knows that he spent time with you." she pointed at Emmaline. "He remembers that he brought her to Maithe House for help, but from there on, his memories and intentions are all clouded. To any outside his mind who wished to look, it will appear that he was kept in the dark by us, locked away. Which, of course, is why he escaped. Why would he wish to remain as a prisoner in the house of his enemy?" She looked pleased with herself. Vali wasn't so sure that was warranted.

"But how will he know what he is meant to do, Morgandy? How will he trigger the trap?" Vali looked at Emmaline, conflicted about how to say this and still honor Emmaline's wishes to keep her in the dark.

"When the time is right, he will remember. And if he does not, a failsafe has been put in place. Worry not." Morgandy's voice was smooth as honey, yet Vali didn't feel one bit reassured by her.

"When did this plan turn into *your* plan?" Lucee asked in an incredulous tone. Her chair scraped loudly as she stood up.

The room was deadly quiet. Morgance rose from her seat and stepped away from her sister, and Vali felt the tension grow.

"That is a good question, Lucee Fearney. I can affirm that I was never consulted on this decision. Ula?"

The third sister stayed by Morgandy, but she shook her head, her face stony. "Neither was I."

Morgance drew herself up and clenched her fists. She glared at her sister for a moment, a measuring look filled with barely reined anger, then she turned on one small heel and stalked off toward the door that led to the forest inside the inner walls of The Maithe.

Lucee watched her for a moment, her heart pounding, then said to no one in particular, "I'd better talk to her," and ran off in the same direction.

Everyone else at the table sat there, afraid to say a word—except Morgandy, who picked up a Cornish hen from a platter on the table and began to savagely tear into it.

"Morgance! Please wait!"

Despite the small size of The Ladies, they could move quickly when they wanted to, and it was evident that Morgance was motivated. Lucee finally caught her outside, where the steps led down to the grassy field between the inner wall of the House and the Forest that it hid inside its walls. She was huffing a little, but did her best to push that down and stop Morgance before she left. Lucee was sure if Morgance went back to House Mirabilis alone, the break between The Ladies would be irreparable.

She didn't dare touch the tiny witchling, so she got in front of her and held out her hands.

"Please, Morgance. Don't leave. May we talk? I don't understand what's happened."

"You saw it laid out before you. My sister has unbalanced us. She has taken steps on her own to meddle, without Ula and myself." Surprisingly, she backed up and sank down to perch on the bottom step of the stairs, looking more like a hurt child than an imperious, otherworldly creature. Lucee had never seen any of The Ladies look like Morgance did right now. It scared her and made her sad.

She decided to sit before her on the ground to make them closer to the same level. *Perhaps that'll restore her usual nature a bit,* Lucee thought. Out loud, she said, "She has seemed off to me lately, not the Morgandy that I am familiar with. Do you know what's changed?"

"Would that I had!" Morgance crackled with anger. "Suddenly she sees fit to test boundaries and strike out on her own. Mayhaps she has grown tired of my leadership and seeks to lead in my stead, but she has said nothing of the sort to me." She crossed her arms across her corset-clad chest, and her face took on a brooding expression. "I do not like this. We marked her behavior when she went into your mind so unexpectedly during our training, but neither Ula nor I saw this coming."

Lucee frowned and said, "I agree, that day was very strange. And even before that, when she challenged me to guard my feelings. I noted that it surprised you when she said that too."

Morgance said nothing, she just stared at Lucee with her now-dark irised eyes. Normally, to be scrutinized that closely by any of The Ladies would be enough to freak her out a little, but today, Morgance seemed open to Lucee, approachable.

"You're my mentors in many things. I've been lucky to have you at my side as I learn my new role with the Eleriannan. I don't know if it's possible, but I want to help if I can. And to be honest, I don't think we can afford for The Ladies to be divided right now. We need you. It feels like Morgandy thinks that she is helping, and maybe she is. I have no way to know right now, not from my perspective in all of this. You see and understand so much more than I do. And I don't think we have much choice but to follow her plans now."

Morgance made a rude, dismissive sound, and Lucee nodded.

"No, I agree, I don't like it either. I've always felt like our strength comes from working together and planning together. But I guess we screwed that up when we started making plans that kept out some of our people, even if we thought it was for the greater good. That's not how we work. We let Camlin lead us, and that led us astray."

Lucee popped her hand over her mouth, gasping as she realized what she'd just said.

"Morgance, that's it. We've been pulled apart from the very beginning. I need to say this to everyone!"

She stood up and offered a hand to Morgance, who looked surprised at the gesture before she carefully placed her small, sharp-clawed hand into Lucee's soft one.

"It has been an age since any have voluntarily touched me or my sisters. You are brave and kind, Lucee Fearney." Morgance's bell-like voice was soft with emotions that Lucee had never heard from the small creature before today.

"You are my family, Morgance. I couldn't do any of this without you," Lucee answered.

They came back to the ballroom to find everyone eating in an uncomfortable and tense silence. Cullen saw her first and the look on his face plainly said, "Save me." If it hadn't been such an uneasy atmosphere, she would've laughed.

"We've gone about everything the wrong way, from the very beginning of this," she announced. Everyone at the table looked puzzled, so she elaborated. "Our strength is our connection to each other, how we do things as a group, a family, a people. We don't enact plans without consulting each other! Yet ever since we let Camlin within these walls, that's all we've been doing and now I see what it's done to us."

She paused to let her words sink in for a moment and noticed Morgandy sitting very straight in her chair, listening to every word. Lucee couldn't read her expression.

"I'm not blaming Camlin for this. It's not like he came here and messed with our heads. But we let him take the lead, and that was our mistake. He approached it like someone who isn't Eleriannan or Gwyliannan, someone who wasn't part of our alliance and doesn't understand how we do these things as one. And because we let him, because we kept secrets from each other, we're now in a real mess. This isn't how we are!"

"Are you—are you saying that he tainted us? Like with the Mealladhan or something?" Merrick asked, concern making his voice crack.

"Maybe not with the Mealladhan. But with his Grimshaw outlook, something he didn't even realize he was doing, and we didn't see as we tried to be respectful of him and his plan. In trying to meet him on his terms, we weakened ourselves."

Those at the table registered their dismay, confusion, and doubt. Lucee addressed Emmaline directly.

"We should never have agreed to keep you in the dark about this. It's one thing for you to ask us not to give you details now that you know to ask to be excluded. But for us to stand by and watch you be hurt because Camlin thought it would be safer...That's not the right choice. You deserve to at least have the option to know!"

Emmaline took a deep breath, then conceded, "You're right. I understood Camlin's motivation and I don't fault him—or you for honoring his request—but I should've been able to make my own choices. I still don't want to know the details, but I'll admit that it was a relief to know that I wasn't wrong, and that he hadn't regressed and run away. He's... well, he doesn't have an understanding of how not to hurt those he cares about. I mean, to him, he was following the letter of his oath. He didn't lie to me. He just shut me out, because he thought that would protect us." She sighed, and shook her head. "The good-looking ones are always such a complicated mess." There were scattered chuckles from those at the table.

"And Morgandy," Lucee addressed the sister, who was sitting in stony silence. "Far be it from me to interfere between you and your sisters when it comes to differences of opinion, or power struggles, or whatever this has been. But we need your strength in these coming days. We need your cunning, and will, and your wickedly insightful viewpoints. And that requires you to have a united intent. We also need you to be forthcoming with the rest of us." She paused, then added in a commanding tone, "And I am not above requiring you to explain yourself to us if you don't offer your thoughts voluntarily."

She watched Cullen's face register alarm at her challenge, and Sousa's reflect his admiration for her courage to say it.

That's exactly how I expected that to go, she thought with a touch of amusement. Merrick, she noticed, looked ready to jump up and battle anyone who dared to contradict her. *Also as expected,* she thought.

"I do not need to explain myself to you or any here." Morgandy stood, with a haughty attitude.

"That is incorrect. I am your leader, and you absolutely need to explain what you've done and plan to do because it affects us all. You could've put any of us in danger simply because we don't know what to expect when we encounter Camlin. That is explicitly *my business.*" Her voice became hard and unyielding as she carefully said the last two words. She was starting to become angry, and she wasn't going to let Morgandy push her into losing her cool.

She was surprised when she felt the light touch of Morgance's hand on her back, where Morgandy couldn't see. A calmness flowed through her. She wasn't sure if that was thanks to Morgance but she was grateful for the grounding energy it gave her in that moment. She was even more grateful—and honestly surprised—when Morgandy bowed her head in submission.

"I am the failsafe."

"*You* are? What does this mean?" Lucee sputtered.

"You put yourself at risk?" Morgance gasped. "That endangers Ula and myself as well! Why would you not have asked us?"

"If you had said no, I would still have done it," Morgandy answered, her voice crackling. Her head was still down. "It needs be done, and I would not have asked another. I would have...disengaged before I took on that task. No risk to you, sisters."

Morgance was as still as stone. Ula, however, wasn't so quiet. She stood abruptly and clenched the table with her clawed hands.

"You would break our bond?" Her voice cut through the room like ice.

"To save us all, I would. Perhaps I have pushed you aside in fear of that day coming. Or it might be as our queen has said. We have moved to decisions without consulting the cohort. We have deviated from our path, and that has changed us in unexpected ways." She looked up, meeting Morgance's gaze. "I chose what seemed best at the time in order to protect those who are deserving of that protection."

Lucee felt nauseated. This was all just too much. It was painful to watch these usually acerbic and disquieting creatures be so vulnerable, especially in front of their entire inner circle.

"I need...I don't know what I need, but I have to focus on something else for a bit. I can't fix what's been done, so we need to find a way to move forward. And I'm starving, I haven't even eaten yet," Lucee grumbled, even though her heart wasn't in it. "Can we take a break, then figure out what to do about all of this?"

"My sisters and I will move this conversation to another room," Ula said and gestured to Morgance, who went to Ula in the meekest fashion that Lucee had ever seen any of The Ladies move.

They filed out of the room, and Lucee somehow managed to make it to her chair before collapsing. Cullen quickly set a plate filled with food in front of her, and she dutifully ate some, not even noting what she was eating. After letting her dine for a moment, he reached out to her.

"You were magnificent, as always. I know you will not believe me, but you said exactly the right things." His warm voice was reassuring and she let it soak in, for once not contradicting his praise.

"Lucee, did you notice how Morgandy addressed you?" Karsten asked in a low tone. Lucee shook her head vigorously, her mouth full of dinner. "She called you queen."

Lucee swallowed her food in one big gulp. "What?"

"She referred to you as 'our queen,' Lucee. I've never heard The Ladies speak of you as anything but your full name before now," Merrick said in an awed tone. "That right there is something."

"And she bowed to your authority. I never thought I would see a day where The Ladies did such a thing." Cullen sounded deeply impressed. "Even Fallon would fight to get their respect on occasion. They are an old power; they bow easily to none, but they did to you."

"Well, I was mad. And right. That's a pretty tough combo to beat," Lucee said in a dismissive voice, but inside, her head was spinning.

The Ladies listened to her! It really began to sink in, and she needed to close her eyes and take a few deep breaths to steady herself.

"They could have had me for dinner, but instead they listened," she finally said, dazed by the realization. "They respect me."

"Of course they do, you ridiculous woman," Sousa said, grinning to take the edge off of his words. "As usual, you underestimate how awesome you are." The rest of the table added their agreement to Sousa's words, and Lucee found herself blushing.

"I dunno," she joked, trying to take attention from her reaction to their praise. "I could get used to being addressed as queen." She leaned over to Cullen and kissed his cheek, then added, "But you're going to have to get used to being called consort. Those are the rules, I didn't make 'em!"

It was a while before The Ladies returned to the ballroom. They were subdued and sullen when they filed in.

"Let us explain what has been discussed," Ula said. She looked tired and drained of all energy. Lucee didn't like the look of it at all. She gestured for Ula to continue, wondering what the otherworldly sisters would reveal.

"I'm leaving the room," Emmaline said as she rose from the table. "I still feel that keeping me in the dark about the details is a smart plan. Could someone come get me if I'm needed? I'll be in the library." She looked over The Ladies as she passed them by, and Lucee thought there was a look of pity on her face.

I hope The Ladies didn't catch that, she thought.

"Morgandy has put herself in danger. We have expressed our dismay at this course of action, and she has agreed that it was unwise to have taken matters into her own hands. What comes next must be an answer that all can abide by, so let us explain what has come to pass," Ula said, her voice gravellier than the usual bell-like tones that Lucee expected from The Ladies.

"When the once-enemy took leave of Maithe House, he pulled a thread that we had left in his mind so that we could be summoned and finish the work we had started previously. What we did not know is that Morgandy had laid out much different framework in his mind than what Ula and I had done." Morgance looked like she wanted to be angry, but she was much too tired to summon the energy.

"My sisters made sure that his most important, yet damning memories and thoughts were given a place to be locked away, in supposed safety," Morgandy explained. "But once they were done, I stole those memories. And I hid them away, outside of him, in a place that none might guess. What I left inside that safe room inside his mind is something else entirely."

"She left a connection to herself!" Morgance hissed.

The entire room was quiet, and it occurred to Lucee that what she was hearing from Morgance wasn't anger at all. It was sorrow.

"What does this mean, Ladies? What trap has Morgandy laid?" Lucee was afraid that she knew the answer, and she truly hoped that she was wrong.

"If the Mealladhan force open that hidden chamber, they will trigger that connection, and they will find themselves entangled in a mighty web, ensnared. Then my consciousness will sweep upon them like a spider. They will be forced to engage in a battle with my mind. Opening that room will also send the one memory I kept there, hidden safely until the right time—the one that tells our once-enemy how to activate the image trap that she laid upon his body." Morgandy pointed to Vali, who looked pale and sick.

"You think that you can destroy it, Morgandy? I hope you are sure," Cullen said. He stood with his hands in his pockets, a stance that Lucee knew meant that he was trying to hide his emotions.

"I do not know. What I offer is a chance to capture our enemy. It is a plan that was agreed upon by myself and…" She paused for a moment, then said, "Camlin. As I have created such an intimate link with him, I suppose I should use his proper name." She made a terrifying face that Lucee suspected was to cover up her feelings about what she had just shared.

"Once we have it trapped, it will be upon the rest of you to decide how to proceed. Perhaps my sisters will have more insight. Or the one who speaks to the Lady of the City." She turned to Karsten, who was sitting quietly and watching the drama unfold. "Or you and your House of Gwyliannan—you may have ideas of which we have not known to dream."

Karsten looked thoughtful. "We have kept my House in the dark about these proceedings, for fear that our plot might slip out. Indeed, since some of those at Tiennan House were once touched by The Grimshaw, and as such possibly by the Mealladhan, it seems a wise choice to keep them uninformed. Some will undoubtedly be angry when they learn that they were excluded, but to minimize risk, I feel that this is the right choice."

"I agree, my friend," Sousa said. "We can deal with that when the time comes, but in this case, it really was important to keep them out of the loop. It could endanger what we're trying to do—and them, if the Mealladhan tried to pull them back in." He turned to Merrick and Aisling. "If you've got opinions, this is a great time to throw them out there. No pressure or anything."

Merrick ran his hand through his hair, which made it stand up at crazy angles. "I wonder how much time we'll have to come up with something. I have exactly zero ideas."

MUSIC: THE MERRY THOUGHTS
Low Violet

I feel like I'm not at House Mirabilis nearly enough these days, but it seems to me like all the important work is here right now. I'm so unsure of what to do," Lucee confessed to the group. "I want to protect everyone. I need to make sure that the House is safe, but I feel like being here in the city is the best way to do that. If I had my way, I would have everyone in one place together, but I'm not going to make that decision for everyone."

She paced back and forth next to the table, her hands clasped behind her back. Lucee generally had more energy than she knew what to do with, so this was her way of working out anxiety over the dilemma laid at their feet.

Cullen watched her for a moment, then casually suggested, "You know that we are going to have to tell everyone a version of what has happened with Camlin, right? If nothing else, to explain Emmaline and how she came to be with us. And if you want to follow the lead of what you said earlier—that we do things together—this would be the correct path, at least in my opinion. And also in my opinion, I suggest that you ask the members of the House what they would like to do. You may be surprised."

Lucee whirled around to face Cullen, her eyes wide. "*Of course!* You are brilliant."

"You said it yourself, that is when we are at our best. I am just parroting you, my lady." He winked and swept her a bow, except he was still seated, so it was more ridiculous than impressive.

"Karsten, can we count on you to give a version of what's happened to the Gwyliannan? Or would you rather I do it?"

"I can take on this task," Karsten said. "But in the future, I would like to see our Houses come together more often to make decisions and plans, for reasons other than strife. Perhaps it is my vision alone, but I dream of the day when we feel less division between our Houses."

"I would like that too, my friend," Sousa agreed. "I've tried to offer the middle ground here, but I can only make the space available; I can't force anything to change. I'm slowly adding things to The Maithe that might make meeting here even more amenable though."

"You are generous with your time and space, Sousa, and please believe me that some of us have noticed and appreciated it. I find myself wishing to come here regularly, even outside of the necessity caused by our shared secrets." Karsten smiled and gestured around the room. "Your hospitality is beyond reproach, but truth be told, I come here for the friendship."

Lucee was amused and pleased to see Sousa blush slightly, obviously relishing the compliment to his household.

"Well, you know, community. It's kinda my thing. Even if I did end up taking a long break from it for a while." Sousa looked uncomfortable, so it wasn't a surprise when he turned the talk back to the subject of addressing current events with the group.

"D'you wanna know what I think? That's good, because I'm gonna tell you." He stopped to grin, then barreled on with his thoughts. "I think that we should keep the main team—that's us here in this room—as close to The Maithe as possible. I know we have the gates, but I would rather have us right here in the building or nearby. We don't know when Camlin is going to make his move, if he's even able to do so."

There was a general consensus of nodding from everyone, and Sousa continued.

"Lucee, obviously you need to address the Eleriannan. Once you've got that done, maybe pop back if they need you, but sleep here? You can let them know that you're getting ready for ArtPark and invite any who want to come plan for the big day to come here as well." Lucee gave him a thumbs up, and he added, "Also, could you stop pacing back and forth? You're gonna wear out my floor!" That made her grin, which she suspected was his goal.

"Karsten, same for you. Go talk to the Gwyliannan and maybe come back here to stay?"

"I will do that. I look forward to more delicious meals here. And getting to better know all of you."

"Souz, I have a commitment that I need to take care of sometime this week over on Greenmount Avenue. I promised them a mural and I have some *plans* for that, if you know what I mean." Vali grinned at Sousa's intrigued look. "I was thinking of asking Lucee and Emmaline if they wanted to go. Karsten, you might want to come too, since you're interested in my work."

"A group seems smart. I'd be surprised if The Grimshaw made any sort of move right away, assuming that they've swept up Camlin already, but it never hurts to have multiple people along. But you didn't want me or Merrick?" Sousa looked ready to jump in at a minute's notice.

"Nooooo, I think that might be a bit much for these folks. They're really great and like me so far, but they're probably not so interested in having me bring along some random dudes with me. Not yet." She shrugged and Lucee had to stifle a laugh.

"We will remain here after Lucee addresses the House," Morgance said, her voice subdued in a way that Lucee had never heard from her before. "And here we will lie low."

"Of course, Ladies," Sousa said, as if nothing had ever happened. Which was the right way to handle it, Lucee figured.

As the gathering started to break up, Vali ran upstairs and brought Emmaline back down with her. She gathered up Lucee and Karsten next.

"I have one important task to do before I go to throw up this mural for the community garden and that involves you, Emmaline. We can do that tomorrow when it's light out, if that's all right with you?" Emmaline nodded in a way that said that she had no idea whatsoever what Vali wanted from her.

"Good! Lucee, I'm guessing that you're going to talk to everyone at Mirabilis tomorrow? Okay. Then maybe we can do the mural the day after that. Does that work for you, Karsten?"

They agreed to the proposed schedule, and everyone went their respective ways. Lucee decided that if they were going to call a meeting at House Mirabilis, they should go home that night and put the word out. She led her small contingent, with The Ladies sullenly bringing up the rear, through the Gate and back to their house. The trek was uncommonly quiet, and at several points during their walk Cullen squeezed her hand. She guessed that he was trying to let her know she wasn't alone, which she appreciated. She just wished that he had some good advice for her. Or that any of her friends did, really.

I'm beginning to think that Merrick got the better deal, she thought and immediately hated herself for the thought. But it was true. She'd spent a lot more time handling big personalities and making unpleasant decisions than most anything else. Merrick got to march in and be the hero, be offered marvelous gifts, and coast through life like usual.

Wait, where was this coming from? She shook her head, uncomfortable with where her mind was taking her.

You know it's true, that's why.

Lucee wrinkled her nose and held onto Cullen's hand tighter.

What on earth, brain?

"Is anything wrong?" Cullen's voice was quiet and gentle. She could only see the outline of his face in the pale moonlight, but she didn't need to see him to take comfort in his caring presence.

"When we're settled, ask me again. Something is bothering me, and I really need to talk to you about it." She tripped a little over a clump of grass in the field and he steadied her, which made her smile.

"Careful, my love. We cannot have you taken out by the vegetation; the other Houses will talk." Lucee awarded Cullen a laughing snort for that, and for a moment, the heaviness she was feeling lifted.

Once they'd made it across the field and into the house, The Ladies disappeared to who knew where. Lucee and Merrick exchanged a glance, and Merrick shrugged.

They were met by Quillan, who somehow always knew when Lucee needed him for a task. She smiled and reached out to ruffle the blue-black feathers that were his hair, and he responded with that adoring look he saved for her and Merrick.

"My friend, you are always right on time," she told him, and he beamed with pride. "I need to gather the House tomorrow for some discussion. Will you kindly pass along the word to everyone?"

He dipped his head obediently. "Shall I say late afternoon? So that all will be awake and aware?"

"That's very clever, Quillan, please do that. And tell me, did we miss anything while we were at The Maithe?"

"Tully and Edana have been working on costumes for ArtPark." His soft voice shook with suppressed laughter as he added, "And Sheridan drunkenly fell over on one of the Drunnog, which did not end well."

Lucee's hand flew up to her mouth. "The Drunnog are the ones who—"

"Look like hedgehogs," Quillan finished for her, whispering.

"Tell me it wasn't the nice lady."

"Brannaugh? It was." His mirth was barely contained at this point, highly unusual for him. Lucee was enjoying gossipy Quillan quite a bit. She noticed that Cullen and Merrick were also holding back laughter, and

Aisling looked like she wasn't sure that it was acceptable to find this tale funny.

"None are hurt," Quillan assured her, "Only embarrassed."

"It's not like Sheridan to be that careless," she said, shaking her head. "Loud, brash, bold, yes. Clumsy, not usually. He must've drank quite a bit."

"We will have to ask him about what happened. With a care for his ego, of course," Cullen noted with a wink.

"Quillan, I believe that we'll unwind on the balcony porch before we go to bed. If anyone looks for me, please tell them that it needs to wait until morning. Is that acceptable?" Lucee smiled again as Quillan bowed, then morphed into his small bird form and zipped away. "He's such a help," she enthused, and Merrick nodded in agreement.

"He has come quite far since he attached to the both of you," Aisling noted. "He hardly spoke to any but Fallon before that. He would never have been able to do some of the jobs he handily does for you now."

I wonder why that is?" Lucee questioned as they walked up the stairs and headed to their favorite spot to discuss things in private.

"You encourage him. Also, it could be that he feels more comfortable, as you have never looked at him as anything but a full member of this house," Cullen mused.

"But he is! Why on earth would I think any differently?"

"I will explain it once we are settled," Cullen said, holding the door to the balcony porch open for the others.

As things often happened around House Mirabilis, the space was ready for them when they walked in. Small, twinkling holiday lights had been strung along the porch ceiling, and candles in glass cages were sitting on the ledge of the porch banister. The large café table had a few fat pillar candles in the center, and there was a large pitcher of lavender lemonade and small herbed scones with butter for snacking on. Four chairs had been positioned around the table, implying that whoever had set up the space knew exactly how many to expect.

Lucee sighed happily and announced, "I love this lavender lemonade. This is just the right thing to drink to wind down." It was her way of thanking the mysterious beings who excelled at making things just *work* at House Mirabilis. She felt it important to show her appreciation.

"Anyway," she said to Cullen, "what is this about Quillan not being seen as a full member of the house?"

"He was left on our doorstep as a babe," Cullen answered. His handsome face grew sad as he remembered. "We were shocked to find him, and at first we were not sure what to do. He appeared as a normal child, no sign to tell us that he had Fae blood at all. As you know, we do not give birth often so the idea that any of our kind would abandon a Fae child seemed unbelievable.

"But seemingly overnight, his bald head became covered with tiny, fluffy feathers, and we knew then that he was one of ours. But none have ever come to claim him or give us a sign as to his origin. Fallon took him in, and he was raised by many of us. He has always been acutely aware of his strange story, and some of the Eleriannan did not fully trust him. Because why would any of us abandon a child? What could be wrong with him? They questioned his very existence. So, he learned to be very quiet and very helpful. And that is how he lived until Merrick soared through our door and smiled at him like he was someone worth noticing."

He hung his head and picked at a piece of scone on his plate. "As you know, we can be quite cruel. Another thing that your arrival has begun to correct. With your kindness, Quillan thrives and so do others who have lived here and been treated as less than." He took a moment to look up at Aisling, who had entwined her fingers with Merrick's at Cullen's last words.

Lucee covered Cullen's hand with her own. "We lift each other up and make each other better. I'm glad to hear that we've done so for our small friend. He's such a valuable member of our household."

Cullen took her hand and kissed it, then turned abruptly to face her. "Ah, but I allowed myself to distract from why you wanted us here! Lucee, what is troubling you?"

"Well, um—this isn't going to be so flattering to me, but something tells me that it's important that I tell you about it." She paused as she sorted her words out, trying to decide how to explain what had happened.

"Let me start by making sure Merrick and Aisling are up to speed on how this started. When I almost died, and Cullen had to come into my mind to pull me towards consciousness, there was a voice that tried to convince me to stay, to not wake up—I'm sure you remember me telling you about that. It cautioned me that Fallon had changed me, and if I woke up, I'd never be the same. Which made me angry because what was the other choice? Stay in a coma forever?"

Merrick snorted at that, then asked, "Wasn't that your dad's voice talking to you?"

"Right. Which, of course, triggered my contrarian side so that backfired spectacularly. But here's the weird thing—that voice has been showing up again on the regular. When Morgance took on training me, she pulled up a scene from my past with Da, and I changed my reactions in her version from what actually happened. Merrick, it was the day Da took away my guitar."

"Oh no, that was a terrible time! But how did you change it?"

"I hit him with the guitar and smashed it. Totally satisfying."

Merrick sat there for a moment, his mouth hanging open, then he doubled over with laughter. "Oh, *wow*, I wish I could have seen that! He totally had it coming, even if it was only through an illusion."

"Trust me, she gave me a replay, and it was quite powerful. Almost too painful. It hurt my head!" Cullen winced, thinking about it. Merrick looked suitably impressed.

"For once, I felt really powerful. But listen, that's not the last time Da's voice has shown up. It was in my head tonight. And it encouraged me to think terrible things."

"Things like what?" Cullen's brow wrinkled in concern.

"Terrible things about Merrick, about...about how everything's easy for him, how he gets all the cool gifts and I get to manage people's problems, just this whole litany of jealous bullshit that was getting egged on by his voice in my head." She felt herself get hot, the heat creeping up her chest and neck and blossoming across her face. She didn't want to tell him the rest of it.

"And—and it... it's stuff that..."

"It's okay, Lucee," Merrick said, his voice kind, forgiving. "You wouldn't be wrong to think that way. I've always felt like you should be angry about how unfairly things have been distributed between the two of us and not just here in our Fae life. I've had it stupidly easy; I know it. And you...you always had to deal with so much bullshit."

He spread his hands on the table and started tapping it with his fingers, a nervous habit she'd seen him do as long as she'd known him. Another wave of heat rushed through her, and unexpectedly, she was crying.

"I don't want to feel like that about you! It's not like it's your fault, anyway. You've always tried to help me out, and you did your best to protect me from Da, which wasn't even your problem to handle." She dropped her head into her hands and let herself sob while her friends sat there silently and gave her the space to be in her emotions.

Finally, her head popped up, and she blurted, "That's what it is. Undermining my support. Just like Da would have tried to do. But I don't think it's actually Da in my head."

"Wait a minute," Merrick protested. "You think something else is in your head?"

"I don't think the voice is coming from me." Lucee paused, wiping her tears away with a frustrated gesture. "I mean, I guess a therapist would insist it's coming from my unconscious desire to belittle myself or some bullshit, but I don't feel like this is my head being a jerk about things. This feels like... something else."

"Lucee..." Cullen's voice shook a little. "Have you thought to ask your Book about this?"

"I haven't. Honestly, all of this all came together just now as I was telling you. When the voice started up tonight, that was the last straw. I knew I needed the insight from my friends to help me see the reality of this."

Lucee reached down through the neck of her T-shirt and pulled up the book necklace by the chain, the thick silver links sliding through her fingers until the pendant rested in her open hand. She looked at it with apprehension.

"This is exactly the sort of reason why Fallon wanted you to have it, you know," Cullen advised her, his voice reassuring.

"If we don't know what's going on, we can't take measures to address it," Aisling added.

"I know, I know. I just—do you know that I haven't asked it anything since the day it told me that I needed to talk to Fallon, and she explained what she'd done to save my life? That makes me wary to use it." She spoke to the object in her hand. "I know, Book, that's not your fault. It's a heavy legacy for you too."

She played with the book pendant for a moment, tracking the knotwork engraving on its surface with one finger. She sighed, a soul-weary sound, and opened the book to the first unmarked page.

"Hi, Book," she said, a tremor in her voice. "Can you tell me who or what is actually speaking to me through my da's voice? I know you won't use names, but if you can explain it to me in a way that I can understand, that would be amazing."

Words slowly began to appear on the page, one at a time.

You have been touched by the thing you fear. It thinks your anger is the key to entry.

As she read it aloud to her friends, she could feel her heart pounding, and a rushing sound tried to drown out her hearing. Her next words escaped her in a sob.

"Are you saying the Mealladhan is inside me?"

She barely heard Cullen's sharp intake of breath or Merrick's small cry of fear.

It looks to enter. It slips you half-truths to unlock your door.

"How—how can I fight it off?"

Your feelings are your greatest asset.

"That's what Morgandy said to me too! But what does it mean? How can I use my feelings to fight it off?" Lucee's pitch raised in desperation, and after a moment, she realized that the book had nothing else to tell her. "Gaaaah!" She dropped the pendant and leaned forward, her head in her hands.

"Do not despair, love. Things will become clear. They always do." Cullen's words were gentle and soothing, and at that moment she wished for nothing more than to collapse into his embrace, but that wouldn't do right now. She needed to be strong, like the leader she was supposed to be.

"I'm okay. I'll be fine." She lifted her head, and looked around the table, at people she loved and trusted the most. "I'm frustrated and confused, and I've got some creepy, asshole mind fungus sniffing around me. But I've also got the best friends anyone could ask for at my side, and a whole community filled with magical badasses. That seems like a pretty good place to be."

"I swear, Lucee, your attitude is amazing. You always astound me with how resilient you are." Merrick was praising her, but Lucee made a face at his words.

"I shouldn't need to be this resilient, but here we are, right? At least my experiences prepared me for things I'd never known to expect." She shrugged and hoped that the bitter feeling in her gut would go away soon.

MUSIC: LOWLIFE
A Sullen Sky

Talking to the Eleriannan the next day went much more smoothly than Lucee had expected. Cullen had advised her to "remember that you're the queen here, and you really don't owe anyone explanations," and she let that guide her. She glossed over much about Camlin's time at The Maithe, allowing her audience to draw their own conclusions about how much freedom he might or might not have been allowed.

Some things really are just need to know right now, she told herself. *That's not breaking the spirit of keeping everyone involved.* She tried not to feel too bad about it.

She announced that because of these developments, she would be spending more time at The Maithe because that was where she expected trouble to raise its head. She was pleased to have most of the house volunteer to spend more time there as well.

"We can begin preparing for ArtPark," Tully volunteered, and her friend Edana, who was standing quietly behind her, nodded in agreement.

"Sousa also wanted me to extend his invitation again for us to come to visit the Heart of the City more often. He and Vali want us all to reconnect those bonds. They're important. And The Lady of the City really would like to see you," Lucee told the Fae, who seemed, as a whole, intrigued by that last bit.

Sheridan stepped forward. "I'd enjoy that! I'm told that the forest extends for untold distances, s'that right?"

"When Brenna tried to fly across the forest, she couldn't reach the other side. She turned back for fear of becoming lost."

There were murmurs of excitement and amazement at that tidbit from Lucee.

"I'd like to explore that for certain. And I've got some ideas about beer brewin' that Sousa might want t'hear." He grinned in a way that said, in no uncertain terms, that Sousa was going to like this proposition.

"Here's a question for everyone: what's to be done to protect House Mirabilis while we're away? The house must have some protections already, am I right?" Lucee sincerely hoped that she was correct. She didn't want to give The Grimshaw any easy targets if she could help it.

"The House protects itself. After the surprise attack on our grounds, and the addition of the gate, we also cast a perimeter protection," Morgance told her. "It will not hold off an attacking horde for long, but it will give enough time to get ready or escape."

"There is a reason why The Grimshaw did not attack Maithe House directly during our battle. Each House is powerful on its own. Possession of a House can only be ceded by agreement, not strife. They thought to force Sousa to swear over Maithe House by death, but it would never have worked," Ula said, a contemptuous look on her face.

"Are you saying that—that The Maithe would have to *agree* to let The Grimshaw have it? Like, make a decision on its own?" Merrick blurted out. Ula made a gesture that implied that it was ridiculous that he even had to ask.

"But Merrick, think about it," Lucee answered. "It totally makes sense. Sousa has said himself that The Maithe has opinions and takes actions on its own. At first, I thought he meant the sort of folks that live here and make life smoother for everyone—I guess maybe they're at The Maithe as well. But thinking back on it, I can see how The Maithe might have a...um...a..."

"Free will? Sentience? A freakin' mind of its own? Sorry, I'm sitting here with my mind blown. Give me a minute." He turned to Aisling, his eyes wide. "Is this something you knew?"

"I have never truly thought about it," she said, her voice soft as she considered this new information. "But you must admit, it makes sense. And it makes your arrival and entrance at this House on the fateful night of that party even more meaningful. If Mirabilis had not wanted you to enter, you wouldn't have been able to cross that threshold."

"Nor you, Lucee," Cullen added, his eyes full of admiration for her. "In fact, if you had not been welcome, chances are good that you would never have seen the House at all. It would have been a blank spot in your vision, something your eyes slid over as you went by. We are remarkably good at hiding in plain sight, and now you know one of the ways that it is possible."

"Huh." Merrick looked suitably awed, and Lucee had a huge grin on her face.

"As always, living with all of you is just a marvel." She spun around in a circle like a big kid, then attempted to get herself together. "Ah, I suppose I should act queenly and composed, but that really isn't who I am!"

"You don't say." Merrick snickered and Lucee stuck her tongue out at him, which caused a ripple of laughter throughout the room.

"So now we bide time until The Grimshaw make a move and prepare for our festival in the meantime?" Edana asked.

"That's right," Lucee agreed. "We prepare, we strengthen ourselves, and we refuse to let the threat of their intentions hang over our heads. The Gwyliannan will do the same, and we'll all gather at The Maithe whenever we're called to do so. It would be a good time to get to know our allies even better, you know. A few parties and shows haven't been enough to build the bond I think we need."

The next few weeks were full of traveling between the Houses. Sheridan showed up to The Maithe one early afternoon and grabbed Sousa for an intense and excited discussion, after which they both mysteriously disappeared. A few hours later, they came stomping up the stairs from a basement space that Lucee and Merrick hadn't even known existed, laughing and covered in dust.

"There's a basement?" Lucee exclaimed. "Is there anything else in this house that you're hiding, Souz?"

"You can bet on it, Fearney," Sousa responded with a wink. "Endless surprises to be revealed. Stick around, you'll get to see them all. Probably."

"Can I see this mysterious basement? I didn't even notice that the staircase kept going down. I'm losing it," Merrick asked. He leaned over the handrail to try and peer into the darkness below, but it looked like the stairs just descended into the void.

"Later, maybe. And when are you gonna get it in your head that you didn't see it because I didn't want anyone to see it? But now that you know it's there, you'll be surprised to know that it connects with the old practice space and my former sleeping space. Just in case you ever need that little fact." Sousa poked Merrick and grinned. "You've still got that key, right? Only three people own copies of that, besides me, of course. You're in an elite group."

"Me, Merrick, you… and Vali? Am I right?" Lucee asked.

"That's right. The three most important people in my life. Don't you forget it." Sousa turned to Sheridan and added, "And you now have seen a space that almost no one has seen in a very long time. I'm looking forward to having your work in the house!"

"You set up a space for beer brewing," Merrick realized, with a laugh. "Of course you did."

"If we're going to be hosting people on the regular, I need to be serving the best, and Sheridan's beer is certainly that! Now, if I could get a stash of mead from Gentry House, we'd be set. But that'll have to come later."

Other things started to change too.

Sousa had been keeping Vali away from the courtyard while he and the other guys worked on their secret, sawdust-producing project. He had managed to drag Sheridan and Karsten in on the work. Vali was itching to know what he had up his sleeve.

Finally, he was ready to reveal what they had been up to, and he gathered everyone else at The Maithe to come see. They filed down to the courtyard entrance, led by Sousa escorting a very puzzled Vali. Sousa was so excited that he was grinning from ear to ear. They stepped through the arched doorway onto the landing that led down to the green space. That was when Vali turned to see what had changed.

A collective gasp came from the group as Sousa and their friends' hard work was revealed. It was a sprawling patio space that stretched along the wall to their right, big enough for any outdoor party and then some.

Sousa had designed it to function as two large outdoor rooms with high roofs overhead that were made with great hewn beams and corrugated steel. The floors were laid with smooth grey-and-green-toned flagstones that looked like they would be cool on bare feet. There was a break in the middle for a firepit surrounded by a built-in couch space, overflowing with pillows. One of the room-like spaces had a big table and many different kinds of comfortable seating. The other had some chairs and an open space where musicians could play if they wished. A stone path led from the landing stairs over to the patio space.

"Oh, Souz…" Vali trailed off, speechless.

"I hope that means that you like it. We worked pretty hard, not to put any pressure on you or anything." He stood there, eager for her reaction.

"It's beautiful! I can't believe that you put this together, right under our noses," she enthused, and Sousa practically glowed with delight. He took her hand and pulled her toward the new construction, and she followed as he started explaining all the details they'd built into the space.

"That's his love language right there," Lucee said as she watched them, and when Cullen looked at her in confusion, she elaborated. "He loves to come up with gifts that are meaningful to those he cares about. But it's not really about the gift so much as it's about making someone feel good. Cared about. If you asked him, I bet he'd say that he did this for all of us. And he'd point out that you guys all helped too. But look at him, and it's obvious—he did this for Vali." She gestured towards the couple, and Cullen's face registered understanding.

"She means the world to him." He tilted his head then, and asked her, his voice quiet enough so that only she could hear, "Do you think he has actually told her that?"

Lucee snorted and waited to answer until everyone else had walked down to look over the new building. "You have met Souz, right? Do you think he's comfortable telling people that he loves them? I'd put money on him thinking this"—she indicated the courtyard space—"is just the same as saying those words."

She took Cullen's hand and started walking down the landing steps.

"We just have to remember not everyone does love the same way. Vali might be fine with how Souz works. Me? I'd be sad. But it's funny, because as a friend, I've never doubted his love. So who knows?"

"Well, never doubt that I love you, Lucee Fearney," Cullen told her. "Because I do not think I can build you a building to tell you how I feel!"

Later, the beautiful tree-like beings known as Ffyn unexpectedly arrived, their branch-like appendages waving around as they patiently waited for Lucee and Vali to come talk to them. For some reason Lucee couldn't discern, the Ffyn didn't seem to reach out with their thoughts to anyone but the two women—but to be fair, she and Vali found them delightful so maybe they sensed that and enjoyed their company best. They discovered that the branch-beings wanted to wander around the forest space and explore, and Vali gave them her blessings.

"You know that the Forest is open to all of us, right?" She smiled as they swayed around her. "Well, you don't need my invitation or blessing to roam around here, but of course you have it." She looked to Lucee with a grin as the Ffyn's happiness washed over them both, then waved as they moved off into the Forest, dipping and swaying as if they were dancing across the courtyard.

"Ah, they always fill me with such joy," Lucee said, as she danced a bit herself.

"They are the best," Vali agreed. "I can't wait to have them show us what they've found."

The Drawback started practicing every other day. Practices weren't necessarily long, but they seemed to raise the spirits of everyone who happened to be around when they took place. Lucee told Merrick and Sousa that she wanted them to be able to run forwards and backwards through any song in their set without thinking about it, just in case.

"I don't think I can sing backwards, Lucee!" Merrick laughed when she flicked one of her guitar picks at him and it bounced off his nose.

"Use some of that magic of yours, you'll figure it out," Lucee shot back, and Sousa punctuated with a snare hit.

Lucee had started noodling on the guitar when they weren't practicing as well. She had found that when she warmed up by doing scales, she felt the same sort of funny pull that she felt when she conjured the sphere of light. As that had been the only real bit of magic she'd been able to master so far, she was feeling desperate to conquer another magical skill. So, she kept a guitar nearby and played whenever she had downtime, hoping that the feeling she got when she played would translate into something more enchanting.

Can't hurt, she thought. *And hey, my playing has never been better!*

Lucee was feeling that tingle—the pull that she associated with doing magic—as they ran through a couple of songs, and she tried not to get too excited as she played. She let herself sink into the music, strumming the chords and then moving into the part with one of her favorite solos. Her fingers ran up and down the frets, each note and chord ringing out cleanly as she moved through the tune—not just with her hands and the guitar, but her heart, like the song was pouring out from her chest and flowing across the room.

She was so intently focused on what she was doing, so lost in the music, that she didn't even notice when Merrick and Sousa stopped playing to watch her, slack-jawed. The music swirled around her, all colors and sparkle and fire and wind, and she had never felt so complete or powerful.

From far away, she could hear something that didn't belong, a sound that was trying to intrude on her moment, and a part of her mind tried to push away the sound, the dissonance. It repeated, then grew louder, and she could sense her concentration slipping, the moment slipping, and she was trying to grasp it and pull it back.

"Lucee! *Lucee!*"

She gasped and stumbled as her guitar made a terrible feedback noise and the spell was broken.

"Ugh, what just happened?" Her head was spinning, and she felt like someone had unexpectedly woken her from a deep sleep.

Her friends surrounded her. Sousa carefully steered her to a chair. Merrick pulled her guitar over her head. Aisling offered her a glass of water, which Lucee gratefully drank.

"You really don't know what happened?" Merrick crouched down next to her chair, his forehead wrinkled with worry.

"Girl, you lit up the room! It was magnificent! It was like you took the music out of you and laid it out in the air before us, a parade of color and energy." Sousa grabbed a chair and flipped it around so he could sit in it backwards, facing her. He crossed his arms on the back of the chair and rested his head there, examining her. "Are you okay? That was a pretty big show, and you look like you didn't expect it. That's gotta be unnerving."

"I have no idea what I did, or what happened," she said, wonderingly. "I was really feeling the solo, I wanted to get lost in it like it sometimes happens on stage, you know how that is." She pushed back her hair, green-and-black braids spilling backwards. "And I felt the sort of tickle I sometimes feel when I'm making the sphere of light. The thing I think of as the 'imminent magic' feeling. And then—well, I was in it, you know? Like I was the music, and it was amazing, pouring out of me, spinning around me, and I never wanted it to end.

"And then y'all wouldn't stop yelling, and I couldn't understand why, and the moment was over like that."

She made a face that was part frustration, part confusion. She looked around at her friends. "So, anyone want to tell me what they saw happen?"

"It was a beautiful, sparkling vision of colors and images, Lucee. But so wild, so uncontrolled! You scared me because I think you didn't know how powerful it was," Aisling said, awe in her voice. "It felt like power was building and building with nowhere to go."

"I guess I can stop saying that I don't have magic," Lucee said weakly.

"You would be a liar to say any different," Merrick said, his eyes wide. "That was unforgettable. But I wonder what you can do with it? Besides the considerable power of mesmerizing a crowd, that is."

"I can try to do it again. See if I can control it better now that I know I can do it, I guess?" Lucee shrugged. "I'd like to try again because that first time was so unplanned. And I'd like to wait to show Cullen, to see what he thinks."

"Show me what?" Cullen said, entering the room with a very full cloth shopping bag in one hand and a bouquet of flowers in the other.

"Oh, those are *lovely*," Lucee sighed, and his face lit up. "Take a moment to get settled, and I'll show you the, um, thing I've discovered I can do. Or hopefully I'll show you. We'll see if I can do it again."

It took some time and a couple of different songs before she found that place where the music took life in her and spun away into something tangible and wondrous. But this time, she was more aware and she was able to rein it in a little so it wasn't so wildly and unmanageably projected. She heard Cullen's gasp when she felt the music first start pouring through her, picking up colors and textures, and oddly, that seemed to enhance her control over it. "I can do this. I can be worthy," she thought, and that thought seemed to add shades and depths to the magic swirling around her.

She finally brought the visions to heel, gathering her playing back into the chorus of the tune, and Merrick and Sousa, bless them, followed her lead perfectly. When they crashed the song at the end, she wanted to fall on the floor. She was so tired.

"Oak and ash, that was extraordinary!" Cullen exclaimed as she staggered over to her chair, her right hand still on the strings of her guitar. She couldn't bear to break that connection.

"Old girl, you really brought it out of me today," she murmured down to the guitar, a blissful grin on her face. She felt Cullen touch her shoulder and say something to her—a compliment? He was always so supportive and she felt a starry darkness around the edges of her consciousness, a buzzing in her ears.

Time seemed to jump because the next thing she knew, her guitar was missing, her head was between her knees, and someone was holding something cool to her head, her wrists. She tried to sit up, but quickly figured out why her head was between her knees, and she stayed there for a while, until the buzzing sound receded and she felt more solid.

"I think I need water. And something to eat," she mumbled and finally managed to sit up without the world tilting and trying to go dark and sparkly. She realized that she was sitting next to a table now, and she leaned heavily on it to help herself stay balanced.

Someone—Cullen—slid a plate in front of her, something that smelled incredibly tempting. "I bought Bàhn mí for all of us from a vendor at the farmer's market," he explained. "It was a surprise treat, but now I suppose it is a treat after a surprise." There was an edge of humor to his voice, but she could tell that he was using it to hide his worry. There was also a tall glass of water and a beer. She guessed that was Sousa's contribution. She drank the water in one long gulp, then took a bite of the sandwich, and followed that with a sip of beer.

"See? I'm okay now. You can all stop worrying," she grumbled, looking around the table at the concerned faces of her friends. "Did it at least look cool? Did you feel anything?" She took another bite of the Bàhn mí, a bigger one this time. It was delicious, just what she needed.

"It was spectacular, Lucee! It felt like a living personification of what the music is all about, both the meaning of the song and the way music feels in general," Cullen told her. He was struggling to explain the experience, it seemed. "It was very personal—yet at the same time, I felt you all through it. I do not know if that is because I know you as well as I do or if a stranger would feel the same."

She nodded, taking in his description and thinking about it while she drank more beer, one of Sheridan's lighter ales.

"I wish I could share how it felt from my end." She wondered to herself what it would feel like if they were mind-connected when she went into that state. Would he feel the power and beauty the same way that she, the living conduit of the energy, did?

"Are you planning to use this in your shows? Because it would be a potent addition if you can gain control of the output."

Across the table, Sousa sputtered and set his beer down hard on the table. Everyone turned to look at him as if he'd grown two heads, and he spread his hands out wide in front of himself.

"Sorry, it's just that it's so obvious that it's meant for an audience, right? And I think for more than that, even, thanks to the power you're generating, Lucee. But it's such an intimate power, it's clear that it's meant to accompany a performer's sort of skill." Sousa combed a hand through his rooster crest of hair. "D'you think that you would feel comfortable trying it out at ArtPark? I know that when we play, we already light things up pretty well, but imagine the reactions to this!"

"I remember our first show at Club Marcada after Merrick joined the Eleriannan, things were pretty flashy—and not from the club lights. I thought that was just Merrick, though... Are you saying it's all of us?" Lucee tried to remember if she'd felt any different that night, if anything had felt like she had just a few minutes previously.

"When we connect, when we feel especially alive and in love with the world and intertwined with everyone around us, it'll often manifest physically in the atmosphere around us. The glow at our first show, the parties you've been to at House Mirabilis and here, the last show at Marcada—you know, people come up to me all the time after our gigs to ask about our custom light rig that we don't have." Sousa chuckled at that. "I tell them that we have a secret benefactor that keeps us in the latest tech."

"Fae Lighting Solutions, Inc," Lucee blurted out, then covered her mouth with one hand as she cracked up. Merrick collapsed with laughter on the table. Cullen and Aisling exchanged tolerantly amused glances.

"I believe that you all need more refreshments and some rest," Aisling said in a soothing voice, which just set the three bandmates off again.

Later, after they had indulged in the suggested rest and refreshments, Cullen pulled Lucee into the kitchen. He handed her the colorful bouquet that he had brought in earlier, now in a rustic milk-glass vase that suited the flowers perfectly.

"Field flowers, but I enjoy their honest beauty over any hot-house assortment," he confessed as she buried her face in them and inhaled deeply. "Look, you have pollen on your nose," he teased her and gently flicked it away.

"But what else is in the bag on the counter?" Lucee asked, pointing to the cloth grocery bag.

"Ah, that is another surprise! I have more flowers, but these are for eating rather than just displaying." He upended the bag and many small bunches of bundled blossoms fell out, making a gorgeous multi-toned pile.

"Wait—eating? Like a salad? Or more like the lavender lemonade at House Mirabilis?"

"Ah, I am sure you would like to know!" Cullen looked extremely pleased with himself. "Actually, you will learn very soon because I want to use these today. They are very delicate and will not want to wait. Would you like to help me gather my ingredients?"

She was directed to find flour, honey, salt, and oil in the cabinets. Each ingredient was in beautifully rustic ceramic containers, except the olive oil, which was in a bottle of hand-blown green glass that gleamed in the light. Lucee stole a bit of honey on her fingertip and sighed happily as it melted across her tongue, sweet without being cloying and tasting faintly of wildflowers.

"All right, you. You should probably leave before you eat all the honey up! Shoo, now," Cullen pushed her out while she protested mildly, laughing.

I wonder what he's up to! Ah, my clever Foxy, he's so full of surprises, she thought as she wandered back to the ballroom in search of her friends.

MUSIC: THE CURE
End

The next morning, Lucee was still no wiser about what Cullen had made for her. He had been late to bed, and she had almost fallen asleep when he came in, looking thoroughly and adorably floured. He immediately headed off to take a shower, claiming that he had dough in his hair and that she had best not ask him details. She would know soon enough.

Today, she planned to follow along with the rest of Vali's entourage—Emmaline and Karsten—as they helped Vali put up the new tag mural at the garden co-op on Greenmount Avenue. Vali had warned her to wear something she didn't mind getting dirty, so she put on the black BDU pants that she'd worn during the battle in front of The Maithe. She added an olive green tank top and a loose, black cotton button-up shirt. She rolled up the long sleeves.

"Looking good and being practical, that's my jam," she said to herself as she laced up her combat boots, and heard Cullen chuckle. "What, you think I don't look good, boyo?"

"You always look a delight. The being practical part raises some doubts, however. Not that I would have it any other way," he hastened to add.

"Okay, Mr. I-Wear-Velvet-and-Silk. I'm sure your opinion carries much weight," she teased him and grinned when he took mock offense.

"I slaved in the kitchen all evening for you, and this is the thanks I get—" She cut him off by throwing a pillow at him.

They teased and joked with each other all the way down the stairs and to the vestibule, where Vali, Emmaline, and Karsten were waiting for her.

"Oh! I hope I haven't held you up! I was—well, distracted." She stuck her tongue out at Cullen.

"Do you see how she treats me when I have gone out of my way to pack food for all of you?" Cullen said mournfully, then grinned and held up a finger to indicate that they should wait. He loped off toward the ballroom and returned a few moments later with four neat canvas bags, each carefully wrapped up.

"These are for breakfast or whenever you would like to indulge. There is also water, I believe it is supposed to get hot today," Cullen explained as he handed out bags. Lucee took hers and stashed it in her backpack, which was waiting for her on a hook by the front door. She then leaned in to give Cullen a tight hug.

"You're the best, I hope you know that," she told him as he beamed at her. She turned to Vali. "Is there anything you need me to carry?"

"Oh, you'll regret asking that," Vali snorted and handed her a sack of clanging cans. "I think that'll fit inside your pack. Trust me when I tell you that it's easier to carry on your back than in your hands."

Vali parceled out paint and tools to the others, and they were on their way. It was a bit of a walk, but nothing that any of them felt was difficult. Leaving in the morning meant that they would have plenty of time to work before it became unbearably hot.

Their path took them past the great white stone and red brick Beaux Arts building known as The Belvedere, once a hotel but now broken up into condos. It had a golden awning out front that Lucee imagined must have been the same as when all the great celebrities of the twentieth century came to stay there.

They turned on St. Paul Street and walked past many brick homes with brownstone steps and stately architecture. There was a long bridge over the Jones Falls Expressway, which took them past the train station, and a few minutes later, they were at Greenmount. Vali pointed out the community garden, which was a few steps from the road down an alley.

"See how it has plenty of light but is still somewhat removed from view of the street?" she asked her friends. "That's part of what I want to play up with my tag, to help them stay under the radar. It's not exactly city-legal." She gestured down the street, where the great wall that surrounded the huge, pastoral Greenmount Cemetery rose up and broke up the neighborhood. "Luckily, the neighbors are pretty quiet." She was awarded with a smattering of laughs for her joke.

"What about over there? Do they mind?" Emmaline pointed across the street, where several newer buildings that housed artists had recently been built.

"This whole neighborhood has been changing. You can see the slow

creep of gentrification," Vali said. "You'd think that would help the people who have been living here for ages, but eventually it'll push them out,
which is bullshit. But people like that think things like community gardens
are quaint and eco-friendly and are probably thrilled that there's one in
their neighborhood." Her voice took on an edge of frustration. "They might
even actually keep the garden going once they've displaced all these nice
people. Of course, they'd talk about it being a tribute to a long-standing
custom or something similar, never mentioning who it was that established
the custom."

She broke off that train of thought at Shanice's arrival, who waved at
the group enthusiastically as she walked up to where they were standing.
Vali introduced her friends to Shanice, subtly making sure that she caught
Karsten's pronouns. She also gave the gardener a small tidbit of background
about each person—that Lucee was a talented guitar player, Emmaline was
a writer, and Karsten was extremely observant and good with their hands.

"I'll be working on the far side, doing some weeding, but if you need
anything just call," Shanice let them know with a friendly grin. After she
wandered off, Vali started handing out paint cans to her friends to organize
by color and explained why she had introduced them that way.

"I like establishing a connection that humanizes everyone right away,
and isn't about what you do for a living, but more about what makes you
who you are. We're all on the same level that way, and she now knows
something about each of you if she wants to start a conversation. Too many
people introduce each other with a connection to their employment, like
that's how worth is calculated." She shrugged and started sketching out
the basic shapes of her mural in beige paint lines. "It's something I started
doing when I lived on the street because being unhoused often means that
self-worth isn't coming from seemingly ordinary things like a job. Anyway,
none of us have jobs to talk about!"

Emmaline cleared her throat delicately. "Actually, that's not true, I'm
still employed. But it's definitely more of a 'send us something when you
feel like it' situation now. It's so freeing!" She was holding the old wooden
ladder that Vali was standing on as she worked on the highest part of the
design. Karsten watched the two of them for a moment, shook their head in
disapproval, and wandered off.

When they reappeared, they had sawhorses tucked under each muscular arm, which they set down carefully by the wall. It only took a second for
Vali to see the plan, and she moved the ladder and let Karsten position the
sawhorses. When they laid the ladder across the tops of the sawhorses, Vali

now had a platform she could stand on—as long as she was careful.

"Wouldn't be OSHA-approved, but it'll do!" Vali found a crate to step up on. Karsten gave her a boost, and she was up. "Where did you find these, anyway?"

"I saw them when we first arrived. By the tool storage. Shanice said we might use them. She holds you in high regard," Karsten answered as they handed Vali a can of the base color for the tag.

The first part of her work was mostly laying out the basics of the design, a highly stylized text tag that spelled COMMUNITY GARDEN. She combined that with a spill of vegetables, fruits, and flowers that surrounded the tag, sometimes overlapping in places. Lucee and Emmaline were both delighted when they saw the design, and Karsten had taken the black book and studied the image intently.

"You have something happening here, something hidden. Protection? And prosperity. And something... complex. I do not understand the last part, Vali."

"Ah, that's because it *is* complex. I'm impressed that you picked it up!" Vali winked conspiratorially at Karsten. "It's a kind of 'ignore me' spell related to how I can disappear when I want to. I designed it using the same principle, but coded against authority figures. It should make this garden and the houses around it fly under the radar of anyone who would want to object to it, like city cops or other city officials who might give these folks a hard time about their illicit garden."

"I did not think—how is that possible? It is not a skill I would think could be extended like that," Karsten sputtered, their eyes wide.

"I have no idea how it works, honestly. I just do it? I've been working to add little charms, I guess you'd call them, into my tags for a while. Once I saw that the ones I added to our gates and the doors at The Maithe worked like I wanted, I've been testing out all these different practical ways to use them." She gestured at Lucee to hand her one of the cans of green paint, and started some of the background, which had a base of leaves.

"If this works, I have some plans to throw 'ignore-me' tags up under some of the bridges around here. It's a good place for unhoused folks to sleep, especially when the weather is bad, but there have been a couple of times lately when everyone's been roused out. And that often ends with them losing what little they own. It's demoralizing."

"Wouldn't it be better for them to go to shelters?" Emmaline asked. She sounded unsure.

"Well, you would think that. But there are a lot of reasons not to want to go to a shelter, even if there's space for you there. As a woman, I never wanted to go because it's dangerous for us. Bad things often happen. It's not great for men, either. Not to say that there aren't decent shelters out there, but they aren't a fix for homelessness. They're just a bandage. If we can't fix the reasons that people become unhoused, it'll just keep happening." She paused and mopped her brow with the edge of the shirt tied around her waist.

"If I could come up with a way to use my talents to cure the problem, I'd do it in a heartbeat. Maybe eventually I'll figure something out, or a group of us will. For now, I'll add my magical bandages to triage the situation, I guess."

Emmaline glanced over at Lucee, and Lucee could see that something had sparked in the eyes of their newest adoptee. She smiled back at Emmaline as encouragingly as she knew how to do.

"You know what? I'm ready for breakfast or whatever we wanna call this meal. Cullen better have fixed us up good because I'm starving," Vali announced, and jumped down from her perch on the ladder rig.

"Look how much you've accomplished already, that's amazing," Lucee observed. "That's a huge amount of the background!"

"Ah, it's just the first layers, but kind of you to say so," Vali answered and pulled out the neat sack that Cullen had given her. "So, what do we have here?"

"Something that Foxy boy threw together last night—oh my..." Lucee trailed off as she found a weighty packet—something wrapped in paper and sealed with a blob of red-orange wax. She carefully ripped it open to reveal what Cullen had labored so hard on the night before.

It was a small round, flat bread—a focaccia—covered in a neat design made with the beautiful flowers and herbs that Cullen had bought at the farmer's market. A light sheen of olive oil and rustic salt across the top glistened in the sun. Lucee heard delighted reactions from the others, and she muttered, "You've outdone yourself this time, boyfriend."

"This is too exquisite to eat!" Emmaline held it up and admired it. "And how did he bake it and not lose the color of the flowers? Unreal!"

"Um, you should keep going. This whole bag is filled with wonder," Vali said, holding up a corked jar of honey and a small round of cheese.

Another bag inside the larger one held hard boiled eggs and a packet with gleaming, jewel-like berries, more than any of them could eat in one sitting. Emmaline, in particular, found the meal enchanting and kept stopping to make delighted faces over bites of each component.

"You are aware that our food is the stuff of legends, yes?" Karsten said with a hint of a smile. "We have many poems, songs, and stories written about the power—and danger—of enjoying a repast with us."

"I'm beginning to see how you've earned that reputation, and I'm glad I get the chance to indulge without suffering consequences," Emmaline answered, a satisfied look on her face. "But here's a possibly foolish question—where is a bathroom around here? Maybe you Fae types don't need that kind of relief, but I sure do."

Karsten obviously wanted to laugh but hid it behind a cough. Vali pointed over in the general direction of a small corner store across the street, well hidden from their view by a section filled with sunflowers and corn.

"Shanice introduced me to the owner of that shop over there, and he'll let us use the bathroom whenever we need. I'll walk over with you and that way he'll know you're with me."

The walk was quick and the inside of the shop was dark and cool. The proprietor was a short, round, dark-skinned man with a halo of white hair who Vali introduced as Bob. He shook Emmaline's hand and thanked them both for their work on the mural.

"Oh, I'm just the paint distributor, that's your artist right there," Emmaline demurred and left the two of them chatting while she went to find the bathroom.

Once she finished and they headed back across the street, Emmaline said to Vali, "Can we walk through the corn and sunflowers? It's just so pretty!" Vali grinned and angled that direction, a skip in her step.

The sunflowers were tall and that part of the community plot was dense with corn. It was much darker than expected between the plants. In the middle of the plot, Emmaline came to a sudden stop. "Something feels off," she said and glanced at Vali, who pointed to her left.

"That's what's off," she said in a toneless voice, and Emmaline turned to find a very confused Camlin standing in the middle of the patch.

"Um, and I mean this with all due respect or whatever, but what the hell?" Vali asked, her voice pitched low so that it wouldn't carry.

"I don't want to be here. I don't want to see..." He broke off and looked at Emmaline with the most conflicted expression she'd ever seen on another person. "It wasn't my idea to come." There was nothing confident about him in that moment, as he fidgeted and his eyes darted back and forth like he was checking for enemies in every corner possible.

"Perhaps you'd best just say what you came to say," Emmaline told him, her voice shaking. He looked like someone had punched him.

"I am not my own man. It gets worse every day. *They* took me back, and *it* is fighting to possess me thoroughly," Camlin confessed, and it was obvious to both Vali and Emmaline what he was referencing. "This is my last chance to—to...Something is telling me to warn you." His face reflected pain as he forced out the last few words. He wouldn't meet Emmaline's eyes as he spoke.

"You're the one who ran away from us," Vali said in a gentle tone, playing along with the script they'd set in motion. She couldn't mention anything about a plan, anything that might indicate that there were memories that weren't available to The Mealladhan. No suspicions could be roused. But she didn't understand why Camlin was standing before them now, or what was fighting inside his head.

"I know." His voice changed slightly, taking on an undertone of haughtiness that Vali recognized as the Camlin she'd first battled with. "I took care of my obligation and used you well. You suspected nothing, as usual." A pained sound escaped Emmaline, and the haughty demeanor broke for a moment. It was long enough for Vali to see a terrible, haunted look in his eyes and for him to spit out, "You're in danger!"

"What do you mean, 'danger?'" Again, Vali saw him frost over.

"You, half-blood, are lucky I care enough to caution you. You would be wise to stay away from the great celebration in the park. The Grimshaw will destroy all Eleriannan who come on that day. They are not finished with you and your Houses."

"Why would you come to warn me? Am I not your enemy?" Vali wondered how he would answer that.

"Y-you were helpful to me." He seemed unsure about what that meant, his brow furrowed. "And she...she is not my enemy."

"I won't stop believing in you, Camlin." Emmaline's voice was heavy with emotion, and Vali could tell that she was holding back tears. She stood stock still, trying to regulate her breathing as a wave of sadness washed over her.

Once she could push back her emotions, she spoke firmly. "Your warning will be taken under advisement, Camlin of The Grimshaw. You should leave us before you're discovered by the others." She reached over, grabbed Emmaline's arm, and started to walk away before any of them could say something else that might put Camlin in more danger than he already was.

"The next time you see me, we will not be so kind." He spoke to their backs, and she shivered but kept walking, practically pulling Emmaline along with her.

"What do you mean you just spoke to Camlin?"

Vali had never heard Karsten's voice sound like that before. Anger deepened their normally soft tones and made Vali cringe.

"Coming back from the store. He was hidden in the corn and sunflowers." Vali made quick work of recounting the whole exchange, and she was gratified to notice Karsten's reaction to some of the same odd phrasings that Vali had caught.

"He said that they are not finished with you and your Houses," Karsten mused. "Not we, but they. He is attempting to fight off the possession by the Mealladhan, or so it would seem. And to warn you of what we already guessed would be happening, their appearance at ArtPark."

"I don't know if he kept the memory about us preparing for that show to be attacked. I suspect that The Ladies might have planted the idea in his mind to drop the suggestion to The Grimshaw, as if he'd come up with it himself." Vali shrugged. Who knew how deep The Ladies had gone? Especially Morgandy, who had become such a wild card of late. "Here's one thing I know for sure—that was more for Emmaline's benefit than mine."

Emmaline had finally stopped crying, but she still had the sniffles and a red nose. She wrenched her gaze up to stare at Vali at the mention of her name. "What?"

"He said that you aren't his enemy. Even while under the influence of the Mealladhan, that line is carefully drawn and enforced. And those parting words? Those weren't for me."

"He was warning me not to expect the Camlin I know."

"Not only will he not be the Camlin you know, he'll be surrounded by beings who will want to hurt you. I think the guilt at putting you in danger is eating at him. This stunt was a foolish risk on his part, and I'm not even sure he understands why he did it."

"He can't, can he? Since so many memories are missing for him?" Lucee asked with a sick expression on her face.

"I do not think he can. It is a testament to his will that he could manage to hold back the power that wrestles for control of his mind long enough to deliver his message, even as disjointed as it was." Karsten looked impressed. "Not many could have done this."

There was a moment of deep silence while everyone reflected on what had just happened and how much sacrifice Camlin was going through in order to attempt his plan. Finally, Vali stood up and said, "This wall isn't going to paint itself. And maybe putting ourselves into the job will help get our minds off of things, at least for now."

Everyone agreed, although with less enthusiasm than before. Vali took a moment to pull Emmaline aside and talk to her.

"Hey, if you're not in the right place for this, you can totally take a break and just chill out in the garden. But—fuck. I hate to say this, but if he shows up again, you need to yell for me. I don't think he will, but I don't want to take any chances."

"I'm not going to go back over there," Emmaline said, her eyes downcast. "I don't think I'm going to be able to stand seeing corn or sunflowers for a while. I guess that's ridiculous, but it is what it is, right?" She tried to give the last bit a joking tone, but it fell flat. Vali felt like she'd been punched in the gut.

"Hey, I dunno if you're the hugging type, but—" She was cut off by Emmaline's tight hug.

"I'm glad it was you there with me. I can tell that you actually care about him," Emmaline mumbled into Vali's shoulder.

"I do. I've tried to give him everything he needs. At least, everything I have the ability to give him. I hope it's enough."

Vali insisted that she could get the tag completed that day.

"I don't want to have to come back to get this finished. I feel that it's even more important to get this activated right away," she told her friends, and they agreed.

"I will keep watch. I should have been doing it from the start," Karsten volunteered in a steely tone—something rarely heard in their voice.

"We were all too trusting, I suppose." Lucee's shoulders slumped, and she shuffled over to her paint cans with a deflated air.

"No, this is good," Emmaline said in a firm tone, and the others looked at her with surprise. "He's okay. He could have hurt us, but he didn't, which means that some of the man that I know is still there, fighting. I mean, it was obvious that he was struggling, or am I wrong?" She looked to Vali, who nodded.

"No, you're absolutely right. But I'm going to assume that eyes are still on him and what he does. I'm going to get this finished now."

Vali climbed on the makeshift platform and got to work, briskly filling out the letters that spelled COMMUNITY GARDEN and creating the vines that wove in and out of the letters in various spots. Lucee noted that Vali seemed to be humming under her breath, and she wondered if that meant that she was doing the thing where she made herself invisible.

No, I can see her... Maybe she's making us all invisible? That would be cool, I guess. How would that feel, how would I know? Lucee asked herself, her mind wandering.

She watched Karsten pace back and forth, scanning the garden and the street beyond it. She admired how Karsten seemed to have no trouble with reconciling being both fierce and gentle.

I should get to know them better, she told herself. *They have been such a fantastic ally. I'd love to call Karsten a friend.*

She handed Vali a couple of shades of red that were destined to create the sheened skin of a tomato. Her thoughts turned to Emmaline, who was standing at the other end of the platform, taking a break.

Lucee watched curiously as Emmaline played with a morning glory vine, coiling it and then uncoiling it around her finger. The plant was growing where they had placed the sawhorse, and one of the tendrils had managed to wind itself loosely around Emmaline's ankle.

"Hey friend," Lucee called to her, "Look down! You might want to unwind that before you trip."

The expression on Emmaline's face when she glanced down and realized that she was entwined with the vine was one of amusement and a little confusion.

"Let's not do that, little friend," she told the vine as she unwound it. "I didn't know they could grow that fast!" She said to Lucee, who shrugged. She was holding a can of orange paint in one hand, and it clanked, which made them both grin.

"It likes you," Lucee joked, then pointed at Emmaline's foot. "Um, didn't you just move that?"

Emmaline's eyes widened as she saw that the plant had somehow managed to embrace her leg again, just that fast.

"What on earth..." she muttered and bent over to disengage the vine. As she carefully removed it, the runner curled around her finger and up around her wrist in a flash. "Ah, it's like a snake!"

Her exclamation made Karsten turn around, ready to defend Emmaline if needed. When they saw the plant continue its journey up Emmaline's arm, they asked, "Is it hurting you?"

Emmaline looked up at them with wide eyes. "Nooo-ooo. It is very gentle, as if it just wants to make contact with me. Is it—is it this plant? Is this normal?"

Vali jumped down from the platform with a sigh.

"I'm an idiot. I was supposed to take you to talk to The Lady of the City, Emmaline. She told me to bring you by and with everything going on, I forgot. I bet it was about this."

She crouched down and reached out to gently touch the vine, which trembled slightly and seemed to cling a little more tightly to Emmaline.

"No worries, little plant friend. I won't hurt you." She looked up to meet Emmaline's gaze and added, "I'd bring The Lady here but after today's events, that seems like a poor plan. I'm just about finished though. We can visit her after we get back if that works for you."

Emmaline sat down and exhaled loudly. "Well, okay then. This day has been filled with surprises." She took a finger and gently touched one of the small flower buds on the vine, and a beautiful blue-purple flower burst open, and began to bloom.

MUSIC: ÁRSTÍ∂IR
While This Way

The walk back to The Maithe felt more dangerous than the trip to the garden had. The paint-spattered group was warier and enjoyed the walk back much less.

"I don't like feeling like this," Lucee confided to Vali. "The city has always felt like someplace safe to me, and maybe that's dumb—I'm well aware of the crime rate in Baltimore—but I've never been afraid here, not once."

"It's not dumb. I've been in some touchy situations in the city, but it's never been something I associated *with* the city, if that makes sense. It's always been about being unhoused, being a woman, being in a bad circumstance. Not because the city is inherently dangerous, or because the people in the city are bad ones."

"You must remember," Karsten interjected, keeping their voice in a low pitch, "This is exactly the feeling that our enemy wants to foster. That is part of their game. To make a place that seemed like home feel perilous, to look at the everyday citizens around us with mistrust. They will feed on that energy and use it to push out those who cultivate kindness and care."

"All the things I was told to fear from the Gwyliannan," Lucee said, her face drawn.

"We all chose the wrong enemy back then." Karsten's voice was soothing, and to Lucee's surprise, they touched her shoulder briefly.

"That we did."

Emmaline said nothing. She just gently played with the morning glory plant from the garden. Shanice had given her a pot for it with her blessings to take it home, as it had been on the list of weeds to pull up. She cradled the pot in her arms as they walked.

"You're not a weed," she whispered to it, and it seemed to pulse happily.

They arrived back at The Maithe tired, dirty, and paint-spattered. After showers and a change of clothes, they reconvened downstairs. Sousa had left a note to let them know that they could be found in the courtyard. They discovered a laid back sort of gathering in progress, with a mix of folks from Houses Mirabilis and Tiennan milling about or gathered in little, comfortable groups.

"It would look like any backyard barbecue if it wasn't for the... well, the Fae-ness of everyone," Emmaline marveled.

"I'd like to say that you'll get used to it, but I'm not sure that's true," Lucee said with a big grin. "It's pretty consistently delightful." She pointed over to the fire pit. "Look at those fools, are they roasting meat on sticks over the fire like marshmallows?"

They were, indeed. Sousa and Merrick both had long skewers of beef, sliced very thin, that they were holding directly in the fire. Aisling was laughing at Cullen as he balanced two sticks, each with what looked to be a sausage of some sort impaled upon it.

"What's this all about, and did you make some for us?" Vali called out and started laughing when Sousa pointed at the stick he was holding in the fire.

"We decided that flaming food was the way to pass the time, and it turns out that it was a delicious idea." Merrick waved them over with his skewer. "We have veggies to roast if meat's not everyone's thing too."

After everyone was sorted out with sticks and food to roast on them, Vali started retelling the events of the day. As she went on, Lucee noticed that everyone around them gradually became quieter and when Vali got to the part where Camlin surprised her and Emmaline in the corn, you could have heard a pin drop.

She didn't mention Emmaline's experience communicating with the morning glory vine, instead shooting her a meaningful look and a subtle gesture that obviously meant that they'd bring it up later. Once she was finished talking, she took out her phone and pulled up the photo she'd taken of the new mural and handed it to Aisling, who walked it around the crowd and showed it to anyone interested.

"I didn't expect that. I guess I should have," Merrick frowned.

"Camlin? No, none of us did," Vali agreed.

"But I feel better after seeing him like that. Maybe that's weird," Emmaline spoke up, her eyes darting between the two of them nervously.

"Not weird, I totally get it," Vali reassured her. "I did too."

"Not weird, but I don't get it," Merrick said. "Can you explain it to me?"

"He's still in there. They don't have him completely. But at the same time, they do have him—which I hate, but that's why he went, right? So, it's working. At least in theory." She was fiddling with a small branch, something that smelled fragrant. Vali looked at it questioningly.

"Oh, I was playing with the herbs planted here, and this broke off," she explained, gesturing behind her to a built-in planter where Cullen had re-homed a few kitchen herbs.

"Those are really growing fast," Cullen marveled, leaning back to run his hand along a rosemary plant in awe.

"Th-they must be healthy," Emmaline stammered, and Vali stifled a laugh.

"So, what now? We've been warned, which really just serves as a confirmation that our plans were on the right track all along. I guess we just keep doing what we've been doing?" Sousa asked with a look on his face that acknowledged that he knew it was a rhetorical question.

"More practicing, more training, more contingency planning," someone—Lucee thought it sounded like Daro—said.

"More costumes, more dancing, more preparing to entertain," Tully answered in a mirthful tone. Some of the Eleriannan around her responded with laughter.

Daro stood up in a huff. "We need to take this seriously. This may well be a battle worse than what we had in the streets before Maithe House. And mortals will be there so we must proceed with caution."

"Ah, you are missing why I countered as I did," Tully said, standing up as well. She took a determined stance. "What will give us supreme luck and empower us in ways that The Grimshaw can never understand or hope to gain?" She paused for effect, and leaned toward Daro with her hands on her hips, but a gleam in her eye.

"The love of the mortals there, my friend. That is our secret weapon. The Grimshaw only bring fear, anger, hate. We will shore our positions with the support of our audience."

Daro stood there, arms crossed over his muscular chest, a resolute statue of skepticism. Tully didn't seem to be fazed by this, however. Instead of continuing to argue the point, she walked over to him, offered up one of her sunniest smiles, and extended a hand to him.

"What if we take some time to sit together and explain our philosophies to each other? I am certain we can find ways to support each other's efforts in a way that will aid us all," she said with a disarming head tilt that seemed to catch Daro off guard.

Hesitantly, he uncrossed his arms and reached out to take her hand, looking about as unsure as Lucee had ever seen him look. Tully turned on her full charm, practically glowing at him as their hands met. She led him away to a blanket spread on the grass. He looked dazed, like he had no idea what had happened but wasn't entirely displeased about it either.

"Well, that was something to watch," Karsten chuckled softly, leaning in toward Lucee and Vali to share their comment. Lucee made an impressed face in return.

"Tully is a force to be reckoned with," Cullen observed. "She seems sweet—and she is— but she is very good at persuasion, as you have seen."

"And Daro is outwardly gruff and unbending, but that is to protect a tender heart," Karsten confided. "Times have not been kind to many of our House, so we can be standoffish and wary. But I do believe that your Tully sees through that. She is a breath of fresh air." They paused for a moment, then added, "As are all of you here in this circle, I must admit. I keep coming back to Maithe House because it feels like hope lives here."

Sousa leaned back, his hands behind his head, a satisfied grin on his face.

Vali leaned over to Emmaline and asked, "Hey, want to go for a stroll? I'll introduce you to my favorite tree. Lucee, you should come along, too, if you want."

Lucee perked up at the mention of her name. "Can Cullen come? Or is this an invite-only party?"

"You go ahead without me, love. Dermot promised to give me some archery pointers, and he should be here at any moment." Cullen kissed Lucee's cheek, then waved her off. "Enjoy your walk!"

As Vali led them toward the trees, Emmaline asked, "Who is Dermot? I don't think I've met him?"

"Ah, you'd remember him if you had," Lucee replied. "He's from Tiennan House, and he's nice but pretty quiet. However, he's got talon hands so that definitely makes him memorable."

"Talons? And he does archery?" Emmaline blinked hard, trying to imagine it. "I'd say that I'd love to see that, but it feels wrong somehow, like I'd be making him into a spectacle because of his hands."

"He does seem sensitive, so that's a good instinct. It's hard to know if gawking is appreciated or insulting when it comes to our friends. On one hand, most of them love an audience. On the other—well, you know how easy it can be to give offense around them if you don't know the proper protocols." Lucee shrugged, then bounced up and down as they approached the great trees. "I always forget how big they all are until we're right up on them! Hello, beautiful trees!"

Vali glanced over to Emmaline and noted the look of deep reverence on her face. "Hey, over there. I know it's pretty overwhelming the first time you get up close to her forest. How are you doing?"

"I, um, I'm fine. How are they *so* big?" Emmaline breathed, her voice trembling. "They didn't look so massive from the courtyard space." She reached out and gingerly touched the trunk of the tree in front of her. It was a tall maple, and it seemed to quiver slightly at her touch.

"Oh! It feels… it feels zingy." She stood still, now with both hands firmly planted on the trunk of the tree, a look of wonder on her face. "It's—it says it's happy we're here?" Her eyes widened and her breathing grew faster. "How's this happening? Do they speak to you too?"

"They do not," Vali told her. "I speak to the one who lives here and cares for them all, though. Do you want to meet her? She wishes to meet you." Vali pointed to a grand oak tree with majestic, mossy branches. Its huge, gnarled roots spread away from the trunk in every direction. Between two of the largest roots was a mossy, green space big enough for several people to sit in comfortably. And standing in that space, close to the tree trunk, was a strange-looking woman—small, wizened, and pulsing with power in a way that differed from the Fae.

"Emmaline, this is the Lady of the City."

The woman's deep brown, wrinkled face became even more so as she smiled kindly at Emmaline. Her eyes, the green-blue color of algae, gleamed from the depths of her wrinkles. The Lady was a grandmother, a queen, a primordial being made from mud and asphalt, brick and sea grasses. Her hair, a long sweep of cobblestone and concrete, changed to the same colors as her eyes where it touched the ground. She swept it back over her shoulder and her movements seemed like a dizzying kaleidoscope of stone and sea, and steel and earth, all slipping and sliding in different directions across her body.

Emmaline's mouth dropped open, and she paled as the woman before her started to approach. She looked at Vali with panic in her eyes, and Vali gestured that she should sit or kneel on the ground, so Emmaline took that advice and sank down to her knees. When the Lady stood before her,

Emmaline's head dropped and she stared at the ground, afraid to look up at this imposing being.

"Ah child, so afraid of me when you have shared a bed with someone who has killed his own kind!" Her deep, gravelly voice was gently mocking, and she laughed when Emmaline jerked her head up to meet the Lady's gaze, her eyes blazing.

"He was used!" Emmaline exclaimed, and the Lady held up a thick hand to stop her.

"Yes, child. Our enemy is shared, and it has used your love as a tool. But now I have seen the fire in you, and it blazes hot once roused. Good, good."

She moved forward, placing her right hand on Emmaline's shoulder, and Emmaline's eyes closed slowly, a peaceful look washing over her face.

"Gifts you were given, and glad I am that they were. But the most important came from me, and I see now that it is waking inside you. You are to use it for the benefit of all, do you understand me?" She tilted her head, and the movement sent rocks sliding and riverbeds shifting across her body, a mesmerizing motion that caused an involuntary gasp from Lucee, who had been quiet until that point.

The Lady turned toward Lucee and addressed her. "Ah, the leader of the undying ones! Glad I am that you joined us; let me look upon you." She flowed across the grass and moss, her hair trailing behind her. Lucee smelled brackish water and ozone as the Lady leaned close and inspected her.

"Careful, child." Her voice was so soft that only Lucee could hear it. "You are carrying worrisome burdens. When the time comes that you need more strength than your proud heart can provide, call my name. I will send you what you need."

"I-I will do that, Grandmother," Lucee stammered, afraid to look the powerful being in the eyes. "I would be honored to have your help."

She was already moving away, back to Emmaline, who had carefully watched her interaction with Lucee.

"Show me what you have learned so far, how you pull the power of the Green through you."

Emmaline looked confused for a moment, then reached into her hair and pulled forth the small branch of thyme that she had taken from the herb garden. She held it cupped in her hands, outstretched before her, and she focused on it carefully. Her breathing deepened slowly, and after a moment, the plant began to move.

Lucee held her breath, watching the branch as it began to grow, tendrils expanding and leaves bursting forth from the plant. She could smell the sharp scent of thyme, which reminded her of freshly sharpened pencils.

After a moment, Emmaline bent and placed the branch on the ground, and as they all watched, roots burst from the end and snaked themselves into the earth. When Emmaline finally withdrew her hand, a small herb bush grew in the fertile soil at the base of the oak tree.

Lucee felt a tear unexpectedly slip down her cheek. She wiped it away with a fist and felt something emotional, something she couldn't put a name to, deep in the pit of her guts.

"Well done, child!" The Lady bent to touch the small plant, and it seemed to quiver with pleasure. "This is just the beginning of what you will be able to achieve if you give it your energy."

She stood back up—though really, it wasn't much of a change in her height—and said to Vali, "You two have much work to accomplish together. And all three of you are my hope, my connection to those who live and move on my lands, and my protection. Glad I am to know you, my children."

She began to move away from them, vines and hair dragging behind her, and Vali called out, "Grandmother! But what about—"

"No. Do not say that name here, Vali Dawe." She did not turn back to look at Vali, and her shoulders seemed to slump. "I have nothing else I can give you to assist in that fight, but know you this: some things cannot be eradicated. Only mitigated."

She seemed to vanish then, melting into air, leaving only the lingering scent of salt and seagrass and tar behind.

"Vali," Emmaline whispered, "*she's* who you serve? That was—I mean, she is—oh, I don't think I'll ever be able to fully get my mind around this."

"You just made a tiny branch into a plant, that's pretty mind-bending too," Lucee said, her eyes glistening with tears. "Sometimes it's easy when we're all bantering and hanging out together like a bunch of old friends, to forget what we're all really made of. But then you spend a while talking to a spirit of place and community like the Lady of the City, and normality just goes out the window." There was a wistful tone to her voice, and she felt an ache, deep down, that she couldn't put a finger on at that moment. A longing, she supposed, but for what?

Vali leaned over to pat the large, gnarled root of the old oak and smiled. "My friend, it's good to sit here with you." She turned to Emmaline and added, "You're welcome here at any time, you know. She wants you to spend some time learning, and there are so many plants to learn from in the forest. It's safe here too. You can sleep under the trees, even. Nothing will hurt you. Trust me, I've done it a bunch of times." She winked at Emmaline, then stood up and offered her a hand up.

"I have no idea how to go about studying for this. I guess I can go online?"

"Oh, I'm certain that our library will give you all sorts of books to get you started. That's how things work around here. Just you wait." She gave a hand to Lucee next, who jumped up and gave her a thumbs up.

"That's true," Lucee agreed. "Just mention that you need or want something and it usually shows up. Just make sure to abide by the usual rules when you find yourself charmed by the helpfulness—no thanking." She was busy trying to brush any possible dirt off her rear, and so her voice was a little muffled as she contorted herself trying to see if it was grime-free.

"You're fine, you goofball," Vali laughed as she reassured Lucee. "You know, they're always warning us about that, but have either of you accidentally said it and had something happen? It's all vague threatening potential outcomes, no solid examples of what's actually happened."

Emmaline turned toward Lucee and Vali, so she was walking backward, facing them. "I said it once to Camlin, in a fight. It was the weirdest response ever."

"No! What happened? You've gotta spill!" Lucee begged.

"Yes, we need to know!" Vali agreed, waving her arms for emphasis.

"It was pretty early on in our friendship, and he was being overly fussy because I wasn't feeling good, and I guess I looked too underfed to him or something. He kept suggesting food to me from the menu at the café where we were always meeting. Finally, he went up to the counter and grabbed a bunch of things I couldn't eat and presented them to me. Of course, he didn't know at the time that my diet was so restricted, and rather bland. Nothing that I was allowed to eat tasted good to me." She shrugged at the dismayed faces that Lucee and Vali made, and went on.

"Anyway, he looked so pleased with himself! And I was upset. I didn't want to explain to this handsome, cocky man why I couldn't eat any of it, and he kept pushing. Finally, I was so angry, I just looked him dead in the eyes and growled 'No, thank you.' And he was like 'Excuse me, what?' in this astonished voice.

"And I repeated it, in a flippant tone at this point because I was beyond tired. And he just sat there and looked at me for a minute, then pushed his chair back, got up, and left. No goodbye, nothing."

"Holy crap, knowing how he looks at you now, that's intense!" Lucee gasped. "He didn't say anything at all?"

"Nope! But get this: he stayed away for one day exactly. The day after that, he showed up and acted like nothing at all had happened. But he

Christiane Knight

started asking me if there was something I would like, and if I said no, he would drop it. And he started asking me more about my illness, I guess to figure out what he could do that was actually helpful." Emmaline raised an eyebrow, then turned back around to face the way they were going, her arms out at her sides in a wide gesture. "And that's all I've got about that."

"That is, weirdly, fucking adorable," Vali cracked up. "And not at all what I expect to happen if I ever slip up and say the dreaded words!"

"Whatever, you both have guys who worship the ground you walk on, you'd be fine," Emmaline teased, "Though let the record show that I don't actually advise testing that, okay?"

"Sousa does not worship the ground I walk on!" Vali sputtered. Her reply was answered by raucous laughter from both her friends.

"Sousa would die for you, you nutloaf," Lucee cackled, and Emmaline nodded vigorous agreement.

"I haven't been here that long, but even I can see that guy adores you and would be lost without you, Vali."

"Hmm. Okay," she muttered and managed to get the attention off her by pointing to the patio. "Looks like more people showed up. Oh, and there's where the archery is happening." She pointed off to their left, where Dermot and Cullen and a few others were taking turns shooting at straw bale targets.

"That looks like fun, I'd like to try," Emmaline said. "Do you mind if I wander down there to check it out?"

"You totally should," Vali answered. She asked Lucee, "You're not going to go see how Cullen is doing?"

"Naw, let him practice without his girlfriend hanging around and making him nervous. I think I wanna chat with Souz and Merrick a bit, anyway."

Vali decided to walk over with Emmaline, so Lucee followed through with her plan to talk to her bandmates. She found them, conveniently enough, sitting together at the firepit, drinking beers. No one else was there, thankfully, and Lucee made a detour to the bar area to grab a beer from the cooler before she went to join them.

"Hey, what did I miss?" she asked as she sat down. Sousa made a *pfft* sound and Merrick waved a hand dismissively.

"Not a dang thing," Merrick said. "How did the walk go?" He leaned back to finish his beer, then looked into the bottle like he was hoping it would magically refill.

"Well, we had a chat with the Lady of the City, so that happened," Lucee answered.

"Fearney, you can't just drop that into the conversation and not follow it up," Sousa grumbled. "What was the reason for her visit?"

"Just...checking in, I guess? And she talked to Emmaline about her new talent." Lucee took a long sip of her beer. "She grows plants now. And they like her a lot. I dunno."

"So, you don't sound excited by that, I'm not gonna lie," Merrick told her.

"Yeah, no. I dunno. I am excited for her. But..." She trailed off.

Sousa, on the other side of Merrick, leaned over him and said, "But you're feeling left out."

"I shouldn't, I know. It's dumb. But everyone else seems to get fancy skills. Me? I can make a glowy light and bedazzle people with my guitar playing. Which I'd argue was a skill I already came equipped with, if I was the bragging type."

Sousa winced at her false bravado. He could hear the hurt in her words, and he didn't like it at all.

"Hey. I was always taught that the gifts that come from the Fae are all about what someone really needs, not what they want. Which is why it doesn't pay to ask for specifics from us because those kinds of bargains always go bad." He made a scary face. "So, what you've received, thanks to your Fae upgrade? It feels like it's about playing off the skills you already have, adding to your strengths. Does that make sense? You're already pretty awesome so the gifts you're getting play along with making you even awesomer."

She made a face and rolled her eyes, but said, "Sure," in a small voice.

"You know what? Don't go anywhere. I have just the thing for you."

MUSIC: TRAITRS
The Lovely Wounded

While Sousa was gone, Merrick drunkenly tried to cheer Lucee up. "Y'know, what Souz is saying makes sense. Look at me! I got all these gifts, and we both know I was a mess before that. I had nothin' going for me but the band and my excellent taste in friends."

He laughed, softly and poked her with his elbow. Lucee sighed but gave him a lopsided grin in return.

"I know, I'm no comedian. I just hate when you get like this, because you are so important to me and to everyone here. Everything would fall apart without you, Lucee! You have the most crucial job out of any of us—leading the Eleriannan, something I sure wouldn't want to do. I know how hard my job can be, yours has to be a zillion times harder."

"You're not really helping here, Merrick," Lucee groaned. "I get the hard job but not the actual power to go with it? You have more power than I do! I couldn't even defend myself with magic if we were attacked by the Grimshaw again. And I hate having to send other people out to defend me."

"But that's *my* job, Lucee. I want you to send me out, even if it scares me, because that's what I'm supposed to do. And it makes me feel like, for once in my life, I've got purpose." He stopped, cocking his head to look intently at her. "Are you telling me that you don't feel like this is your purpose?"

"I don't know, Merrick. I really don't. I feel like I'm severely outclassed and under-armored. I love our Fae family, and I want to do this job. But maybe I'm just not good enough?"

Merrick made a rude farting noise. "That's bullshit, and if you don't know it, you're hiding the truth from yourself. You're a force to be reckoned with, and everyone who meets you sees it. Why don't you believe it?"

Lucee looked down, avoiding his gaze. "I want to. I hate feeling like this."

Sousa broke the tension by arriving with a big package wrapped in plain brown paper.

"I knew this was gonna come in handy one of these days, and this seems to be the day. Fearney, I'm gonna show you how long I've known that you're special. Open this!"

"What the actual what, Sousa?" She took the package, which was a long rectangle and heavier than she expected. "How long have you waited to give this to me?"

"Hey, why don't you shut your beer hole and open it, and all your questions will be answered," Sousa answered with a big grin.

She raised an eyebrow as she tried not to laugh at "beer hole" and tore into the package. The brown paper revealed an unmarked cardboard box, which she also had to tear open, exposing a black, pebbled surface.

"A guitar case?" She wondered, as she pulled it out of the box. It was a high-end hard case with reinforced corners and a lock.

"Open it, would you?" Sousa urged her.

"Okay, okay—oh my good goats, what did you do?" She gasped as she flipped the case open to show the beautiful guitar inside. The purple-and-green sparkles in the clearcoat picked up the light from the fire, making the guitar gleam with a bewitching energy.

"*Da-aa-mn,* that guitar is gorgeous," Merrick said, impressed. "Souz, where did you get that?"

"Lucee knows."

She picked it up gingerly, as if she didn't believe it was actually in her hands.

"Merrick, the first day that I met Sousa, I showed him this guitar at Tom's Music. I played on it and then we jammed in the store, and he asked me to be in a band with him. I never knew what happened to it. I'd put it back, and the next time I went back to the store to look around, it was gone."

"Because I bought it with the intention to give it to you in the future. When you needed it."

Lucee didn't say anything right away. Instead, she strummed a chord on the guitar, then made a face.

"Oof, storage didn't do the tuning any favors," Merrick grumbled. Sousa dug into a pocket of his BDUs and pulled out a packet of strings and tossed them into the open case.

"Sorry, if I'd known I was going to get this out today, I would have restrung it first."

Lucee shot him a thumbs up, then took her time to change the strings, lovingly turning the tuning knobs until each string was pitched correctly.

"I dunno how she does that by ear," Merrick muttered. "That's magic she's always had." Sousa snorted at that.

"Hey, you should plug into the amp over there," Sousa gestured to the covered area to their right, which had some equipment set up and ready to go. "I figured that at some point we'd be doing parties out here, so I prepared ahead of time."

Lucee started to sling the guitar over her head, then cracked up laughing. "You found a strap that had purple and green sparkles. How did you manage that?"

"Called in a favor. Wait until you see the picks I got; they glow in the dark." He grinned at her, obviously absolutely delighted with himself.

When she turned on the amp, they heard the typical electric buzz noise. She plugged in and gingerly strummed the strings. A rich tone poured out, and she ran through a couple of chords with her eyes closed. Sousa made an encouraging sound, and her eyes popped back open.

"So, let me ask you this, Joseph Sousa," she asked in a crisp, tense voice. "What in the world possessed you to buy this for me, then hold onto it for ages? What is going on in that weird Fae mind of yours?" Her hands were shaking, and she did her best to disguise it, gripping the guitar tightly.

"Y'know how some people put things away for a rainy day? This is similar, but the rain can be replaced with a crisis of confidence in this metaphor." He shrugged. "Besides, that guitar was meant to be yours and I didn't want to see it end up with the wrong person, especially one of those useless pieces of stage decoration at Tom's Music. After you rocked it like that, you know one of 'em would have grabbed it up, trying to steal a chunk of your energy. Tell me I'm wrong."

"You are...you aren't wrong. I guess." She grew quiet and looked down at the guitar hanging there, a perfect fit against her body. She cradled the neck like it had been made to fit her hand. And the tone was perfect, with a clarity that plenty of more expensive guitars lacked.

She looked back up at Sousa, and she could feel the tears starting, even as she willed them to stay put. To her surprise, he was watching her with a look on his face that matched how she was feeling pretty well, at least as she saw it.

"Look, I never ask anyone to play music with me. You were the first one in so long that I can't even tell you. It's lost to the seas of time and memory. But you? As soon as I met you, I wanted to know you. I was afraid you wouldn't want to be in a band with me, that I'd never hear from you after that first day. And you brought Merrick, and I went from being this sad, lonely guy rattling around in a big, empty house to someone with actual friends and purpose again.

"You saved me in a very real way. I was disillusioned, hurting. You brought the magic back into my life. That is, until this dingdong over here crashed a Fae party, then the magic got really real." He shot a big grin at Merrick, who gave him a crooked, drunken smile back and spread his arms out as if to say "Sure, that was me."

"But how? You were this punk guy who really had his shit together. I couldn't believe you actually wanted me! Do you know that for the longest time I thought you were just humoring me? It took months before I finally caught on that you were serious. No one but Merrick ever believed in me before I met you." Lucee exhaled hard, trying to gather herself together. "Can someone grab me a chair? I guess I'd better play this ridiculously extravagant gift so that I can learn to feel like I deserve it."

"That's the Lucee I know and love!" Sousa exclaimed and fetched a chair for her. "By the way, the best way I know to show your gratitude is to rock out with that thing like you have never rocked out before."

Lucee sat there for a moment, her fingers over the strings, gathering herself before she dared to try playing anything on the impressive instrument. She remembered how she felt on the first day she met Sousa, when she'd lost herself playing for him - how the songs blended together and became a story she was telling him, and him alone, as she played. Then she recalled the energy she'd channeled during their last practice, and the ways she'd centered herself, heart and soul, into the tunes.

She let those memories flow into her playing, as she first started with the simplest thing she knew: Beethoven's Ode to Joy. Easy, careful fingerpicking grew into strumming with picking as she built the tempo and intensity. She glanced up and saw Cullen, watching from the back of the patio. He was casually leaning against a post, but his eyes were locked on her with the intensity of love and admiration, and a wave of happiness washed through her. She shifted into a version of This Is Not The End by The Bravery, singing along with the chorus as she played. She heard Merrick singing harmony next to her, and somewhere Sousa had pulled up some kind of hand drum and was playing along.

She decided to shift the mood and hit the opening chords of their song, We Got A Fight, and heard Sousa's whoop of joy from far away as she attacked the riffs with an intensity. Merrick was singing the lyrics, and she could feel them rolling out in front of her, riding across the notes she threw in front of them like a road rising to meet each word. Colors swirled in her vision, and she could see them reflecting off the crowd of friends that had gathered to watch them play, drawn by the sound of her guitar and Sousa's joyous yelling. Some of them were dancing around. She saw Tully spin by, pulling Daro with her, and a Ffyn, swaying its branches gracefully in time to her playing.

But it was Aisling—standing perfectly still in front of them, with her arms thrown back as the music and colors and images washed over her, and a look of sheer joy on her face—that finally brought Lucee to tears.

She didn't stop playing. Instead, she brought the emotions that she was feeling into the song, colors changing to reflect Lucee's emotions and thoughts. The mood of the room shifted along with that change, and people started swaying together, arms around each other. She found herself surrounded by her friends, and they were applauding her, cheering her. It was overwhelming, and she stood up, trying to get some room for herself and get herself back together.

"Move back, give way, make space for your Lady!" She heard the crackly, demanding voice of one of The Ladies cut through the crowd, and the crowd obeyed, stepping back far enough that Lucee felt like she could breathe again.

"I told you that your feelings were the key," said a small voice, meant only for Lucee to hear. She looked down and found Morgandy standing there beside her, with her sisters not far behind.

"I still don't understand what's happening," Lucee grumbled, though her heart wasn't really in it.

"Does it matter what you call it? It is obviously a power that brings people together, using the skills you already possessed," Morgance said. She sounded tired, and Lucee looked at her with some concern. "You are ready to face your foe now, as ready as you could hope to be."

"Eh, what's the talk about foes doing in our celebration? Let's focus on the joy of this moment for now, all right?" Sousa had kept his tone light, but his face sent the firm, unspoken message: drop this line of talk for now. Let Lucee have her win.

Lucee had already lost focus on the interaction nearest to her, though, searching for the one person whose opinion mattered the most to her. Cullen had not moved closer - in fact, he was still standing in the exact same spot. He had watched her entire performance intently and with admiration, even though she hadn't been aware enough to realize that. When she finally spotted him through the crowd, he did something so very Cullen— yet a thing he'd never done for her before.

He dropped into the courtliest bow she'd ever seen him give, and when he rose up, his right hand went to his lips and he threw her a kiss. Her hands seemed to clasp over her heart of their own volition at his salute to a smattering of pleased trills and applause from those around her.

"How very eighteenth century of you!" she called out to Cullen, trying to cover the emotions that were threatening to take over. He answered with a cocky grin and a wink that made her laugh, breaking the imminent flood of feelings before they spilled out in front of everyone.

Sousa yelled out, "I've got a keg of Sheridan's best here! Who wants to help me drink it?" He mugged for Lucee when there was a loud shout of approval. "There, that'll get them away from you and give you some time to relax," he told her, then led off the thirsty horde.

She had bent down and started to put her new guitar back in its case when she heard the soft sound of a throat clearing, and looked up to find Cullen standing there.

"Is there anything I can help with?" he asked. He had a look about him that she couldn't quite put a finger on. It made her edgy.

"You know, that's what guys used to say to me at the end of the night at parties when I'd be trying to clean up, and they didn't want to go home alone." She framed it as a joke, but after she said it out loud, she realized it didn't sound very funny. Cullen, however, seemed to take it in stride.

"I certainly do not want to go home alone." He smiled sweetly, then walked over to unplug the cord to the amp. "I would loop this for you, but I have already learned that I am hopelessly incompetent at doing that properly, so let me just hand it to you instead."

"Can I confess something to you?" She was suddenly as nervous as she'd felt when they first realized their attraction to each other.

"You may tell me anything and everything, Lucee." His voice was light and carefree, but he stood stock still, waiting for what she was about to say with a focused intensity.

"I thought I wanted to prove myself to you. I thought I needed to impress you with my skill, my ability to be just as magical as anyone else in this house." She paused for emphasis, then continued. "That was dumb."

"You have nothing to prove to me. I have never needed anything but the Lucee I met in our garden on that autumn day," he replied, his voice soft and neutral.

She looked up to meet his gaze, and there was something there, a whisper of pain and sadness, that she hated seeing.

"I've hurt you. I didn't mean to, but I did. I was so busy focusing on what I thought I lacked, I didn't consider the way I was making you feel. I'm sorry. And I think I get it now. At least, I hope I do." She stood up, then folded her arms across her chest tightly, gripping her arms with her hands.

"What has hurt has been watching you beat yourself up over something you thought was missing, then looking to me as if I had clues to give you that might tell you where to look. As if I could see you as anything but perfect, because of who you already are." His voice was rough, and his eyes sad. "You have all the parts of being a mortal that draw us to you like moths to flame, and you are utterly unaware of that power. In fact, you discount it, yearning for the things that we have given others to make up for the fact that they do not possess half of your charm and grace and experience. And if you asked them, they would agree with me wholeheartedly."

"You wouldn't say that about Merrick."

"Sand and storm, that is exactly who I mean!" His eyes flashed as he expressed his frustration and then he held his hands up and took a deep breath. "Lucee, we give gifts that match the needs of the receiver, at least as much as we can sense those needs. Merrick needed gifts from all of us, both to assist in his newly assumed role and to compensate for things he had yet to achieve on his own. He needed to learn lessons that you already knew."

Cullen took a step toward her, and she desperately wanted to close the gap and hug him close, but she knew she couldn't yet. Not only did she not deserve to be let off the hook that easily, but he needed to say all the things to her that he had been carrying inside him.

"I'm listening."

"I know, and I am grateful for that." His small smile felt like a beam of light breaking through the darkness to her. "Look, I did not even consciously realize all of this until today, while I watched you meld music and magic together effortlessly.

"I tried to teach you skills with a completely wrong mindset, and The Ladies knew it. That is why they went about your lessons the way that they did, digging into your past, where all the self-deprecating talk comes from. You do not need to have the skills that Merrick has, other than self-protection and whatever practical things you pick up along the way. You do not need to shift your shape or cast an illusion of water. You just need to be able to lead, to have the confidence to do that job and believe in your decisions. You need to be able to see yourself the way we all see you. Like how I see you."

"I keep trying, Cullen. I really do. I mean, the fact that all of you believe in me, and count on me - I know that means something. But there's knowing and *knowing*, and I can't seem to fully beat back that voice of Da, whispering in my ear that I'll never be good enough." She scuffed a boot across the flagstones, frowning.

"Well, I will keep telling you these things until you can only hear my voice, drowning out the lies that your father told. I will say them until you can believe them too. Because you are magnificent, and that man is a fool not to have seen it." With those last words, he stepped close to her and held out a hand. "As long as you allow me in your life, Lucee Fearney, I will be your champion."

She took his hand, then pulled him in for the hug she'd been longing for.

"Looks like you're stuck with me forever, my Fox-fox. Or until you get tired of my nonsense," she told him, her voice muffled as she leaned against his chest.

"Forever sounds perfect," he agreed as he hugged her tightly.

"Are you two done being all romantic and goosy? Because there is *beer* over here with *your* names on it!" Sousa's voice rang out across the courtyard, ruining their sweet moment perfectly. Lucee softly bashed her head into Cullen's chest a couple of times.

"I swear to the ghosts of all the fields of hops that man helped destroy, he's so lucky that I love him. And that y'all are immortal and he probably won't get liver disease."

"Probably," Cullen agreed, laughing.

MUSIC: TWIN TRIBES
VII

The weeks before ArtPark were filled with preparations, plans, and—of course—parties. Lucee and Merrick and Sousa practiced until they felt like they could play their songs in their sleep, as Merrick put it. Tully had put together outfits for them, although Sousa had a lot to say about wearing a shirt while drumming.

"It's going to be a million degrees out there! That shirt had better be sleeveless, Tully. Otherwise, it's just going to end up in a crumpled pile on the stage behind my kit."

She rolled her eyes at that. "Yes, yes, I know about your *requirements*, don't worry."

"Have you ever seen Sousa in a shirt with sleeves?" Emmaline asked Vali as an aside.

"Only sleeves I've seen on him are on his leather jacket! And that was over a sleeveless shirt, of course," Vali chuckled. "He says he gets too hot, and I can corroborate that he definitely puts off some heat. No need for a heavy blanket if you're bunking with Souz!" That made Emmaline giggle.

"You two are both the oddest couple and yet the perfect match for each other," she said.

"That's a fair assessment," Vali agreed. "I can't imagine being with anyone else, but we are definitely weirdos. I'm glad that we're so well aligned philosophically because that's the part that makes living together work the best. We're both pretty driven to take care of our communities in the ways that make the best sense to us."

"He was really great at the community clean-up along the Jones Falls last week," Emmaline said. "He had everyone organized and kept people laughing so it was actually fun to stand on the bank of a smelly stream and pick up trash. That's pretty impressive."

"Wanna know a secret?" Vali leaned in conspiratorially. "Having Daro and Karsten from Tiennan House around so much lately has really convinced him to start taking action outside of our little group. They do so much in their neighborhood to help the mortals who live there. It has started to really push Sousa to do the same. And of course, he sees me and now you working at the community garden and bringing food around to the tent encampments. Suddenly, he's realizing that he could do so much more."

"And he's good at it!" Emmaline approved. "People wanted to know when we would meet next to do more clean-ups, because they had a great time and he made them feel awesome about their involvement. That's just what people need these days, a win that helps them feel like they're making a difference."

"I bet next month we have even more volunteers. But hey," she said, changing the subject, "I wanted to mention—I'd like you to stick by me at the festival, if that's good with you. I think Camlin wanted it that way, and I'd feel better about that too. Is that all right?"

"Honestly, Vali, I don't know who else I'd attach myself to otherwise." Emmaline smiled with relief. "I feel pretty comfortable with everyone here, I guess. But I feel closest to you and Lucee. And I like Karsten pretty well too. But I clicked with you the strongest," she said shyly.

"It's funny, because in another life I dunno if we'd be friends. I would probably serve you coffee or tea and we'd trade jokes, and then we would forget about each other until the next time you came into the coffee shop. But here, as Fae adoptees, we're friends, and I'm glad." Vali bumped into Emmaline playfully and grinned.

"Well, I've never really had many friends, so at least I found the coolest ones possible when I did," Emmaline announced, bumping Vali back.

"Are you going to be okay on Sunday? This is a lot to handle."

"I—ugh." Emmaline gestured wildly, making circles in front of her. "That's how my feelings are right now, to be honest—a wild mix of everything. I'm excited, I'm scared, I'm anxious. There's a part of me that's hoping that we go and The Drawback plays, and it's just a lovely summer festival experience, and then I turn around and Camlin is standing there and he's fine. And it's over, the bad thing is defeated and we never had to risk anything at all. The end." She breathed in deeply, and Vali saw that she was wringing her hands.

"But that's not how this works, I know. We're with the Fae but it's not a faery tale. Chances are good that there will be a fight, and people will get hurt, and I might lose—I might lose Camlin forever. That's the price we all pay for fighting the bad guys. That's the price I personally have to pay for getting a chance to live again. And Camlin's paying for the poor choices he made. I hate it, but the possibility that somehow we could all walk away with our lives and loves intact gives me hope." Emmaline looked at Vali intently, her eyes steely and determined. "At least I've been given the chance to love, and feel loss, and fight. I'm going to remember that, no matter how it all turns out."

Merrick's voice rang out in the ballroom, where everything for Sunday's event was staged.

"I'm going to take a stroll down to the festival to see how it is going, get the lay of the land for tomorrow's events, and just to...well, spy. I'd like a couple of people to come with. Who's interested?"

Out of those in the room who raised their hands, he chose Karsten, Tully, Daro, and Sousa. Aisling also joined, entwining her small hand in Merrick's before he could say otherwise. Vali bounced up and pushed her way into the group, next to Sousa, who grinned at her.

"This is a good mix. We can look over a lot of different aspects of the grounds this way," Merrick said. "We'll be back in a while, try not to drink all the beer before we get back!"

"Hey, bring me a funnel cake!" Lucee yelled at them as they left. "Bet they forget," she muttered to no one in particular.

Sousa parked the van a few streets over from the park, and they trooped across the blocks and blended in with the crowds headed in the same direction. The Dell, the part of the park where the festival was held, was an unusual space. The bulk of it was hidden from view of the roads that surrounded it, as it curved downwards into a sunken, open area thickly surrounded on all sides by large trees. Sidewalks snaked across the open grass area in the middle of the park, and along some of the stacked stone retaining walls. Antique-looking iron lampposts dotted the way beside the sidewalks, adding an ageless air to the space.

To access the park, one had to either descend a series of stairs, or travel a path that sloped down through the trees. Entering the park felt like stepping outside of the city and into someplace quite different. It was a bit like the Forest inside The Maithe, Vali decided. It had that same magical feel, a wonderful place to choose for an event that brought people together for a joyous day of activities.

They came in through one of the entrances that had stairs, moving along in tandem with a group of random people who were also attending ArtPark. The first thing Vali saw were colorful towers set up at each quarter of the park: north, south, east, and west. Each one was a different color and covered with different symbols.

"Wow, that's impressive," she said to the group, pointing to the towers.

"Did you catch the symbolism?" Merrick asked. "The colors represent the four directions or quarters. They're casting a circle!"

Daro looked at each tower, and made a sound of recognition. "This practice is not one I am familiar with, but I understand what they intend to represent. The green and brown is Earth, correct?"

"That's right—north is associated with Earth, and the rocks and leaves they have decorated the tower with reflect that. East is Air, and that's why they have that tower covered with all those yellow and white flags and streamers. South is Fire, and they did a pretty great job of representing fire on that tower, with those glistening panels that look like flames!"

"And then west would be Water? I see the sculpted blues that flow around that structure. Very clever," Daro agreed. "Is the intention to keep bad things out, or the good things in?"

"Maybe it's to concentrate all the positive energy," Tully guessed. She linked her arm through Daro's, and he turned his attention to her and smiled at her in a way that Vali had never seen him do with anyone else.

Interesting, Vali thought. *I'll have to point that out to Souz.*

Music echoed around the Dell, and Sousa pointed to the south, where a covered stage was set up.

"Bless them for having a roof on that thing," he said. "Otherwise, we'd be roasting under this full blast Baltimore summer sun."

"I'm imagining you playing in just boxers," Vali laughed.

"If that!"

Merrick made an appalled face, and everyone cracked up.

"I don't want to have that mental image stuck in my mind! Sooooo... let's take a stroll around and see what's to be seen," he said, gesturing for everyone to start moving.

There were vendor tents set up along the gentle curves of the sidewalk that meandered around the edges of the park space, with a mix of arts, crafts, and food. Sousa grumbled when he noticed that beer drinkers were supposed to stay in the beer garden area, but cheered up when he saw that rule didn't seem to apply to the performers. The members of the band currently playing were definitely swigging from bottles of beer.

Tully chuckled when she saw a troupe of acrobats and stilt walkers go by.

"They're pretty good, but I guarantee that we will be unforgettable," she said, a smug smile on her face.

"Now, now, they're only mortals. They're doing the best they can," Merrick pretended to scold her, which got a laugh out of Daro and Karsten.

"There are a lot of people here!" Aisling pointed to a long line at a food booth. "What could be so amazing that people are willing to wait in the sun?"

"Oh, that's my friend Penzy's booth! She does Baltimore classics—snowballs, freshly made crab chips, lemon sticks," Merrick told her.

"I am afraid you're going to have to explain. None of those things sound like food!" Aisling looked skeptical.

"Snowballs are big cups of crushed ice covered with flavorings that have names that often don't tell you what they're supposed to taste like. My favorite's skylite, for example. If you're feeling fancy, they'll put a big dollop of marshmallow on top. I think you'd like them." Aisling's face didn't change from her suspicious expression, so Merrick continued. "Crab chips are just potato chips with crab seasoning on them. Spicy, really good when they're fresh like that. And a lemon stick is half a lemon with a special peppermint stick in the middle. You suck on the peppermint and get lemony mint juice. It's something that every kid who grew up here knows about."

She wasn't convinced, so Merrick took the group to the side of the tent to yell hi to his friend, and came away with a sky-blue snowball with several spoons and a couple of lemon sticks.

"Penzy was outraged that you'd never had either of these, so she hooked us up. She said that if you like them, come back tomorrow and she'll get you some more. She also said that they've been non-stop busy since the festival opened and that she had heard that we were bringing some really great entertainment with us." He stopped and gave Sousa a hard look. "Any idea how she might've heard something like that?"

"Well, I wanted our friends to not be completely unexpected," Sousa said, uncharacteristically meek. "I probably should have let you all know that I let that slip to the organizers, but this way if there are any questions about who is or isn't supposed to be performing, people will know that they're with us. Course, if things really go south, they might not ask us back again, but we'll worry about that later." He shrugged, sheepishly.

"Ah, hell. Okay, I hear you, that's probably not the worst idea," Merrick agreed, then started laughing when he saw Aisling's face after her first try of the lemon stick.

"It's so sour!" She scrunched up her face and tried it again. "But I can't seem to stop myself from going back for more!"

Tully seemed more interested in the snowball, which she was sharing with Karsten. They pointed at each other's blue-stained lips and laughed like children. Daro, on the other hand, really seemed to enjoy his lemon stick and had almost finished it.

"It reminds me of something I had as a child," he said in a pleased tone. "I will certainly have another tomorrow. Quite the delicacy."

Vali watched as a group of people passed by Daro and swiveled to stare as they walked past. Despite toning himself down a bit for the day with the help of glamour, there was no hiding his imposing form or the uncanniness that he exuded naturally. She overheard a woman whisper to her friend as they went by, "Did you catch the look of that brother? He's a little weird but *fiiiine.*"

True that, Vali thought as she tried not to laugh.

She heard someone call her name, and she whipped her head around, trying to spot who could be looking for her in a crowd like this. She heard it again and realized that it was coming from one of the park benches—a thin, dirty man, hidden behind Penzy's tent in the shade of some trees.

"Hey guys, I'll be right back," she told her friends. When Sousa made a move to follow, she shook her head. "I'll just be right over there. Someone I know wants to talk to me for a sec and he's not the type to hang around for strangers."

"Be careful? I'll be watching from over here," Sousa replied, frowning.

"It'll be fine. That's Jimmy, I know him from around," she assured him. He nodded, knowing that by "around," she meant her time living on the street.

She walked over to the bench and sat down, not looking directly at the man sitting there.

"Hey Jimmy, what's going on?" she asked in a noncommittal tone. He was an edgy, anxious guy, so she was always careful not to do anything she knew could push his triggers. Thanks to that, he'd often sought her out to talk to when things had gotten bad for him as she had a way of being able to calm him down. In turn, he often rewarded her with info and gossip he'd heard around his usual places in the city.

"Vali. I was lookin' for you, but since you been holin' up in that big place, I don't see you much," he said, his voice rusty-sounding. She guessed that he didn't often talk to people these days, and she felt a twinge of guilt.

"Sorry, man, I'll have to get out more so I can catch up with you. I owe you a coffee anyway." She kept her voice upbeat but didn't smile at him because she knew he didn't like that.

"I'm glad you been off the streets, though. It's been weird out here lately. And I seen you with your new friends, and I'm thinking you need to know about the weird. *They* seem okay, but the weird ones? They ain't right."

He had her attention then. She tried hard not to turn to look at him, to see if he was scared.

"What's not right about them? I do wanna know, you got that right."

"People get mean when they're around, Vali. People are fightin' and ac-tin' crazy when these dudes show up. They're tryin' to cause fights in the streets, in the shelters, in front of the liquor stores and on the street cor-ners. Comin' up and talking crazy shit meant to start trouble between the gangs or setting neighbors against each other. Even messing with us street people, and bad stuff happened in tent city because of them. Lowden got stabbed, did you hear?"

Vali shook her head, wanting Jimmy to go on, her heart sinking as she listened to him.

"They came around stirring up shit, and Benny stabbed Lowden, and the cops came and cleared everyone out and tore down the tents and trashed all our stuff. Now we can't sleep there, and they talkin' about ma-kin' it so that we can't sleep anywhere. And now some of those tent guys are mad and wanna revenge. You know that ain't gonna go well."

"No, you're right, Jimmy. That's bad news. So, what's these dudes look like? Do you know?"

"Like—like your friends, but not pretty. Pretty ugly!" He laughed, a harsh sound, then coughed a few times. "Not right, but these guys are scary not right. Like they'd be just fine in a horror movie, you know?"

She did know.

"Have you seen them recently? And are you staying somewhere safe?"

"I been sleepin' here. But they've been here, and I don't wanna be here anymore." He paused, then did something he'd never done before in the en-tire time she'd known him—he moved to put a hand on her arm. She knew Sousa was probably losing his mind over it, but she didn't care. This was serious if Jimmy was willing to touch her.

"I saw you and I 'membered what I heard, that you run with the pret-ty ones now. And they got power. And... I heard you got power too." He paused to take the hand from her arm and run it through his tangled, grey hair. "If you can stop 'em, if you have any way to do it, you need to do it, Vali. These guys mean to ruin everything." His voice suddenly became very clear, not at all raspy or slurred. "You've got to stop them before they make things worse for everyone."

She did the thing she didn't want to do and turned to look him in the eye. For a moment, he held her gaze, his filmy blue eyes clearer than she'd ever seen them. He looked terrified.

He grunted, then, and broke her gaze, backing up on the bench. She quickly looked away.

"I'll let you be, Jimmy. And we are going to do everything we can to stop the bad ones. I'm glad you told me all of this."

He wouldn't look at her anymore. It was like he'd said everything he could, and now he couldn't even see her. She got up and walked back to her friends, who had watched the whole thing from where they'd stood, and shook her head, sadly.

"That was a disturbing conversation."

"Did he—what did he say? If he tried to hurt you..." Sousa trailed off at the look on Vali's face.

"He's a friend and he brought me news from the street about our enemy. It's not good. I don't want to tell you here. Let's wait until we get back to the van." She took Sousa's hand and squeezed it.

"Let's go say hi to the folks running the music and we can get out of here," Merrick agreed. "I just want them to know that we swung by, and see if there's anything we need to prepare for tomorrow."

They managed to get over to the backstage area just as one band finished their set. Merrick and Sousa took a few moments to chat with the stage manager and let the sound person know that they thought the sound was fantastic. That was never a bad plan before a performance. Vali watched them from a distance, but her mind was still on the conversation she'd had with Jimmy, and how much it had creeped her out.

She refocused herself to find Karsten looking at her with a worried look on their face.

"I'm good, friend," she told Karsten. "The reality of this is just really starting to hit home. It's that feeling of inevitable disaster and impending doom. I just can't seem to shake it."

"To say that you should not worry would be foolish," Karsten replied in their soft voice. "But we are forewarned, and we are strong. And if we do fail tomorrow, we will not stop fighting. That is how we are made. We will fight for the good in the world until the fight is over, or we are." They kicked a small rock with one booted foot, eyes downcast. "I am sorry that my words are not more uplifting. A day like today deserves joy and hope. I can only offer determination."

"Karsten, I'd rather have your honest words than hollow and empty ones of positivity. We know what we're facing. At least we can say that, and prepare properly." Her mood took a sudden shift and she noticed that Karsten still showed proof of their snowball experience. "Hey, your lips are still blue! That's a great summer look for you."

Karsten's head snapped up, and they looked at Vali with confusion for a moment, then they started to chuckle. Then they threw their head back and laughed loudly. Tully, who shared a similar blue lip tint, looked over at the pair curiously, and that sent Karsten into another laughing fit.

"I needed that laugh, Vali," they said once they got themselves together. "There is the mirth that a day like this one deserves!"

"What's so funny?" Sousa asked, rejoining the group with Merrick trailing behind.

"Blue lips in the face of adversity," Vali answered as they started walking, and she heard Karsten muffle a guffaw from behind her.

Sousa looked confused but shrugged it off, and they made their way through the crowd— bigger than ever now—and back to Sousa's van.

"Tomorrow, we'll be able to park this bad boy in the performer's lot. Which is good because I don't like leaving it on the street, even if it would be unwise for anyone to mess around with Fae property," Sousa said as he opened the van's doors and let everyone in.

Once Sousa had pulled into traffic, Daro, who was sitting in the middle row of seats next to Tully, spoke up.

"Can you tell us what the man on the bench said to you, Vali?"

Vali turned in her seat in the front of the van, and recounted the conversation, word for word to the best of her ability. Merrick was frowning, and both Daro and Karsten looked alarmed at what Jimmy had told her. Tully had her hand on Daro's, as if she was trying to comfort him.

"They always go for the disenfranchised," Daro growled. "They know just where to start trouble. The more unrest they can cause, the more they can drive people away from being in the city, the more power and control they amass."

"It's curious," Merrick noted. "The way he talks, you sound a bit legendary in his network. He's wanting you to do something about beings that terrify him, in a way that implies that he is totally convinced you could pull off."

"All of us. He was referring to all the Fae." She ran a hand through her purple hair, tousling it further. "I am a bit legendary, I guess, in that world. The really tough luck folks, they knew if they came to me with their problems, a lot of the time those problems would get solved. Not always in the way that they wanted, but in ways that worked for them. Like Jimmy—because of some people I knew through working at the Frisky Bean, I was able to set up a situation for him where he could reliably get his disability checks. It's not much money, but it's more than nothing, and it helps him. No one else ever bothered to do that for him."

"That's because you actually do shit instead of talking a good talk," Sousa said, a proud tone in his voice.

"That's what we all do now," she said. "At least we try. And people on the street, they talk, they pass news around. I'm guessing that they don't know exactly what we are, but they know we accomplish helpful and possibly impossible things. So, we're powerful and worth appealing to or something."

"That's exactly how it was in the old times," Aisling mused. "You could appeal to a Fae court, and they might help if they felt so inclined."

"Powerful, but capricious," Sousa added, and Merrick snorted at that. "What?" Sousa demanded.

"Didn't think you knew words that big, that's all," Merrick smirked.

"You're lucky you're in the back of the van, bucko—oh, but look, we're back at The Maithe now!" Sousa came to a screeching halt in The Maithe's small parking lot, and Merrick made a rude noise.

"You're not going to do anything about it unless you wanna play bass and sing along while banging on the drums."

"He's got a point, you know," Vali said to Sousa and turned around to throw a wink to Merrick, grateful that he'd found a way to lift the mood, at least for a little while.

"Guess you're right. But just for that, you get to tell all of this to Lucee, dude," Sousa informed Merrick.

MUSIC: NEW MODEL ARMY
Bittersweet

After Merrick and his small group had left to go check out ArtPark, Lucee decided that she needed to go someplace calm and quiet so that she could get her head together. Between worrying about what would happen the next day at their show, and if The Ladies would recover, and if they could win without anyone getting hurt, she felt like everything was pressing down on her. It was obvious that Cullen agreed, because he took one look at her after her friends left, and grabbed her hand, pulling her toward the courtyard space.

"Even if we are not alone out here, it must be better than the cacophony in the ballroom," he told her, and it was true. When they emerged outside, into the gentle sun shining on the green space The Maithe hid, Lucee immediately felt calmer.

"Oh yes, this is glorious," she said, and Cullen spun her around, trying to get her to smile.

"Hey, there's Emmaline." She pointed toward the trees, where they could see the long-haired figure of the quiet woman. "What is she doing, can you tell?"

"I have no earthly idea—oak and ash, she gathered the Ffyn! Look at how they bow to her."

Lucee could see them now, gathered in a messy, uneven row along the edge of the woods, their branch-like appendages swaying and reaching out to Emmaline as she moved around them. She stopped at one and Lucee inhaled sharply as she watched Emmaline's hands move over the Ffyn's trunk-like body because the touch of the gentle woman seemed to cause the Ffyn to change and grow.

"Look, Cullen, they are growing—are they leaves? Are the Ffyn actually trees? I have never been sure."

"None of us know, exactly. But they do seem to be growing. I wonder what their plan is?"

"Oh, they look more like willow trees now, don't they?" Lucee recognized the look her friends were taking on, and thought they were even more magnificent to behold.

One of the Ffyn must have noticed the couple because it waved branch-like arms in their direction, and Emmaline turned to beckon them over. When Lucee got close enough, the first one that had been transformed brushed her delicately with its tendril-branches, and Lucee felt the consciousness of the being touch hers, as they had before.

She felt the Ffyn's joy at seeing Lucee, but also sadness. It ached in a way that felt unfamiliar, the mournfulness of a being that was used to expressing only happy emotions. She hated that it was carrying that feeling and grew more disturbed when the vision of Ffyn fighting in these new shapes came to her.

"They changed in order to defend us better," she told Cullen. "They felt that their help wasn't enough during the battle at The Maithe. Oh, my heart." She covered her face with her hands and tried to get her emotions together. These gentle souls should never face such challenges!

"They sensed that I could assist them, and came to me," Emmaline explained, a guilty look on her face. "I didn't like it, but who am I to deny them? This wasn't how I wanted to be useful to this house, Lucee." Her voice cracked on the last sentence. One of the Ffyn trailed a few long, feathery branches across her face, and Lucee felt the comfort that it projected to them all.

"If anything happens to any of you, I'll be heartbroken," Lucee told the Ffyn. "I want to dance with you while your branches try to touch the sky. Don't disappoint me, friends."

She felt the long, supple branches wrap around her, and she was embraced by one Ffyn, then another, until each one had touched her with a mental caress that told her how much she was loved and respected. One by one, they withdrew, moving with their swaying steps away from the woods and across the field, to the trail that led to the Gate.

"Where are they going, Lucee?" Emmaline asked, and Lucee shrugged.

"They didn't say, but my impression is that they are finding their way to the Dell for the big event tomorrow. I have no idea how they'll manage it."

"They have their ways," Cullen told them. "Some mysteries are beyond even my kind, and the Ffyn are certainly one of those. But if they say they will be there, then you may rely on them." He pinched the bridge of his nose, lightly, his face reflecting a weariness that Lucee hated to see on him. "The Grimshaw cause pain and destruction even when they are not here in front of us."

"I don't know if it makes anything easier to bear, but they were quite proud to do this," Emmaline told them. "They showed me an image of what they would become, and the impression is that their ancestors once were warriors with that form."

"I can't even imagine that," Lucee replied. "I'm trying to picture that in my mind and utterly failing. They're just my friends who love to dance and spread joyous thoughts."

The three walked across the grassy field to the courtyard space, and Lucee sat on one of the stone steps with a sigh.

"People are going to get hurt again, and this time it's on my watch, and I hate it," she said. Her shoulders slouched as she leaned on her knees, her arms wrapped around her legs. She just wanted to crawl into a hole, she was so tired of all the sadness and uncertainty leading up to an event that should have been nothing but fun.

Cullen said nothing, choosing instead to gently run his hand up and down her back in a comforting manner. She turned a little to reward him with a tiny smile.

"I don't know how you do it," Emmaline said. Lucee lifted her head and turned to stare at Emmaline.

"How *I* do it? Girl, it's nothing compared to what you're carrying around! I don't know how you hold it together. At least I've got Cullen..." Lucee trailed off as she realized what she was saying, but Emmaline waved it off.

"Don't censor yourself on my account, Lucee. I won't lie, this is really hard. I miss Camlin terribly, and I am so worried for him, but he's trying to make up for some horrible choices, and I respect that. If nothing else, at least I'm now in a place where I feel like I could do things that matter, and that's thanks to him in a lot of ways." She took a lock of her long, dark hair and twisted it around her finger, and Lucee knew that Emmaline wasn't as calm or as accepting as she seemed.

"You know that's it's okay to be angry about this, right?" Lucee asked, her voice gentle.

"I'm not sure what good that would do," Emmaline answered, a sharp tone creeping into her voice. "It won't banish The Grimshaw or get Camlin back. It won't change the fact that I might never see him again after tomorrow. Sometimes I catch myself wishing that he'd just let me die that day, so at least I wouldn't have to face the idea that he might not be able to escape The Grimshaw this time. How fucked up is that?"

"No, I get it. I hate that you're feeling it, but I can't say I'd feel differently. All I know is that we're going to do our best to get him back, no matter what. And I know that doesn't mean much to you because you still don't know us that well. But if there's one thing we don't do around here, it's leave our friends in trouble!" Lucee stood up, delivering her last sentence fiercely, and she felt Cullen stand next to her, as if to co-sign her speech.

"She is right," he said. "Ever since Lucee and Merrick joined the Eleriannan, they have done nothing but teach us the value of unfaltering friendship. Vali and Sousa are the same way. We Fae have learned from the best about the value of loyalty. And even though Camlin was once our enemy, that is no longer the case. We will do everything in our power to return him to us, Emmaline."

"You talk about him as if he's one of you now."

"If I have anything to say about it," Lucee declared, "he is. And guess what? I don't throw my power around much, but I'll fight anyone who wants to argue differently about this."

"Trust me when I tell you that she is absolutely not lying," Cullen agreed. "No one wants to butt heads with her when she makes up her mind."

"Hey!" Lucee retorted with a laugh.

Emmaline stood up and paced around for a moment, her hands trailing over some of the herbs that had recently grown around either side of the steps up to the patio. As she touched them, they leaned toward her, like eager children looking for attention.

"I don't understand you, any of you." Her voice quavered. "But I'm really glad that I'm a part of you now."

"Damn right you are," Lucee told her, grinning. "Hey, Cullen, do you think there could be some of that lavender lemonade around here? I'm awfully thirsty after all this talking."

They found some lounge chairs and a table and pulled them to the grass. They sat and drank lavender lemonade and ate some scones that Cullen found in the kitchen, talking until Merrick and the others came back from ArtPark.

"This looks like some sort of Victorian lawn party!" Sousa joked when he saw them, then he retrieved some more lawn chairs and handed them out until everyone had a seat. Vali brought over beers for him and herself, and she sat on the grass at Sousa's feet, leaning back against him.

They recounted their adventure to the trio, and Lucee frowned when Vali finished talking about what she'd learned from Jimmy.

"Is it wrong that I feel absolutely no surprise about this?" Vali shook her head, and Lucee continued. "Yeah, it just seems like the kind of dirty pool they'd play. But it's telling me something else. Once we're through everything tomorrow, Vali, I want to pick your brain about what else we can be doing to help. Playing music to inspire people is great, but I want to take more concrete action."

Vali grinned the widest grin possible. "That's what I've been waiting to hear from y'all. There are real steps we can take that would make life a lot better for people. More water and neighborhood clean-ups, community gardens, beautification through art, free food handouts, and finding ways to get safe places for people to stay all immediately come to mind. We could easily do all of this."

"I feel like an ass that I've never thought to do any of that before," Sousa admitted sheepishly. "I spent so much time focusing on the wrong things."

"Not wrong, just a little myopic, I guess," Vali told him, patting his knee. "Which is understandable. You've had to break free of being so jaded for so long. It makes sense."

"You're way too forgiving of me, but I'm not going to tell you to stop," Sousa said, then took a swig of his beer. Merrick chuckled at that.

"Vali's good for you, man. Actually, she's good for all of us." He raised his beer to Vali, who surprisingly blushed.

"I just have a conscience that won't stop, that's all," she mumbled. "*Anyway*, the stage setup looks great, Lucee. Everyone near the park is going to hear your guitar."

"Badass! I'm really looking forward to the concert portion of our jam-packed afternoon." She left the part about the impending fight unspoken, but everyone seemed to feel the weight of that implication, and things grew quiet for a while.

"Has—has anyone seen The Ladies recently? I don't want them to get left behind or anything," Merrick stammered, breaking the silence.

"I will ensure that they know our plans for the day," Karsten quietly assured him. "That is a simple enough thing for me to do."

"I haven't even seen them recently," Lucee said. "I guess they're done training me?"

"They're holed up in a room away from everyone," Sousa said. "One of the tower rooms, which feels appropriate. I mean, I guess if I had a dungeon that might be better, but a tower works. Apparently."

"Souz, do you think they're going to stay here after all is said and done? I feel like tomorrow is a turning point for House Mirabilis. Maybe I'm wrong, but it really feels as if The Maithe is the future of the Eleriannan." She looked at Daro and added, "I don't know what that means for the Gwyliannan, either. But Tiennan House seems more vital to everything than Mirabilis does. We don't add anything to the area where House Mirabilis sits. It feels like we go there to hide. Again, maybe I'm wrong?"

"You and Merrick breathed life into House Mirabilis. But I don't think you're incorrect here—you know how I felt about the static nature of the Eleriannan," Sousa answered, his brow furrowed.

"I see changes," Tully said, a wistful look on her face. "Everyone knows that I have been the loudest voice when it comes to bringing people to our House. I annoyed Sousa greatly with my sales patter." Sousa chuckled at that, and she smiled at his response, but her normal glow seemed subdued.

"But as I've learned to look beyond our walls, I've found so many things to want, and to fight for." She reached a delicate hand out to Daro, who took it in his own muscular one like she'd offered him a treasure. "I'm beginning to see that my real life and purpose lies outside of House Mirabilis. I don't think I am the only one either."

"I... I did not see that coming," Cullen said, "But maybe I should have. You have really grown, Tully—I suppose we all have. Mutantur omnia mutamur in illis, as we once said."

"Things do change," Merrick agreed. "I'd say that adaptability has become something of a skill for us all. And that most certainly wasn't the case when we first met last year." His tone was clearly self-deprecating.

"We're all good for each other," Lucee said. "Now we need to try and be good for those outside of our circle. I don't think we can do that while holed up in House Mirabilis. It's something I want to go over again once we're through tomorrow's trials."

The discussion turned to impressions of ArtPark and what they expected might happen on the next day, and Cullen leaned in close to Lucee and spoke so only she could hear.

"Do you plan to move us all from our House?"

She turned to face him, trying to gauge his feelings on the matter, but he was unreadable.

"I'm not planning on making anyone do anything, that's not how I roll. But I'm going to lay out some of the things I've been thinking about, and we will see how the House reacts to my ideas. What do you think?"

He hesitated, and covered his reaction by taking one of her hands in his, quietly tracing patterns on the back of her hand. Finally, he looked up, his face pained.

"I am afraid that there will be too much change, and I will find myself inside a life I no longer understand. But then I look at you, and my friends around me, and I feel like perhaps this is the best way to build a new life. One filled with things that I was too small-minded to even dream of having before I met you." He squeezed her hand lightly. "Change is painful for our kind, but was that not why Fallon wanted you to lead us? She saw your optimism and strong moral compass, and made sure we would have a way to follow that."

"I don't want to make a decision for everyone." Lucee screwed up her face like she'd eaten something distasteful. "People should be able to choose their own fates."

"Another difference between you and Fallon," Cullen told her. "She would have ordered, in a way that none would have even known they could object. Such was our way before we took in mortals and they shoved us into modern times." He winked at her, and she made a *pfft* sound back at him.

"That's what I don't want to do, shove. I want to convince with brilliant arguments and the promise of adventure because I think we've got a lot of that ahead of us."

"Well, you have convinced me at least." He kissed her nose lightly and she wrinkled her forehead.

"Not to belittle that accomplishment, but I think you were going to agree with me anyway. I have some advantages with you that I don't with everyone else in the house." She raised an eyebrow, and he rewarded her with a grin and another kiss on her nose.

"Could you two stop being cute and jump into this discussion, like people normally do when they're getting ready for a fight?" Sousa broke in.

"Sorry, didn't know there was a pre-fight protocol," Lucee said, rolling her eyes.

"We just want to try and make sure we're all on the same page." Merrick shrugged and added, "Not like anything's going to be predictable, not with this group."

"All we can control is what we do and how we react," Karsten said in a reasonable tone. "We can at least get a good idea of how we plan to start the day and work from there."

Everyone agreed with that assessment. Vali offered to sketch out the layout of the grounds, and after retrieving her backpack from the library, she used one of her sketchbooks to draw out the festival in as much detail as everyone could remember.

"Here's the stage area, and you can see the towers at each direction." She colored each one, using the proper colors, and wrote their correspondence next to each color in a key she put at the bottom.

"That's really cool," Emmaline said. "Earth, Air, Fire, Water."

"They have big art installations in each area that reflect those concepts too. It's pretty stunning," Vali told her. She went on to draw in the rows of vendor tents, and she noted where benches were, as much as she could remember.

"I'm expecting the Ffyn to be hiding in the trees—there's a lot of woody spaces off to stage left, too, a great place for us to regroup or cool off. In the middle of the Dell, there's no shade, so keep that in mind." Sousa pointed to an area and Vali swirled in some green to represent the treetops.

"What time does the band play? And when will you arrive at the site?" Daro asked.

"When I talked to the stage manager, she said that she wanted to keep us until later in the day—not the headliner, that's going to be Bright New Day. So probably around four-thirty? And we'll get there before the festival opens so we can unload and park the van close by," Sousa told him.

"We're opening for Bright New Day? That's going to look awfully good on our resume," Lucee crowed. "If we can manage to pull this whole thing off, our band calendar is going to be booked solid."

"Sure, as long as The Grimshaw don't eat us and we can do something against the Mealladhan, we'll have gigs coming out of our ears." Merrick's tone was skeptical, and Lucee frowned.

"Speaking of things I'd rather didn't eat me, I think I'm going to see if I can find The Ladies and catch them up on our plans. Souz, you said they're in one of the towers?"

"Left one, I think. It's a climb up those stairs, just warning you."

"Great, I was hoping to get some cardio in today before I chat with my three favorite creepy people."

He wasn't wrong about the climb. Lucee had never been higher than the third floor and by the time she'd made it to the last full floor, she was huffing and puffing. She eyed the door that led to the tower room and muttered, "There had better not be more stairs behind that."

There were. She grumbled a curse and decided that before she climbed them, she had better announce herself.

"Ladies? Hello? It's Lucee, I wanted to tell you about the plan for tomorrow!" she yelled up the stairs. She waited a moment, but heard no answer, not even a sound of movement. "Ladies? I need to talk to you!"

No sounds, and now Lucee was starting to get worried. It wasn't like Morgance, at least, to ignore her. What if they were in trouble? Were they even living in the tower at all? Maybe Sousa was wrong.

"Fine," she sighed. "I'm coming up, and if you're up there, you'd better remember that I called for you twice."

These stairs were steeper than the main staircase, dark and narrow. She wondered how they ever got furniture up into the tower rooms, with stairs like this. When she came around the bend and into the room itself, she was on edge.

The first thing she saw was a pile of cushions in the middle of the room. It was otherwise mostly bare. The light coming through the skylights cut into the ceiling revealed a dusty table with some bottles on it, and an old trunk with what looked like clothing spilling out.

Lucee's eyes darted all around the room, searching for anything she'd missed, anything to make sense of what she was seeing—or more properly, not seeing.

There was no one there, no one at all.

MUSIC: PINK TURNS BLUE
Walking On Both Sides

Lucee was in a panic. Where could The Ladies be? She ran to the other tower as fast as she could manage, hoping that maybe she'd checked the wrong room. This tower had a slightly different entrance—a room was attached and a ladder ascended directly into the tower room. She knew even before she climbed up to look that there was no way The Ladies would have chosen this room. It looked like it had sat empty for ages and the floor was thick with dust.

"What the hell, Morgance?" Lucee complained. She walked back out into the hallway and yelled, *"Ladies!* Dammit, come *out!"*

Nothing. Not the slightest sound. She knew she was wasting her time; they weren't in the building. Lucee flew down the spiral stairs so fast that she almost stumbled several times and had to catch herself.

She burst through the courtyard door and ran to where her friends were, yelling for Sousa. She found him by the firepit, roasting sausages on sticks over the fire.

"Whoa, what's happened?"

"The Ladies are gone." Lucee panted, trying to catch her breath.

"Oh? I thought for sure they were staying in the Tower." He didn't look too worried.

"Well, they were, but they're not there now—not anywhere on the top floor. And we need them! Why aren't you bothered by this?" She wanted to shake him until he was as freaked out as she was.

"It's like this," he explained in a patient tone. "The Ladies are going to do whatever they want. No one I know can control them, and they've been pretty unstable lately. So, although I didn't expect this, I didn't *not* expect it either. We'll be fine." He picked up one of the sticks and checked the sausage on it. "This is almost ready if you're hungry."

"Sousa! I'm too worried to eat! Morgandy was supposed to be our fail-safe! What do we do now?"

Before he could answer, Karsten spoke up. "I believe that they will be there tomorrow. They have sacrificed too much already not to come."

"How do you know?" Lucee whirled around to face Karsten. "They just disappeared!"

"I trust them to not abandon the cause, or you. Have faith in your people, Lucee." They pushed back a few tendrils of snake-hair and nodded encouragingly at Lucee.

"Basic communication would make it a lot damn easier," Lucee complained.

"Look, just eat this, drink a beer, and try not to worry so much," Sousa told her and handed her the stick and a mug of Sheridan's ale. "That's all we can do at this point because whatever's going to happen is what'll happen."

"'It is not in the stars to hold our destiny but in ourselves,'" Cullen quoted, adding, "I am not disagreeing with you about worrying, but I do think being prepared for every contingent is a good way to keep those worries at bay."

"Ah, but there's no way to be prepared for everything, is there?" Sousa took a bite of sausage and waved his stick around to punctuate what he was saying. "I think we've done all we can and anything else is just winding us up without purpose. But what do I know?"

"Ugh. You know what? I need to take a walk. Maybe that'll calm me down."

Lucee stalked off, but not before she heard Sousa suggest to Cullen to let her go off on her own for a bit.

"Sometimes I hate that you know me that well," she grouched to herself as she stomped up the stairs and through the stone entrance that led into The Maithe. She blew off some steam by taking a lap around the building, and when she got to the ballroom, she found Merrick sitting on the edge of the small stage. He was leaning back, kicking his feet into the air like a little kid, and Lucee sighed privately as she walked over and sat down next to him.

"I think Souz should put more mirror balls up. What do you think?" he asked her, his focus on the large one that hung above the open ballroom floor.

"Might clash with the amazing chandeliers, but what do I know about setting up ballroom spaces in giant old buildings, right?" She let herself fall back so that she was on her back, looking up at the ceiling. "I think part of the magnificence of this room is its simplicity. There's a lot to be said for being simple."

"Is that really what you want from life? Because it seems to me that you'd get bored if that was the case. Even though complex also means sometimes that things are challenging in ugly ways."

"My friend, the philosopher and champion of the Fae, always telling me what I don't want to hear." She knew her voice was sharper than she meant it to be, but she didn't seem capable of stopping herself.

"Okay, but hear me out. Maybe you *need* to hear what I'm saying. Look, you haven't been your fun-loving self lately, and yeah, things have been tough for a while, but get this. You can lean on us, you know. You aren't doing this alone."

"But guess who bears the responsibility when things go wrong? The buck stops here, boyo." She sat up abruptly, frowning. "I'm scared out of my mind, Merrick."

"Hey." His voice was soft, comforting. He sat up as well so he could look her in the eyes. "I'm scared too. Y'know what scares me the most? Having to possibly fight Camlin again. I barely beat him the last time, and that was only with help. And now? Now I know him, and here's the worst part—I like him. And I know that if I have to fight him, it's not really him in charge. So, I'll have to hurt a guy who doesn't deserve it. Hurt or worse..." He trailed off, and Lucee closed her eyes, feeling sick. She hadn't thought about that aspect, at least not much.

"I'm sorry. I've been so selfish; I wasn't even thinking about how this was affecting you. I mean, it's easy to worry about Emmaline; she's in the direct line of getting her heart broken. But you're actually in harm's way—physically and mentally—and I didn't even consider that. I'm an ass."

"No, no, no! You're the furthest thing from an ass. You have more to protect than just me. In fact, it's kinda my job to be the one at risk, or at least that's how it's become." He shrugged, and it surprised Lucee how honest that gesture felt.

"You like it. You like being responsible and protecting people."

"I guess I do! Is that weird? It feels more respectable than just wanting to play music for a crowd. But lucky me, I get to do both. And so do you. We get to do it together, which is even better." He leaned over and hugged her, to her surprise.

"Hey, you never hug me first. You feeling okay?" she joked as she hugged back as tightly as she could manage.

"It's not that I never hug first, it's that you never give me a chance to hug first," he replied, grinning as he let her go. "You are a world-class hugger, that's your thing. I'm actually amazed that I beat you to it this time."

She pretended to punch him, and he overacted a dramatic flinch.

"And you are the cheesiest, that's your thing," she teased.

"Guilty as charged! Now are you feeling up to rejoining everyone, or do you need more time alone?"

"I want more time alone, but I think I should stifle that urge and come back to the courtyard. Enough moping on my part."

"That's a good thing because someone's got to stop Souz from drinking *all* the beer."

When they rejoined the others, everyone acted like wandering off was normal, for which Lucee was grateful. Even Cullen didn't say anything. He just hugged her and handed her a beverage. She took a sip and discovered cool water with lemon and strawberries. "Tomorrow is an early day. I thought you might want to be clear-headed," he whispered in her ear.

She nodded and squeezed his hand, glad that he thought about details like that for her.

"What did I miss? Anything interesting?"

"The Houses are gathering. Everyone seems excited." He gestured to the field and the trees. Lucee saw a few more firepits set up in the field with the shadows of beings gathered around them.

"It's a regular campground out there," she said. "I guess it was a good thing the Gate is inside this space rather than in the House itself, or things would be getting crowded fast."

"Like this place is not big enough to hold all of our Houses and more!" Cullen laughed.

"You don't have to tell me. Don't forget that I climbed to the top of The Maithe today. We need to talk to Souz about getting a dang elevator up in there!"

Lucee spent the rest of the evening moving from group to group, socializing and reconnecting with the folks she hadn't seen recently. She didn't recognize some of the Gwyliannan, so she pulled Daro over, with Tully in tow, to introduce her to his people.

"Those two have become close," Cullen quietly observed.

"I like it," Lucee said. "They seem to balance each other well. Look how much Daro smiles now!"

It was true. Daro was generally solemn and reserved, but with Tully around him, he was often downright cheery. And Lucee noticed that effect spreading to the other Gwyliannan, who were generally quite nice but not the type to make a joke or cultivate a light mood.

Lucee nudged Cullen and murmured, "Look, I see some who like it less than we do."

He looked in the direction she indicated and saw a group of the creepy-looking Stickmen called ArDonnath, lurking near the edge of the woods. They glowered darkly and when Daro laughed, they came together, muttering.

"Well, that is unnerving," Cullen groaned quietly. "I suppose this means that they disapprove of the friendship between our courts as well."

"You know they just hate fun," Lucee said, trying to lighten the mood. "I'm sure he's aware of the situation, but we might want to mention it later just in case. No one wants a bunch of angry shrubbery in their court."

"That was hilarious, my love, but you had best keep those jokes quiet," Cullen replied, trying to stifle his laughter.

She heard some music start up, drifting across the field from a gathering nearer to the forest's edge. A violin sang and cried out, and an untamed sounding percussion gathered underneath those sobbing notes. Lucee felt the tune surge through her, leaving her with an inexplicable longing for something unknown, and her heart started to pound. She noticed that she was clutching Cullen's hand tightly and leaning against him. They had stopped to listen without realizing it.

"Wow, I can feel that in my soul," she murmured. Cullen pulled her toward the small gathering and she followed, eager to see the musicians and to be closer to the music.

They were congregated in a loose circle around the fire, which glowed with an eerie green-and-gold light. Lucee stumbled to a halt when she realized that she only recognized one of the beings in this circle—the grand, primeval form of The Lady of The City. She had a great, round drum in one hand, holding it at shoulder height as she beat the rhythm in a pattern that was slowly growing in complexity. Bits of steel and glass reflected the light of the fire as she played.

Four other beings were with The Lady of The City, and each was as remarkable as she was. The woman playing the violin was tall, thin, and looked as if she could have been a progenitor of the beautiful Ffyn. Her skin was dark, and every muscle and line reminded Lucee of nothing more than the grain of a fine wood. She swayed gracefully as she played. Long hair—mossy green and brown with leaves caught here and there in the tresses—waved back and forth with each movement. Her eyes were closed as she played, but Lucee knew that if she opened them, they would be the same color as a pine forest.

To her left was a being with a wooden flute, and Lucee couldn't make out even one of their distinguishing features. Everything about them was in motion. Filmy grey-and-blue robes seemed to constantly shift. Silver hair floated in silken waves where it escaped the hood that obscured the being's face. The flute seemed to produce the most ethereal notes, nothing like what Lucee expected to hear from it. She felt a shiver down her back when the being played a scintillating trill.

The other two moved as one, and they were the liveliest beings in the circle. They were red haired with golden-brown skin, and they seemed to shift from male to female and back again as Lucee watched. They danced together in a pattern that brought them close, then spun them away from each other in entwined circles and arcs. They each held gnarled wooden staffs covered with bells and ribbons at the top, which they shook in time to the music. Occasionally they brought them together with a clash of sound.

"Do—do you know who they are?" Lucee whispered to Cullen. She couldn't take her eyes off the majestic, resplendent beings.

"I have never seen such as their like before," he answered, in a hushed, respectful tone. "They are no type of Fae I have encountered. They are old, and powerful in ways that are frightening." He was holding Lucee's hand as tightly as she was holding his.

"No reason to be afraid tonight, my children," The Lady of the City called out, her voice rough and deep, a strange counterpoint to her drumming. "These friends have come to watch over you and your efforts tomorrow."

"Oh!" Lucee exclaimed, relief washing over her. "You're kind to lend your help!"

The sound of laughter, light and low tones all jumbled together like many voices, washed over her, and she reeled in confusion.

"Ah, you have misunderstood." The Lady of the City rose, her small stature becoming more imposing as she spoke. "Watching is not the same as aiding." Her drumming never stopped and the cadence of her words matched the beat so that each word was punctuated by a thump on the drum.

"You will...watch but not help? Please, I'm only a small being. Help me understand." Lucee tried to keep a note of panic out of her words, but she was sure she was failing.

The Lady threw back her head and laughed. "Ah child, no need to remind us how small you are. You are speaking to those most elemental and ancient! But it is for those reasons that they do not offer to interfere." She winked, and the wrinkles in her face moved like layers of earth and stone shifting past each other. "They are interested in what will take place and how that will change the energies around me and my land. What happens there may have greater consequences across many realms."

"You cannot give us support at all?" Lucee's face fell, and she felt Cullen drop her hand and move to stand behind her, his hands on her shoulders in a comforting stance. Met with silence, she took a moment to steel herself and push away her disappointment before addressing the strange beings.

"I understand, I think. This is a job for Mortals and Fae to accomplish. It's our burden. And you are hoping that we will do well, but you have to watch us do our best and hope that it's enough."

"Ah, now she begins to see clearly," The Lady of the City rumbled, pleased.

"So, may I ask a question and request an answer, if that's possible?" Lucee didn't wait for permission, instead blurting out her question before someone told her no. "If I were to ask for you to contain the effects of our fight tomorrow so that they were only between those who chose to step into the battle, would that be considered interference?"

The music came to a sudden stop, and all five of the beings in the circle around the green fire turned towards Lucee.

The Lady of the City burst into a loud cackle. "You must admit, she is clever!"

Cullen made a muffled noise that could have been a laugh or a suppressed cough. His hands tightened slightly on Lucee's shoulders, and she decided it must have been a laugh at her audacity.

The uncanny beings came together in a huddle, discussing among themselves, though Lucee couldn't hear any words being exchanged. Finally, they broke apart and looked to The Lady of The City, who nodded once, then spoke to Lucee and Cullen.

"You intrigue them. You are courageous and foolhardy at once, which they attribute to your Mortal side. But you also appealed to them for the safety of others, not in regards to your own success—or your own safety, for that matter. This was pleasing to them."

She moved toward Lucee, and for once Lucee didn't find her tilting, shifting textures and colors as disorienting to watch. When The Lady stood before her, Lucee fell to one knee so that she wouldn't tower over the powerful being.

"You are polite at the times that matter and brash when needed. Those are commendable traits, Lucee Fearney. Here is what you will do tomorrow. Call our friends here, each under their sign, before the sun is high in the sky. All you need do is acknowledge them and they will do the rest." She leaned forward, her eyes twinkling. "And if you were to acknowledge me as well, you would bring great honor to your Grandmother."

Lucee bowed her head, both out of respect and because having The Lady of the City so close to her made her nervous. "I can do that, Grandmother."

"Ah, wise child! Clever girl! You have my blessings for tomorrow. Now leave us and get some sleep!"

There was a flash of light and a gut-wrenching feeling, and then Lucee and Cullen found themselves standing alone at the far end of the field near the pathway to the entrance of The Maithe.

"Well, *that* was interesting," Cullen spit out, visibly thrown off by what had just happened. "I have to say that I am glad they decided I was not worth their attention because I am quite unnerved."

"I feel like… Maybe I should keep this interaction to myself for a while? Though telling Vali might be smart as she's connected with one of those beings." She grabbed Cullen's hand and pulled him toward the exit. "I guess since we were sent to bed by forces as old as time. We should probably obey."

They were silent until they reached their room.

"I have to admit," Lucee said, once they were settled in the bed, "this interaction has upped the ante for what freaks me out now. It used to be that I was always in awe and a little afraid of many of the Eleriannan and Gwyliannan. And of course, I'm scared of The Grimshaw. But those folks, tonight? They're so…so…ugh, I don't even know what to call them. Not god-like because they're so different from that kind of energy."

"Elemental. That is the word you are looking for." Cullen's voice was flat, like he'd been stunned into an emotionless state.

"I suppose it is, but are you okay? You seem a little broken." Lucee raised up a little, trying to see his face in the darkness of their room.

"I feel a bit like…like perhaps what an agnostic might feel like if they were put face to face with a god. I have always known that such beings existed but only as an abstract concept. Not as a concrete reality standing in front of me whilst my beloved argues them into giving a damn about us."

"You were—were you afraid?" Lucee couldn't fathom that idea.

"I was shocked, afraid, and impressed by you all at once. How is it that nothing throws you for long, Lucee?" His voice trembled a little, and she didn't understand why. "From the day we met, nothing has fazed you in the slightest for any amount of time, including being attacked by ArDonnath and almost dying."

"And then being turned into a Mortal-Fae mishmash. I know, it should freak me out more than it does. I dunno, Cullen, I just roll with things because the alternatives don't make any sense to me. No matter what weirdness the world throws at me, be it magic or controlling parents or Stickmen trying to kill me, I'm still me and I'll figure it out or die trying."

"Sooooo..." He pulled her down into the circle of his arms and kissed her on the top of her head. "Not to be the voice of logic on such an evening such as this, but if you know this so well, then tell me why you are so resistant to believing in yourself?"

"You know what? I'm really tired. Goodnight, Mr. Foxy-fox."

"I will take that as a concession that you shall consider my words, then."

"*Fine*, fine. I'll consider your words. Now kiss me or I'm going to sleep."

MUSIC: RHEA'S OBSESSION
Between Earth and Sky

The morning was surprisingly uneventful with absolutely no hiccups at all. The van was loaded up and ready to go, and everyone began to gather in the ballroom.

Lucee noticed that Sousa was wearing the shirt that Tully had made him. It was a sleeveless tunic sewn from some loosely woven, reddish-brown material with unfinished-looking edges. He'd thrown it over some jeans with huge holes in the knees and his combat boots.

"I'm shocked he's not in BDU shorts," Lucee commented to Vali. "I didn't even know he had jeans."

"Well, that's because he didn't until recently. I got those from a thrift store and he immediately busted the knees out of them trying to show me some trick on one of those mopeds he's still got in the practice space. He's lucky that's all he busted." Vali laughed.

"What a dingdong," Lucee agreed. "Good thing he's got you to keep him mostly together now."

"I don't know if even I can do that." Vali winked at her.

"Oh hey, look at Merrick and Aisling! Always gotta be the best-looking couple around, jeez."

Aisling had another of Tully's creations on—a gauzy summer dress that matched her black-and-lavender hair perfectly—and she had captured all that hair into a loose, fat braid down her back. Tiny jewels shone here and there amidst her locks. Merrick was in his customary black, but instead of a T-shirt topping his black jeans, he wore a shirt that Tully had made for him. It seemed to be made from the same material as Sousa's shirt, but his colors were black with hints of dark blue and Merrick's shirt had short sleeves, unlike Sousa's. Lucee could see the tattoo on his wrist that the Eleriannan had given him when he'd pledged himself to their court. The circlet of oak leaves stood out against his pale skin.

"Hey Lucee, Vali. Are you ready for today?" Merrick called from the entryway to the ballroom.

"I just wanna play music," Lucee said. "And eat a dang funnel cake since *someone* didn't bring me one yesterday." That got a laugh from her friends, who were all too familiar with her love for sweet, bready food.

"You and I both know they're best when you eat them fresh while you spill powdered sugar all over your nice clothes and Tully watches you and cries about it," Merrick teased her.

She stuck out her tongue at him, which to her seemed like a reasonable response, and got another laugh from everyone.

"I wouldn't dare get powdered sugar on this ensemble," she declared, and spun around to show it off.

Tully had nailed it with Lucee's outfit. She'd repurposed a ballerina tutu into a sundress for Lucee, and it suited her well. The forest-green tulle of the skirt was soft so it wouldn't feel scratchy against her guitar. The base of the dress was a watercolor swirl of lighter green and browned purple on satin with small brown sequins at the neck and here and there on the dress. She glittered when she moved but not enough to hurt anyone's eyes in the sun.

Lucee had paired it with green fence-style fishnets and her combat boots, and she'd taken her green-and-black braids and pulled them back into a small ponytail. One or two had escaped and hung down around her face artfully.

"You are a sight to see," Cullen told her and took her hand to kiss it.

"Ah, you're going to make me blush," she said.

"That is always my goal."

Cullen, of course, always looked well put together, but this day he had chosen to play himself down a notch. Lucee wasn't sure if that was so that he could stay watchful in the background or so that he could give the spotlight to her. It didn't matter. He was as handsome as ever. He had on a simple outfit of brown trousers and a brown-green waistcoat over a white dress shirt. He'd left the top buttons undone and rolled his sleeves up. A few sprigs of lavender and sage tucked in with his pocket square made Lucee smile.

"Everyone else will be following, I believe—have you seen Emmaline today? She can ride in with us, if she doesn't mind being squished in," Sousa asked the group.

"Here I am," Emmaline spoke up from the entrance. "Karsten is giving me a ride on their motorcycle. I've never been on one before and it sounds like so much fun!"

She was wearing a short, simple black gauze sundress with patch pockets that had mauve roses embroidered on them, over leggings and boots. She spun around to show it off. "You don't think it'll be a problem on the motorcycle, do you? I don't want to get caught in the wheels!"

"Tuck it under you when you sit. And hold tight to Karsten," Tully advised in a tone that suggested that she had some recent experience in similar situations.

"So that covers most of us. I'm assuming that you'll ride with the Gwyliannan, Tully?" Sousa asked, and Tully nodded a blushing agreement. "That's going to be a sight to see, all of Tiennan House rolling up on their motorcycles!"

The group split up with plans to regroup at the Dell. Sousa was able to drive down to the stage area for unloading, then he moved the van up to the closest parking area for entertainment. With Vali helping, they quickly got everything up on the stage, and since they were so early, they got the invite to do a sound check right then, which did a lot to soothe Lucee's nerves.

"We sound great!" she shouted to Merrick, and Sousa yelled in agreement.

"You do, and you've got a simple setup, which makes my life easier," their sound person said. "I'm Meesh. If you need anything at all, like more vox in the monitors, just tell me. Meesh is short for Michelle, but no one calls me that if they want me to like them." She grinned in a way that said that she was joking, but they'd better not call her Michelle. "The stage manager is Bo, and if you want to make her happy, be here early for your set. You go on at four-thirty *sharp*. Be here before that and we'll make you look and sound amazing. Thanks for being here before opening. Your brownie points are accumulating!"

She waved them off, and Cullen whispered to Lucee, "Brownie points?"

"Not like your Brownies, I don't even know how that would work! She means like 'good will,' I guess you could say. She's pleased with us." She paused to think about it a minute, then added, "It's not an actual physical thing, but if you gather enough good will, you definitely can cash it in. Like in this case, it builds our reputation as being a great band to book because we're prompt and easy to work with."

"And wait until they have seen the lighting and effects you will be providing," Cullen said smugly.

"We'll probably confuse the heck out of them," Lucee agreed.

Merrick thought that staying together in a loose group was to their advantage. Lucee remembered what The Lady of The City had told her and tapped Cullen on the shoulder to get his attention.

"I need to stop at each of the towers and call to the—the *beings*—we met last night. I don't think I should mention this to the others, you know? Like, I get the distinct feeling that the interaction was meant just for me and you."

"Just you, I think. I happened to be there, but I most certainly was not a part of that exchange. I could have been a sack of potatoes, for all the attention they paid me." Cullen snorted. "I will come stand with you as you connect with each one, though. Do you understand who to honor at each tower?"

"I believe so, using what Vali drew out on her map as a guide. I know there's supposed to be a proper order if one is casting a circle, but I don't know it. Should I start here?"

"With the Red Tower of the South? No, you should go to the North to begin. Perhaps you *should* mention a version of what you are doing? At least to Merrick and our inner circle."

When she explained to Merrick that she wanted to hail the beings of the four directions, he nodded as if she'd said the most sensible thing in her life.

"Sure, that seems like a great ritual to start off the day! And honoring The Lady of The City at the end makes me feel dumb for not thinking of that myself. Let's do it!" He strode off to the Green Tower. As they drew closer, Lucee could see leaves and branches on it, all made of fabric and wire, moving in the gentle breeze.

As she moved to the front of the group and stood before the tower, she realized that she had no idea what to say. She put her hands on the tower and closed her eyes for a moment, imagining in her mind the being that had played the violin, her woodsy skin and wild hair. She took a deep breath, and could smell pine and fallen leaves.

"Spirit of Earth, I see you, I stand with you. I honor you here. Be with us today, if you will. We play in your name today." Just when she thought that could never be good enough, and she certainly had messed it up, she heard the sobbing wail of a violin and the leaves of nearby trees fluttered madly.

She breathed a deep sigh of relief and she felt Cullen's hand on her shoulder, confirming that she'd done well. From behind her, Lucee heard Vali make a small gasp.

"I felt that," Vali explained. "Like it moved right through me!"

Lucee gestured her up to the front of the group with her. When they came to the Yellow Tower, which was covered in streamers and banners, she motioned for Vali to stay nearby.

"Spirit of Air, I see you, I stand with you. I honor you here. Flow around us today, if you please? We will play in your name today." Lucee thought of the one with the flute, their robes and hair shifting all about them as they played and those same ethereal notes floated above, crystalline and evocative.

Cries of delight came from the crowd, and Lucee realized that it wasn't just her Eleriannan, or even all Fae at this point. Mortals—strangers—were mixed through the group. They all seemed enchanted, willing to believe. Maybe it was the general ambience of ArtPark, with the kinetic sculptures scattered around like magnificent, otherworldly beasts roaming the grounds. Or perhaps it was the magic carnival-like atmosphere starting to build as festival-goers and performers streamed in. Whatever the reason, she could feel the energy building, and she decided that she was going to embrace it.

"Follow me to Fire!" she cried out, and there was an answering a shout from those gathered.

Lucee found herself skipping, the tulle skirt of her dress bouncing up as she led everyone to the Red Tower. The fabricated flames attached to the structure shimmied, and their material crackled in the breezes, just like a real fire would. She glanced to her right and saw that Tully and Daro were there. Daro was a solemn, regal figure as usual, but Tully was glowing and exuberant, swirling her skirts and laughing joyfully. Lucee couldn't tell by Daro's face, but she suspected that he was loving every minute of it.

Cullen was on her left, his enjoyment much more evident in his expression. She felt a rush of affection for him, and a feeling of being so incredibly lucky. She tucked that feeling aside for a moment as they stopped before the Red Tower, and she stepped up to speak to the Elements, remembering those red haired twins at the campfire with their boundless energy and dancing patterns.

"Spirit of Fire! I see you. I stand with you. I honor you here. We welcome your strength, your energy! We will play in your name today."

The cheering was loud, and Lucee was a little in awe. This was much more than she'd expected! But now she looked toward the Blue Tower, and she realized that a water spirit hadn't been in attendance at their meeting the night before.

She glanced at Cullen, unsure. Bless him, he knew what she was thinking because he gestured that she should go ahead.

"Call on them all, my love!" he shouted over the din of the people. "Cast your circle!"

She walked up to the last tower, the station of Water, and smiled at how the artists had made it so that the bottom of the tower seemed to flow out over the ground beyond it. They had made raindrops from glittering crystals that hung on gossamer strings. They were attached to protrusions that came from the corners of the towers. When Lucee stood in front of it, she realized that they'd rigged it with a misting system. It gently sprayed her with droplets of water. She closed her eyes and let the feeling take her over for a moment before she spoke.

"Spirit of Water, hello! I see you and stand with you. I honor you here. You bring us life and cleanse us when we need it, and we welcome it. We will play in your name today."

A burst of mist sprayed from the tower, and it swirled out in a moist cloud that enveloped the crowd. They cheered and raised their hands as one.

"They think it part of the entertainment!" Cullen whispered to Lucee.

"I hope that means that the Elementals were pleased," she whispered back. She raised her voice to announce, "Now to the center!"

In the center of the field, the crowd surrounded her, and she looked at all the faces—Fae and Mortal, friends and strangers. She felt the same sort of feeling she got when she was up on stage playing with The Drawback. There was a connection with the audience that said they were all undeniably, miraculously linked together. She stood in that energy, feeling it gather within her. Then she spoke.

"Grandmother! Lady of The City, the embodiment of where we now stand, where we live and love. We see you! We are here to honor you today, we who are both a part of who you are, and yet so often unaware of how we fail to respect and care for you. Not today! Today we will play in your name. Today, we recognize you all around us."

She looked around the circle, meeting the eyes of as many who stood there as she could.

"Take care of our Grandmother today and from now on, my friends. Be careful how you tread upon her. And *throw your trash away.*" She gave the crowd a big grin to soften her words a little. "Go, have fun! And come to the South Stage by the Red Tower at four-thirty to see The Drawback play!"

That got her a big laugh from the crowd. They cheered and then slowly broke up, wandering off to look at the vendors, art, and other performers. Lucee was left with her friends surrounding her, all looking a little stunned at what had just happened.

"Lucee, that was amazing," Vali told her. "Did you—were you told to do this? I'm getting this feeling of deep satisfaction through my connection to The Lady of The City, but, of course, she won't tell me anything outright.

She claims that would be too easy." Vali rolled her eyes in response to how ridiculous she thought that idea was.

"We—Cullen and I—had a chance meeting with Grandmother and some of her, um, friends," Lucee explained. "It was suggested that we pay our dues today since we'll be watched for what we do here. And I asked them to help protect the innocent attendees if they would. I mean, no pressure or anything, right?"

"Oh wow. You met other beings like The Lady of The City? Really?" Vali's eyes were huge.

"Not like her. I mean, they were obviously wild and powerful but not tied to a place like she is. They were—"

"Elemental beings," Cullen broke in. "Which is why Lucee was at each tower, addressing them. They were beautiful and impressive and honestly, terrifying. They made me feel quite insignificant."

"That makes sense," Merrick said. "My understanding from the occult books I've read is that elemental beings really don't care much either way about puny mortals. I guess Fae don't give them much pause either, though you'd think otherwise."

"For a creature that far removed from our worries and desires, I suppose we are all puny," Karsten mused. "But are we to do anything else to appease them? And is there anything else we should know?" They wiped a bead of sweat from their forehead, and Lucee realized that it must now be noon or just after.

"First, let us get out of the sun!" She smiled and pointed to a shady spot under the trees, with a softly sloping hill of grass. "We can spread blankets there and make a base camp if we like."

As they did just that, Lucee explained how she and Cullen had stumbled upon the Elementals and The Lady of The City and how they had not promised help to the Fae.

"Brave of you to appeal to them for anything at all," Daro mused. "I would wager that they are not the type to entertain foolishness."

"Well, they did brand me 'brave and foolhardy,' which, I mean, that's fair. At least the foolhardy part, if nothing else," Lucee joked.

As the time passed pleasantly, other groups of people joined their encampment in the shade. Many had brought their own food, including the Fae. Of course, none could match the sheer opulence and variety of what had come with the Fae contingent.

Despite the fabulous repast, Lucee was thrilled when Cullen offered her a hot funnel cake from one of the vendors.

"Foxy, you are my hero!"

"I should hope so! I had a mighty struggle to keep that powdered sugar off of my waistcoat—look, Lucee, across the way! I think I see the Ffyn?"

She looked where he was pointing and was delighted to see her friends in their new leafy guises, sweeping and swaying through the crowd, who gave them a wide berth but seemed utterly enchanted by them.

"I wonder how the mortals are explaining it to themselves," Vali said as she watched the Ffyn circulate through the fair.

"Poorly." Sousa snorted. "They'll marvel at the artistry and come up with a bunch of implausible explanations. It'll be legendary."

"Um. But check *that* out," Merrick said, his voice tense, as he pointed down the field toward the north.

It looked like a cluster of people walking with branches held high above their heads. But as Lucee focused on them, it became clear that they weren't human people, not at all. They were ArDonnath—or as Merrick had dubbed them, the Stickmen. They moved in an ungainly fashion, their stick-like limbs jutting out at uncomfortable angles. They looked like beings made from a collection of small trees damaged by wind and weather. Each wielded a branch, like a bludgeon, above their head as they lurched through the crowds.

Although to Lucee, there was a palpable feeling of malice coming from them, the festival-goers seemed excited to see them. It was obvious that they assumed their appearance to be part of the entertainment.

"Oh shit," Sousa growled. "I don't know what's going to happen, but this cannot be good."

"What do we do? Do we go fight now?" Lucee felt a sickening panic rise in her. This wasn't how she envisioned any of the day's possibilities turning out.

Before anyone could answer, there was a collective cheer from the grassy center of the Dell. A circle had formed around the two groups of beings, who were at opposite ends of the circle in a standoff. Lucee saw the Ffyn wave their branches around in a way that probably seemed charming to the audience, but she knew it was quite a menacing gesture aimed at the ArDonnath.

Three things happened next in quick succession.

First, a loud growling noise rose up from the Dell and echoed. It drowned out the crowd, and then it faded away and left an eerie silence behind.

Secondly, a pulse of energy surged from the center of the circle outwards. It pushed the mortals away from the ArDonnath and Ffyn. The pulse kept going, moving past the throngs of festival-goers and performers, the vendor tents, and the soundstage. When it blew by Lucee, she felt a calming, protective force move through her. It seemed to stop at the borders of the park.

And finally, there was a strange sensation, like a wrenching in the gut. Lucee realized that everyone seemed to be standing still—or at least the mortals who had just come out to enjoy a weekend festival seemed frozen in place.

"What just happened?" Vali squeaked out, and Lucee could hear Sousa cursing behind her. She realized that she could move just fine.

"Was it The Grimshaw?" Merrick asked in a panicked voice.

"I don't think so... Look there," Lucee said, pointing to the field.

The towers in each corner of the Dell were glowing with an otherworldly light.

MUSIC: CRYING VESSEL
The Abyss

T he Elemental beings really are here." Merrick's voice had a catch in it. "We need to see if any of the other Grimshaw are around—"

A great clashing sound drowned him out as the Ffyn and ArDonnath crashed together in battle.

"Oak and ash! They will tear each other apart!" Cullen gripped Lucee's shoulder protectively as they both watched the tree-beings and the Stickmen slash and rip at each other.

Lucee gasped in horror as two ArDonnath jumped at one of the Ffyn. One tried to encircle the Ffyn's waving branch-like limbs as the other slashed at its trunk. The ArDonnath were almost successful until another Ffyn seemed to expand in width and encompass the slashing Stickman with its leafy canopy. There was a shriek, and branches flew everywhere. They were not the branches of the Ffyn.

Lucee felt like retching when she saw that, and even more so when the captive Ffyn managed to break free, its leaves slashing the ArDonnath all over its body. A sap-like liquid seeped from the cuts on the Stickman, soaking into the ground where the Ffyn threw its mangled form.

"This isn't right," she managed to get out before a loud shout rang across the field, followed by the thundering sound of booted feet rushing in.

"Arswyd!" Cullen hissed, and Lucee heard Sousa's shout of anger echoed by Merrick and Daro.

There were at least twenty of them, all terrifyingly intimidating. Lucee recognized the two who had tried to push her and Cullen around in Hampden while they'd been on their date. The others were just as ugly and brutish with their huge ungainly bodies and toothy sneers.

Eleriannan and Gwyliannan stepped forward from locations all over the Dell, where they had been entertaining mortals or just enjoying the day while they added a little magic to it with their beauty and oddness. Watching them walk towards the fracas in the middle of the field was like watching them step away from a greyed background into a foreground filled with colors. Everything came into extreme focus as they approached the circle of Ffyn and ArDonnath.

"We need to get down there!" Merrick cried out, and in the blink of an eye, he'd morphed from human form into that of a large raven and soared off.

"Merrick, wait!" Lucee cried out, but it was too late. With a roar, most of the Fae followed suit, running down to the center of the Dell.

Lucee looked around her in a panic and realized that Vali and Emmaline were still there. Tully was hiding behind a tree a bit further back. A small noise at her left startled her until she realized it was Quillan, appearing from who knows where.

"My lady, will you fight?" He pulled a gleaming sword from thin air.

Lucee knew that sword. It was the same one that Fallon had given her during their last battle with The Grimshaw, and she had used it to kill ArDonnath. She still had nightmares about that day, and seeing the sword now brought them all back in vivid detail.

"Will you hold that for me for now, my friend? I'm not quite ready," she told Quillan, hoping that her expression wasn't showing the nausea and fear she was feeling.

He nodded, a solemn but trusting look on his face.

Of course, she thought. *He thinks I can't fail. Oh please, don't let today be the day I prove him wrong.* "Can you help Tully get to somewhere safe? Maybe see if there are others who aren't fighting, so they can be in a group together?"

Again, he nodded, and Tully started to protest, but Lucee held up a hand.

"Look, I've already watched a bunch of my gentlest friends become fighters today. Can you please keep yourself out of this so that my heart has something beautiful and untouched to fight for? Please do it. For me." She looked imploringly at Tully, who nodded and indicated to Quillan that he should lead her away.

"Be safe," Tully whispered to her friends as she and Quillan left, carefully sticking to the shade of the trees to keep attention away from themselves.

Lucee turned to Vali and Emmaline, and she did her best to project calm and assurance.

"Look, I think that something weird is going on here. It's not like Merrick or Souz to take off like that without thinking. They're both clever guys. Can you even see them out there?" She didn't even want to mention Cullen, or she knew she'd break down.

Vali squinted as she tried to make sense of the fracas in the field. Lucee realized that, unlike last time, it seemed more like a brawl than a battle—she couldn't see many actual weapons. At least, she couldn't see any yet.

"I can't —wait! There's Sousa, back to back with... Daro? Wow. That looks intense. And I see Merrick, and he's... he's... oh, Lucee. We need to do something, now." Vali sounded like she wanted to cry.

"Point him out," Lucee insisted and followed where Vali was pointing until she focused in on Merrick. And then she saw why Vali was so upset.

He was doing his best to get to a cluster of Arswyd, who were concentrating on pushing around the one they'd surrounded. A flash of blond hair in the midst of the circle told her all she needed to know.

"Cullen!"

She started to bolt forward, but strong hands caught her and pulled her down to the ground. She tried to break free, screaming in frustration and anger, until a slap across her face made her stop in shock, and she looked up into the deep algae-colored eyes of Morgance.

"Lucee Fearney, heed me now! That is not your path. Let the Blackbird save your lover. You have a different destiny."

The tiny creature and her sisters held Lucee down until she finally relaxed in their grip, and then they stepped back and allowed her to sit up.

"Enough of this. You must focus. The Mealladhan affects us all now, and you can see the results." Morgance gestured to the field, where they could see bodies being thrown about and hear the shouts of anger and of pain.

"How do I save them? What should I do?"

"We must work together, all of us," Ula said, gesturing for Vali and Emmaline to come closer. "We all have our parts to play now."

"Who has seen Camlin?" Morgance asked.

"No need to see him, I know where he is," Morgandy spoke up, her voice sounding far away. Everyone turned to stare at her, and Lucee saw Morgance's hands tighten into fists.

"What have you done?" Morgance hissed at her sister.

It struck Lucee at that moment that Morgance wasn't angry with

Morgandy. She was scared for her. A sinking feeling started in Lucee's guts. This was not going to be good news; she just knew it.

"You know. I am still connected with him, enough to trace him down. Enough to start this fight with the Mealladhan," Morgandy said in a matter-of-fact tone. "It is done, and we must do what needs be done."

She pointed at Vali and addressed her. "You must stay by me so we may finish what we started. And the other one—where has she gone?"

"What?" Lucee jumped up, realizing that Emmaline was nowhere to be seen. "Emmaline!" she shouted, then muttered, "Great, just fucking great."

"She ran off?" Vali was incredulous. "Now? She knows how much danger she's in!"

"Does she want to help or to hinder? That is the question I have," Morgance growled. "Has her connection to Camlin strengthened her or left her weak?"

"I have no reason to doubt Emmaline," Vali said. "But we don't have the time to debate now. We need to put a stop to this!"

Lucee, trying to see where Cullen had gone in the midst of the melee, nodded absently.

"I'm going to do that, now. I want you to find Camlin and do what needs to be done. I'll give you a distraction."

Before anyone could stop her, she jumped up and took off toward the mass of fighting Fae.

"Dammit, Lucee!" Vali yelled out, but it was too late. She was already halfway to the fight. Vali turned to The Ladies, exasperated, and said, "Fine, let's go do this and hope we don't need to rescue her in the process."

"Can you move about while invisible?" Morgandy asked her.

"I haven't really tried before, but crisis is a good teacher," Vali answered. She closed her eyes and took a determined stance, her fists clenched and her feet spread a bit apart. A few slow, deep breaths later, she faded from view.

"Good, now follow us and see if it holds," Morgance said, and they started moving to the left under the shade of the trees. They broke away and headed towards the fighting once they couldn't walk along the trees anymore.

Vali looked down as they stepped into the sun and she realized that she could see the barest hint of her shadow.

The Ladies aren't saying anything, so I'll assume it's business as usual, she thought. She couldn't see for herself how it looked, because to her, she seemed normal and visible.

She was actually struggling to keep up since they were moving so fast. When they hit the outside wall of skirmishes, The Ladies—despite their small stature—neatly cleared a path by physically grabbing anyone near them and violently pitching them aside. Vali wouldn't have believed it if she hadn't seen it with her own eyes.

"There. He lies ahead near the middle of the fray," Morgandy cried.

As they moved forward, they heard Lucee shout, "STOP IT!" and a bright light flared, almost blinding Vali with its intensity.

"What the hell was that?" she muttered, and then she realized that whatever Lucee had done, it had worked at least momentarily. All the fighting came to a halt, and dazed Fae and Grimshaw turned to look for the source of the light.

"This is our chance! Move quick!" Morgance hissed, and Vali hurried to catch up to them. Dodging through the crowd, most of whom had stopped to fixate on the spot where Lucee was, she saw the extent of the damage that the two forces were dealing to each other. It reminded her of a massive bar-room brawl where people were busted up, but few had debilitating injuries.

We're just beating the snot out of each other! This is so different from the battle at The Maithe; what is going on here? She felt like the answer was nagging at the back of her mind, but she didn't have time to focus on it at the moment, as she was busy trying to keep up with The Ladies.

Lucee, on the other hand, found herself standing in the center of the melee between ArDonnath and Ffyn. She stretched out her arms, trying to keep the two arboreal factions apart.

"Stop it, both of you! This is wrong, and I am *sick of it!*"

She knew she must sound ridiculous, but the sight of her gentle Ffyn armed for battle and viciously attacking the ArDonnath was more than she could bear.

"We are all the same people! We don't have to be friends, but there's no reason to tear each other apart!" she shouted, even as she felt her stomach twist while she declared it. She knew she didn't fully believe what she was saying. The Grimshaw could never live peacefully with the Eleriannan and Gwyliannan. And others in the crowd knew it too.

"Why should we listen to you? You, who live in great houses and look down on us while we hide in the dark corners and sewers and abandoned places!"

Another voice growled, "You are mortal-born, you are part of the problem!"

"Yes, I was born mortal and came to the Eleriannan. But I was brought in to foster change for the better, to help break the cycle of different sides hating each other for reasons that have been lost to time and history!"

"You have done much to bring Eleriannan and Gwyliannan together." She heard a voice she recognized. "But we will never partner with The Grimshaw! And you should not want that either!"

Lucee threw back her head and growled in frustration and looked for the right words that could knock sense into all of them.

"We don't have to partner with each other! But we cannot solve these issues by trying to hurt each other either. Look," she leveled her voice into a reasonable tone, as she decided to change tactics, "I don't know if you are aware of this, but you Grimshaw are being controlled! Your decisions aren't your own, and if I was a being as strong and powerful as you all are, I'd want to know."

"Lies! You lie!" The anguished shout rang across the open field.

"What would I gain from such a lie? It's obvious that you hate us. I don't aim to change that. But if you are going to fight, don't you want it to be on your terms?"

Lucee watched as confusion spread across the faces of The Grimshaw. Even her Fae allies seemed surprised by what she was saying and looked off-balance. She took the opportunity to keep talking. Maybe it was working?

"Your hatred of us is being used to manipulate you into trying to take us out, to create a version of the city you think will benefit you. But what if I told you that it would actually reward the thing inside you that feeds from you? And when all your enemies are gone, how do you think it'll create enough conflict so that it can continue to feed?"

For a moment—a few bright seconds of hope—she saw her words stir inside the friends and foes in front of her. The Grimshaw were actually listening to her!

And just as quickly, hope slipped away, like the sun on a cloudy day.

"Very clever words from the mortal-born one, so clever that she had you all believing her! She has cast a spell over you, and I am ashamed that any who call themselves Grimshaw could be taken in by this weak once-mortal's magic and lies!"

The crowd parted, as if they'd had no choice but to move, as Camlin strode into the open circle within. He seemed to gleam like silver in the afternoon sun, once again as powerful and arrogant as he had been before his defeat at the battle at The Maithe.

Lucee looked him up and down, both as a show of defiance and to try and size him up. Was there anything left of the Camlin she'd grown to know? The sneering reaction on his handsome face said no, but she didn't want to believe that.

"If you knew me as well as you'd like your followers to think, you'd know that my magic is weak at best," she shot back at him. "I don't need magic or lies. I haven't had a reason to lie when the truth is so damning."

As she talked, her mind was running through her options. Where were her friends? What had happened to Merrick and Sousa? She didn't dare think about Cullen.

Facing Camlin alone wasn't something she thought she could handle, but now she was locked in so she'd better do her best or go out swinging.

"Why don't you tell them about the Mealladhan, Camlin?" she said in a sickeningly sweet voice. "Tell them how you and all of them are controlled by their emotions? Or shall I call on the Mealladhan myself and remind it that it tried to get me, but *it failed*?" *Oh Lucee, you are walking the tightrope now,* she thought.

Camlin threw back his head and laughed. "Like we would want *you!* The one who admits herself that she is weak?"

He stepped forward, a threatening gesture, and she forced herself to hold her ground and move her hands into a blocking position. She couldn't take him if he attacked her, but she could at least go down trying if it came to that.

"You are mistaken. I never said I was weak, only my magic is. But my mind and will are strong, too strong for your puppet master. The only one who has cast a spell is the Mealladhan," she spat at him.

She could sense the nervous movement of the Grimshaw and her Fae around them. With a single word from Camlin, they could start fighting again, and she would be in big trouble.

Where was Merrick?

She felt a shift in the air, a strange tingling. Some of her braids escaped from their tie as she whipped her head around wildly, trying to see what was happening. She heard Camlin's sharp laugh—something she had never heard in all his time staying at The Maithe—and then a voice cut through the atmosphere, silken and persuasive.

"You'll never be good enough for them, you know. It's why you can't work the powerful magic, like what they gave to Merrick so eagerly."

The voice came from Camlin's mouth, but it was Da's tone, his accent, and his mocking of her abilities. She felt a dizzying surge of confidence. This was a game she'd already beaten.

"You're still tugging at that thread? My purpose isn't the same as Merrick's. We're different people. And my da doesn't hurt me anymore. I've got my real family now."

"Ah yes, your *real* family." Camlin's eyebrow shot up, and his voice changed, becoming honeyed. Reasonable. "You were brought in without ever asking your consent first. You were a failed risk that Fallon took, a hope to mend the crumbling Eleriannan and best the Gwyliannan once and for all. Although I suppose assimilating them is close to beating them, isn't it?"

An eerie silence fell at his last words, then murmurs and grumbles from some of the Gwyliannan in the crowd. Lucee swallowed nervously and tried to keep her face neutral, but Camlin—or the Mealladhan, speaking through him—knew it had scored a point.

"What, Gwyliannan, have you not seen your so-called leader parading about with the golden-haired Eleriannan on his arm? Do you think he brings her to your House? Or has he been... absent of late?" Those icy blue eyes of Camlin's were twinkling with amusement as the displeased noises grew in the crowd.

Lucee felt the Ffyn starting to get restless, and she didn't know how much longer she would be able to hold the center of this space, or keep the factions from resuming their fight. Camlin would surely destroy her once that happened.

She looked around the circle, at the bruised and bleeding faces and bodies of her people, and those of The Grimshaw. They were all looking worse for the wear at this point. Confusion, anger, and wariness showed on their faces. She had no idea what to do next, none at all.

Clever Lucee, out of words, your only weapon.

The thought—hers, or those of the Mealladhan—echoed in her head.

"And what about the disgraced leader of The Grimshaw? To whom did he bring me, a damaged mortal, for saving? Was it not the Eleriannan?"

Lucee's attention snapped back to see Emmaline push her way into the circle, coming to stand between her and Camlin.

"What is this nonsense?" Camlin sputtered, visibly flustered. His calm arrogance had been replaced with confusion.

He can't remember what happened, Lucee realized. *The Mealladhan is realizing that there are gaps in his memory!*

"You were left to die by The Grimshaw! You wanted to use me to get back on your feet and to further your healing. And what happened instead?" Emmaline crossed her arms across her chest, glaring at him—an expression Lucee had never expected her to use with Camlin.

No—it wasn't for Camlin at all. It was for the Mealladhan.

"I-I don't remember." For a moment, he sounded more like the version of Camlin that Emmaline knew.

"You took care of me, that's what happened. You nursed me, and we became friends, then more than friends. And when I was dying, you took me to the door of The Maithe and begged for them to help me." Emmaline took a few steps forward, her arms open. "The Mealladhan left you, and you became your true self, the Camlin who was only angry because the world had been unfair to him. Not a killer, not a leader of other angry Fae. You were someone who wanted to help others. And the Mealladhan took that from you because it is using you. *All* of you."

Her voice was calm, loving, reassuring. As she talked, she continued to move closer to Camlin, as if she was approaching a once-wild animal that she knew she could tame.

He stood there, nervously watching her, his hands clenching and unclenching at his sides as she spoke. Lucee could see beads of sweat on his pale forehead.

Emmaline was so close to him now—too close. Lucee felt a hot wave of nausea mixed with hope as she heard Emmaline speak to Camlin in a voice so soft that only those in the center of the circle could possibly have heard it.

"You told me that you would rather die than see harm come to me, Camlin. Here, take my hand and we can go home and start again."

She held out her hand to him, and everything seemed to stand still in time. Lucee saw Emmaline's elegant hand extended, and watched emotions wash over Camlin's face, restoring his face from haughty to handsome, softening his energy.

He took a deep breath, and suddenly it was the Camlin that they knew, the one that loved Emmaline, standing there. Emmaline's face lit up in recognition, and as he reached out to take her hand, Lucee could see her radiate happiness.

His hand enveloped hers, and a rapturous smile blossomed across his face as he stepped closer to her. Lucee could feel her own smile in response, a wash of relief overcoming her as she watched the lovers reunite.

"That was beautiful, my *love.*"

And Lucee could only watch in horror as Camlin's smile changed to a cruel grin. He yanked Emmaline, pulling her against him as he wrapped a strong arm around her so that she couldn't escape.

MUSIC: HAPAX
Shining Lover

Vali could hear everything that was happening in the circle so when Camlin stepped out, she knew that it was time for The Ladies and herself to take action. They had come to a stop in front of her, and she crouched down so they could confer.

"What's our plan, Ladies?" she whispered, mindful of the Grimshaw and Fae fighters surrounding them. Although they seemed locked in on what was happening between Lucee and Camlin, and she was still invisible as far as she could tell, she didn't want to draw unnecessary attention to The Ladies.

"We must get to *him* as soon as possible. I can see his struggle to surface, but he is being overpowered." Morgance's voice was a soft hiss, uncannily by Vali's ear.

"You will know when to act if you watch me," Morgandy told her. "Stay close, be alert."

Morgance pushed her way forward, followed closely by Morgandy and Ula with Vali trailing behind, still wary that they would be noticed.

Vali sucked in her breath sharply when she was near enough to see through the crowd, and spied Camlin standing there, taunting Lucee.

"You were a failed risk that Fallon took, a hope to mend the crumbling Eleriannan and best the Gwyliannan once and for all. Although I suppose assimilating them is close to beating them, isn't it?"

Vali heard his words and winced. That was close to home!

She almost missed the dig at Daro and Tully, implying that Lucee was to blame for their partnering and subsequently, the time they were spending at The Maithe. She could see that Lucee was unsure of how to answer him. There were unhappy murmurs spreading throughout the crowd, and Vali could feel the tension growing.

"Oh shit, that's Emmaline!" she cried, then clapped her hands over her mouth.

The once-sickly woman was still wan, with shadowed eyes, but she stood bravely before Camlin and tried to reach the man hidden by his monster.

As Emmaline testified to what he had done to save her, in front of his followers, Vali noticed that The Grimshaw seemed uncomfortable. There were growls of anger and confusion at Emmaline's next words.

"You were someone who wanted to help others. And the Mealladhan took that from you because it is using you. *All* of you."

"What is she saying? What is using us?" Vali heard one of the Grimshaw, one who must have once called himself Gwyliannan, ask those around him.

There you go, asking the right questions, she thought. *Oh no, Emmaline, don't get so close!*

She watched with her heart pounding in her chest as Emmaline said something to Camlin that Vali couldn't hear from her vantage point. It seemed to lull him, calming him down. She could see his expression change, soften, until he looked like the man Vali had come to know and actually like.

Emmaline extended her hand and stepped forward, and for one hopeful moment Vali thought that this could be over, that Emmaline could actually have won him over through love. It could be that simple, that poetic.

Abruptly, Camlin's smile turned sick and twisted, and Emmaline was in his grasp – no, the grasp of the Mealladhan, using Camlin's body.

Vali would have sworn that she saw a flash of pain in Camlin's eyes before he disappeared under control of the Mealladhan.

She was vaguely aware that she had shouted when Camlin grabbed Emmaline, and it became clear to her that she wasn't the only one as the crowd became restless, agitated. She could hear cries of outrage, bewilderment, and animosity, all jumbled up together—from both sides of foes. No one seemed to know what to do next.

"Move! Now!" A small clawed hand grabbed Vali's wrist with eerie accuracy and pulled her to the fore of the crowd. Camlin didn't even glance their way, to her surprise. Vali realized that if he couldn't see her, and he underestimated the power of The Ladies, there was no reason why he would bother to guard against them.

Lucee, however, noted them. She was smart enough to not look directly their way, but Vali saw her stand taller as soon as they came in view.

"Now what, Camlin? Or should I say Mealladhan?" Lucee challenged him.

"It seems to me that the wisest course of action is to eliminate all sources of weakness." Camlin's voice was oily, the kind of attitude that made the normally peaceful Vali want to punch people. "If I take care of this problem, then everything else will fall into alignment as it was meant to be. But here is the question."

He paused, looking around the circle with a penetrating gaze.

"Do we kill her, or do we keep her?"

Vali made a noise of repulsion, and Morgance jerked her arm hard.

"We must wait," she hissed between clenched, pointy teeth.

Lucee wore an expression that matched how Vali was feeling—repulsed and outraged with a hint of fear that she was struggling to hide.

"You won't do either of those things if I have anything to say about it," Lucee said. Her tone was brave but she wasn't fooling Camlin, and it was obvious to Vali that she knew it.

Morgance jerked Vali's arm again, but not quite as hard this time.

"Look there." She moved Vali's hand to indicate where to look, which was at Emmaline.

She was clearly terrified, and was doing nothing to try and conceal it... wait, was she playing it up? Vali's glance was pulled downward at another of Morgance's arm jerks, just at the moment when Emmaline opened her left hand and what looked like seeds fell from her palm onto the ground at her feet.

"Now things begin to move in our favor," Morgance said, and Morgandy turned to look at her, a determined look on her face. Vali was struck by the tiny cracks that covered her skin, like those on an old porcelain doll. It occurred to her that she'd never seen The Ladies this close in daylight before today.

"Move when I move," Morgandy said to them. Vali had the fleeting, incongruous mental image of the four of them as a small, freakish army made up of her purple-haired punk self, flanked by spooky, childlike supernatural creatures.

A rumble of thunder echoed across the Dell, and Vali looked up in surprise—she hadn't noticed the gathering clouds until now.

"Just what we need, a late summer storm," she muttered, and Ula hissed at her to be quiet. Vali noticed that she wasn't the only one to be caught off guard by the threat of rain. Others in the crowd were complaining as well.

It's not like our fight's gonna get washed out, she thought. *Huh, I wonder why no one's started fighting again? We're all just sitting here, waiting for the drama to end. It's weird.*

It was weird. Everyone seemed to be captivated by what was happening between Lucee, Camlin, and Emmaline. Vali couldn't figure out why. Were they waiting for Camlin to order them to start fighting again? Was the Mealladhan stretched too thin? That was an intriguing thought, but she was distracted by Camlin's next words.

"If we take her in, as one of our own, that would be a nice, tidy victory. And of course, our leader gets to have his little mortal-born plaything." Camlin jerked Emmaline tighter against him, and she whimpered. "But if we kill her, we hurt our enemy and put everyone in their place."

It was plain to Vali that the Mealladhan was threatening its own host with that suggestion. As much as that disgusted Vali, she recognized that the Mealladhan had just admitted that it didn't have as much control as it wanted the Fae to think it did.

The rain was starting to come down harder, and mud squelched under her booted feet.

Another rumble of thunder broke, and Lucee shouted over it. "If you hurt her, you'll lose!"

"That is a ridiculous statement, and you know it," Camlin answered angrily. "Either way, I win!"

"Is it? Your followers already begin to see that they are being manipulated. Even your host sees it - even now, he is fighting against you! Killing her is designed to squash his rebellion, and any possibility of theirs."

"Way to put it all out there, Lucee," Vali muttered. "Are they listening, though?"

If the reactions from the Grimshaw around her were to be judged, they were indeed listening, and they did not like what they were hearing. The crowd, who until that point had seemed rooted in place, started to edge forward. The inner circle collapsed into a much smaller space.

Lucee held her hands out, stretched to either side, and called out, "Stand back, give him room!" Her eyes darted nervously around the circle, and Vali could see that her control of the situation was rapidly slipping.

"Now?" she whispered to The Ladies, and Morgandy held up a finger, cautioning her to wait, then turned it to point to where Camlin held Emmaline.

"There," Morgandy hissed.

Time seemed to slow down to a crawl.

Vali saw Camlin pull a gleaming silvered knife from a sheath on his belt, and put it to Emmaline's neck. There was a loud shout from the bystanders, both Grimshaw and Fae. Camlin's face became hard, his icy eyes slitted, as he heard the shouts, and Vali saw the hand that held his prisoner clutch her cruelly.

Emmaline closed her eyes and seemed to steel herself, and Vali saw her mouth move but couldn't hear the words she was saying. There was another loud rumble of thunder, and silence fell after just long enough for Vali to hear Emmaline's voice in the hush.

"Forgive me."

She gestured with her left hand, a sweeping motion unrestricted by Camlin's arm that held her captive. There was a strange rustling sound, and Vali's mouth fell open as she watched morning glory vines wrap themselves thickly around Camlin's ankle and calves, then pull him rapidly down to the ground. One snaked around the arm with the knife and jerked it away from Emmaline's throat, and she gasped with relief.

Somehow, he still kept a grip on her, but the vines wove themselves around his limbs, tethering him to the ground.

Morgandy shouted, *"Now!"* and charged forward. Her sisters and Vali followed. Vali stumbled over one of the Drunnog and some pieces of an ArDonnath as she burst into the center of the circle.

"Move this child!" Morgandy shouted as she lunged for Camlin. Vali tried to pull Emmaline free, but Camlin, fully possessed by the Mealladhan, hissed and dug his fingers into her. Emmaline cried out in pain and struggled to break loose. Morgance pushed Vali aside and as Vali watched in horror, Morgance sank her sharp teeth into Camlin's arm.

He screamed and tried to shake the Sister off, and Vali was able to finally pull Emmaline away.

"Go! Run!" Vali shouted.

"I can't! I need to be here to hold him with the plants!" She reached into a pocket in her skirt and pulled out more seeds. "I can keep back the others with this!"

Before Vali could answer, Emmaline spun around, throwing the seeds in a circle around them. Morning glory vines sprang forth immediately, arching upwards towards the rain coming down, then falling over to find each other and twine together.

"They're encircling us!" Vali gasped, realizing what she was attempting to do.

"They look fragile, but they'll keep people back," Emmaline panted, pushing some of her long, rain-soaked hair out of her face.

Pulling Camlin down seemed to have broken the weird truce between the factions because all around them, fighting resumed as if someone had taken everything off pause.

"What is happening?" Emmaline cried out.

"Look at The Ladies!" Vali shouted, pointing to where they had gathered around Camlin. She felt Lucee's hand on her shoulder, and Lucee gasped as she saw what they were doing.

The vines had pulled Camlin down spread-eagled against the ground. Morgance and Ula were kneeling on either side of him, brows furrowed in concentration, each with one hand on him and the other on Morgandy.

She knelt at his head, her small clawed hands on either side of his face. Morgandy had a terrible, pained expression, and whatever she was doing to Camlin was obviously awful for both of them, as he was writhing beneath her hands.

"What do we do?" Lucee asked, and Vali shook her head.

"Stand back. Wait for them to call on us."

There was a blood curdling scream from Camlin, and Emmaline fell to her knees, arms wrapped tightly around her. Morgandy shrieked and threw her hands upward, and Vali could see something forming in front of her, floating above Camlin's prone body.

A darkness formed, a moving mass that ebbed and flowed in the air like a swarm of something living, a cloud made up of many small bodies. It shifted between deep grey to browns, then a sickly green, then back again, and Vali could see gleams and sparkles of light— electricity—crackle through the shifting apparition. She could see Morgance on the other side of the cloud, and the expression on her face was the closest thing to fear that any of them had ever seen from her before.

MUSIC: REV REV REV
One Illusion Is Very Much Like Another

A static feeling shot through the women in the circle, and the words of the Mealladhan crackled all around them and vibrated inside them. *You have ousted us from our main host, and now what? We still hold all these creatures in our thrall, and they will destroy your people. Then what will hold us back?*

Emmaline put her hands over her ears, trying to drown out the reverberating words, to no avail. Laughter cackled around them, and Vali grit her teeth, trying not to let anger take hold of her. Lucee, however, was tired of the Mealladhan and its games.

"You know what? This has gone on long enough. You need to leave and not come back." She stomped her foot for emphasis, not caring if it seemed childish.

What do we care what you demand? So weak, you could not even fight our host with magic. Even your words were soft. Go on, try to strike at us. Surely you can summon enough strength to deliver one blast?

The cloud oozed forward, and Vali gasped as Lucee stepped forward to meet it.

"I have no need to prove myself to you."

What about your people? They watch you in your weakest moments. They see you failing.

Images of Lucee trying to defend herself against Cullen during her lessons flashed before them all, as vivid as if everyone on the field had suddenly appeared in the room with the couple as they sparred. The exclamation that she had made when she hit the ground echoed across the field.

"Ha! You try to humiliate me, but I'm not ashamed of that day anymore. There's no shame in learning through failure," Lucee crossed her arms, a brave stance. "You'll have to try harder."

Beyond the swarm of energy that was the Mealladhan, Lucee could see The Ladies had joined hands, still on their knees, their heads bowed together. Whatever they were up to, she knew that she needed to buy them time.

"All I see is a creature that makes itself stronger by gathering up the energy of others to bolster it. Without all the beings that you suck the life from like a parasite, you are nothing at all!"

The Mealladhan gathered itself into a dense mass, and its color changed to a red-tinged grey. Before Lucee could react, it enveloped her, and everything outside of the mist became obscured and muffled.

You think you are better than us. You meddle in the world around you and call it aid, but it serves to bolster your ego and put forth your own agenda. All this power, all the opportunities at the fingertips of all of you, Mortal and Fae, and what do you do with it? Fight! You look to rule as much as your foes do, and so we delight in encouraging you to tear yourselves apart.

As it berated her, she could feel it looking for weak points where it might gain entry into her, and she fought to keep herself calm and push her anger away.

"My whole goal is to stop the fighting and bring positive change. I don't want more power. I want to use the power we already have to help others."

You cannot! Not without spreading your own corruption as surely as we spread throughout your people and increase our own colony. Every being wants power. And power corrupts. Power will change you.

The Mealladhan abruptly shifted colors to a neutral grey with little bursts of sparkling energy that tingled Lucee's skin. She couldn't see beyond the cloud at all now.

I thought you once-mortals were all dangerously useless, but you have proved me wrong. At least a few of you are worthy to become my hosts. Together, we could create change that would be better for your people, a future away from the spreading corruption of mortal filth and destruction. You sink all your energy into a lost cause. Why not rally behind those who can actually create a world you dream to see?

A vision appeared before Lucee's eyes, and it was difficult for her to shake off its beauty: clean city streets, shining structures and gleaming windows, green flowering trees on either side. The ribbon stream of the Jones Falls cut through a cityscape where the banks had no trash, and the clear water had fish moving through the stream while herons stalked them. No cars on the roads, no traffic, no... people? Where were the people?

"You paint the picture of a barren paradise. What of those who live here? Where are they in this vision?"

It showed her a party where The Drawback played to an audience of mostly Fae creatures.

"Where are the mortals? You would push away the heart of the city in order to remake it!"

You and I both know that they are the source of their own suffering, and they pull down the world around them in their desire to conquer all. They have no understanding of balance; they use everything until there is nothing left to use.

"So, we teach them! We offer better examples; we use our strengths to show them different ways to move in the world!" Lucee could feel her voice crack under the strain of her desperation. The thing was—she wasn't so sure that she was right, and that scared her more than anything. What if the Mealladhan had a point? What if mortals—humans—would never learn? Where was the line between stubbornness and digging her heels in because she didn't want to admit defeat?

She could feel the pressure of the Mealladhan waiting, knowing that it understood that it had scored a hit on her. She mentally scrambled, trying to justify her stance against the reality that the Mealladhan had forced her to face: humans, historically, had made reliably awful choices. She could feel a pit of despair opening inside her, and a cold wave of fear took over.

She was losing.

She realized that she was clutching her book necklace, and the conversation she'd last had with the Book came back to her, rising up in her memory.

It slips you half-truths to unlock your door. Your feelings are your greatest asset.

What banishes fear? What keeps belief alive?

Hope.

"I will not give up on the Mortals. I can't because I *was* one, and I've seen how far I've come in just the past year! I believe that they can do better, that we all can do better. I believe that there must always be room for redemption, for hope." She gestured around herself, indicating the people outside of the cloud that was the Mealladhan, even though she couldn't see them.

"None of us are perfect. We're all flawed. We have all made bad choices, which cause harm well beyond our small, personal worlds. But we keep going! We keep trying to improve, because growth is always possible. If all I can do against corruption and pollution and cruelty is to go out there and lend a helping hand in the fight against it with acts of love and service and joy, then so be it. My job is to show that there can be another way and to help others find that path. I will never stop believing. I will never let my hope die."

Lucee was met with a silence so profound that at first, she thought that it had somehow taken her hearing. She stood there in the soundless dark of the Mealladhan and wondered if this was the end for her.

The thumping of her heart in her chest broke that silence. It seemed to echo around her, and she felt a movement in the malevolent cloud. Anger, confusion, then panic rushed through her—not her emotions, but those of the Mealladhan.

And then reality crashed down all around her as the darkness pulled away abruptly, and the sights and sounds of the field bowled her over with their sudden return. She fell hard to her knees, the pain unnoticed as she focused on what was happening in front of her.

Morgance and Ula stood flanking their sister Morgandy, each clutching one of her hands. Morgandy's small form stood with her legs apart, and her hands away from her, and Lucee realized that her sisters were bracing her, holding her upright.

But what Lucee couldn't look away from was the horror of Morgandy's mouth wide open, a pointy toothed maw out of some nightmare, as she sucked the huge black-greyed cloud of Mealladhan into her.

Somewhere far away, Lucee thought she heard screaming, then realized it was herself and that she couldn't seem to stop.

Morgandy's eyes rolled back into her head, and swarms of the grey energy rose up from every direction, pulled from The Grimshaw into that terrifying void that she had opened up.

After what seemed like a lifetime of nightmares, Morgance yelled out, "Vali, now!"

Lucee watched in horror as Vali gestured to Emmaline to move the vines away. She ripped at Camlin's shirt with strong hands. She seemed to grasp something intangible to Lucee, a thing that looked like a black smudge. She ran to The Ladies, her face as serious as Lucee had ever seen it.

"Hold her well, I need to place it in the right spot," Vali shouted, as Morgandy's body began to writhe in the grip of her sisters' hands.

The tiny, monstrous being began to kick and curse as Vali ripped at the black cotton of her bodice, and a terrible wail escaped her as Vali slapped her hand with the smudgy thing in it across her bared breastbone.

A great, blinding flash blew everyone in the circle back, and Lucee felt the wind violently knocked out of her as she crashed against the ground. She laid there for a moment with her eyes closed, regathering her wits. She didn't have it in her to move, even if she was in danger. She could hear yelling and screams from around her - some of pain, some of confusion. She didn't recognize any of the voices.

"Lucee? Talk to me, are you okay?"

She could hear her name from far away, like it was coming over a loud-speaker somewhere.

"Lucee! Open your eyes, girl!"

"You can't be hurt; we've got a show in a little while!"

Oh, someone was a smartass.

"Can't play if I'm dead," she mumbled, and she heard an uncharacteristically nervous laugh from... Sousa?

"You're not dead, but later on you might feel like it," he told her. "Open your eyes, you need to see what's happened."

Lucee groaned but did as she was told, and her reward was the sight of Sousa and Merrick leaning over her, their faces changing from worry to relief as she squinted up at the both of them.

"Lying in the mud is doing wonders for this dress," she grumbled, and they each took a hold of one of her arms and gently helped her to a sitting position.

"Everyone's a muddy, wet mess. We'll look like we're starting a new fashion trend." Merrick's voice said he was joking, but his face betrayed the distress he had been feeling.

Lucee looked around her, and tried to make sense of what she was seeing.

There was a huge scorched mark in the middle of the circle, where the three Ladies sat, looking worse than Lucee had ever seen them look. Morgandy was singed from head to toe, and she sat between her sisters much like a rag doll might, legs and arms akimbo. Her face seemed vacant; the black pupils of her eyes were huge but empty looking.

Morgance and Ula clung tightly to her, their expressions taut and determined. Lucee wanted to cry when she saw their faces.

"Did she—she ate the Mealladhan," Lucee stammered, trying not to cry.

"She pulled it from everyone and took it inside her. And Vali locked it inside her with the tattoo sigil she put on Camlin." Merrick's voice dropped in volume, and he added, "I don't know if she'll ever be able to release it safely. And she won't be able to unless Vali removes the sigil."

Lucee didn't know what to say about that. Every aspect of it seemed horrible to her.

"What about Camlin?"

"He is free. But he doesn't remember his time with us, not at all. He is trying to come to grips—again—with the idea that he was used, and Emmaline and Vali are with him. But look at everyone else, Lucee! Look around, it's amazing."

She squinted at Merrick again, then carefully turned her head as she took stock of what was happening between her Fae and The Grimshaw.

There was a general sort of mass confusion in the crowd of recently opposed beings, but hatred seemed replaced with curiosity and, weirdly to Lucee, a grudging respect. The Grimshaw looked as dazed as she felt.

"The Mealladhan had them so controlled that they barely knew what was happening," Sousa told her. "Some of them will never like us, and that's fine. But I foresee some of them coming back to the Gwyliannan, maybe. If you can manage to hit the right pitch with them, you know?"

"Me? You want me to address everyone and—do what, exactly? Help me out here, Souz. My head is spinning." Really, she wanted nothing more than to go find a quiet spot and take a nap. She felt so off balance. "And while I'm asking questions, have you seen Cullen?"

"I'll find him," Merrick offered. "You talk to this horde. I think I'm getting the better deal," he added with a wink, before he morphed into his raven guise and took off over the field.

"You'd better hold me up, man," Lucee grumbled to Sousa, who obliged her by giving her a hand up. He stood behind her and to her left, ready to catch her if she wilted.

"I have no idea what to say," she muttered, then shouted to get their attention. "Hey! Eleriannan! Gwyliannan! Grimshaw! Let's talk!"

Despite Sousa's muffled guffaw at her opener, it worked. She found herself in the center of a very attentive audience, desperately in need of someone to explain what had happened.

"Look, for starters, let's just establish that we're all Fae or Fae-adjacent here, so I don't have to keep using our faction names over and over again when I'm talking about all of us, okay? No insult meant, I'm just really tired and I'm sure you all are too.

"Some pretty shocking things have been revealed today, and it's pretty disorienting to realize that you've been used by something that was controlling your thoughts and actions in ways you never even suspected. We don't expect things to suddenly change because the Mealladhan isn't inside you anymore, but can we try to work on making a way for all of us to coexist? Maybe even understand each other better?"

She paused to look around the circle, making sure to meet the eyes of any Grimshaw who was bold enough to do so. She didn't smile, but she would give subtle head nods to those who looked receptive.

"What of our leader?" called out a tall, dark-skinned Grimshaw from the edge of the gathering. Lucee wondered in passing if she had once been from Tiennan House. She had the same sort of elegant, yet stern demeanor as Daro did.

"We're not holding him. We're trying to help him come back to himself," Vali replied, raising her voice so that she could be heard. She was sitting cross-legged on the ground next to Camlin, who was sitting up, but was still half attached to the ground thanks to Emmaline's morning glory vines. Some of the blue flowers had begun to open.

"I may be able to assist you there." Karsten's low voice carried across the circle. The vines that had kept people back parted to let Karsten through, and they knelt before Camlin and Emmaline.

"Wh—what is this?" Camlin stumbled over his words, trembling.

Lucee heard some rumblings in the crowd from Grimshaw, and turned to yell at them, her fists on her hips.

"Don't you dare talk crap about Camlin now after he gave up so much to save your asses! He didn't have to put himself in danger like he did, and in fact he could have just stayed away from the Grimshaw and avoided getting sucked back in by the Mealladhan. But instead, he went back so that he could break *you* all free, and we came along to help. We all risked ourselves to help you, but your *leader* did the most. You should honor him because not many would do what he did!" Her eyes narrowed and she shot daggers around the crowd, daring any of them to mock Camlin again. To her satisfaction, some of the Grimshaw stepped back nervously when she focused on them.

She turned back to Karsten and Camlin, and saw that Karsten had extended their hands to the pale Grimshaw leader, encouraging him to take them.

"You and Morgandy arranged this before you returned to The Grimshaw. Just try to trust me and you will see. I know that it is a lot to ask."

"I arranged this with who?"

"The one who took the Mealladhan out of you. She has given herself over to be a container for it, at least for now. It was a great sacrifice, one that she took from you. She believes that you have important work to do."

Camlin sat there for a moment, and Lucee could see that he was considering all that Karsten had said, and possibly calculating what that meant for him. He looked from Karsten to Emmaline, who hadn't left his side. It was obvious that she was trying to keep her emotions in check. She was doing her best to school her face into a neutral expression, but her nervous, sad eyes gave her away.

Camlin raised his chin, his jaw clenching, then he reached out and took Karsten's hands.

At first, nothing seemed to change. They just sat there, eyes closed, hands locked together. When Lucee started to worry that something else bad had happened, Camlin let out a loud gasp, let go of Karsten's hands, and fell back, tears streaming down his face.

His hands flew to his chest, where the sigil tattoo of the heart had recently lived, and his face took on a stricken expression.

"Morgandy keeps it now," Karsten gently told him. "You carried it long enough. She said that you deserved a chance at some life."

"I don't know if I do." His voice shook, and he swiped away the tears on his face using the back of one hand. "I fell right back in with the Mealladhan. I tried to hurt the one person I cared about more than anything in the world." He wouldn't look at Emmaline, Lucee realized.

"But you came to warn me, to warn us! You fought it off long enough to come find me and tell me to beware, and that showed me that you were still in there, even when you were forced to use me as a bargaining chip. Look at me, Camlin!" Emmaline grabbed his arm and shook it until he finally met her gaze.

"You knew you were risking losing yourself and you did it anyway. You are a hero today, even if you don't see it. You helped to save all these people." She gestured wildly around the circle.

"And if you want to really cement the deal, could you please back me up when I tell the Grimshaw that I'd like for us to all gather and parley?" Lucee broke in, then looked up and the now mostly clear sky and added, "Parley *after* the show, though—crap, it's got to be close to our time to play!"

Sousa clapped a big hand on her shoulder. "Leave it to you to get back to what really matters!"

"So, what now? Can we count on you to come parley with us after we take care of the rest of this day? We can arrange with Camlin where and when to meet." Lucee addressed the crowd as earnestly as she knew how to be, and her reward was unsure looks and puzzlement. Finally, Camlin stood up and spoke, his tone firm and loud enough for even those in the back of the gathering to hear him.

"I will bring The Grimshaw to parley. Let us find a way forward together."

He blinked in surprise when there was a shout of approval from the horde. Lucee couldn't tell which faction had shouted, or if it was all of them together.

"Sounds like a date! Now, how do we break this weird time bubble that we're in?" She looked around, then it hit her - she was still missing important people. "And could someone find Merrick? And you know, my boyfriend? Because this is starting to get ridiculous."

MUSIC: AGNIS
I Am the Light

Maybe I need to let the Elementals know that we have solved the problem, at least for now?" Lucee wondered aloud, and Camlin tilted his head, puzzled.

"Elemental beings are here?"

"They played referee, I guess you could say? They're the ones who made it so that our brawl didn't affect the mortals here. I also suspect, even though they said they wouldn't directly interfere, they helped keep things from going beyond fistfights. But the hard work, that was all us, just so you know. And by us, I mean everyone here." She raised an eyebrow and gave him a meaningful look.

"If they are here, they would be aware of all that has transpired. If they have not let time resume as it was, there is a reason for that," Camlin mused. Nearby, Vali nodded thoughtfully.

"There's something we're missing," she added. "There has to be. The Elementals don't think we're finished."

A small flock of birds swirled into the center of the circle, and transformed into Quillan, who dropped to a knee in front of Lucee. In an instant of clarity, she knew that whatever he was about to tell her was why they were still held in this arcane space.

"My lady, you must needs go with me," Quillan told her, his eyes cast downwards.

"What's happened?" she asked as her heart sank.

He didn't answer, instead grabbing her hand and pulling her along with him. The crowd parted for them as they moved through it, reshaping itself behind them to follow. Lucee didn't notice any of that, however. She focused on what was before her.

It became clear as they reached the shade of the trees. She first saw Merrick, pacing back and forth across the grass. The next thing to come into focus was the clear sphere that she knew came from Merrick's magic, standing larger than her friend himself. Trapped inside it was an angry, panicked Arswyd, trying desperately to break free.

And lying on the grass nearby was Cullen. He wasn't moving.

Lucee didn't know when she dropped Quillan's hand and started running, but it both felt like an instant and a lifetime to get to where they were. She tripped and tumbled down right before she reached Cullen and ended up crawling on her hands and knees to him.

She could see that he'd been beaten badly. He was covered with cuts and bruises, but she couldn't see bleeding beyond that, not yet anyway. She fought the urge to get violently ill and forced herself to question Merrick.

"Tell me. What happened."

Merrick's voice was strained, and hoarse, as though he'd been yelling.

"I could only catch one, Lucee. They had him and one held him while this one… He wasn't conscious when I got here. They were beating an unconscious man." His voice broke, and he had to pause for a moment. "I don't know how he is. I'm so sorry."

Something clicked in Lucee's head, like a wall coming down between her grief and the parts of her that needed to be clinical and take care of things.

I'll lose it later. I need to take care of this now.

She bent her head to his chest, listening. A heartbeat. Breath. He was alive. That was something she could work with.

Out of the corner of her eye, she saw Aisling and Tully as they ran to where she knelt with Cullen. Suddenly, she had an idea.

"I need anyone who might want to help to gather around," she called out. "I need your energy!"

I can't heal him. But maybe I can give him what he needs to heal.

First, though, she needed to clear away anything that could hold her back.

"Merrick? I need you to release the Arswyd."

"What?" His voice cracked. "No! He beat—"

"Just do it, okay? He wasn't in control of himself. I can't hold him accountable for something he did while the Mealladhan inhabited him. It would be wrong."

She turned back to Cullen and took his hand, wincing as she saw how bruised and battered his knuckles were. He had tried to fight back, but it hadn't been enough.

"I don't know what I'm doing," she said to those around her. "So, I'm winging it. Maybe this is a waste of time, but I have to try. If you can put your energy out there, concentrate it on us, maybe that will help." She felt a tear slip down her face, but she did her best to push back her fear and doubts in herself.

She felt hands on her shoulders, and looked up to see Sousa and Vali standing above her.

"You can do this," Sousa told her, and Vali nodded encouragingly.

People started to move forward, gathering around them. She saw Tully and Daro join hands with Emmaline and Aisling, and more faces she knew beyond those—and many she did not.

There are some Grimshaw in this circle, she thought and realized that Camlin had come to stand by her.

"I would help, if you will allow that from me," he said, pulling up his sleeves. Lucee looked at the tattoo on his forearm, then up at him, confused.

"Vali made this for me, but I think you might need it right now. If you can bear to touch me, that is." He hunched his shoulders, ready to be rebuffed.

"Do it, Lucee," Vali whispered. "You've gotta trust him."

Lucee looked down at Cullen, his handsome face puffy and bruised, his battered body sprawled on the ground before her, and she knew she would take any risk to help him. She swallowed hard, steeled herself, and reached out to touch Camlin's arm.

She felt her eyes close—not by her own will—and a strange lassitude came over her, a deep, calming peace. For the first time in a long time, she found confidence, strength that had always been a struggle for her to achieve. Now, she was at ease, and she knew what she needed to do.

She kept her eyes closed, trusting her mind to do the work that needed to be done next. She could feel her friends all around her, and those she led—and even those who had recently been enemies were there and seemed to be on her side, at least in this moment. She visualized sweeping her arms around, gathering up all the energy that was offered into a huge, sparkling swirl of vitality. It filled her arms, and she saw herself stumbling up to the oaken door that she had imagined the first time she had joined Cullen in mind work.

"I would knock, but I don't think you're able to answer, so I'll see myself in," she said, and pushed on the door with her foot. It swung open easily, and she felt a rush of relief. At least he hadn't locked her out!

To her surprise, she found herself on the stage at the far end of the field. She looked to her left and saw the Fire Tower glowing in the late afternoon sun. It looked as though it was pulsing with fire, and she could have sworn that she could feel heat coming from it.

"I don't understand what I'm supposed to do," she mumbled, and she realized that there was a crowd in front of the stage, shouting at her.

"Play! Play! Play!"

"What the—okay, fine. I'll play. It's obvious that I have no control over what's happening here, at least I can do something I'm good at."

Her guitar was set up next to a mic at center stage, so she walked over to it. The ball of energy in her arms started to quiver, then shake violently. She gasped and let it go, and watched in amazement as it burst into thousands of twinkling lights, which drifted up above her. It hovered in the air over her head like a cloud made of stars.

She looked up at it in wonder, then bent down to the guitar and picked it up, pulling the strap over her head with a sigh of pleasure. The purple-and-green glitter in the finish of her instrument reflected onto her face as she strapped it on.

"This feels right," she said into the microphone. "I don't know what to play for an audience inside my boyfriend's head, though. All of this is uncharted territory." She laughed, feeling the utter madness of this moment. "So, I'll play something I love beyond measure because that's how I feel about Cullen. I hope that works."

She was thrilled to find that this vision—which she seemed to be deep into without much control on her part—had thought to include her guitar pedals. She stomped on the ones she needed to begin the swirling, shoegazey opening to a song she had written back when she had first met Cullen, and she hadn't been sure that they would work out.

She didn't have the keyboard backing, so she imagined it kicking in after the opening, to meet the flowing sound of her guitar, and she heard the crowd cheer.

All right, she thought. *Let's see if I can conjure up some drums and bass too.*

She sang the opening lines plainly, over the guitar and keys, with no effects on her vocals. She sent them out to the crowd, a love letter to them, and to the Fae shape-changer that she couldn't imagine her life without. The energy cloud above her head swirled, building more power. Lucee could feel the potential of it in the air, ready to release at any moment.

At the chorus, the bass and drums came crashing in, and she felt the lyrics pouring out of her.

And the whispered voices lure us
as we dance across the mist
embracing sweet forgetfulness
in the garden where our secrets rest

A sweet guitar solo, notes that shimmered and then disappeared, sent tiny sparks out across the audience. They reached up to try and catch them, laughing with joy.

Finally, she felt it - the potential had been reached; the power could contain itself no longer. She saw a movement at her side, and realized that Merrick was there, fingers thumping away on the strings of his bass. Behind her, Sousa's drums supported her guitar and lifted up the song as surely as Merrick made certain they still had a tether to the ground.

Maybe this was all for nothing, but she had never felt more powerful and sure of herself as she did in this moment. She sang the next words straight to Cullen, calling out to him in the way she knew best.

Would you take my hand once more
journey through that distant door
if I kissed you there
would you close your eyes?

Come back to me, she thought, and she felt the twinkling, gyrating cloud above her head spread out, flowing away from her and the stage and over the heads of the listeners. Stars burst forth from it and went twirling, careening away in big, gentle arcs and loops that made Lucee think of fireflies. The crowd cried out in amazement and Lucee could hear those cheers and exclamations echo all around them, building and growing until that was all that she could hear.

She felt her eyes closing, caught up in the moment, the reverberations of music and cheering and that energetic cloud. The sensations built until all she could hear was a loud buzz... and then that faded away, and all that remained was the thump-thump of her heartbeat.

Open your eyes, Lucee.

"I'm afraid."

You're the bravest person I know.

"...Cullen?"

She forced herself to open her eyes, and found herself standing behind the stage facing toward the Fire Tower. It looked much more subdued now that the sun had moved below the line of trees. Her hand was clutching the neck of her guitar like something bad might happen if she let go, and she could feel the strings biting into her fingers.

"What..."

"Turn around, Lucee!"

She whirled around to see Merrick and Sousa sitting on the stage steps. And propped up between them, looking beat up but most certainly awake, was Cullen.

"So, I'm alive," he said, with a sheepish, lopsided grin.

Lucee stood there for a second, trying to process everything. And then she gently dropped her guitar on the ground and flew over to the stairs, where she swept Cullen into a crushing hug. She almost pushed Merrick and Sousa off the steps in the process.

"Ow," Cullen protested mildly, but he was hugging her back as tightly as possible.

"I want some of this too," Merrick said.

"What the hell," Sousa agreed, and Lucee found herself in the middle of a huge group hug.

"What the hell is right," Lucee's muffled voice came from the pile of huggers. "We just fixed this guy. Maybe we shouldn't crush him so soon?"

Laughing, Merrick and Sousa let go, and Sousa got up so that Lucee could sit next to Cullen.

"So, I don't understand how we got back here? And"—she looked around meaningfully—"it's almost dark! What the hell happened?"

"You tell me, Fearney. We all woke up here, same as you. I don't know what the hell you did, exactly, but it was unlike anything I've ever seen, and that's saying something." Sousa stepped back and looked around, then came back to where they were sitting. "Looks like the headliner is getting ready to play? Like... did we actually play a set?" His eyes were huge.

"I guess we'd better go find everyone and see if they know what happened."

"That sounds like a plan. And hey! Are you gonna pick up that guitar, or is that what my presents mean to you?" He winked at her, and his teasing felt like a return to normalcy that she didn't realize she had needed.

The band on the stage, Brand New Day, kicked off their first song. Lucee grinned and shouted "Sorry, can't hear you over the music!" She grabbed her guitar before he could think of a suitable retort. When she turned back from stashing it with the rest of the band's gear, she found herself alone with Cullen. He gave her an unfathomable look and indicated that they should go sit off to the side, under the trees.

"Less noise," he shouted, and she nodded.

He was still wobbly so she helped him—not the easiest feat, as he was taller than her. They fell to the grass and Cullen made a pained noise.

"Well, I will be feeling this for a while. But it would have been worse without your help." He looked off into the distance, a blush on his cheeks.

"Why are you—wait, are you embarrassed? Because that's ridiculous, you know."

"Is it? I made a big show of wanting to fight the creatures who tried to push us around, and they found me and almost killed me. You had to swoop in and save my life. I do not know why you want me around. I cannot defend you and I am obviously more of a liability than an asset." As he spoke, he picked up a fallen leaf and methodically tore it into tiny pieces. He would not look at Lucee.

"Cullen. Don't do that." She reached out to touch him, and he stopped tearing at the leaf and sat perfectly still. "You are not a liability. Hey, look at me."

Reluctantly, he turned and met her gaze. She tilted her head and looked at him with empathy in her eyes.

"Everything I do is made better by you. I don't need a hero to fight for me, Cullen. I don't need that kind of support. What I need is someone who will listen to me, and tell me when I'm doing things wrong, and cheer me when I need it. You partner with me in all the right ways, and that's something I've never had until you came into my life.

"Please don't want to be someone different, and don't discount how you matter to me. You've always believed in me, but I guess you need to know that I believe in you too."

"Oh, I have never doubted you, Lucee Fearney, not for a moment." He paused, then added in a subdued voice, "So… I suppose that means that I must listen to you now."

"That's right. If I can learn to believe in myself, so can you."

She leaned forward and threw her arms around him, drawing him into a sideways hug. He sighed deeply as she leaned her head against his shoulder.

"Don't fight any more Arswyd, okay? I don't know if I can pull off an epic concert rescue like that again."

A short while later, Sousa and Merrick returned with their friends. Lucee struggled to help Cullen get to his feet, so Vali immediately ran over to the couple to assist. Then she enveloped each one in a tight hug.

"We did it," she whispered into Lucee's green and black braids while she squeezed her.

"One day I'll figure out how," Lucee laughed, stumbling from the ferocity of Vali's hug.

When Vali let her go, she found herself facing Camlin. He was holding Emmaline's hand like it was a delicate, precious treasure.

"I owe—"

She cut him off. "No, don't say that."

"I know what it means. Still: I owe you." He closed his ice blue eyes wearily as a small blast of energy burst away from them and outward, ruffling hair and clothes as it sped away.

"Dammit, now you've done it. Camlin, I don't want your obligation!" She almost stomped her foot on the grass but managed to control herself.

"This is an obligation I'm taking on voluntarily. I want to try and bring everyone together, and to join you in your work. I'll do everything I can to make this happen. That's my oath." He glanced at Emmaline, who gave him an encouraging nod, and then he turned to address Sousa. "And we hope that we are still welcome to stay at The Maithe? It would make it a lot easier to be of help that way."

"You two always have a room at The Maithe. Besides, Emmaline is one of us now—and you are too, if you want to claim that title."

To Lucee's surprise, Sousa stuck out his hand. It must have caught Camlin off guard as well because he stood there and stared at it for a moment before he took it in his own.

"People don't generally like to touch me," Camlin mumbled.

"You're really gonna have to get over that, we're a bunch of huggers here," Lucee told him, grinning. "And if you are ready to get working on that obligation, the first step is getting a meeting between us and The Grimshaw to happen. Can you do that?"

"I think you will be pleasantly surprised by how much they also want that."

Lucee could hear the guitar from the band on stage combined with cheers from the audience as it echoed across the Dell. She smiled, looking out at the field and the people who had stuck around for the end of ArtPark.

"We missed all of it, but I'm good with that," she said to herself, then louder to her friends, "We should pack up and get out of here. I haven't had anything to eat besides a funnel cake all day, and I am *starving*."

That idea got an enthusiastic response from her friends, who started heading to the backstage area to grab the gear and haul it to Sousa's van. Camlin awkwardly offered to help Cullen get to the parking lot, which made Lucee and Emmaline trade wide-eyed grins.

Before Lucee could follow them, she heard her name quietly called from the shadows under the trees behind her. She turned slowly, not knowing what to expect.

The Ladies waited for her there—Morgance and Ula standing tall, with Morgandy slumped between them. She had a veil over her face, while her sisters were unveiled, but their expressions were blank.

"Ladies, we owe you much," Lucee said, as she dropped to one knee before them. "What can I do now to help you?"

"There is naught to be done," Morgance told her. "All is as my sister planned, and now we wait to see if she shall return to us, or stay a prison of flesh and will."

"Morgandy remains, somewhere inside the mycelia trapped inside her. She will fight the Mealladhan and return." Ula's voice sounded convincing, but her expression told a different tale.

"She could be like this from now on? What does that mean for the two of you?" Luce couldn't comprehend the horror of it.

"We are...lesser, without her," Morgance admitted. "She took care to sever her link to us before she consumed the Mealladhan, so we are not in danger."

"But this also means that we cannot reach her." Ula's voice was the closest thing to sadness Lucee had ever heard from The Ladies.

"We plan to stay at Maithe House, with your leave," Morgance said, and Lucee's eyebrow shot up at that. When had they ever asked her permission for anything?

"Of course. Anything you need will be provided. But I hope that you don't remove yourselves from our Council. I still need you, Sisters." Lucee bowed her head, respectfully—and to hide her fear that they were truly withdrawing.

"We will not leave you, but you must face the coming days without us at your side, Lucee Fearney. You are ready to lead on your own."

Morgance stretched out her hand, and opened it to reveal a small velvet bag of the deepest green.

"You lamented that none had given you gifts, but it turned out that none were needed. Still, that request resonated with us, and we have now rectified our oversight. When you are alone, open this." Morgance watched as Lucee carefully took the pouch from her. "Now go back to your people and use the skills you learned with us."

She pointed away from them, and Lucee turned to look. When she looked back to where The Ladies had stood, they were no longer there.

EPILOGUE: KILLING JOKE
Euphoria

I t took a few weeks for things to start to resemble anything approaching normality.

When they had left ArtPark, no one was sure what exactly had happened to the mortals who had seemed to be frozen in time. The hours had obviously kept marching on for the Fae, as the weather had changed and the sun had moved. But the mortals had to have been aware of *something* because the internet was abuzz with how "amazing" and "stunning" ArtPark had been for attendees. Even the local news had called the festival "one for the ages, an event like nothing that Baltimore has seen before." Emmaline decided to do an online search to see if she could find evidence of what others had experienced.

"Look at these videos I found!" she announced while they gathered for a casual dinner in the library. She turned her laptop so everyone could gather and watch what the festival-goers had recorded.

A long shot of the field, with the Ffyn and ArDonnath fighting, and people were cheering them like they were at a medieval reenactment.

A troupe of dancers moving through the crowd, in a cloud of glittering veils and otherworldly auras. The clip was out of focus.

Flares of energy coming from all of the towers, a shower of sparkles blowing across the mortals, who gasped in awe as they watched from the field. That clip was out of focus too.

The Drawback on stage, with Lucee singing her heart out. Colors swirled behind her, like a high-tech lighting setup that Lucee knew damn well wasn't part of the stage lights. There were lights moving through the audience as well, and there was an audible observation from the person recording. "How are they *doing* that? It's so cool!"

The comments section for that video was filled with praise for The Drawback, some going as far as to say it was the best live show they'd seen in ages, and that they'd loved every track.

"I-I don't remember playing anything but Garden of Secrets?" Lucee racked her memory, trying to recall any other part of a set.

"Look, someone posted the setlist in the comments," Merrick said, and pointed to where they mentioned every song the band had planned to perform that afternoon, with the addition of Garden of Secrets.

Lucee looked around the table, and saw the same questions echoed in everyone's eyes there.

"So, we're all in agreement that this is weird, even for Fae magic?"

"Not necessarily." Sousa declared authoritatively, then took a swig of beer. It was a new batch that Sheridan had been working on, a citrusy lager. Despite being light, it had become a favorite around The Maithe.

"Do go on," Merrick said with a skeptical look. He had been watching a video of what looked like a giant fireworks or pyro display in the middle of a crowd in the Dell, but stopped to listen to what Sousa had to say.

"Is that when Vali trapped the Mealladhan? Daaamn." Sousa raised his eyebrows, impressed. "Anyway, time and reality can run in very different directions when the veil is pulled back. All those old cautionary tales about traveling within the Faery realm are based on real experiences!"

"So, you think that the Mortal guests saw a *version* of what was actually happening for us? But how did we manage to do a whole gig without remembering it? That seems, well, improbable?" Merrick rolled his eyes. "I know, I know. It's all improbable from a mortal's standpoint."

"Stop trying to understand it from that angle, then," Sousa told him, in a tone that implied a "duh" at the end. "What have we told you before about Fae magic?"

"And this wasn't even all Fae magic," Lucee added. "Because the Elemental beings definitely added their own weirdness to the mix. I don't think we can logic through to understanding all of this, Merrick."

"We need to focus on the future," Vali declared, and nudged Camlin, who was sitting on the floor next to her. They had been pouring through her various sketchbooks, trying to come up with ideas for her next big piece of graffiti.

"What's all that for, anyway?" Merrick gestured with the piece of pizza in his hand.

"If you get sauce on any of these sketches, I'll lock you in your room for a week using one of 'em," Vali glared up at him, then winked. He wisely

296 | Christiane Knight

pulled the pizza slice back in, then took a bite of it as he gave her a contrite look in reply.

"This is for part of the proposal we've been trying to come up with to offer the Grimshaw," she explained. "Camlin says that some of them don't want to live anywhere fancy, at least not yet. And by fancy, they mean an actual house with amenities, which I understand. You get used to living the way you live, and if you're resentful of those who seem to have more, it becomes a way to rebel against them."

"But I want them to have the feeling of being responsible for something positive, with the rewards that can give them," Camlin added. "Do you know the big warehouse along the light rail tracks near Woodberry?"

"The one that some folks tried to make into artist's lofts illegally? Wasn't that shut down?" Lucee asked.

"It was. Because the landlord didn't do everything that was needed to make it safe to live in," Sousa chimed in. He paused for a moment, then added in a nonchalant manner, "So... I bought it. And I gave it to Camlin."

He grinned as everyone in the room who hadn't been in on the idea stared at him in shock.

"And my plan is to turn it over to the Grimshaw who want to live there, providing that they put the work in to fix it up and make it safe." Camlin's face lit up as he explained the idea. "I'd like to see them take the space and make it a place for artists again, but it'll be up to them to find the vision that makes the most sense for them. Vali and I will be helping them see possibilities. It turns out that they have a deep respect for all of Vali's efforts to help us escape the control of the Mealladhan."

Vali shrugged and grinned at that. "Just doin' my part. We all deserve to be free to make our own decisions and mistakes. Just wait until they're responsible for this building, they may find it more challenging than they like!"

It turned out that Vali wasn't the only one who had gained the respect of The Grimshaw.

A few nights after the discussion in the library, Camlin gathered The Grimshaw to parley with the other Fae. They had decided to meet under the trees north of the field of the Dell at midnight so they wouldn't need glamour unless they chose to use it.

Lucee stood with Cullen at her right side and Sousa on her left. Merrick and the rest of her friends from The Maithe and House Mirabilis gathered behind her.

Daro and the Gwyliannan from Tiennan House made their own group. Once they assembled, and The Grimshaw stood before them, Tully made a point of walking over from the Eleriannan to stand next to Daro and take his hand.

"You can see that we are doing much to erase the divisions that kept us fighting for reasons that have long passed." Daro's voice rang out, and everyone turned to give him their full attention. "We may still keep a sense of belonging and yet expand our boundaries of who and what we belong to, as I have recently learned. I am Daro of the Gwyliannan, and now I also find myself a member of this greater alliance."

Once the murmurs from Grimshaw had ceased, Lucee spoke up.

"We wanted to meet with you to extend a hand in peace, and hopefully in friendship to come. We recognize that you were controlled and your actions may not have been your own. I want to stress that I say 'may not' because it's important to me to not assume anything. I don't want to sweep any grievances that you may have with us under a rug. We can't build something bigger if we're not honest with each other, right?" She held her hands out at her sides, a hopeful look on her face.

"Look, we're not politicians, so we're speaking from the heart, and hopefully it all comes out right." Sousa stepped forward. "We've all said and done some shit that is going to be hard to get past, but I think we can do it. And I guess Camlin's told you what we put on the table to show that we're earnest. We've also got room at The Maithe and at Tiennan House for those who want to try something different, but the goal isn't to split you up, it's to give you options. What do you think?"

The Grimshaw gathered around Camlin, muttering and hissing back and forth. Lucee watched them, confused about how she was feeling. The ArDonnath grouped in a cluster together, and they seemed to Lucee to be the least interested in what was offered. She looked at the various kinds of Fae that made up The Grimshaw, and how different many of them were from the Eleriannan. There were thin, goblin-like beings and the beefy and coarse Arswyd. Several tall, willowy creatures with great antlers that rose above their heads stood toward the back. They had eyes that glowed a spectral green, like strange deer people from a nightmare. And of course, there were the defectors from the Gwyliannan, incredibly beautiful and odd Fae entities.

Finally, The Grimshaw grew quiet, and Camlin came to the front of the group. Before he could speak, there was a commotion behind him, and a large form pushed to the front—an Arswyd. It strode up to Lucee, and she realized that it was the one she and Cullen had encountered in Hampden on their date—the same one that had cruelly injured Cullen.

She heard Cullen inhale sharply and sensed him tense up. She had to work hard to keep herself from doing the same, and tried to appear relaxed as the Arswyd stopped in front of her.

It towered above her and was easily twice as wide as she was. It just stood there for a moment while the entire gathering seemed to hold their collective breath. Lucee, however, decided that if this was how her attempt to bring peace between the factions was going to end, she would go out as bravely as possible. She stood up taller and raised her chin so that she could look the Arswyd in the eyes. To keep herself from clenching her hands into fists, she stuck them in the pockets of her BDUs. Her fingers grazed The Ladies' velvet pouch, still unopened, and she felt a wave of strength.

The Arswyd fell to one knee before her.

Lucee felt the entire assembly of Fae exhale in relief, and her legs trembled. The Arswyd bent his huge head and addressed her, his rough voice humble.

"Y'didn't have to let me go, an' you did. Even though I almost killt your man. I owe you."

At the pronouncement of debt, there was a rush of energy that burst away from the two of them. It blew around the clothing and hair of those gathered in the field, then faded away.

"Oh! You...you shouldn't have done that—oh, wow. I don't even know your name," Lucee stuttered. His unexpected action had left her unsure of what to say next.

"I'm Ang. Guess I'm yer man now, 'til the debt's paid." Ang kept his head bent. He seemed afraid to look at her now that he'd pledged himself.

"But we went through all of this to set you all free!" Lucee wailed, and then caught herself. "No, I get it, I don't mean to insult your honorable offer, Ang. C'mon, stand up, let's talk about this."

She glanced over at Cullen, knowing that he would be affected by this, as he suffered the most at Ang's hands. He was quite pale, but he nodded subtly to her.

Ang surprised them further at that moment by turning to Cullen and addressing him.

"I dunno how yer gonna feel t'have me around, but I hafta make up for what I did. I'm sorry."

Cullen stood there a moment, blinking, obviously dumbfounded. Finally, he inclined his head and answered in a level, measured tone.

"I accept your apology. Let us move forward and make some changes, as Lucee urges us to do."

That's not the end of this, Lucee thought to herself, *but it'll have to do for now.*

The factions parted that night with some plans, and ideas, and a budding peace.

Most of The Grimshaw decided to move into the warehouse space, and Camlin and Emmaline traveled between there and The Maithe regularly as they started work on making the building livable. Emmaline planted a garden for them in the courtyard of their new home, and discovered that the Arswyd were naturals at growing things.

Some of the former Gwyliannan decided to rejoin Tiennan House, and one or two even took up rooms at The Maithe. The ArDonnath would have nothing to do with either house and instead claimed themselves a plot along the Jones Falls, near the Round Waterfall. They were less and less inclined to answer calls from Camlin, and he confided to Lucee that he wasn't sure how much longer they would honor their truce.

Tully and Daro decided that they should split time between Tiennan House and Mirabilis, much as Lucee and Cullen did with Mirabilis and The Maithe.

And one stormy September evening, Lucee came stomping up the stairs and burst into the library where Merrick and Sousa were drinking coffee. They were watching Vali as she tried to teach Emmaline how to shape her vining plants into working sigil shapes.

"That's never going to work, is it?" Merrick was saying as Lucee came into the room.

"Um, you guys... you aren't gonna believe this one. The people who organized ArtPark called."

She paused, letting the tension build.

"They *loved* what we added to their event...and they want us to host their official Halloween Ball!"

Camlin looked up from the book he was reading, a sly grin on his face.

"This feels like a job for The Grimshaw, just saying."

"Look," Lucee told him, "no one gets to eat anyone, you hear?" She grinned, and added, "Not this time, anyway."

CPSIA information can be obtained
at www.ICGtesting.com
Printed in the USA
LVHW022030290422
717484LV00012B/1343

9 781736 850336